What readers are saying about *Waves of Deception*:

I think women would be wise to leave this book lying around for the men in their lives to take a few lessons from on how *not* to mess up a relationship. Shreeve gets into a woman's head and heart for expectations and fears I wouldn't have imagined.
—Peter Wilks

Shreeve has a unique ability to create characters and scenes in an almost, written 3-D illumination—weaving the intrigue/romance with the unexpected family connections very comfortably. Definitely a "stay up all night, page turner." The "steamy" parts are handled in a classy, sophisticated way and just enough of it.
—Sue Leth Stevenson

I'm delighted with such well-developed characters in *Waves of Deception*. The plot moves briskly from start to finish. I found myself staying up way past my bedtime to enjoy it. I loved the continuation of so many characters from *The Wind Remembers* and how well they blended into this plot.
—Carolyn Moore

WAVES OF DECEPTION

Sequel to THE WIND REMEMBERS

Nothing is secret that shall not be made manifest;
    neither anything hid, that shall not be known and come abroad.

                ——Luke 8:17

To Carol,
Enjoy Dierdre's struggles to grow up and fall in love with the right man. Christine is my dear friend.— yours too!

Caroll Shreeve

WAVES OF DECEPTION

Caroll Louise Shreeve

WAVES OF DECEPTION

*To those who have despaired of ever making
wise choices in matters of the heart.*

Romantic Suspense

Front Cover design by Killian Group
Back Cover, Spine design by Aaron Campbell

Library of Congress Cataloging-in-Publication Data
ISBN-13: 978-1502840493   2014
ISBN-10: 150284099

Published by Synergy Books Publishing,
St. George, Utah, USA

WAVES OF DECEPTION

Table of Contents

PART I

Strong Medicine

WAVES OF DECEPTION

Chapter One   *Living on Pause*

From behind her sunglasses, Dierdre Ingram's eyes explored his hard-muscled body stretched out on the sand next to her. His rosy skin and golden chest hair glistened with suntan oil. Dierdre experienced an overwhelming urge to touch him, stroke him, be intimately touched in return by his strong, sensitive fingers. She'd come to relish their lovemaking and knew she was falling for him—hard. Passion was a powerful antidote to severe loneliness, and she knew plenty about both.

Almost impossible to believe, she'd found a man with all the attributes she wanted for a long-term relationship. He had charm, humor, good looks, and great moves in the sack. *He's even a wealthy trust-fund baby with no children. Marriage? Maybe yes, at last.*

Her desire for him had become a consuming need. Especially since he'd encouraged her more vulnerable side this getaway weekend. Under his devoted probing, she'd let her usual protective guard down. He appeared to be aware of her need for him and teased her about it over brunch at the hotel he'd let her arrange and pay for. When the server interrupted his nibbling on her ear to deliver the bill, he'd said to her casually, "Catch you later on that."

Enamored, she'd risked feeling safe with him. Touches of the intimate sort could wait until they were alone in their room. Considering the public beach, she decided on a more socially acceptable request.

"Darling," she breathed, leaning close enough to lightly brush his ear with her lips. "Slather some suntan lotion on my back." Trailing her finger down his chest, she added, "Pretty please? I can't reach it as well as you can."

He scrunched his haunches into his beach blanket. "Don't think so. I'm comfortable now."

Surprised by his uncharacteristic refusal on such a little matter, she flirted her fingers slowly down his shoulder to his elbow. "If I were Madonna you would."

"Yeah, but you're not."

Dierdre sucked in her breath. She'd been verbally slapped, shot by a sniper with the cruel tool of sarcasm.

"You sorry son of a sea biscuit!" She whapped his thigh with her rolled-up magazine. Sand stirred and stuck to his legs. She inhaled salt air and choked down the urge to scream at him.

He reached up and removed his sunglasses, his face amused.

"Touchy, aren't we? Surely you don't think you're still in runway-model league at your age, do you, honey?"

Dierdre fought to breathe. Sheer panic made her gather her things with what little dignity she could manage, pull her wrap around her bikini, and tie it tight. The urge to touch him had turned to the desire to commit murder.

Or should it be suicide for falling for another control freak? She lectured herself. *He's the kind of man who sucks you in with charm, waits until you're hooked, then takes you apart one vicious stab at a time.*

She rammed her belongings into her tote, stood and accidentally on purpose kicked sand onto his well-oiled body. His stunned recoil gave her delicious satisfaction.

"Go screw up somebody else's life you chauvinistic jerk. You'll find your shit at the bellhop's station in the lobby."

She left him cursing and picking sand grains off his Adonis tan, while her sandals slapped up the steps to the hotel's back entrance. Her heart raced and her face burned.

Where were the red flags she'd missed? A rich man letting her pay for a nice hotel. *Ah, I should have caught on right then. But if I hadn't fallen for that, too, I wouldn't be the one in control now who gets to throw the rat out.*

Up in their room, while calling for bell service and piling his expensive clothes in the hall, it occurred to her there might never have been any other flags. *Some bastards are smooth.* She tucked a tip for the bellman into one pricy leather loafer and stepped back into the room.

Dierdre threw the deadbolt, turned the shower on full blast, and had a good cry.

Is there a genuinely good man on the planet for me who doesn't turn out to be a deceiving jerk?

* * *

Dierdre lit a meditation candle and took a lotus pose before the seated Buddha statue on her condo balcony. She inhaled deeply first through one nostril, then the other, allowing the scent of nearby jasmine blossoms to exhale slowly through her parted lips. For some time she attempted to clear her mind of troubling thoughts while she performed her breathing ritual and prepared her inner self to move to a peaceful state. It was beginning to work.

The doorbell rang.

It might as well have been a clanging fire engine. Dierdre jerked back to the mundane moment.

"Damn it!" She rose, blew out the candle, and padded barefoot back inside to answer, peeking through the security lens in her door. "Tiffany." Dierdre undid the latches and opened to her neighbor friend.

"What brings you around so early, Tiff?"

They embraced briefly. "Rarely do I de-stress with you at an early hour." Dierdre closed the door.

Tiffany gestured to the clock above the coffeemaker. "It's after 10:00 girlfriend, not early in my book. I've already walked Sophie and solved Sudoku over my first mug of java."

She pulled a stool up to the breakfast bar. "My life's so dull I thought I'd drop by to see what perks in your world. Living vicariously is the best I can do. I came to suck some excitement out of you and your memorable men."

"Suck is the operable word. Exciting is out, and memorable is nasty." Dierdre filled two mugs with coffee, picked up a pack of cigarettes, and led the way to the balcony lounge chairs.

Tiffany collapsed into a lounger and kicked off her sandals. "Oooh, sounds juicy. Tell all. My shoulders are at your disposal."

Dierdre lit up, offered a cigarette, which was declined and leaned back to take a deep drag. She exhaled and watched the little cloud dissipate over the balcony railing. "He turned out to be a despicable jerk."

Tiffany raised her hands above her head in apparent disbelief.

"You mean the guy you were beginning to think was Mr. Right? The rich, blond god you spent last weekend with in the Keys?"

"The very SOB."

"I'm so sorry. What happened?"

It didn't take long for Dierdre to bring her friend into the picture of how the disaster unfolded. They sat sipping coffee, Dierdre smoking, relieved to have the pissy episode off her chest. Silence thickened between them like a meditation.

After a while, Tiffany set her mug on the stand at her side.

"Classic passive-aggressive twit, honey. Don't you waste another second on him. You were simply victimized."

"Victimized or not," Dierdre smashed her spent cigarette in an ashtray, "I'm running out of time to make a good catch."

"You're in your twenties, what's with the running out of time? A little early to worry about your biological clock, don't you think?"

"Look, Tiff. I'm turning thirty next month. I don't want kids. I'd be no good with them. It's not my clock; it's my klutz. I'm striking out in the relationship department. I told you what he said about my looks. He meant they're fading fast." She pulled another cigarette from the pack and lit up.

"Bull pucky. Everyone we know thinks you're drop-dead gorgeous." Tiffany reached over and patted Dierdre's arm. "So plan a smash of a birthday party. Give your ego a boost and set your emotional stage for a new man."

Dierdre inhaled, exhaled, inhaled again. She let the smoke escape her nose in a whoosh.

"Guess if I can't avoid the turning of a decade, I might as well celebrate in some terrifically memorable way. Since I'm a twin, a thirtieth party has to include Suzanne and her husband Taylor. I'd love to find a man like him. Kind, honest, a real hunk of manhood, hardworking, reliable, and I bet hard-loving, too."

With the reunion idea blossoming, her mood lifted.

Tiffany rose with her empty mug. "Would they come to Florida?"

Dierdre stood and tucked her cigarettes into the pocket of her shorts. She picked up her mug and stepped back inside the condo. "I bet if I arranged a tropical-island cruise they would. Let's go look at the calendar. If I'm not scheduled to be cruise director on some voyage near our birthdays, I'll book a vacation on a sister cruise ship without having to work and play nice."

Tiffany offered a fist bump. "That's the spirit."

Dierdre put her filter tip between her lips and responded with her free fist.

"I'll phone her in Utah and start commitment wheedling. She'll have a ton of excuses why sharing a birthday cruise would be impossible. I'll get Taylor to help me talk her into it."

When Dierdre slid the glass balcony door into place behind them, she smiled for the first time in three days. A resurrection period, she thought, snapping the lock into place with finality. Time to come back to life and make something good happen. *I've been living on pause long enough.*

* * *

The prickly plants reminded Gregory Armstrong of how it felt to hobble through the desert in the dark with a rifle barrel nudging his back. The blistering desert filled him with the old fear. It wasn't the sun beating down on his tee shirt or the sand and dust at his feet where gypsum crystals sparkled that made him afraid. It was the spicy smell of sage and the way its branches scratched his legs while he climbed the narrow red-dirt path.

Memories of sand burs digging into his bare feet, the real terrors of the nasty man a year ago began and almost ended for the boy in the desert. The man's life ended but for Gregory scary didn't, might never. He wasn't telling anybody about it either. Feeling afraid was his biggest secret.

The insistent nudging, hurting and the man's ugly voiced words hurrying him bare-footed faster through the sharp stones, the silky dirt, and the stickery shrubs. Today it was the desert's fault he shivered in the June heat. He'd tried to tell his mom and Taylor not to come. He couldn't tell them *why* he didn't want to because then they'd know how much he was afraid of the desert. He didn't want anybody to know. He hated knowing it inside himself.

Mostly, he'd been able to close his mind to the memory of that scary-night kidnapping, even when he visited Grand Pop's mews with Taylor for his falconry apprenticeship. The gyrfalcon's sharp beak and talons, which punished the horrible man didn't frighten the boy as much as the desert, the scratchy bushes, the smells, and the desert strangeness.

He pressed his thumb and fingers against his nose to shut out the sage smell. Breathing through his mouth, he swallowed sobs, hiccupping them down. It didn't matter he'd celebrated his tenth birthday months ago. Fear was no fun. Today, hiking through this canyon with his family and their friends he felt younger than his five-year-old sister Mitzi, holding their mom's hand behind him. Shuddering, he stepped aside and let them go ahead. He felt safer with his big new dad at his back.

* * *

Taylor's hand closed over Suzanne's fingers. His comfort enveloped her like the soft night embraced them all. She lifted her gaze to the velvet sky pierced with stars, the Milky Way a scattering like a brush stroke she might have splashed across her watercolor paper. Tilting her head toward her new husband, she kissed his cheek.

"Happy?" He whispered at her temple, moving his hand up her arm to draw her closer to his flannel-clad shoulder.

"With you near, I'm always happy." Smiling at him in the firelight, while gesturing to the others at the campfire she whispered, "A year ago was a nightmare. Tonight is bliss. Who could have imagined things would have turned out so well?"

Mitzi, Greg, and Cosma Stargazer's two sons, Cloud and Stellar, taunted the coals with oozy marshmallows crispy and melting on their willow sticks. Creamy drips sizzled in the embers.

Johnny Carlisle did his best to break chocolate squares into bite-size pieces he handed to Cosma, dropping the empty candy papers into the flames. Glittering cinders drifted up and disappeared in wisps of fragrant cedar smoke.

Cosma squished the kids' hot marshmallows and Johnny's chocolate squares between graham crackers and made S'more sandwich cookies. Humming, she handed the sweet-smelling treats around on paper plates.

"I like this camp-out business," bubbled Mitzi, biting into her S'more. While laughter circled the campfire, she licked melting chocolate from her lips and fingers.

Gregory scooted close to the fire. "We could've made S'mores in our fireplace at home."

Suzanne feared he'd melt his sneaker soles but said nothing. This trip was all about him, though she hadn't told him so. Taylor, Johnny, and Cosma were part of the conspiracy. Only the four kids were oblivious, she hoped.

She sipped hot cocoa and watched her loved ones. Her son seemed troubled. She wondered if he'd overheard her remark to Taylor about last year. She prided herself on rarely being careless enough to mention Greg's terrifying kidnapping. He hadn't wanted to come to the desert; she and Taylor knew that much. Though this campsite was hundreds of miles away from the Sun Tunnels they'd visited on the solstice last summer, the desert wasn't pleasurable for Gregory. She and Taylor decided some time ago they wanted him to have a fun camp-out to erase the horrors of last year. No tents set far apart from the others. Not this time.

"I wish our Aunty Dreedra could be here," said Mitzi, reaching for another S'more. "She'd ask Cosma to play some drums."

Johnny chuckled. "Dierdre would make some great brandied coffee, too. Hot cocoa's okay, but her brew is . . . special."

Suzanne giggled and told Taylor how the campfire at the Sun Tunnels had included the sort of coffee Johnny remembered, prepared by her twin Dierdre.

Cosma rose to her feet. "My drum's in the camper. I'll bring it out here." She turned to her sons, "Boys, do you want your jackets now?"

Stellar mumbled, "Um hum," nodding with his mouth full.

Cloud, fourteen and three years older than his brother, shook his head no. Suzanne observed how he often went shirtless in the sun and donned only a tee when the air cooled in the evening. His strong Apache-Piute cheekbones, deep-set dark eyes and coppery skin had inspired her to make more than a few sketches of him. His brother Stellar's complexion was lighter because his father was a white man, his hair a curly auburn contrast to his brother's jet-black mop.

Suzanne was pleased the boys got on well. She'd expected Stellar, closest to her son's age, to become a quick friend, but was surprised Gregory followed Cloud with his eyes. He often stretched to do whatever the older boy found interesting in the desert landscape—even when she was certain it probably scared him to enter strange caves or gently tease scorpions with sticks.

Stellar gulped a swallow. "We don't have to do a whole ceremony tonight do we? You always make us go to bed right after you finish."

Cosma's rich laugh rippled through the dark. "I think tonight the drum's message will be enough of a ceremony."

"Good," said Gregory. "I wanna stay by the fire . . ." His voice trailed away while he swiped fingers around his gooey plate.

Suzanne and Taylor got to their feet and refilled their cocoa from the thermos, offering more to Johnny and the kids. They resumed their places, backs to the sandstone boulders still warm from the sun, and reached for each other's free hand.

Somewhere beyond them in the darkness a coyote yipped and was answered by another.

Suzanne shivered. "How about some camp songs?" she suggested across the glowing coals to Gregory in particular.

Cloud's strong voice cut through Suzanne's softer one. "I know an Indian ghost story my Grampa Blue Thorn told me. This place is perfect for a scary story about a pack of hungry wolves."

Suzanne watched Gregory's startled face. Her heart pounded. She imagined his did too.

Uh oh. That's the worst possible idea.

* * *

Cosma Stargazer listened to the coyote's conversation echoing in the cliffs. She unwrapped her deer-hide drum, closed the camper door behind her, and hurried back with it and Stellar's jacket to the campfire. *If what Suzanne believes is true, the spirit talkers will frighten Gregory.* She stepped into the firelight.

"The trickster coyotes are calling for joy rhythms." Cosma held her drum in front of her hips and moved toward them all. "Did you hear them call to one another? They say the door into the realm of the spirit is opening. They wouldn't tease about a sacred thing like that."

Mitzi scrambled to snuggle into the blankets at Suzanne's feet. "I heared those coyotes. Do they bite? Are they coming closer and closer?"

"No, Love, they're far away from here." Suzanne patted her stepdaughter's arm and pulled the blanket over her legs.

Cosma sat down next to Johnny. "The cliff echoes bring the coyotes' talk closer than they dare come. They have new young ones and will not venture near our fire." She looked at Gregory, willing him to return her gaze. "Coyotes fear people—with good reason."

Cloud moved to the other side of Johnny. "I will not hurt a coyote or a wolf. It's enough that they fear me." He sat cross-legged stripping a willow stick of its bark with a penknife, his center-parted hair a dark waterfall to his shoulders. "A ghost story would tell you how to treat a wolf to gain its respect," he muttered.

"No ghost stories tonight," said Cosma. "Perhaps tomorrow in the daytime when Mitzi will feel safer." She caught Suzanne's look of relief and turned her attention to Gregory.

"The drum reminds us the first sound of the universe was a vibration. A cosmic noise birthed nature, the planets, and Earth Mother. Drum music is the dance of the stars and the hum that lives in our bodies. Music reflects to us a mirror of ourselves. The drum is caller of spirits, healer, and teacher. Listen. Feel the rhythm of life within each of us."

Cosma looked into Johnny's eyes, noted his nodding encouragement, and began with her fingers, her palms, and then her flat hands to make a sound pattern. It echoed from the cliffs and returned to them. She watched Gregory and Stellar tapping their fingers on their knees in time to her rhythms.

While the drum calms his heart, the boy is forgetting his fear of the coyotes. Still, Gregory may not sleep peacefully in the desert tonight. This place is alive with reminders for him.

I must be prepared if the spirit of the dead cowboy roams with the call of the coyotes and comes to visit the child who watched him die while the falcon screamed.

* * *

Chapter Two   *Mind Traffic*

Dierdre hung up the phone in frustration. She turned to Tiffany at the kitchen counter.

"Suzanne and Taylor are camping with the kids for two more days. Her voice message says they'll be out in the Utah desert, no phone service. Darn it. Birthday-cruise plans will have to wait 'til they're closer home."

Dierdre stubbed out her fourth cigarette of the morning.

Tiffany refilled her coffee mug and opened Dierdre's fridge. Over her shoulder she remarked, "Those cigs are going to zap what's left of your youth—inside and out. Find a healthier alternative when you're stressed. Relax. Your sis is bound to say 'yes' to your cruise idea. You all out of soy milk?"

"Check in the door. Should be a carton, third shelf down." Dierdre poured herself another mug of coffee and spread the newspaper across the counter. "The only things likely to relieve my stress are shopping for fabulous new shoes, soaking up a mani-pedi, or a new man—not necessarily in that order."

"You've got a paper there. Find us a good chick flick at the Megaplex, preferably something with a George Clooney or Brad Pitt type guy, so tonight we can *both* live vicariously."

The phone rang. Dierdre reached for it and checked caller ID. "Stranger," she mouthed, then warbled, "Hello?" in case it was a mysterious man.

"Oh, Stan," her smile and arm sweep included Tiff, "of course I remember meeting you at Kristin's party. Yes, I'm the brunette who was with my gorgeous blonde friend Tiffany." She rolled her eyes to the ceiling and back to Tiff. "Dinner with both of us? Tonight? Kind of short notice, isn't it?"

She sipped and listened for his comeback.

"Your brother's in town and you're hoping we're both available? As a matter of fact we were just making plans for the evening. What do you have in mind?"

Tiffany tilted her head in close enough to listen.

Dierdre lit up, waved her match to put it out, and tucked it next to the last deceased one in the ashtray. "Dancing afterward? What club?" She inhaled. "Marriott Hotel on the beach? Kind of pedestrian, but could be fun. Not Dutch treat, I hope." She exhaled away from the phone.

Tiffany gave her a thumbs-up.

"Meet you there at seven?" She checked for a go-ahead nod from Tiff. "Guess we're up for that. Thanks, we'll see you at the Marriott." She hung up. "Ah, give me a man with a great ass, great shoulders, a brain, and some class."

They gave each other a high five and chimed, "Double date for the evening on their dime! Woo hoooo!"

* * *

Around six-thirty, Tiffany closed her apartment door behind them. "Don't you think it's odd, Dierdre, that Stan didn't offer to pick us up?"

"It's the twenty-first century, honey. Gender equity and all that. Perhaps his brother's staying at the Marriott. Let's just be happy they're two-warm bodied men picking up the tab for the evening."

Approaching the parking lot, Dierdre clicked the remote for her red Mustang convertible.

"After my recent fiasco, I'm not going to be first to fork over for the tab. We have two men waiting to meet us and take us to dinner and dancing. At least one of them we've met. He's very good-looking and dressed like he can afford to treat us like queens. Cross your pinkies Phil is as appealing as his brother Stan."

Behind the wheel, she eased the Mustang out into the Miami traffic. Accelerating along the shore road where palm trees swayed in the Florida breeze and the Atlantic waves lapped at the beach, they shared an up-beat, expectant mood for fun.

* * *

Dierdre moved into Stan's muscular arms for their third dance, absorbed in the way his hair waved about his sun-tanned ears. "You're a superb lead, Stan." She inhaled his musky cologne like a man dying of thirst sucks on a wet sponge.

"And you look divine in that clingy red dress. Dancing with you is a pleasure," he said, smiling appreciatively into her eyes. "You really know how to move."

She loved that look and his praise, but didn't want to let him know how attractive she found him, at least not yet.

Her most recent poor read on a dysfunctional relationship on her mind, she chose to be more elusive for the time being.

"Your brother's a good dancer, too." She nodded toward Tiffany and the handsome, body-builder-type Phil across the floor. "They appear to be getting on really well."

He smiled a little oddly she thought and nodded, guiding her off the dance floor with a warm hand at the small of her back.

Dierdre looked forward to the next opportunity to be in Stan's arms, or perhaps they'd trade partners. Phil's powerful arms looked equally inviting, and his salt and pepper mustache begged to be touched. She wondered if Tiffany thought so too.

When the combo took a break, they all returned to their candle-lit table, where fragrant, pale lilies nodded in a sparkling glass vase. Dierdre slid into her side of their banco, managing to stay intimately close to Stan's thigh. She smiled as Phil pulled out the chair opposite for Tiffany. The night had been stimulating already, a great way to erase the bruising reality of the weekend in the Keys resort.

The server brought another round of cabernet sauvignon. The foursome clinked stemmed glasses of ruby-red wine.

Stan proposed a toast. "To a lovely evening with two exceptionally beautiful and fascinating ladies."

"I'll drink to that," added Phil. "This has worked out even better than Stan and I hoped. He told me the two lovelies he met at Kristin's party would make us both happy. Ladies like you two really are fun."

"And what had you two hoped would make you happy?" Dierdre asked, peering coyly over the rim of her wineglass. She wondered what they would propose to polish off the wonderful evening and hoped they'd plan another one in the near future.

"Well, you know the drill when a couple of guys like us want to be out and about with some winsome women," Stan offered, sipping his wine.

Tiffany perked up. "Guys like you two?" She looked puzzled. "I guess you don't really look much like brothers, but I'm a bit confused about what you mean."

Dierdre came to her friend's aid, since to her also they looked entirely different from one another in height and build. "Fraternity brothers perhaps?"

"No, love," said Stan, chuckling. "Phil and I aren't brothers, we're partners, gay partners. We carefully select gay women for social evenings out in public. You two lesbians were a knockout combination to enhance our pretense of a terrific hetero-foursome."

Tiffany spilled her drink down her cleavage.

Dierdre sputtered and watched red splotches grow to the size of quarters on the white tablecloth.

* * *

Gregory listened to Taylor's snoring across the tent space until he grew drowsy and dozed off in his sleeping bag.

The fourth time, he awoke startled. Sweat streamed from his face and trickled down his neck. He sat up, rubbed his eyes with the backs of his fists, and remembered the nightmare that kept returning. All that came back was feeling naked and lost, running from something chasing him in the dark, something that wanted to kill him if it could. Something mean with sharp teeth. Maybe it was the man's big black dog.

He unzipped his sleeping bag and crawled out of it. Dragging it soundlessly, he arranged it along side Taylor's and scooted himself back into it. This time when he zipped it up to his chin, he fell asleep with the comfort of his big step-dad's strong arm right next to his own.

* * *

Dierdre's mind swam from some far away, dreamy place to her own Miami bedroom. Dripping rain stirred her to wakefulness—alone—in her king-sized bed. Without opening her eyes, for a while she listened intently to the soft splats of water droplets drenching her narrow balcony. Soon, the first rays of light pierced the pale-peach sheers and nudged her eyelids open. The Atlantic wind blew the rain in sheets against the sliding-glass doors, blurring the swaying palm trees to smudgy-gray shapes reminiscent of her dreams.

Marooned in the middle of the immense bed she was an island in a sea of coverlets. So often alone, she longed for the strong, caressing arms of some imaginary lover. The sort of real man who'd been coming and she hoped would *not* always be going— from her bed, her heart, her life. Rarely did she admit fearing never being understood and loved for herself. Her terror of abandonment lived on her back burner cooking right along with the fear of appearing foolish.

She felt weary of this interminable aloneness and envied her twin, Suzanne, for the loving relationship she had with Taylor. She imagined Suzanne thought of her as strong and independent, bent on going about life her selfish, indulgent way, regardless of anyone else's needs. Giving the appearance of an independent spirit was essential to Dierdre's protective armor. She usually avoided showing her vulnerability to anyone and developed great personal strength over years of disappointment, disillusionment, and longing for something more. Giving in and letting go in the Keys had been her undoing. She wouldn't succumb again so quickly. To her face, her twin—and more than one lover—had described Dierdre as one tough cookie. She didn't feel tough and as far as cookies were concerned, her armor like them was definitely crumbling. There was nothing sweet about that.

It's time I had a man of my own. A partner. A man I can respect, who'll treat me with respect in return. I want a good man I can rely on to be my friend, my lover, my confidant, my renewable source of strength and security. Well, he doesn't have to be too good, but he must be interesting and stimulating or I'd be bored silly and come to resent him. Then things would fall apart again.

Fully awake, she sat up and threw off the lace-edged linen sheet holding her in against the bed's emptiness. *What is it with me? I take risks but seem to be missing something with every man I brave caring enough about to let him know what I really feel for him. If the rain can wash the world clean outside, it's past time for me to wash away my resistance to learn something new about my judgment skills when it comes to men.*

Her silk robe was a splash of tropical colors where it lay across the white-eyelet comforter at the foot of the bed. She slipped it on, belted the sash about her narrow waist and padded barefoot to the kitchen to turn on the coffeemaker.

Today, I'll begin to scrutinize every man I encounter for partner qualities. When I do meet a good match, I'll be more likely to recognize and snare him before somebody else does, leaving me alone again.

* * *

Later that day, Dierdre led the way to her bedroom's walk-in closet with Tiffany in her wake.

"Help me pick out something to wear to Mario's gallery opening tonight. I'm thinking white slacks and something wispy on top. Not too contrived-artsy, more Mediterranean for the theme of his paintings."

Tiffany stopped at the make-up table in the bedroom. She called, "Is this your mom in this photo? Don't think I've ever noticed it before."

"Just found it in a stored box of Mom's things. Seemed inspirational with that line up of stunning men on either side of her, so I picked up a nice frame yesterday."

Dierdre returned from the closet with a couple of tops swinging from hangers laced through her fingers. She joined her friend at the table. "Which do you think would be most appropriate?"

Ignoring her, or so it seemed, Tiffany, bent down for closer examination of the picture. "Do you know who any of these gorgeous guys are by name?"

"I'm guessing one of them is likely my mysterious father, though she never admitted it to Suzanne or to me when we'd ask. Definitely something important about that photo because she kept it under glass on her nightstand, never framed and hung on a wall. That's how Sis and I came to the not-so-funny jokes between us twins about our virgin birth. Those handsome guys are likely all balding in their fifties to seventies by now. What a shame. As for names, she mentioned an Eddy, a Tom, and Wes somebody. Don't recall the others or know who's who."

She met Tiffany's eyes in the mirror. Her friend had a serious expression and asked in a quiet sort of voice, "Dee, did it ever occur to you your mom may not have been sure which one got her pregnant?"

"Whew, that's not so sweet of you. I don't think Mom was a loose woman, just a romantic one. Men were always falling for her, and I suppose a few found their way into her lacy linen."

"Nicely put. Bet she'd be proud of your discretion." Tiffany pointed to one after the other of the surfers in the photo. "Not a nerd in the group. Your mom attracted some fine specimens for sure. Of course, looking like that in a bikini, why wouldn't she?"

"When a guy's eighteen to twenty-five, super fit, tanned muscles and all that sun-bleached hair, they're *all* fine specimens." Dierdre laughed, took a few steps back and shook out a soft cotton top in one hand and an organdy see-through in the other. "Okay, help me pick."

"Are you wanting to knock some artist's beret off, set a few wives to wringing their hands, or look innocently appealing?"

"Honestly, Tiff. You are a gas." Dierdre laughed. "Is it possible to accomplish all those with *one* blouse?"

"Oh, Honey. You are hopelessly devious. I have to run. You're on your own."

After Tiffany left, Dierdre set up the ironing board, turned on the radio and laid out an unopened pack of cigarettes. Between her sister Suzanne's and Tiff's admonishments, if she wanted to protect her health and find a great guy, she'd better lay off the smokes. It was nearly killing her, but she was doing it. She told herself she'd keep one new unopened pack around for the superior feeling of control. She could indulge if she chose, though Tiff called it falling off the wagon if she succumbed.

Adding distilled water to the iron and setting it on steam, she poured herself a tall glass of water and was sipping it, half listening to the radio. A traffic report interrupted the broadcast with news of a terrible accident on the freeway. A driver on a car phone, lost control and plowed across a lane and hit a car head on. The pregnant mother and her two children were life-flighted from the accident scene. Red Cross urged people with Type B Negative blood to donate. The unusual blood type was in critically short supply and if the donor had RH blood as well, the mother's nearly full-term baby would more likely be saved.

Dierdre set the glass down a little too hard on the counter. While she mopped up the splash, her mind flew back to her own unexpected pregnancy in college. Like her father, her fiancé ditched her at the news. She'd chosen to have an abortion and finish college, with mixed regrets. She thought of her precious niece Mitzi, a little five-year-old just starting out in life and Gregory, the nephew she treasured even more after his terrifying kidnapping last year. She missed them so much and decided at that moment the children must be included in her invitation to Suzanne for a birthday cruise.

Ten minutes later, the radio alert repeated, tugging at her heart. Innocent kids, a pregnant woman with responsibilities, a young family that needed a mother. Dierdre held the steam iron in the air. She with everything but a good man and a family, standing there in a pricey condo, owning a closet full of expensive clothes and a hot, red Mustang convertible in the parking lot—her B Negative blood with that special RH factor racing through her veins. She unplugged the iron and grabbed her car keys.

* * *

Dierdre removed her Vuarnet sunglasses, a gift to herself in Paris a few summers ago. She tucked them into the side pocket of her Gucci bag. Waiting less than a heartbeat for the Red Cross receptionist to look up from the pile of forms on her desk, she cleared her throat for attention.

When the woman volunteer smiled and gestured to the pen on the sign-in clipboard, tan wrinkles appeared like quotation marks at the corners of her eyes. *She's not even being paid to welcome me, nor all the others behind me. I never volunteer for anything. Correction Dee Dee, for a change you're doing it now.*

Dierdre felt awkward at the newness of a procedure that appeared to be quite predictable to other adults in the waiting area.

"I'm here to give blood for that pregnant mother I just heard about on the radio newscast."

"Then perhaps you have the B-negative blood we're needing to rush to the hospital emergency room?" The woman's Red Cross patch stitched to the pocket on her ample breast rose up and down while she talked, a distraction of sorts.

Dierdre nodded. "I've never giv . . . donated blood before. What do I do?"

The woman handed Dierdre the pen and tapped an unpolished, clean fingernail on the information material. "Take this pamphlet to a seat over there and prepare to answer the questions on that form. When you return the information to me, I'll assign you to a waiting room."

"You mean, to part with my blood I have forms to fill out and waiting to do?" Dierdre already regretted her hasty decision to come for something involving a needle, let alone document forms and waiting her turn.

"Standard procedure, Ma'am. It won't take too long . . . and the need is great."

Dierdre knew if the unopened pack of cigarettes on her kitchen table were within reach at the moment, she'd be tempted to rip off the plastic with her teeth and chew her way through a few filter tips. *Why did I do this?*

"I'm in a hurry," she said, in her most urgent voice.

"Thank you so much for coming to donate . . ." The woman turned the clipboard to read the name. "Ms.

Ingram, we'll get you through the process as quickly as possible."

Dierdre took a seat with the others and read the first couple of pages emphasizing the physical reactions she might experience within minutes or hours of having a pint of her blood removed. *Hmmm, light-headedness, fatigue, etc.*

I get light-headed over a great set of male shoulders and survive it just fine. I doubt this will be anything I can't handle. She flipped to pages about the reasons *not* to donate. Did she take prescription medications in the drug column? Had she recently used illegal recreational drugs? Had she shared needles? Had she given blood too recently? The questions about sexual partners, explicit sexual contact—protected and unprotected, partner and personal lifestyles, the list went on *ad nauseum.*

Good lord, the Red Cross certainly does a thorough job of protecting whoever receives my blood. I should be so careful in interviewing my romantic partners. She couldn't bring herself to refer to them as a string of lovers, occasionally even one-night stands. She wondered how she could ever be certain of her sexual partners' other lovers. *Only if I dare to ask, even then, the chumps will lie to get what they want. Good thing I insist on condom and diaphragm protection.*

Returning the information pages to the desk, she was ushered to another chair in a cubicle-sized room where a nurse sat at a wee desk with a computer.

"Look, all I want to do is give blood for that woman who's been in the auto accident. You know, the one who's expecting a baby and has a couple of little kids all life-flighted to hospitals this morning."

The nurse smiled warmly. "She'll be so grateful for your donation. Answer these questions on the computer for her protection. Once you finish this critical formality you'll be out of here in fifteen minutes and your blood will be on its way to her." She rose and closed the door, leaving Dierdre in privacy.

The computer questions were the ones she'd reviewed in the pamphlet, so whipping through them was almost a breeze. She'd visited foreign countries with her cruise ship job, but never for long enough to endanger herself with blood parasites, eboli, Hepatitis C, and the like. The questions that slowed her down were the sexual experiences and partners in the last so many months. *I've been behaving like a needy teenager or . . . a slut. Time to put on the brakes and be sensible about my future, let alone the blood I'm donating!*

Simple, direct questions really stopped her. Had she ever been pregnant? *Yes.* Delivered a full-term baby? No. Miscarried? *Hum. Not exactly.* She had the RH factor with her negative blood and had never had injections or transfusions. That was a big plus. Her blood would be especially precious to an RH-negative mother. She signed her confirmation of truthful answers on the computer and opened the door.

In minutes, after checking for needle marks, a blood-pressure check, and a test prick of her finger to confirm blood type and iron level and negative HIV, she lay back on the padded recliner with the fat arm rests for securing her donating arm. Dierdre chose her left arm, just in case she had something imperative to do with her right fist, like sock her most recent hero disaster smack in his sunburned nose.

The nurse checked the inside of her extended arm at the elbow for a good vein, marked it with a black felt-tip pen, and prepped the area with iodine on a cotton pad. A row of four donors chatted at her side with their nurses or each other. *We're a frappin' assembly line of bleeders!* She grimaced, bracing for the stabbing moment to come.

Dierdre took a few deep breaths and let them out slowly while the needle gently, expertly went in and was taped firmly into place. Relaxing, she watched in fascination while her life force flowed dark red into the tube leading over the armrest to the gravity-fed vinyl bag at floor level.

She tried to imagine the young mother's feelings a few miles away in the hospital's ER. *If she's even conscious she's probably agonizing over her young children's injuries and wondering if her unborn baby has injuries as well.* Dierdre shivered involuntarily. *Her family will be gathering. Oh, God, I hope she makes it and the children too.*

"Do you want a warm blanket?" asked the attending nurse.

"No, no I'm fine, thank you." Every so often, Dierdre squeezed the foam-rubber ball in her palm, as she'd been instructed, to keep her blood flowing into the tube at a good rate so it wouldn't clot.

She closed her eyes and ventured to recall her abortion decision more than a decade ago, the "procedure" as she referred to it, if she let herself think of it at all. Somewhere over the border in Canada, she'd gone to a little clinic she'd been told about by a college roommate. She'd chosen not to confide in Suzanne until it was over. Dierdre certainly didn't ask sister Susie to accompany her to the clinic or drive her back to school. Her twin would have tried to talk her out of it.

Though she ditched him shortly afterward, she'd bribed her fiancé into driving her there and back with keeping his aborted child secret from his high-society family. She never told her mother either, especially since her mom had brought up illegitimate twins without financial or moral support from anybody. Like most difficulties in her life, Dierdre had toughed it out alone as her mother had done. *This going-it-alone shit is getting really tiring. I'm kind of resenting Mom passing it on in our DNA.*

"Your first time, your chart says. You're doing great. I think you'll finish your pint in under five-and-a-half minutes."

The nurse had broken her train of thought, but not before Dierdre pondered why she'd had a change of heart about risking examining her feelings in relation to Suzanne, her family, and her friends. She'd leave exploring the men moving in and out of her love life like the surge and ebb of the tide behind in her condo, least she burst into a tantrum or a flood of tears in public.

Something about giving my blood to another woman in need brings back the turning point in my spiritual life last summer when Gregory was kidnapped by that vile man. Dierdre relived the desperate terror of realizing every aspect of the unbelievably scary situation was outside her control to do anything to help her nephew. *I hate not being in control!* She was still amazed she'd found herself on her knees, praying for his safe return. *My knees for god sakes—me.*

Dierdre couldn't remember praying since she was a little girl wishing for *her* daddy, *a* daddy, *any* daddy. Somebody big and strong, smart enough to help her mother. Some kind, big-daddy man to hold her and her sister and make every scary feeling go away. Her prayers had gone unanswered so little Dee Dee had stopped praying for anything, let alone what she really needed or wanted. *What was the point?*

Now she meditated more often than she used to, sitting cross-legged before a flickering candle flame, a Buddha figure, a few crystals, some gathered nature flotsam from the beach or a fragrant stem of jasmine. Nature for her was the epitome of beauty and sign of the Almighty. *Nature is the godness I respect.*

Until crashing to her knees in prayer for Gregory's merciful return, when she'd made promises to the God she doubted, the way she'd been told atheists did in foxholes, she'd been well . . . *above* prayer—as if it were a weakness—not a power she could count on. But now, those promises to be a better person, to give and care for someone in need even when it was inconvenient or perhaps painful, well those promises nudged her to take action. Dierdre believed in action, was proud of the way she could make decisions and just do what needed to be done, whether others were able to or not. *Perhaps today . . .*

"All finished! Good job." The nurse shut off the intake tube, filled a few vials for testing, removed the needle, and swabbed and bandaged Dierdre's inner elbow. "Have some juice and snacks before you leave, take it easy today, no heavy lifting or heart-racing activity for twenty-four hours."

Well, those instructions alone should leave my man-crave on my back burner. She smiled her thanks and gathered her things.

When she looked at the vinyl bag of her very own blood, Dierdre felt a sense of awe. She watched the tagging process noting her B-negative blood type, donor code, and RH information and the attached sample vials. *So clinical, so efficient. At last I've done something selfless for someone else. It feels good to give.*

Okay, God. I'm working on my payback promise. Thank you for returning our dear Gregory to us unharmed. Help me go on being useful to somebody besides myself. Please use my blood to save that young mother and her unborn baby. I guess you knew I'd be listening to the radio to hear the need for just my kind of blood. I'll be expecting your nudges in the future. You better be there to help me know what to do because I have 'avoiding-the-uncomfortable' down to a fine, selfish art.

* * *

That evening, Mario's festive gallery opening was well underway when Dierdre arrived alone and signed the guest book. The newspaper photographer for the arts and society pages brushed by on his way out, leaving the eager columnist schmoozing the socially prominent for story quotes. The hum of conversation and laughter flowed around her from a mixed crowd of painting enthusiasts and the upper-crust types intent on being where it was important to be seen.

The ultra-sleek elite in their expensive casual wear, accented with Rolex watches, custom-designed jewelry, and more than a few Botoxed faces, milled about greeting each other with perfect-teeth smiles. Their champagne in sparkling flutes, they toasted Mario's gala opening. Dierdre passed by a halo of designer scents wafting from their silk and crisp-linen shoulders. She nodded hellos to a few people whose names were emblazoned in her memory bank as habitual long-journey cruisers.

She paused at an unframed, three-inch deep gallery-wrapped canvas, painted by Mario with nuances of subtle to vibrant color, perhaps an interpretation of a tidal pool. *Hard to tell what it's supposed to be, but his colors are lovely.* Interrupted, she stepped aside for the gallery owner to paste a red sold sticker on the title placard. The price tag would have paid off her Mustang.

Accepting a champagne flute, she sipped the bubbling gold liquid and strolled around the gallery, pausing occasionally while admiring one after another of Mario's happy child-like paintings. Her birthday cruise a new priority, the prices exceeded her budget.

A noisy group of artsy types in campy attire held sway in the middle of the gallery. Everyone else had to weave through or walk around them. She enjoyed their swinging shoulder-length hair, dangling earrings, batiks from India, and zany tee shirts. Artfully ragged jeans, intricate tattoos, and Birkenstock sandals completed the earthy look, reminiscent of sixty's flower children. Only beards and sans-bra boobs helped her make quick distinctions between androgynous men and women. The love children hugged one another freely and lingered in twos and threes before the paintings, sipping wine or beer. She caught phrases while they discussed aesthetic points and Mario's painting techniques. By the paint splotches on some jeans several were artists themselves.

On the fringes of the earth children and black-tie cocktail sets were tourists dressed more traditionally than the artsy group but less impressively than the affluent élite. All vied for the prestige of posting red sold stickers and being interviewed for local social columns. Some tourists had cameras slung around their necks, though posted signs warned "no photos please or cameras will be confiscated". Even without cameras, many wore un-pressed clothing with crease marks from hangers and the crush of luggage giving them away as vacationing non-locals.

Dierdre paused to listen near a well-informed group discussing Mario's style of painting with acrylics and mixed media, including meticulously applied gold and silver leaf. She learned a few were art teachers and painting professors on vacation from distant schools.

I wonder if any of these men meet my wish list. Single, bright, romantic, no kid problems, and trustworthy. Wealthy would be a plus. Eyeing the affluent men in Armani slacks, she set her empty flute on a passing tray and searched for any inviting man not wearing a wedding ring.

Catching her eye, Mario came eagerly to her side in a white, open-neck silk shirt and shockingly tight, white leather pants. *My god, it's a good thing those don't have pockets. Coins or a handkerchief would get him arrested.* She choked back a giggle.

"Dierdre Ingram, my darling glam girl! So good of you to come to my little soirée."

He embraced her in an affectionate bear hug. The gold medallion on a chain strategically draped on his hairy chest bit into her cleavage. She pulled back and managed her best smile, imagining a dent on her person where there shouldn't be one.

"Wouldn't have missed it," she enthused. "Fabulous turnout. The pleasure for me is watching you emerge as a contemporary Florida artist of merit. You've come a long way from styling my hair."

Mario beamed, his dark eyes taking her in. "Thank you. And you dressed as for Amalfi—my Mediterranean home, my passion, my art. If I did portraits I'd beg you to model for me."

"Thank you, dear one. You do know how to make a woman feel beautiful, even without scissors in your hand." She chuckled. *So dramatically romantic. Showmanship sells.*

His eyes searched the crowd, ever noisier as champagne and wine flowed. Dierdre relaxed her smile. New bottles were being expertly popped at the bar. "Such fun. You're pulling off your opening-night in elegant style."

Apparently spying someone, Mario tightened his arm around her shoulders, guiding her across the track-lit space to the hors d'oeuvres table.

"You must meet two of my dearest friends. The three of you are among my most enthusiastic fans."

He drew her by the hand to a man whose back was turned. Appallingly familiar wavy hair curled around a nice set of tan ears. She inhaled sharply.

"Stan," said Mario, tapping him on the arm.

Her dinner-dance partner from the Marriott turned and faced her. He smiled, nodded hello, and tugged the sleeve of his companion who also turned.

"And Phil, meet my darling Dierdre," Mario added. "Too many guests tonight to worry about last-name intros."

Oh, Lord. Dierdre smiled and put out her hand. "Yes, we've met, Mario. Stan and Phil are not only enthusiastic art patrons . . . they're very good dancers."

Mario bowed. "Then I'll leave you three to catch up while I greet my other guests." He glided away in Florentine loafers without socks, running gold-ringed fingers through his black hair, looking every inch the Italian heartthrob.

"Dierdre," Stan began. "We—well I in particular—owe you a most sincere apology for mistaking you and Tiffany for . . . well, you know."

Phil stepped closer and whispered, "We both deeply regret causing you and your lovely friend any embarrassment. We had a terrific evening dining and dancing with you ladies and would never intentionally hurt your feelings."

Well, I'll be damned. Two sweet, charming, and handsome men who can actually apologize like true gentlemen. Gay. What a waste for me.

Dierdre smiled warmly. "How kind of you both to express regrets for . . . a misunderstanding . . . on both sides. Apology accepted."

I've got to get out of here before there are any more surprises from my past.

This time she shook their hands more comfortably. "Nice to see you again. Good-bye. I'll pass the word to Tiffany."

Heading for the door, she waved to Mario, too surrounded by adoring art collectors to move in her direction for a farewell hug. He blew her a kiss.

In the parking lot, a salty evening breeze caressed her arms while she unlocked her car and laid a Mace atomizer within reach on the passenger seat. Driving home with the top down, the pale moon flickered through the silhouetted black lace of palm fronds skirting the shore road. A wistful longing enveloped her, as if more than the moon and the sea called like enticing sirens from some enchanted place. Perhaps the place was as close as her heart.

Are gay men the only types who can behave like gentleman, even say they're sorry? My romances with straight guys haven't promised kindness and sensitivity for the long term. Am I destined to go through life without a good man who prefers women?

* * *

The bubble bath with an uplifting book hadn't erased her anxious mood. Dierdre tucked a terry bath sheet around herself and moved to the kitchen. She brewed some Lady Grey. *I need a dose of serious pampering to shake me out of this funk.* Running through her mental checklist, she decided on a massage. *Anthony always puts me right. He's been my honest friend for years, one of the few men I can trust.*

At eight, she phoned for an appointment. Two hours to kill. Too flighty for meditating, Dierdre sipped her tea, carried the steaming mug back to the bedroom, and pulled on workout sweats. She popped in a yoga tape and unrolled her foam mat, putting herself through stretching poses and deep breathing. Even Downward Dog wasn't going well. Finishing Sunrise Meditation, she rolled up the mat and returned to the kitchen to reheat cold tea.

The phone rang. Too early for Tiff. She checked caller ID. No one she knew. *Whoever this is would be an improvement over roaming this condo alone. Even a forbidden solicitor would be a welcome change.*

"Hello?"

"Sorry if I woke you, Ms. Ingram. Maintenance here. We're evacuating your building. A gas-line leak has been detected in the parking garage. Leave your apartment immediately." The man hung up.

"I don't need this now," she blurted, lifting keys and handbag from the knob rack by the door. Grateful to already be dressed, she dashed for safety.

After hanging around for an hour at the farthest end of the condo lot with neighbors in their bathrobes and sweats, the gas-company truck pulled away. Her apartment was still standing and the marine breeze blew the remaining rotten-egg odor away.

Dierdre drove to her favorite spa. She parked the Mustang at the end of the lot where it was less likely to be dinged, put the top up, locked the doors, and walked briskly to the reception area of her massage therapist.

"Morning, Nadia. I know I'm a little early but perhaps . . ."

"You've plenty of time. Anthony's running a little behind."

"You mean at this hour I'm not his *first* client?" *Heavens, every little thing is irking me. Get a grip Dee.*

"The senator's wife had an emergency schedule change."

"Well bless her sweet political heart," Dierdre snapped. Regretting the sarcasm, she squeaked, "Sorry," picked up a towel, a locker-room key, and gave Nadia a forced smile.

A steamy shower, followed by a cool one, soothed her angst. Donning a plush velour wrap, she took her time in the hallway looking at framed local-artist paintings far less impressive than her sister's watercolors. Thinking of Suzanne, she hoped by tomorrow they could make contact and begin plans for their birthday cruise.

Nadia approached. "Take the Vine Room, Dierdre. Anthony will be with you in a moment."

After an hour of hot rocks, essential lavender oil, and a deep-tissue massage to gentle music, Dierdre felt on the way to being restored.

"Anthony," she ventured, while his capable hands soothed the tension in her neck.

"Yes?"

"You have a clientele that . . . well, includes a broad range of women—in age I mean—right?"

"Of course." She felt his hands stop moving. "So, what are you asking?" His fingers moved expertly to the small of her naked back and along her hips.

Dierdre swallowed, closed her eyes, and went for it. "Women in my age range, too?"

"Certainly." She heard him chuckle. "You wondering how you compare in the beauty department?"

"Yes, yes, I'm losing my confidence in every area of my life, especially my bod."

He pummeled her thighs and moved to her tense calf muscles. "You are beautiful, Dierdre, exceptionally so, whether compared to other women of your own age or any age. However, well, it's not my place to say . . ."

She took a breath and held it for a few beats. "Go on."

"It might be time to think of what you're going to do for a money-earning skill when you can't truck as easily on your sensational looks . . . in a few years, of course." He kneaded her left calf until it relented.

Dierdre couldn't think of a comeback. He'd struck the very nerve driving her to sleepless nights and anxious days. "Thanks for your honesty, friend. . . . I think."

She bit her lip and let him finish, feigning sweat where tears wet her cheeks.

* * *

Chapter Three   *Secrets and Dreams*

In the dark tent, Gregory's screams woke Suzanne. She switched on the Coleman lantern. Next to her, Taylor held her son tight against his chest, stroking the struggling boy's back through his sleeping bag.

Gregory squirmed and fought with his fists, gasping, "Let me go. Let me go!"

Taylor loosened his grip, sat up, and gathered the boy close to his body, pulling him free of the nylon bag. "Wake up, Son. You're having a bad dream. You're safe. I've got you. Shhhh now shhhh."

Suzanne held the lantern high until she could center it behind them on the closed cooler lid, so as not to blind Greg with the glare when he came fully awake. Across the tent, Mitzi was a mound of restless wiggles, her sleep disturbed, too.

Taylor met her eyes and mouthed, "He's soaked with sweat. These nightmares are getting worse."

Her breath white in the air between them, she whispered back, "Maybe I was wrong to insist we bring him back to a desert place to put his unreasonable fears to rest."

She patted the boy's shoulder and fingered through the wet bristle of hair at his temples.

"Greg, Honey, it's safe to wake up. We're here with you. No one's going to hurt you." She shivered.

Taylor tugged his own jacket loose from a stack of clothes within reach. He kept Gregory embraced against him while he tucked the jacket around the boy and rubbed him vigorously. "You're okay now," he said. "Take some deep breaths. Open your eyes to see you're safe here with your family."

Gregory snuggled his head under his stepfather's chin, nuzzling closer for reassurance like a nursing puppy.

Mitzi wakened to the commotion and sat up. "What's the matter, Gregory?"

Suzanne crawled to her side. "Your brother had a bad dream, Sweetie. He's awake and fine now. You can go back to sleep. It's a long time until morning."

Mitzi settled back into the warmth of her mummy bag. "Good, I'm not all finished sleeping yet." The fringe of lashes closed and she drifted off to sleep again.

Suzanne turned back to Taylor and her stepson. "Would you like a drink of water, Gregory? She asked, pulling on her hoody in the chill.

"Mmmmh, guess so," Gregory mumbled, turning his face to her, but not letting go of Taylor. "It was a scary dream . . . a black dog as big as a car, with huge, sharp teeth . . . biting my leg, wouldn't let go. I couldn't get away. Thought he was going to tear my leg off, make me bleed and die." His words tumbled out between heaving breaths. "The stinking bad cowboy was taking me away again." He reached fingers to his neck. "I could feel his knife at my throat . . . like before."

Suzanne opened a bottle of water from the box on the floor and let him grasp it.

"Drink a little, Darling. You've been hollering and breathing hard. Your throat's bound to be dryer than usual out here in the desert air."

Gregory pulled away from Taylor at last. Wrapped in Taylor's jacket, he took a few swallows, looking from one to the other of his parents.

"I want the nightmares to stop." Tears rolled down his cheeks, glistening from eyelids to chin like tiny rivers in the lantern light. "The stinking cowboy and his big, bad dog are always waiting for me when I close my eyes."

Suzanne and Taylor exchanged knowing glances. She spoke gently, "Cosma told me she has an idea for making your nightmares go away. Could we talk to her about it in the morning?"

Gregory sipped from his bottle of water and vehemently shook his head. "Nah, Cosma's nice but she's kind of weird. She'd probably pound her drums and make me drink something disgusting. I'd feel stupid anyway. Don't even ask her."

Suzanne's heart sank. *I've brought him out here away from home and only made things worse.*

* * *

Outside, Cosma Stargazer stepped back from the Armstrong family's tent. Waking to Gregory's screams, she'd come running and had been about to call out to them an offer of help when she overheard the boy's answer to Suzanne. It seemed the adults had brought their children camping for nothing. Helping the child with his nightmares had been a wasted effort. *We've only increased his anxiety with the familiar desert things bringing back that horrible night when I met his family.*

She raised her eyes to the inky sky cluttered with sparkling stars and stood motionless in the cold, thinking. She fingered the beaded wrap on the thick braid at her shoulder. How she wanted to forever silence Gregory's night terrors.

How can I help him if he doesn't trust me? Even if I can earn his trust, can I help him face his fears without chasing away his right mind?

Great Spirit, if my purpose in this world is healing, I need your way to be clear to me for this child's recovery. Show me soon. I will wait for your wisdom.

Behind her in the darkness her Apache-son Cloud touched her arm.

Startled, she jumped, barely controlling the urge to gasp loudly in alarm and be discovered for eavesdropping by the Armstrongs.

Her son tugged at her sleeve, pulling her further away from the tent, back toward their camper. In the silky dirt, they fell into soundless steps together.

"Mother," Cloud whispered, "I will help you free Gregory from his night screams. He looks up to me. He'll change his mind about you." He patted her arm as if he were the elder in their family.

Cosma realized her first-born had followed her to the Armstrong's tent, and had also overheard Gregory refuse her help. She put an arm around Cloud's shoulder, grown nearly as tall as she. Like his grandfather Blue Thorn, it had become obvious stealth with the owl's wisdom would be Cloud's lifeway.

Calmly, she accepted how her prayer to Great Spirit had been answered. The guide she prayed for, she herself had delivered to the planet fourteen years ago.

How Gregory would be healed of his private pain was a mystery. But the sureness she felt that it would be so, took root in her heart and filled her with peace.

Following Cloud inside the camper, while he climbed to the bunk above her, she lifted the blanket on her man, Johnny, and slid in beside the comforting warmth and strength of his big, awkward body she adored.

He pulled her to him. His lips found her ear. "Is the boy alright, Love?"

"Not yet," she said, between soft kisses, "but he will be now. I am certain, though when and how are up to Great Spirit . . . and Cloud."

"Then you are mine for the rest of this night." Johnny undid the bead wrap on her long braid. His fingers combed through the length of it and freed handfuls of the black abundance touching their bare shoulders and flowing over her generous breasts.

"For this night and all the nights to come," she whispered in return, kneading his powerful back muscles to pull him close, as if her deep love for this man could erase the ridged scars her fingers caressed— and the horrific memories trapped in each one from the same evil man that—though dead, still held the boy in the nearby tent captive.

* * *

Gregory dreamed. Stinking Man and his black beast held him captive in a dark place deep in the earth. He sucked for air, clutching about him for help. None came. His tied hands hung from wrist ropes. The only good thing was he could touch the dirt with his sore feet. His full weight didn't hang from his hurting wrists. He twisted in the air, tried to call out, but the gag in his mouth choked him. Tears streamed down his feverish cheeks. He awoke screaming in the tent. Taylor and Suzanne comforted him all over again. Exhausted, Gregory lay awake in the crook of Taylor's arm until morning, afraid to close his eyes or try to sleep.

* * *

In the morning, tired from their sleepless night, Suzanne poured pancake batter onto the camp griddle, forming a fist-sized bubbling circle. The steaming aroma rose to her nose. She turned aside and called to the group around the picnic table. "Who's going to eat this last flapjack? I hate to waste batter."

Mitzi dipped a handful of her 'pretty stones' into a plastic cup of water, then one by one lined them up by size next to her paper plate, waiting for them to dry. The boys, Cloud, Stellar, and Gregory studied a trail map with Taylor and Johnny, discussing best views, petroglyph sites, animal tracks they might come upon, and how long it would take to reach and return to camp from each hiking site.

None of them responded about food. Suzanne flipped the pancake onto a plate, slathered it with butter and set the plate in front of Cloud. "You're the growth-spurt young man of the moment," she said, handing him the agave syrup.

Cloud drizzled the golden stream onto the pancake, cut wedges with a fork, and took one to his mouth. "We'll all share it," he mumbled, sliding the plate and fork to Gregory, who hesitated only a moment before laying the map aside. With sticky fingers he popped pancake bits into his mouth, then licked his fingers and wiped them on his jeans.

Suzanne pretended not to notice the sticky residue she'd have to spot-treat once they were back home.

Cosma climbed over the picnic bench with her mug. "Since it's our last day, I'll help Suzanne clean up the breakfast mess so you hikers can get an early start with your snack packs and water bottles."

She touched one of Mitzi's shiny-wet stones. "That's a gypsum crystal. Very special energy. It catches the light in tiny sparkles, doesn't it?"

"The sparkles winked at me in the red sand," Mitzi said. "That's how I found my pretty crystal." She dropped it with her other favorites into the pocket of her shorts and brushed the red dust left behind out onto the ground. "I don't like long hikes. I get tired, and Mommy says I'm too big to be carried."

"I've brought my watercolors." Suzanne stuffed used plates into a plastic trash bag and tied it shut. "Would you like to stay here and paint with me, Mitzi?"

"Um hum, that's the bestest idea."

"Best idea," Suzanne corrected, stuffing the bag into the fat metal can with the hinged lid to keep animals out. She replaced the heavy rock on top.

"That's what I said." Mitzi shrugged her shoulders. Moving syrup, salt, pepper, and ketchup, she helped make room on the table for painting supplies.

Cosma chuckled and dabbed sunscreen on Stellar's nose and the back of his neck.

"You men take good care of these boys." She looked with affection on Johnny and Taylor, busy gathering cameras, backpacks, and binoculars to entertain the boys.

Taylor brushed Suzanne's hair with his lips. "See you later, Honey. I'll grill tonight so you women can relax by the fire."

Gregory moved to his side. "Since Mitzi's not coming, can we follow the petroglyph trail that takes longer?"

"That okay with the rest of you men?" Taylor secured Gregory's backpack onto the boy's shoulders.

He caught Suzanne's eye. They exchanged questioning raised eyebrows.

"Fine by me," called Johnny, herding Cloud and Stellar toward the trailhead.

"Let's take the left fork along the dry wash."

They were off.

Cosma tapped Suzanne's arm lightly. "I'm going to gather fresh plants I'll need for Gregory tonight at the campfire. I won't be gone long. Gives you a chance to paint with Mitzi."

Suzanne nodded. "But, how can we persuade him to allow you to help him?"

"Cloud offered to make sure Gregory trusts me. He must have his own idea."

"Whatever works to stop these terrible nightmares is welcome."

Suzanne spread paints and brushes on the table and tore sheets of stiff watercolor paper for herself and Mitzi, taping them to boards. It puzzled her Gregory was eager to take a longer hike when he'd done nothing but complain about hiking every day they'd been camping. She noticed Taylor wondered why as well and watched while their boy uncharacteristically hurried past Taylor to catch up with Cloud.

Maybe trusting Cosma will come through Cloud. What a fascinating friendship our boys have formed. What idea could that Apache have in mind?

Uncomfortable misgivings stirred her insides, until she became absorbed in painting and directing Mitzi to stay focused with brushes and paints on her paper too.

* * *

Later, with Mitzi down for a nap in the tent, Cosma returned to camp with her sage and cedar bundles and observed Suzanne tucking her rinsed watercolor brushes into their linen carrier. Taped on the end of the picnic table, her two watercolor sketches of rocks and rabbit brush and Mitzi's colorful painting dried in the soft breeze.

Before the boys and men returned from their hike, no doubt starving, Cosma opened the ice chest next to the table, lifted a couple of bottles of water out, and handed one to Suzanne. She had looked forward to time alone with her friend and had hurried back to make certain they could have a private conversation. She was particularly pleased Mitzi was down for a nap. *It will be easier, more straightforward to question her.*

"Thanks. I need to hydrate after painting in the desert for a couple of hours."

"Hydrating is important, especially for you," Cosma said, sipping and smiling at the woman she still found to be such an unusual best friend for herself. Suzanne the Christian churchgoer and Cosma the Indian shaman who communed with Great Spirit. Last summer she'd felt closer to Suzanne's more metaphysical twin Dierdre, until the kidnapping of the boy. Gregory's kidnapping had changed everything for all of them.

She came back to the moment, waiting with anticipation to question Suzanne, finding it hard to suppress her curiosity.

"Why *especially* hydrating for *me*?" Suzanne cocked her head and raised her eyebrows.

Cosma sat down across from her on the bench of the picnic table, enjoying the prodding direction she was taking with her words. "Do you have a secret you feel like sharing?"

"Wha . . . ?" Suzanne's fingers paused in the act of tying closed the brush-carrier ribbon. Her mouth opened like a fish just hauled in, gasping for a last breath.

Setting her water bottle on the table, Cosma laughed gently. "Last evening you passed up wine with our campfire meal and you skipped your strong-coffee ritual with Taylor this morning. Are you two going to have a baby? Is that why you didn't prod Mitzi to go along for a hike today? I mean one of you always ends up carrying her back to camp. Not smart for you to risk a fall or a strain if you're pregnant."

Suzanne's eyes were wide. Abruptly, she sat sideways on her side of the table, fidgeting with the ribbon, tying and untying it. She met Cosma's steady, warm gaze, shrugged her shoulders and smiled back.

"Well, if you aren't psychic, you're some savvy observer." She sighed. "I'm only a few weeks late. No nausea, just a little queasy around food. If I *am* pregnant, we'll know soon. I don't want to take chances with anything that might harm an infant. We so much want a baby together."

"Of your own, you mean. Very wise to be careful." Cosma clinked her chilly plastic water bottle against Suzanne's. "Celebrate the possibility, probability—shall we?"

Suzanne's face lit up, apparently with hopeful joy. "Will you keep my secret until I'm sure? I turn thirty soon. I miscarried Steve's baby. Then he got cancer, so we didn't try again. I'm cautious of losing another . . . you understand. I haven't told Taylor because he'll start treating me like I'm fragile. I'd like to wait until he notices I'm different and asks me what's up."

"He adores you and will enjoy playing father-hero. You must let him. He's taken on Gregory and Mitzi and loves them as if they were his own. He even shows love for my boys the way Johnny does."

"And you, Cosma?" Suzanne looked expectant. "What about you and Johnny? If anyone adores anybody around here it's you two. Are you going to m . . . have babies of your own?"

Cosma laughed and rose to start the lunch meal soon to be begged for by their returning hikers. She admired the way Suzanne did not assume she would marry, since only one of the fathers of her boys had been a husband.

"We've been talking about the M and B words—marriage and babies. I feel Great Spirit has led me to this good man, his falcon, and his need for someone . . . me. Yes, we will marry, but when and where have not been decided. He loves me and has asked me if I could accept him for a husband, but feels he has so little to offer the boys and me in the way of a home and financial security. Plus he worries about his impairments and necessary medicines to calm the tremors that can surprise him."

"How do you feel about all that?" Suzanne rose and sorted through the bags of food for lunch items, talking over her shoulder.

Cosma moved to her, opened her arms in an embrace, the first between them since Gregory's kidnapping.

"You and I are blessed with these fine men to father our children. As for Johnny, he has more than a healthy amount of what I want—what you already *have* in a husband—a loving heart and a kind way."

* * *

At noon, the sun was high and hot. The hikers paused on a ledge above a sparkling stream punctuated with red-sandstone boulders as big as hay bales. In the lead, Taylor stopped and put up a hand.

"We're more than halfway back to camp. Let's break for water before we go explore that shaded wall of petroglyphs Cloud spotted from below. It's not listed on our trail map, probably because it's harder to get to. Should be interesting."

Johnny shook a few tablets into his palm and uncapped his water bottle. "Sounds good to me." He downed his meds in one gulp and passed water out to the boys.

Gregory sat on a rock next to Cloud and opened his backpack for a candy bar. He broke it into three pieces and shared it with the Indian brothers on either side of him.

Stellar shoved candy in his mouth and handed his brother a fistful of dried cheat grass before he took the bottle from Johnny. "This what you wanted?"

Cloud nodded. He unfolded a length of cattail leaf brought with him from the stream bank. Working on his knees, he wrapped the grass inside the leaf and pierced the little bundle securely with mesquite thorns to form a fat pad with a lump on one end.

"What are you making?" Gregory leaned close to watch.

"Something for our last campfire." Cloud patted Gregory's shoulder and smiled up at Johnny who also watched with interest. "You'll see tonight. It's a special thing for my mom to use."

Gregory backed away, chewing his lower lip. "Is Cosma going to burn it to make smoke for her pipe?" He gulped down the rest of his candy.

"She'll know what it's for." Cloud broke off four stiff mesquite branches the size of long wooden fireplace matches and stripped them of their tiny leaves and black thorns. He chose one bent twig and three straight ones. Tucking them into a pocket of his backpack with the leaf bundle and several thorns, he zipped it shut and accepted a drink from Johnny. Smiling with satisfaction, he stood and gestured to the other boys.

"Let's go. Is your camera still charged, Stellar? Mom'll want to know what sacred symbols from the ancient ones we found scraped into desert varnish on pink sandstone."

"What *you* found, you mean." His eyes adoring, Gregory followed on Cloud's heels. He hurried to keep up on the deer trail winding higher through the rocks and weeds.

No verbal warnings came from the men or the Indian boys about rattlesnakes, scorpions, or poisonous lizards. By silent agreement, watching for hazards was taken care of for Gregory, who for the first time all week seemed more like a happy boy.

* * *

Chapter Four   *A Change of Plans*

Dierdre perused a stack of cruise brochures, making notes on a pad. Occasionally, she sipped iced tea from the frosty glass on her patio table. She inhaled salt air and sweet jasmine, prompting the thought that a tropical birthday vacation held the most promise of fun for Suzanne and her family, drying their lives away in Utah's high-desert country.

Without her weekly phone chat with Suzanne, she felt uneasy, set adrift somehow. Waltzing around the unopened package of cigarettes on the kitchen counter without ripping it open was especially challenging this afternoon. Still, resisting the nicotine craving gave her a sense of pride and strength of character she hadn't felt for a long time.

Pausing, ballpoint in hand, she mused, *I wonder if I'm ready for a serious relationship and the feeling of belonging I have with my twin. That belonging she has with Taylor and the kids. Living family-less isn't all it's cracked up to be anymore. Will I ever be able to lean on someone else or am I doomed to always go it alone no matter how lonely and aimless my life gets?*

The phone rang. She laid the pad and pen aside and went to pick up.

Caller ID showed a call coming in from an unknown area code. *Probably a wrong number or a solicitor for something I don't want or need.*

"Hello?"

"Dee, I'm calling from a hospital emergency room."

"Susanne? What on earth has happened?" Dierdre's heart tightened in her chest.

* * *

Cosma held Johnny's free hand. His other lay still, palm-down on the white sheet. An IV needle bandaged into a vein on top secured the tube dripping saline solution. It hung from a bag on a mobile pole above his cranked-up hospital bed.

She bent and brushed his stubbly cheek with her lips, whispering, "The doctor assures me you're vitals are stable now. She says you're going to be fine in twenty-four to forty-eight hours. Exhausted probably, but recovered."

Johnny's gaze met hers. She observed his dilated pupils, so dark and large his brown eyes appeared onyx like her own and Cloud's.

"What happened? Don't remember much. It's all mixed up." His soft words came out more deliberate and labored than usual. "Damn. I ruined the campout . . . where are the boys? Taylor's family?"

Cosma's heart brimmed with tenderness for him. "Don't worry John-Love, you're more important than a campout. You had a seizure, epileptic they suppose. After you were carried down to camp, Taylor let me rush you here in his truck. The boys helped him and Suzanne take down and pack up their tent and all our gear. They just arrived half an hour ago in our camper. Suzanne and Mitzi are in the hall on the phone to Dierdre. We're all relieved you're going to be fine. Taylor and the boys have gone to find a motel for all of us until you're released to go home."

The dazed expression on Johnny's pale face told her, under sedation he couldn't take in all she'd just explained and make sense of it.

She rubbed his hand, her voice intimate. "Your job is to rest and let the Phenobarbital and the IV restore you to normal. Once you're out of here I'll take over. You know what a healer I can be."

He closed his eyes, pulled his hand free, and turned his head away, sighing as if the world sat on his chest. "I'm afraid . . ."

She waited. Fearing he'd forget his train of thought without telling her what he feared, she stroked his brow with bent fingers. "Afraid of what?"

Johnny turned his head back to her on the pillow and opened his eyes, coming from far away in an effort to focus on her face. "You don't need . . . my problems. The boys need a dad . . . like Taylor."

Cosma laughed softly. "I'll decide what I need and what my boys need. You don't get to decide *everything*." Her kiss was gentle, her tongue moistening his parched lips until she felt the stirring of his response and stood looking down at him, aroused by his sweet vulnerability and her deepening love.

He smiled a crooked, drugged sort of smile and drifted off to sleep.

She pulled a chair near the bed and sat next to him caressing his shoulder, grateful that he was safe, peaceful in the sureness that she would be his woman no matter what. She must convince him of her devotion. She fingered her bead-wrapped braid, deep in thought.

* * *

Dierdre carried the remote phone back out to the balcony, cocked between her ear and shoulder. She carried pen and pad.

"Suze, give me the hospital name and a number besides the pay phone where you can be reached." She was nearly delirious with relief that Suzanne and none of the others in her family were the ones needing hospitalization. "But what happened to Johnny?"

Suzanne's voice was ragged. "I'll call you again in a few hours. Mitzi's starving and we're all stressed and tired, but relieved of course. Johnny's grand mal seizure didn't cause a whole series of them or make him or anyone else tumble over a cliff. Just wanted you to know we'll be a couple days later getting back home. Didn't want you to worry we were stranded in the desert."

"Of course I'd worry. So you're going to stay until Johnny's out of the hospital? You'll let me know a motel number where I can reach you and tell me for sure when you're going to get home, right?" Dierdre sank into the chaise lounge and doodled on the pad. "When you're up to it, tell me everything."

Suzanne said, "Will do. Wait a minute. Mitzi wants to talk. Be fast. I'm out of quarters."

"Aunty Dreedra, we don't get to do our campfire and S'mores tonight. Can we cook 'em with you sometime soon? Your gooey ones are the bestest."

Dierdre felt a surge of adoring energy. "Tell your Mommy I have a birthday surprise for her and S'mores for all of you—very very soon."

The little voice bubbled with hope. "And for Johnny and Cosma too?"

Quarters used up, the phone's auto-voice asked for a deposit. With none forthcoming it clicked dead.

Dierdre sat stunned at the thought of planning a trip for *two* families, the money, the trouble of scheduling, all the complications. Yet, the more she thought about it, *Haven't I been wanting a family, a feeling of belonging? Why not an extended family including Johnny, Cosma, and her boys?*

Her mind raced with ways to make the thirtieth birthday party on a cruise ship a smashing affair with memories to last a lifetime. Now to get them all to go along with my idea. Gads. How to pay for so many?

Dierdre put down the note pad and lit meditation candles before her Buddha altar. She spread her yoga mat and sat lotus style to begin her breath work, relieved to be back in touch with her twin. Her mind formed prayers for Johnny and possibilities.

* * *

Taylor and Stellar left to make a last trip to the camper for the two-handled cooler. Cloud unzipped a backpack pocket and removed the twigs and leaf-wrapped bundle of cheat grass. The leaf edges had curled dry. He spread the items out on the motel- room windowsill and shoved the backpack under the bed.

Gregory stepped behind him. "We didn't get to have our campfire. Can that stuff still work sometime? I mean for what your mom wants to do with it?"

Cloud smiled at him. "I'm letting it dry so it will work even better. Let's go swim in the pool. Taylor said he and Stellar will join us after they bring the cooler."

"Shouldn't we all go to the hospital?" Gregory held his sneakers by the laces, looking undecided.

"Mom said there's nothing to do for Johnny but wait for him to rest until he's better. She wants to stay with him. Taylor said we should get in some swimming to forget about all that happened on the trail. Your mom and little sister are coming too."

Gregory shuddered. "It was awful. It scared me to see Johnny choking and shaking on the ground . . . his eyes rolling around. I didn't know what to do."

Cloud turned his back, dropping his jeans and underwear. He stepped into swim trunks, pulled them up, and faced Gregory. "You did everything Taylor told us to, like ramming that stick between his teeth so he wouldn't choke or bite his tongue through. Good thing us boys took turns carrying the big guy's arms and legs. Taylor couldn't have carried him down to camp alone on a good trail, let alone the steep rocky one we were on. Your dad needs to rest, too."

"I hope it doesn't give me nightmares." Gregory pulled his tee shirt over his head.

"One of these days, your nightmares will go away." Cloud knew if anyone could help the kid, he could because Gregory would have to trust somebody sooner or later. His mother assured him if his heart stayed open to Great Spirit he'd be told what to do to help his friend. Cloud believed his mom. *Great Spirit is a powerful ally.*

Gregory changed into his bathing suit. With a bath towel over his arm, he followed Cloud to the pool.

* * *

Sitting beside Johnny's bed, gazing out the window at the moon and stars, Cosma sensed the growing tenseness in his body and turned back to him.

Is he about to have another seizure? Her hand paused above the nurse-call button while she observed the thrashing of Johnny's arms and legs, his head moving back and forth on the pillow, his eyes darting beneath his closed lids, breath rushing in and out, hands grasping air then covering his face. Sweat formed on his forehead.

He's dreaming, not having another attack. Thank Great Spirit! Better a nightmare than a seizure.

She rose and took both his hands in hers, the one with the IV needle taped into it, the free hand as well—crooning to him as if he were a frightened child.

"Shhhh, John-Love. I'm here. You're safe. Shhhh now, Love. Your Cosma is here."

She repeated the words softly, filling him with her comfort, willing him to trust her and leave his nightmare behind in whatever godforsaken-place it dwelled in his mind. The indentation from his skull to his jawline formed a jagged lightening bolt, a still-discernable scar plastic surgery had not fully erased. How he'd survived the brutal attack amazed her as much as it had his doctors. *Like an old warrior you are.* She caressed his hands, his sweaty face.

His arms and legs stopped thrashing, his head stilled. He began to breathe normally. His eyes fluttered open and rested on hers with such kindness and gratitude her heart swelled with tenderness.

"Bad dream, Babe," he whispered.

"About Bo?" She kept his hands in her own and brought the one without the needle to her cheek. Turning it over, she kissed the palm.

He nodded. "God, I wish I could go to sleep without Bo beating me again and again. Wish the seizures would stop too. He did all this to me. I can't be the man you deserve."

His measured but stronger words came out slowly with great effort. Tears formed at the corners of his eyes. He blinked them back. "On the trail, we climbed up to the wall of petroglyphs Cloud spied from below. There was an image of an eagle flying above some men with headdresses chasing antlered elk or deer. A spring trickled water down the dark rock. The sun sparkled on the slick places, the light flashing, flashing, flashing. That's all I remember."

Cosma sat on the side of the bed. Listening, she continued to stroke his hair where the scar ended in a sort of broken line.

"That flashing light probably brought on your seizure. The doctor said changing your medications will help prevent them in the future. Somehow we'll find a way to put an end to the bad memories making you vulnerable to nightmares and seizures."

"I heard Gregory's screams. If nightmares like this are what he's having, it's hell. Poor little kid."

"Only Gregory knows all of what all happened to him at the hand of that brutal kidnapper and his dog before Suzanne and you found them in that cellar."

Cosma breathed deeply and calmed herself now that Johnny was fully conscious.

He spoke quietly, his chest heaving while painful words tumbled out between his lips. She strained to hear each one, a litany of his losses, things he'd never discussed so openly with her before.

"The boy's so young. Bo cost me my wife. She divorced me, took my sons. Bo killed my dog, stole my gyrfalcon, destroyed my life as a full man. Gregory's got his whole life ahead of him. Not fair to a kid. That bastard left so damn much pain in his wake. Should have let *me* die. Dying was too good for him." His big shoulders shook. Tears coursed down his cheeks.

Cosma dried them with the back of her hand. "You have us for family now. My boys will never replace the sons, but Cloud and Stellar have come to love you as I do. Your sons will get in touch when they're of age and can return stateside. They loved you, still do. We'll do our best to give you new . . ."

"*You* and your boys are everything to me now," Johnny interrupted. "Maybe as a vet I can afford some help with this PTSD stuff the doctor talks about, even if my injuries didn't come through military combat. I might be able to help the kid, too."

For the first time that evening, Cosma chuckled. "You came through combat alright. So did Gregory. You're a couple of true warriors, and so is our Suzanne."

The nurse entered, changed Johnny's IV drip bag with an injection in the tube. When she left, he motioned to Cosma and winked, pointing to his lips.

"Ahh, something I can do for the patient that no one else can." She smiled and leaned down to him.

His free hand grasped her braid and gently pulled her face within an inch of his mouth. "You got that right."

Their prolonged kiss said everything between them. Cosma's heart swelled with love for him.

At last, Johnny relaxed against the pillow. His eyes closed on his smiling face.

Cosma returned to her vigil in the chair, her mind awhirl with renewed purpose.

Bo Rodman might be dead but his spirit still terrorized her John-Love and young Gregory. She knew freeing them both wouldn't just bring *them* peace, freeing their minds was essential to her family's happiness and Suzanne and Taylor's as well.

Great Spirit, guide me to use your powerful wisdom to heal my loved ones.

* * *

Chapter Five *Soft and Strong*

Dierdre spent the evening driven to create a keepsake arrangement in her living room, quite unlike her lifelong aversion to sentimentality. She'd cleared the top of a bookcase and the wall above it. Soon nostalgic mementos collected over the years were brought from closets, boxes, drawers, and albums. Framed photos of herself; she and Suzanne; their mother with them on the beach at Salt Air on Great Salt Lake, Utah; and pictures from Suzanne and Taylor's wedding reception last autumn. All smiled from a gallery-like display, which grew to take over the entire wall. Seashells collected with Tiffany, an empty champagne bottle celebrating her promotion to cruise director three years ago, and amazingly—her baby shoes—the tiniest black patent-leather Mary Janes, matching ones her twin wore in their toddler days.

She poured a cup of decaf and surveyed the entire effect, surprising evidence of her inner recognition that she wanted—needed—family and friend meaning in her life.

The doorbell rang. Who at this hour?

She peeked through the peephole on her apartment door. *Tiffany.* Unchaining the security device, Dierdre gestured a welcome to her friend, shooed her inside. "What's up, girlfriend?"

Tiffany set her handbag on the coffee table. "Saw your light and no extra man cars out front. What're you up to without a date on a Friday night?"

Dierdre laughed and lifted her mug. "I've been having fun. Want some brew or a glass of wine?"

"Too late for coffee, even decaf. I vote for wine. Show me what . . . "

Dierdre pointed to her new display, retrieved a wine glass from the armoire bar and poured.

Tiffany studied the items on the bookcase and the wall of photos. "Wow, Dee! What made you step out of your minimalist shoes to go schmaltzy? This shrine thing is quite the earth-shaking alteration in your taste." She accepted a stemmed glass of Chardonnay.

"It's hardly a shrine, Tiff. I'm developing my softer side."

"Lordy, girl. Next thing you know you'll be picking out a homey type to marry. I'm feeling the cool breeze of being left out of your ever-shifting life."

Dierdre cozied up on the couch, patted an adjacent cushion, and gestured Tiffany to sit.

"Actually, dear one, I'm admitting to myself it's time I waded into life's commitment phase." Dierdre clinked her mug with her friend's wineglass. "To our friendship."

"It is great to have a friend you can confide in, isn't it?" Tiffany kicked off her shoes and relaxed into tufted pillows behind her head.

"Speaking of which," Dierdre added, "I expect a phone call from Suze any minute. She called earlier from a hospital.

* * *

The following morning, a call to the cruise-liner reservations office left Dierdre ecstatic. Ideas she proposed to the events coordinator were enthusiastically welcomed. Funding a birthday cruise for two families suddenly became more financially feasible, if she could talk Suzanne and Cosma and their men into it.

When Suzanne called that evening, Dierdre listened intently about Johnny's condition. She was determined to get him and Cosma onto a ship with her sister's family, as soon as he could travel.

"So is he coming along okay? I mean when will he be out of the hospital and able to get out and . . . do things again?"

Suzanne sounded more upbeat than earlier in the day, explaining she'd napped by the motel pool. "Cosma says he's doing great, except for worrying about the trouble he caused. She's so in love with him there's no way she'd be upset about something he had no control over. I think she's going to suggest they marry because then he'll believe she really loves him. He'd never ask her first. Wouldn't that be great?"

Dierdre's ideas roared into overdrive. She paced the room, phone to her ear, passing and re-passing the tempting cigarette pack, still unopened on the dining table. She smiled at herself in the mirror above the fireplace. "Where do they want to get married?"

"I've no idea if the wish has gone that far, Sis. Any suggestions from your end?"

Dierdre inhaled deeply and let her breath out slowly. "I think the Caribbean would be nice, don't you? A honeymoon cruise is so romantic."

Suzanne's laughter made Dierdre's smile widen.

"Dee, it's a fabulous idea, but I doubt they'd have the money for such a luxury."

With the cruise topic open, Dierdre plunged in. "Actually, my dear twin, we should *all* go so you and I can celebrate our thirtieth birthdays aboard ship or on some lush tropical isle."

"Dream on. We Armstrongs don't have deep enough pockets either. Taylor is still paying off the two trucks he bought for his tree business. I wouldn't go without him, even to run away with my twin for a birthday in paradise." Suzanne laughed like when they were teens planning the impossible.

Expecting resistance, Dierdre was undeterred. "Okay, here are some possibilities. If you'd teach watercolor workshops on board and Cosma scheduled tarot readings and drumming ceremonies for guests, I can get your fares comped. I've checked out having Johnny go on a reduced or perhaps comped ticket as a disabled Korean vet. I've saved up a bit as my birthday present to us. It will help. I'm sure I can come up with other money ideas. The captain can marry Johnny and Cosma for less money than a big wedding would cost."

"Dee, what about the kids?"

"So we'll add them all to the package deal and get a group discount. Cruise lines do it all the time." Dierdre plopped onto the couch in a fever of anticipation.

The phone was silent. "Suze? You still there?"

"I'm here. Here with a secret I haven't even told Taylor. A cruise may not be a wise idea even if we can scrape up the money. "Ah . . . I think I'm pregnant."

Dumbfounded, Dierdre nearly dropped the phone. After a pause she burst into giggles. "Talk about upstaging your twin. I thought I was dropping a happy bombshell. Amazing news! Thrilling, really thrilling."

"Gotta go. Taylor and the kids are back from the pool, starving. Bye for now."

Dierdre clicked the remote phone to off and sat tapping it absently in her lap.

A baby. The enormity of her feelings glued her to the spot. Darkness filled the apartment while she sat thinking. It was a long time before she stood, switched on a lamp, and re-cradled the phone in the kitchen. She lit the gas under the teakettle and watched the blue and pink flames lick its sides, her mind in a distant fog.

Now turning thirty is going to mean something entirely different to my twin than to me.

* * *

In a fury of splats against Suzanne's Blazer windshield, a summer cloudburst erupted in a downpour. She parked in the closest vacant space near the clinic entrance and cracked her driver's-side door wide enough to put up an umbrella. She slid out under its meager protection, shut the door, and hurried up the wind-swept walk. If not forced to hurry through the rain, she would likely have dawdled along the flower-lined way until a moment before her obstetrics' appointment. Suzanne hoped for confirmation of her pregnancy and feared warnings of complications like those she'd missed out of ignorance when she miscarried Steve's baby. If she and Taylor were truly expecting, she wanted to do whatever was necessary to make certain their baby was born healthy.

After filling out forms, having her medical insurance card recorded, and waiting the few minutes that felt like hours, she was shown to a private pale-green examination room where she undressed and donned a crinkly paper robe. At least it was dryer than the clothes she'd worn in. The nurse took her vital signs, specimen cup, blood samples, and left to deliver those necessities to the lab. Suzanne sat on the padded examination table with a paper blanket over her knees, eyeing the steel stirrups with trepidation. Feeling vulnerable and embarrassed, she waited.

Oh, Lord, she prayed, *I'm so afraid to lose this baby. Please help me do whatever I have to for . . .*

Her doctor entered. The nurse closed the door.

* * *

By the time she returned to her car, the rain had stopped. The moment she drove in the driveway with the windows down, an aroma of grilling hamburgers assaulted her senses. Her stomach went queasy.

Thank heaven, Taylor cooks tonight. Ascending the back steps to the house, nausea grew more urgent. She rushed through the kitchen, tossed her handbag and keys on the counter, and flat-handed the swinging door, praying their only bathroom would be empty.

Minutes later, pale in the mirror, she washed her shaking hands and smiling face and slowly drank a glass of water. Through the window Gregory and Mitzi greedily munched Taylor's fat burgers at the backyard picnic table. His "Natural-born Griller" apron hugged his trim waist with ties accentuating the hard-muscled body she fairly worshipped.

I'm about to make you a happy man—as happy as you've made me.

Opening the fridge, she took out the covered bowl of strawberries she'd prepared before her doctor's appointment. Placing it on a tray she added dessert dishes and spoons, then descended the back steps and went outside to the picnic table, hungry only for one of Taylor's loving hugs and the proud approval she imagined in his eyes.

* * *

The phone was ringing when Dierdre unlocked her apartment door. Closing it with her hip, she dropped packages and purse on the nearest chair and hurried to answer. Hoping it was Suzanne, she picked up. Caller ID wasn't familiar. "Hello?"

"BJ here, Dierdre. You free tonight?"

She pictured the Southern blond hottie she'd met last summer at a Fourth of July Sea Bass Bash held in a shanty take-out restaurant on the beach. They'd clicked immediately and dated off and on. Off had been the case for a couple of months, prompting her to move on to the trust-baby brute she'd recently dumped.

Her mood was shaky on the point of man flesh, the supremely handsome ones like BJ in particular. Bored and lonely, she hesitated before answering.

"Long time no hear from you, *kimo sabe*. What d'you have in mind?"

"Forgive the long silence. I stayed at my sister's place in Hanau, Germany a couple of months. Should have told you. I've snagged a pair of tickets to a little review my niece has a part in. Hoped you'd go with me so I can show up with a classy lady on my arm."

His excuse was lame. *Me for arm candy. He's probably been catch-of-the-month with every German girl in Frankfürt. However, a date with him might shore up my flagging ego. Better than sitting home tonight.*

"Throw in dinner and dancing and I *might* be persuaded, BJ"

"Can do, Sugar. Pick you up in an hour."

"You have a lot of faith in my speedy *toilette*."

"Pretty as you are, you could throw on a beach towel and look divine."

He always lays his Southern schmooze on so thick. She laughed at the giddy way such compliments, especially delivered in BJ's Southern-gallant style, made her heart beat a little faster. She hung up and undressed on the way to the shower. Soaped up and blithering shampoo bubbles she heard the phone ring and sped through a condition rinse. Just as she stepped onto the bathmat—Suzanne was leaving a message.

Wrapped in a towel, her head swathed in a terry turban, she punched the blinking-light button and waited. "Call me!" came the demanding voice message.

"That's more cryptic than usual." She towel-fluffed her hair with a free hand while pressing redial.

Suzanne answered. "That was quick." She laughed. "Dee, I'm going to have a baby for sure. Taylor's as excited as I am. He swooped me up in his arms and whirled me around 'til I feared I'd toss my cookies. Even the kids are thinking up baby names."

Dierdre swung from feelings of happiness for her twin, to envy, to concern. "Did you ask your doctor about traveling, you know, like on a cruise?"

"She said not 'til through my first trimester."

Dierdre's heart sank. *Hmmm, three months, so two more months to wait.* "Guess we'll have to delay our birthday celebration a bit. Okay, of course. Your health and safety with the baby must come first."

"Glad you understand, Sis. I've got to go for now. It's been a long day and Taylor insists I put my feet up while he does dishes."

"You lucky darling. Okay, Suze. Keep me posted. Bye for now."

Forty minutes later, Dierdre misted her throat with Obsession and surveyed herself, front and back in the full-length mirror inside her closet door. White ankle-length pencil skirt, slit to the knee; sea-green silk blouse cut low, and two-inch heels on silver-toned sandals. She'd finished snapping on a wide silver bracelet when her doorbell rang.

"Damn, he's twelve minutes early." Irritated at being rushed, she undid the dead bolt. "You're cutting my 'get pretty' time awfully short, you know."

"I knew you'd look and smell divine, finished beautifyin' or not." He grinned.

They hugged. He ran his hands over her back and down her backside. "Missed you, Sugar."

She stepped out of reach and scanned his tan face to read his smoldering eyes. They told her he was in schmooze mode. *Figures.* "I'm sure you had plenty to keep you occupied since we last . . . got together."

"Got it on, you mean." He chuckled and reached for her again, this time brushing her breasts with both hands. "I came a little early just in case you weren't quite dressed. We have time to enjoy a passionate quickie and still make the show."

Dierdre's blood boiled. "You've practiced getting right to the point, BJ."

He laughed, his smile wide over too-perfect white caps, a dimple in one cheek, a spoiled-boy look. "What can I say, Sugar. You're a hell of a lay."

Dierdre resisted the urge to smack him. She unsnapped her bracelet and deposited it in a sparkling crystal ashtray not used in weeks.

Phoenix-like she rose from the ashes of old ways of living her life.

Looking him square in the eye she assumed her firmest cruise-director tone. "I think you left your fine Southern manners and a great deal of your charm with your German *fräuleins*—hookers? You'd better get your not-so-smart ass out of here."

His smile faded in surprise. Eyes wide with shock, he shook his head in disbelief. "But Sugar, geeze I'm sorry. What's your problem?"

She backed him to the door, opened it, and stood with her hand on the knob.

He stepped backwards into the hall, protesting and apologizing in monosyllables. "I don't get it. I know I haven't called in too long a time, but . . ."

"Please don't bother calling or coming by. I've always wondered what BJ stood for. Now you've shown me . . . Big Jerk."

She closed the door and shot the dead bolt.

Turning, Dierdre leaned against the door, listening with satisfaction to him cursing his way down the stairs to the foyer below. She smiled to herself—then burst out laughing.

Oooh was that ever a kick. She pounded her fist against her palm and lifted both fists in the air like a victorious athlete.

On her way to change out of her glamour clothes and into pajamas, she patted the unopened cigarette pack with the kind of affection she used for Tiffany's shih tzu.

"I'm getting through my little tense moments without you filtered lung busters. Proud of myself, too."

Her skirt and blouse hung back in the closet, she picked up a romance novel.

I think I'm done with narcissistic handsome types who behave like God's gifts to us girls. It's time to consider the sort of men who don't look like Cosmo cover models with ecstatic beauties fawning all over them in those chest-baring perfume ads. The next time I'm going for character as well as charm.

Before dropping off to sleep, she mentally lined up the last several super-handsome bozos she'd fallen for and ground them down her mental garbage disposal.

* * *

Cloud turned off the computer and loped down the stairs with the kitchen in mind. By their hushed voices he could tell his mom and Johnny were having one of their secret conversations. Stopping on the bottom step, he strained to catch what they were saying. Things between them had gotten even more lovey-dovey since Johnny came home from the hospital.

After camping, he hadn't left for his own place like usual. Cloud liked Johnny's kind ways, his tough pride, liked him well enough to trust him. He hoped this time his mom would marry this one. He'd been in more than one fight at school when bullys said bad things about her.

He waited . . . listening. He couldn't make out more than a word or two, but did hear the word 'married', which made him happy. He crept back up a few steps and came noisily down again, whistling.

Entering the kitchen, he went to the refrigerator and opened it, pretending to look for a snack.

Out the corner of his eye his mom rose from the table, trailing a hand down Johnny's shoulder as she moved to Cloud. "Your brother's bike tires wouldn't hold air when he tried inflating them. He'd planned to go over to Gregory's for the afternoon. Now he's bummed, watching TV in the basement."

Johnny scooted his chair back and stood. "It's Saturday, when I help Taylor with the falcons. If you want, you boys can come too. Gregory wants a falconry lesson. Could be a guy's day out."

Cloud turned to them, grinning innocently. "You sure you two wouldn't rather have the afternoon to make your own plans?"

His mom gave him one of her half smiles used whenever he figured something out she didn't expect. If Cloud wasn't mistaken, Johnny blushed, studying his boots. The silence lasted so long he heard birds in the trees outside, traffic going by, and the kitchen clock ticking at the speed of his heart. He waited what felt like hours for one of them to say something.

Johnny raised his head and gave him a long look. "I guess you know your mother and I, well we love each other. But I . . . well I have my health problems. I don't know that I'm the best hus . . . partner for her or stepfather to you boys."

"Do Stellar and I get to have a say in it?"

His mom clasped her hands around her braid. Calmly, she said, "Cloud, you are wise beyond your years. How would you feel about Johnny being my husband and your father?"

Her chin quivered and her eyes shone with tears she probably wouldn't let fall. Whatever he said next mattered like never before. Not in the habit of getting involved in her relationships, his chest tightened because his answer was scary important to all of them and especially himself. He smiled.

"Stellar and I have wanted the four of us to be a family for a long time. Let's all be Carlisles."

Cloud felt his mom's arms reach up and hug him tight. He was stunned to see it was Johnny's rugged face that streamed with tears. His big shoulders shaking, his smile lit up the kitchen. He pulled them both into a bear hug and laughed a deep rumble against Cloud's ear.

* * *

Suzanne finished her leisurely bath, wrapped her wet hair turban-style in a towel, donned a terry robe, and returned to the master bedroom. Taylor, already showered, lounged on their bed in boxer shorts. He looked up from *American Forestry Magazine* and smiled. His tanned, muscled body and the damp curls at his temples nearly made her melt. He'd shaved and smelled of her favorite aftershave.

"Taylor, I . . . feel so, so . . . different." She unbound her hair, which fell about her shoulders in ringlets. Fluffing it with the towel she approached the foot of the bed.

"Come here, Baby." His voice was soft, enticing. "Let me take off that robe and decide for myself if you feel any different."

"You know that's not what I meant." What he did mean made her feel sexy and youthful. Laughing, she moved to him, confident in their love.

He sat up, took her hands and pulled her to him. His back against the pillows, he kissed her palms and sent tingles throughout her body, arousing her most secret places. He let go of her fingers.

Her arms went around his shoulders while he untied her robe and searched with gentle hands for the blossoming of her breasts, explored the rounding of her belly. He cupped her breasts and rolled over, taking her nipples in his mouth, teasing back and forth between her breasts until she hummed little noises in her throat.

Suzanne grasped handfuls of his hair and held on while his head moved over her body, exploring with lips and tongue. Dizzy with desire she lifted her hips against him, in touch with his hard eagerness, his boxers throbbing against her bare body.

He lifted his head and met her eyes. "Did you ask if it's safe for the baby for us to make love?"

She laughed softly. "We *are* making love."

"Don't change the subject." He chuckled and lowered his head to her belly, blowing air bubbles against her navel until they laughed together.

Suzanne brought her hands to his face, raised it, and looked tenderly into his eyes.

"She said if we are gentle I should be fine until the last couple of months, barring any . . . problems."

His furrowed brows spoke his concern for an instant before he grinned. "No monkey sex?"

She pretended to be serious, pursing her lips. "We didn't discuss monkeys."

Playfully, he tackled her and slipped her robe from her shoulders, spreading it beneath them. "Let's see if we can make love—gently—like human lovers then. Because, Suzanne my Sweet, your scented body is making me crazy."

"Funny, you have no effect on me whatsoever." She giggled. "But I will make every effort to be quieter than a mama monkey."

He covered her mouth with kisses.

* * *

Taylor left the loan company office patting his jacket pocket where he'd tucked the paid-in-full loan papers. With Gregory in the passenger seat of his truck, in twenty minutes they parked next to Pops' barn.

Before Taylor was even out from behind the wheel, the boy unbuckled his seatbelt, escaped the truck cab, and hollered to Cloud, Stellar, and Johnny just inside the cavernous doorway.

Climbing down to the driveway, Taylor waved to Johnny, who stepped out into the sunshine. He appeared to be in an especially upbeat mood.

"Afternoon, Johnny." He shook his friend's hand and noted its firm grip. "You're fully recovered, I'd say. Is Pops at the mews?"

"Just packing up seed for the pigeons and doves. Boys are raring to get out with the falcons."

They followed the three kids kicking through the barn's straw-covered dirt floor. They could hear Pops filling water jugs at the outdoor sink.

"How's Suzanne doing?" Johnny asked, pocketing his sunglasses. "Any morning sickness?"

"It comes and goes, sometimes at odd hours. I think she's mostly excited about being pregnant." Taylor patted his friend's shoulder. "You doing okay in my mobile home?"

Johnny hesitated. "I haven't been there much since I got out of the hospital." He blushed and cleared his throat. "Cosma wants to keep a close eye on me. I'm staying at her place for a while."

"That's a woman for you." Taylor added, "They like to keep the tether short on their end. Of course, like using an enticing lure with a falcon, it's not all bad when they get what they want."

Johnny stopped in his tracks and touched Taylor's sleeve. They faced each other.

"Cosma and I are getting married. We're gonna be a family." His face broke into a grin that lit him up like kids' faces on Christmas morning.

"That's great! Wait 'til Suzanne hears about you two getting married. The phone lines between our women are going to burn red hot." Taylor laughed heartily. "The boys are happy I bet." He whapped him affectionately on the shoulder. "When? Where?"

"We haven't planned that far yet." They moved on to the back entrance where the boys crowded around

Taylor's dad, helping him tote water, seed, binoculars, and an empty pigeon carrier. They headed off toward the mews with Johnny and Taylor following.

"I've some news of my own," said Taylor. "Could affect you and Cosma and your boys, if you keep an open mind and my secret."

Johnny, with a puzzled expression, walked at his side. "News? Shoot."

Taylor, puffed with pride, blurted, "I haven't told Susie yet, but I just paid off our two trucks this morning. Without two hefty truck payments a month our budget can breathe. I'm thinking it's time my bride of a year has a honeymoon with her old man. Dierdre says we should all take a cruise. She's told Suzanne her ideas for how to cut the costs to the nub. Why not a couple of couples on a honeymoon with our broods?"

Johnny's eyes misted. His jaw worked. He shook his head in denial, disbelief, resistance.

Taylor gripped his shoulder in brotherly fashion. "We'll work it out. Don't say no 'til we explore all our options, okay? If necessary, what are credit cards for?"

* * *

Chapter Six   *Waves of Recognition*

Two in the afternoon Miami time, Dierdre took a break from her cruise director duties to get some fresh air on deck. She imagined spending seven days smiling until her face ached. It was the first time she could recall her stolen moment didn't include smoking a cigarette. She looked through her splayed fingers resting on the deck rail at the last of hundreds of guests coming aboard. They dragged and rolled their luggage up the ramp for check in.

When travelers stepped away from showing passports and tickets, the ship photographer snapped smiling groups, posing couples, bewildered or chatty singles—all of them with enough money to afford a luxury cruise experience. That evening after dinner, and before she hosted the welcoming stage show, they'd be ogling posted photos of themselves to buy for their cruise souvenirs.

Dierdre wished this could have been the birthday cruise she'd looked forward to sharing with Suzanne. She missed her twin more than usual. Their time to party would have to wait until it was safer for pregnant Suze to travel in airplanes and on moving water. For Dierdre it was just another launch day on the job to usual destination points in the Caribbean.

She inhaled salt air deeply, struggling to pin to earth the shifting going on inside herself, a different sort of restlessness. The Atlantic breeze tossed her hair and whipped her white slacks against her ankles. Waves lapped gently at the ship's hull and the pier where another liner's aft section squared up to theirs. Their deck also filled with cocktail crowds. In two hours both ships would put out to sea. The waves on the open ocean would be as shifty as she felt. It occurred to her she'd been so self-absorbed her usual bubbly self wasn't the persona greeting the new crop of cruise guests. They brushed by asking directions to their cabins, the purser's office, the casino, the library, or the hair salon. She'd supplied automatic answers with automatic smiles. *I'd better shape up. This is the job I love for heaven's sakes.*

Dierdre hurried back inside, slipped through the chandeliered main dining room, and with a practiced eye checked the white tablecloths, sparkling stemmed glasses, shiny flatware, and recently freshened flower arrangements. Nothing must be out of order which could give chronic complainers something to make a fuss about. Uniformed servers and sommeliers arranged wine bottles, polished glassware, and moved chairs, sprucing up from guests of the previous cruise who'd disembarked that morning.

Catching sight of her windblown appearance in a mirrored wall, Dierdre took the elevator to her cabin level for a quick freshening up of her own. Retrieving her key from her jacket pocket, she opened her door and stepped inside.

He stood next to her bed smiling.

At least he's dressed this time. "What in hell are you doing in here?" Her hand hadn't pulled the door shut; her heart pounded with indignation. "How did you get into my room? I *never NEVER* give out keys."

"Take it easy, Babes. We can see each other plenty. I got this gig in the Starlight Lounge." He stepped toward her. "I told the steward you were expecting me."

Dierdre shook with unreleased fury.

"Look, Daniel, you may think I want to pick up where we left off, but you're wrong. Get out! I can't believe you'd risk getting Becker fired, you arrogant, selfish . . . twit."

She stood aside and opened the door wider. "Now!"

"Damn you!" His face fell; his shoulders slumped. He sidled past her searing her with a glare. "You're one confusing broad, Miss Cruise Director. You can bet I won't bother you again, no matter how much you flirt with me backstage."

She gripped his arm. "Stick to your music, Daniel. If I hear one word of gossip about what you and I were to each other on that cruise to Bermuda last year, I'll figure out a way to get you fired. We treat each other as professionals—period. Savvy?"

He ripped his arm away. She let go, shoved him into the corridor and slammed the cabin door. *Thank heaven it locks automatically.*

At the vanity she combed her hair and tied it back with a ribbon, her fingers shaking. Practicing some Zen deep breathing, Dierdre calmed herself until her reflected expression in the mirror looked less like she'd been chiseled out of cold steel.

Too many of my chickens are coming home to roost. Daniel's always been a sweetheart. I treated him like dirt. Still, presuming to sneak into my room and wait for me. What the hell did he expect! Wait 'til I give Steward Becker a piece of my mind.

* * *

Dierdre left the Cruise Hotel Manager's office and returned to her cabin with paperwork she'd been handed. Instructed to consult the Excursion, Food and Beverage, Human Relations Managers, and the Officer in charge of on-board lectures, Dierdre prepared her ammunition. With the network of ship experts to help her organize ways to utilize the talents of her twin, Cosma, and perhaps their men, she believed her persuasive arguments for booking a birthday cruise would prove irrefutable. She'd even enlisted backup with the medical team for Suzanne, should any emergency arise. Dierdre wanted an answer to every argument when she laid out her plan to Suze.

In half an hour she was due on deck to facilitate guest entertainment for the duration of the cruise. The ship wouldn't dock at their first destination port in Cozumel until tomorrow, so keeping passenger spirits and energy high was her and all staff's first priority. Whatever the employee undercurrents of jealousy, romantic affairs, job competition, illness, and numerous grievances, the show of effortless congeniality and impeccable customer service must be flawless.

Dierdre was glad her job entailed the fun of cruising and not the challenges of mending spats and behind-the-scenes drama Human Relations had to deal with. However, she was more than a bit envious of HR Abby's "ship husband" arrangement with another officer for six months at a time. Sharing a cabin and the comfort of a steady man for long periods of several cruises would be a welcome trade for the dating scene with staff on board, which often included a succession of men and as many disappointments—ending in what she was most sick of—loneliness and regret. Not to mention uncomfortable surprises like Daniel.

I wonder if I could pull off an arrangement like Abby has with Rick. But would I wish for more permanence once we ended each cruise? The wait on land between cruises is the loneliest time of all.

The tap on her shoulder surprised her. "Ma'am?" She turned. A young woman in her early twenties stood with an incredibly handsome older man in dark glasses. *Why sun glasses here inside the ship?* Dierdre smiled at the girl, took in what she supposed to be the mid-to-late-forties fellow's white-tipped cane. She ran through her homework mentally to place them by name. *Oh, he's the blind guest.* "May I help you?"

"Dad and I don't agree on the location of our cabin. He was told one thing by a steward, and I'm going by the cabin map in our packet." The young woman handled herself confidently, as if she were much older. Probably used to managing for her father.

Her brunette Italian bob, short over one ear, long from the crown to her chin on the other was swingy and chic. Silver hoops sparkled from her tanned ear lobes. The names clicked.

Dierdre gestured for the map, consulted it, and smiled. "I love it when I have an answer, Megan and Randy Keene. You're one deck lower. Take the stairs you came down or use the elevator to our left."

"But, but how do you know our names?" Megan stammered. We've never met and we're not wearing tags." Her perfectly waxed and shaped eyebrows furrowed in confusion.

"My job is to study passport photos from reservations. I'm to greet you by name on your arrival." Dierdre laughed and handed the map back.

Randy held out his free hand. "And you are?" She liked his deep voice, a rich baritone. His wide, white-toothed smile formed deep creases running to his impressive jaw. Broad shoulders added to the look of a fullback. *I wonder if he's always been blind.* She shook his hand. *A firm but gentle grasp.*

"I'm Dierdre Ingram, Cruise Director. We're delighted to have you aboard and will do everything we possibly can to make certain you have a memorable cruise vacation."

He dropped her hand and stepped back. "Yes, of course . . . our vacation. You sound like a lovely lady. Is she as beautiful as she sounds, Megan?"

"Yes, Dad. She's beautiful all right." Megan giggled and looked at his dark shades as if he could see her reaction.

His laugh was contagious. "I'm sure we'll meet again, Ms. Dierdre. Perhaps by the pool. It's been a pleasure."

Megan took her father's arm and turned him in the direction of the elevator. She waved at Dierdre. "Thanks for your help and your warm welcome."

Dierdre watched them maneuver among other passengers lugging roller bags, most consulting maps while they jostled and apologized passing each other in the corridor.

Realizing she'd been standing like one mesmerized while she watched the retreating blind man outside her cabin door, Dierdre stepped inside.

That's the first time I've felt truly complimented by a man who thinks I'm beautiful when he can't even see me. Funny, it never occurs to me that looks don't always matter. Why-the-hell can't I find a single, available—sighted—no-kids, hunk like that gentleman to make a new love life worth all the risks?

* * *

Dierdre exited the ship elevator wearing her favorite clingy red dress. Snug at the waist and hips it flared mid-calf. She'd accented it with a ruffled black-organza bolero and black Spanish boots. The effect was exotic and sexy, and she emphasized it with a practiced runway walk. On stage she'd top the outfit with a flat-brimmed black flamenco hat set at a sauciest angle over one eye. Dangling jet earrings and hot red lips and nails completed her wow appearance. Dressing like this gave her an adrenalin rush as good as being on stage.

Turning heads followed her progress through the corridor to the gaming tables in the casino. She tried not to be too obvious noticing herself in every mirrored wall she passed. The click of dice and soft tumbling sounds on the craps table filled her with anticipation. *It's going to be a fun kick-off evening and a great cruise. I'm sure of it.*

Swishing between guests and greeting frequent cruisers by name, she sensed the stir of admiration following her and loved having the power to make it happen. Suddenly, like a magnet, her eyes were drawn to the grinning mid-forties man in the cream sports jacket. His sky-blue shirt, open at his tanned throat, matched his incredible eyes—Tyler.

He lounged against the balcony rail watching her. He lifted his tumbler in greeting. As if in slow motion, they moved toward each other.

"Tyler," she breathed. "It's been a long time since Martinique." Her pulse hit an erratic pace. *Oooh, he has the same effect on me as before.*

"Too long, sweet thing. I'd nearly forgotten how gorgeous you are in red—or out of it," he whispered. "You'll knock 'em dead tonight." His free hand lightly caressed the small of her back, leaving a trail of shivers.

"Traveling alone again?" Dierdre hoped his answer would be yes. Their month-long affair had nearly been her undoing two years before. They'd kept in touch for a while by an occasional phone call. After a few weeks the many-states-apart distance fizzled their romance.

"Not exactly, but something could be arranged, if your schedule is somewhat flexible." He sipped and studied her over the rim of his glass. Smiling, he set the empty tumbler on a passing server's tray and took her hands in his.

A sleeze-ball red flag flickered and was promptly ignored. The guests around them blurred. Inhaling his expensive scent, Dierdre's senses quickened. She said, "Perhaps before the show we could take drinks up on the lido. I have half an hour and after the last show we could get reacquainted in the moonlight."

His smile widened to a grin. "Dazzling and as romantic as I remember you. It's a date, if we're not too old for that sort of thing." He hadn't let go of her hands and rubbed his fingers tenderly along hers. "Let's take our drinks up for a few minutes."

They chose a pair of deck chairs facing the ship's foaming wake. The moonlight glittered along the stern rail and broke into sparkling shards on the roiling waves.

He handed her a glass and helped her settle into a chair.

"I think you've improved on perfect." She clinked her glass against his. "To old friends."

"Cheers," he replied, pulling the other chair next to hers and seating himself.

They sipped in silence, looking into each other's eyes until for Dierdre the tension was unbearable. "I want you to kiss me so much if I didn't have this glass I'd need one under my chin."

Tyler threw back his head and laughed. "I think we should do something about your mouth-watering urge." He set his glass on the deck, took hers from her hand, and placed it next to his. "Give me a taste of those lips. I'll watch from the audience and do a bit of my own drooling."

Tyler pulled her to her feet. His mouth came down on hers, all soft. The tip of his tongue explored her lips and parted them gently.

Dierdre, dizzied with desire, reached her arms around his shoulders and melted into him. They consumed each others' kisses for what felt like eternities. She moved her hands against his chest.

The string of recent misjudgments about men made her pull herself free. She smiled up into his eyes. "Mmmmh, Tyler. I have to cool it. I can't walk on stage in this state of . . ." She laughed. "Disarray."

"Ahh, ever the professional. No dishevelment shall be tolerated." He smoothed her hair, set her back in her chair, and returned her wine glass. "I too cannot betray my overly apparent desire for you, Madame. Whatever reputation I may have among the ladies and gents, it would not do to be so obvious as to impersonate a young stud just returned from an evening in the back of dad's Cadillac."

He picked up his glass. "My dear, we do still have some electric chemistry."

"You are an incredible kisser. My anodes are fried, Tyler Hamilton."

He leaned close and kissed her cheek. "Ever the quip queen on stage or off."

She bit her lip and stared into her wine, swirling it in her glass. "Tyler, why did you say you weren't *exactly* alone on this cruise? Is there a woman waiting in your cabin? Am I about to experience a broken heart or an embarrassing confrontation—or both? I cannot let this go any further between us until I know."

He didn't answer. She checked her watch and reality set in. Reluctantly, she excused herself to hurry downstairs to the theater and prepare to MC the cruise's opening-night entertainment.

* * *

After the closing dance number and her farewell remarks to the audience, the stage curtains closed and Dierdre retreated backstage. She congratulated dancers and musicians, the comedian, and the stagehands.

"Marvelous send off for the cruise guests. Thank you all for your hard work and terrific enthusiasm."

The lead singer hung back, beaming. "That new opening number went great for a first-run tonight, don't you think, Ms. Ingram?"

Affectionately, she tapped Tony on the shoulder. "Good thing you're a pro. We all owe you thanks for covering the timing glitches with your snappy adlibs. The audience loved them and probably thought it was all part of the script. Think you could do it that way every time?"

He hugged her for a 'yes' and hurried off to join the rest of the cast heading to dressing rooms to shed costumes. Dierdre stepped out of her stiletto heels and exchanged them for ballet flats from her tote bag. She wanted to make a faster escape to meet Tyler on the Lido deck. Shouldering the tote, her hat in her hand, she took the back stairs and collided with a big young man coming up in a bigger hurry.

"Pardon me," he said, pausing to steady her without dropping his guitar case. "You okay, ma'am?"

Dierdre released her death grip on the stair rail and caught a restorative breath. She recognized his jacket color for the disco lounge's musicians. "You're new with us."

He nodded, swishing long, auburn hair out of blue eyes amazingly rimmed with thick, black lashes. "My first cruise. Heard there's a jam session about to start with some of the stage dudes. Sure didn't mean to crash into the cruise director. Bet that could get me fired." His sweet sun-starved face blushed with embarrassment.

"No harm done. Fortunately I changed out of high heels. You can sense we're out in open water with plenty of wave action." She laughed her reassurance. "Slow down. Pace yourself with the roll of the ship."

"I will," he said, stepping aside to let her pass.

She smiled and glanced at his name badge.

"Wilson, you might consider tying your hair back or a salon appointment with Jody so she can find your nice eyes. You'll be busy with more than jam sessions when the girls can see them."

His blush deepened. Nodding, he carried his battered guitar case up the remaining steps toward the instrument noise at the back of the darkened stage.

Smiling to herself, Dierdre walked to the nearest elevator musing about Wilson's naïve personality and youthful eagerness. *Was I ever that young and sweet? What I'd give for those eyelashes. Why do guys get that kind and we girls have to enhance like mad with mascara and liner? Not fair.* She chuckled.

"You're flirting style is less sexy than it used to be with me."

Dierdre jerked in alarm, the chuckle died in her throat. The familiar voice had a sinister quality she'd never heard in it before. The grating tone was nastier than their parting encounter in her cabin when he'd bribed the steward to let him in. He emerged from the connecting corridor.

Her back stiffened. "You startled me, Daniel." She edged to the elevator doors, disconcerted about the instinctive warnings churning her gut and the clammy sweat gathering between her fingers.

He beat her to the button and pressed 'up' before she could reach it. In the back of her mind, a sea of red flags waved like Russian May Day. She'd caught all the nuances of bitter sarcasm in Daniel's remark and wondered how long he'd stood out of sight in the shadows waiting to catch her alone.

What's he up to? Am I in danger? Her sister Suzanne's life-shattering, near date-rape ordeal came to mind. *Oh God.*

"Let's keep it professional," Dierdre said quietly, grateful the elevator doors were opening. *Empty of cruise guests—damn it!*

With an elbow she pressed the button for her deck level and moved to the corner. Back squared to the wall, she held her tote bag high in front of her hips like a shield.

Daniel faced her while the doors closed behind him and the elevator began to rise.

"That long-haired boy isn't your customary type." He raised his arms, trapping her with flat palms planted on either side of her shoulders. His sneering face within inches of hers, he ground out the words, "Not someone like me, but I suppose young and innocent could be more fun for you with your years of considerable affair experience."

His spittle spattered her cheeks. She willed herself not to wipe it away or express her disgust with a withering look. *This is damn scary.*

Experience had sounded like it had a TH in the middle. He'd never lisped before. She smelled whiskey on his breath. Escape instincts in overdrive, her immediate goal was to avoid panic and an embarrassing scene for passenger guests she prayed would be there when the elevator doors opened at her deck.

Dierdre stared ahead, refusing eye contact or response. *Drunks aren't rational. I've got to stay calm and show him I'm not intimidated.* Averting her face from his alcohol breath and venomous words, with her tote against his chest and her hat on the floor at her feet, she shoved him away.

Daniel hurled to her side and rammed his hand up behind her tote, raising her dress skirt between her thighs. It hurt like when she came down hard on the bar of a boy's bike as a kid. She bit her lip to keep from screaming.

Shocked, her pubic bone in agony, she sucked in her breath. "Take your goddamn hand off me!"

Hobbling to the button panel, she reached for the emergency alarm lever.

Daniel lunged and grabbed her hand. "Please don't bother, Baby. Believe me, your bod's not worth losing a job over."

Dierdre wrenched her hand free, hissing, "I warned you not to behave in some stupid way. Don't you *ever* say anything so rude to me again! And never never touch me! I can't believe I . . . we. You are nothing but a drunken creep. Stay away from me."

She pulled her skirt down and retrieved the hat, still holding her tote in front of herself while he leered and had the audacity to sniff his fingers and grin. Her stomach turned over.

"You've made me wish this door would open to a cliff I could push you over. My job may be in jeopardy if our affair gets out, but you'd better not pull a sniper attack on me ever again."

The elevator bumped gently to a stop at the staff floor. The doors slid quietly apart. She punched the hold button to keep them open and waited, hiding her shaking hands from him. No one hurried down the hall to enter. *Damn. No one to help me.* Her heart pounded. Close to panic level, she gritted her teeth, reached in the tote for a stiletto ready to spike him in the eye if he tried to touch her again, and held her breath.

Daniel smoothed his hair back and stepped out of the elevator laughing at her. With both hands wiggling fingers up, he gave her a crude come-on gesture like a street-gang teenager.

She didn't follow him off. Fighting for professional control, Dierdre pressed the door-close indicator. Daniel's leering grin faded in a sandwich between the merging panels. Once the doors closed completely, shutting out his physical face, his horrible image lingered as if it were pasted on the inside of the doors. The chilling illusion made breathing a sigh of relief futile. She leaned on the deck number for the administrative staff offices. His mocking laughter seeped in around her while the elevator started up. She didn't release a normal breath until his laughter faded completely away below.

Minutes later, Dierdre finished filling out a Safety & Security request form, signed her name and official cruise-ship role at the bottom, and recapped the pen with shaking fingers.

The subject on the request line read: We need security cameras in *all* of our elevators. Dierdre handed the completed form to the Maintenance Manager.

"I was just accosted in the theater-area elevator by a drunk. If there were cameras he might never have been so foolish. Just as important, I'd have proof to press charges, which now I don't."

"He actually laid a hand on you?"

She nodded, shivering with how violated she felt. "*Very* intimately—the jerk."

"Gawd amighty. Would you recognize him again? I can call a security man to find him." The manager studied the form in his hand and looked up at her. "Beautiful, sweet women like yourself have to be careful. Do you carry Mace?"

"Until now, only when I leave the ship." *How nice of him to call me sweet and beautiful. Daniel wanted me to feel like a sleaze with no redeeming qualities.*

"I'd recognize him all right. I'm reporting him to security immediately because he's on staff. I don't want any more trouble with him for me or anyone else. I'll carry Mace too. Please reprogram my cabin-key cards."

She handed them over, her fingers still trembling. Fighting back tears of outrage, the throbbing of her privates was so distracting she could barely concentrate.

Tapping her key cards on his palm, he said, "More on-ship drama with employees? Worse than guests. Never ends, does it?"

She shrugged her shoulders. "On all my cruises . . . never before."

He reformatted keys to her cabin and returned them. She left, breathing easier since she'd taken action instead of brushing off the whole embarrassing incident. After her twin's experience with the drunk at the dance over a year ago—whose warning signs she deeply regretted ignoring—now Dierdre took danger seriously. This time she was the one in peril. She filled out a sexual-harassment complaint with Daniel's name on it in letters no one could miss.

I hope to get his sorry ass fired and put off when we dock. Cruising with him on board is a frapping nightmare. I'll never know when he might show up and humiliate or hurt me again.

It wasn't the first time Dierdre found herself wishing for a personal hero to lean on, not just for sharing private pleasures. *My diversion with Daniel backfired big time. I'm not going to repeat that mistake. Tyler will not be entering my cabin tonight, no matter how tempting he becomes.*

Arriving on the Lido Deck, Tyler waited with glasses of chilled Chardonnay and deck chairs. Suddenly vulnerable feelings overwhelmed her. *I have to be alone.*

He stood to greet her, offering a glass. "What took so long? The show ended well over an hour ago."

Finding out why he wasn't alone on the cruise no longer seemed important. She planned her escape.

"It was an unexpectedly emotional employee problem I had to follow up on." Dierdre forced a casual smile. "I'm drained and a drink will put me under. Forgive me and ride down the elevator with me to Staff Corridor, please?"

* * *

Next morning while showering, Dierdre gently soaped her tender inner thighs. Looking down, she was shocked to see ugly blue-black bruises. She rinsed and toweled off, pulled on panties and photographed her upper legs before dressing. *The brute! How could I have missed seeing him for the controlling creep he is before we ever climbed into bed together?*

Having hardly slept, her hands still shook while she applied make-up. Annoyed beyond belief, she had to nix the third attempt at eyeliner and cleanse her lids with cold cream. *I know Daniel's counting on me to keep quiet about our little fling to save my reputation with the captain and crew. Well jerk, if I learned anything from Suzanne it's that pride isn't going to keep me, or anyone else safe.*

Before reporting for duty, Dierdre stopped by the Security Office and popped the camera chip into a computer, printed out her photos, dated them, and asked the clerk to tuck them into an envelope and attach them to her harassment complaint against Daniel.

"You'd better have the med staff re-photograph your legs—and anywhere else—to verify evidence of your sexual harassment in writing, or your complaint may not go anywhere," he said, examining the pictures. "It will be tough enough to pin anything on the guy without witnesses. Do it right away this morning, while he's perhaps exhibiting a hangover. Might prove he was inebriated last night. Should work in your favor."

"You may be right," Dierdre said. "I'll go there now and, and . . . get verified."

Oh, lord. I suppose I'll have to take my panties down too and not for fun either.

Daniel's leering face came to mind. She shuddered with revulsion and hurried to the med lab.

Better get it over with before I lose my nerve.

* * *

Chapter Seven   *Special Requests*

Before 6:30 in the morning, Dierdre picked up the thank-you size envelope someone had slipped under her cabin door.

The elegant script on the front read:

Ms. Dierdre Ingram
Sundancer Cruise Director

I wonder what this is about. She opened her door a crack. *No one there or walking away in either direction.* She stepped back inside and went to the table she used as a desk. Slitting the ivory envelope under the flap with a nail file, she pulled out a stiff, formal card edged in silver scrollwork. The message in the same lovely hand script read:

Please join Dad and me for dinner this evening after the show. Solar Ray Lounge, midnight buffet. Dad would love your advice regarding an important matter.

Randy and Megan Keene
RSVP by voice message, Cabin 24-E

How strange, but intriguing for sure. Why on earth would a blind man need my advice? Ha, perhaps how to avoid a satisfying love life. I could give him plenty of examples. But then, being blind, he's probably got that one nailed.

Dierdre waffled about accepting the invitation since she'd already agreed to have drinks with Tyler Hamilton before tonight's show. She'd had to leave for opening night just when he was about to explain why he wasn't alone on this cruise. She was simply dying of curiosity and dread. Terribly attracted to him, their spark was still there, as if over a year hadn't passed. Reestablishing a relationship with him had given her hope Tyler could be the much-needed change in man-luck she sought.

Looking over the dinner invitation again, she reconsidered. *Oh, what the heck. Might as well make a couple of guests happy and treat myself to a diversion from my frustrations about Daniel, Tyler's cabin guest, and all the rest of the deceiving jerks in this world.* Her ego and her body still smarted from Daniel's assault.

On the cabin-to-cabin phone, she punched in the numbers for Cabin 24-E. With no answer, she left her acceptance message and dressed in white capris and a black and white Ralph Lauren sweater to introduce the morning lecturers in the theater.

Later in the afternoon, main-deck activities kept Dierdre occupied facilitating light-hearted shuffleboard contests and handing out Sundancer tee shirts, caps, and tote bags to the winners.

Still in capris and a wide-brimmed hat banded with nautical ribbons, she went on to host the skeet shooting with clay pigeons and the golf drives into the wake, both off the stern from the lower deck.

My arms are red. I've had enough sun today. Slathering herself repeatedly with sunscreen, she kept up a lively banter with the guests until breaking to leave time for a shower and an evening-wear change before meeting Tyler at the cocktail hour.

Toting several carryalls, Dierdre passed through the lounges, nodding and smiling to guests. She went up several deck levels to return the remaining prizes to inventory. That accomplished, she walked to the nearest stairs to return to her cabin level.

The head of security approached. "Ms. Ingram."

She waited. He stepped near and spoke quietly.

"Your papers charging one of our employees with drunkenness and sexual harassment have been reviewed in your favor. Do you want Daniel arrested and formally charged State-side or will dismissal and putting him off ship when we return to Miami be okay? The captain would like to avoid, you know . . . unhealthy publicity for the cruise line, while taking your comfort and safety into consideration, along with that of our cruise guests, of course."

Dierdre hesitated. "It was more than harassment. I specifically wrote 'assault'. I know a USA-based corporation doesn't own this liner. Arresting him aboard ship isn't likely?"

"No, Ms. Ingram. But once he's back in the States it can be handled."

"Still, I live in Miami and I'm afraid he'll come looking for me, perhaps finish what he started. Is a restraining order possible once we're ashore?"

He scratched his head and adjusted his cap. "I'll check. If it can't be directed from ship to shore, I'm on good terms with the Miami PD. We have a cruise-line attorney who can help you fill out a restraining order. The captain says he'll cover any medical or legal expenses. One way or another we'll see Daniel leaves you alone on board and in Florida. He's sobering up in the brig for now. Upset with himself, so I'm told."

Dierdre sighed and relaxed her shoulders. "That's a relief."

"Since he claimed he can't remember laying a hand on you, it's a good thing you and the doctor provided photos of physical evidence and exam reports. Though his blood-alcohol level said otherwise, Daniel swore he'd only had a couple drinks and wouldn't hurt you for the world."

The security manager tipped his hat and went his way.

He wouldn't hurt me for the world—my Aunt Millie. If I had an Aunt Millie, she wouldn't buy it either.

Dierdre retreated to her cabin, breezed through a cooling shower and refreshed, dressed in her MC outfit, a sassy little nautical number with Katherine Hepburn slacks and a striped Coco Chanel jacket. Hurrying to the salon in the main gallery, Jody styled her hair while an assistant touched up her nails.

Arriving at the bar a few minutes early, she ordered a Crown Royal on the rocks with a squeeze of lime. Perched on a stool, an empty one next to her for Tyler held her stiletto tote. She planned to grill him about who shared his cabin and why.

No more accepting these betraying men on face value. I've been way too trusting.

The Crown Royal went down well and warmed her while she nibbled pretzels, satisfying the desire for salt, and cushioning the alcohol blow to her empty stomach.

In the bar mirror, she watched Tyler's approach in casual slacks, loafers, and a white-collared-and-cuffed sky-blue shirt. He checked other women out as he came. She moved her tote while he signaled the bartender and ordered a scotch on the rocks. He patted her arm and sat, turning to face her. "How's my lady this evening?"

"I'm fine this evening. But I'm not *your* lady, Tyler. Not anybody's lady, really."

He laughed casually, pulling out a gold cigarette case. "Well, you *are* a lady aren't you?" He opened it, offering her one.

Shaking her head, she declined, smiling. "So let's pick up where we left off again, right before that young woman this morning interrupted us and jabbered nonsense all the way to my cabin. You didn't get to explain why you're not alone on this cruise, an obvious change from our previous 'your-cabin-or-mine' relationship."

His drink arrived and he toasted it toward her. "Cutting right to the chase, I see."

She clinked her glass against his. "That's my plan. Spill the truth straight up, like your drink."

"Okey dokey. The jabbering woman is Holly Crane. She shares my cabin."

Dierdre set her glass on the bar before she could toss it in his face or accidentally pour perfectly good whisky into his lap.

He grinned. "You look surprised. Don't think I can attract a lady in her twenties?"

The urge to kill. Act cool, Dee Dee. Though her stomach knotted convulsively around salty pretzel bits, she did act cool. "Why didn't you introduce the jabbery darling? Holly's a little young . . . perhaps? She looks about fifteen, but if you say she's in her twenties, guess you're legal."

She sipped the remaining watery whisky slowly, squelching the urge to commit a felony in public.

Tyler lit a cigarette.

Dierdre craved the entire pack. Already sick of his detached attitude, she swirled the ice cubes in her glass and waited to see if he'd explain or let her go on wondering for the fun of it.

He laughed heartily, as if he were talking about the weather instead of piercing her heart.

"Holly's only been with me six weeks." He inhaled and blew a smoke ring, nudging it with an extra puff of breath.

Dierdre set her face into an aloof smile, as if nothing he was saying mattered to her in the least. *I'll be damned if I'll let on how much this hurts.*

"She's the nanny for my daughter Brittany, who's also in my cabin." His exhaled smoke ring went wobbly and dissolved over the bar.

Making Dierdre squirm with his dropped phrases and long pauses amused him, or so it seemed.

"You've never talked about a child." Dierdre cradled her glass in both hands, tempted to clunk him in the head with it, wrestle the cigarette out of his dying fingers, and smoke it herself. "How old?"

"Eight. I just got custody last month." He puffed, watching her with apparent amusement.

Dierdre almost groaned aloud. *I hoped Brittany was his spaniel. A single man with a school-age kid? That kicks Tyler off the top spot on my potential-husband list. Drat!*

He downed his scotch. "Would you dance with me after the show?"

"I have plans. Perhaps another time."

When they parted company, it was clear to her their reunion romance had sunk at the bar while at sea. She hoped he caught on to her cooled interest in him and drowned somewhere close enough so she could watch him flounder, holler for a saving float ring, and go down while she sipped a martini and waved.

At least I still managed to not only save myself the humiliation of sleeping with Tyler again, but I didn't succumb to my cigarette crutch for the twelfth day in a row.

After the curtain call, Dierdre didn't change out of her stage heels. She took her time climbing the stairs. *Daniel might be locked below deck, but backstage elevators by myself give me the heebie jeebies.*

Several decks up, she joined Randy and Megan at the midnight buffet. She hadn't had the stomach for food after Tyler dropped his Brittany bombshell. She passed the ice-sculpture centerpieces on the buffet tables and caught sight of the Keenes. Megan got to her feet and offered a chair at their table.

"We're so glad you could join us, Ms. Ingram."

"Please call me Dierdre, Megan." She took the chair. "Hello, Randy. How kind of you and your daughter to invite me to dine with you."

He smiled beneath his dark glasses and extended a hand, shaking Dierdre's firmly. He'd somehow avoided knocking over the little vase of rosebuds centered between them. "Our pleasure. I've looked forward to talking with you personally."

His rich baritone is perfect for the stage or radio. At least he brings a daughter old enough to take care of herself, as well as him. Pity handsome Randy isn't a soul mate possibility on my radar.

"It's been a long day, but after a show it takes me a while to wind down so I can sleep. Lovely of you to have me join you for dinner. I rarely eat after the show, but there wasn't time before. I've worked up a mammoth appetite."

Megan reached for the water pitcher and filled her glass. "Let's go through the buffet lines and pick out what looks appetizing." She stood and addressed her dad. "What would you like me to bring you?"

Unrolling his napkin, Randy felt for the silverware and placed it on the table, fingering lightly across the cloth for where it should be arranged to leave room for a plate.

"Coconut shrimp sounds good, if they have what they did last night. And mango salad and a couple of those dinner rolls I can't resist. Maybe some cheesecake later to go with my coffee?" He waved them away.

Dierdre stashed her tote under her chair and followed Megan to the buffet. Megan's couture style caught her attention. *She has fantastic taste and access to somebody's deep pockets.* Megan's pastel-silk dress, belted at her slim waist, flowed to handkerchief points at the hem, swishing enticingly at mid-calf. *This girl doesn't shop off the rack. Her jewelry is expensive and exotic. Does Randy give her a hefty allowance or is she a self-made exec somewhere?*

Plates full, they returned to their table. The three took their time dining and discussing the activities Randy and Megan were involved in on board. Megan recounted spending her hours with a good book in a bikini on deck and working out in the exercise room between snacks.

Over dessert, Randy sipped a coffee with brandy. "I've spent hours in the library so I can use my Braille computer for research. I'm a writer—well novelist wannabe—I have to admit."

Dierdre toyed with the last of her mahi mahi, imagining she was being scrutinized by both of them and not sure what gave her that feeling. "I'm curious to know what it is you want my advice about, Randy." She gazed at her distorted reflection in his ultra-dark glasses while he chewed discreetly and swallowed.

He brought his napkin to his lips before laying it aside. "I came on the Sundancer to do some preliminary research. Passenger types, their interests and intrigue, highlight experiences you've had as cruise director, destinations—the best and the worst. Your valuable personal insight."

Dierdre drank from her lemon water thinking how to be honest and not destroy his illusions. *Creative people can be so touchy. Few handle disappointment as well as my sister.* "There wouldn't be anything I'd be permitted to tell you that couldn't be found in one of our brochures."

His face fell, at least what she could see of it below his invisible eyes.

"Oh," he said. "How disappointing. I counted on a behind-the-scenes point of view from someone high up and in the know."

"I'm so sorry. I hate to disappoint you. If I think of anything . . . uniquely interesting that I'm allowed to tell you, I'll let you know. Promise," she added, hoping her voice carried her sincere concern, since he couldn't see her expression.

He smiled. His even white teeth in his tan face made Dierdre's heart stutter. She realized Randy Keene was an exceptionally handsome man. Trying to gauge from his daughter's age what number in the forties rang true for him, she calculated it at early to mid forties.

The servers cleared the long buffet tables of everything but the flower arrangements. A chamber group assembled on the modest dance floor nearby. The keyboard player led off, supported by a violinist and a cellist, all long-haired young ladies elegantly gowned in unadorned black. They began with well-loved Gershwin and Cole Porter show tunes.

"Would you like to dance?" Randy stood and held his hand out across the table toward her. "If you'll lead me to the dance floor, I think I can take it from there. I'm pretty good at sensing how close the other couples are so we don't mow anyone down." He laughed at himself and waited for her.

What? He walks with a white-tipped cane but leaves it at his chair to dance? I imagined blind people have shins of steel from walking into things. Oh, godfry, I hope he can dance or I'll be dragging him around the floor like Raggedy Andy. Me looking and feeling the fool to the frequent cruise guests who know I dance most steps very well.

"I . . . well, certainly, Randy." She swallowed her discomfort and smiled bravely.

Dierdre looked at his daughter who smiled and winked. "You'll give him a break from dancing with me," she said, opening a fashion magazine plucked from her enormous Hermes handbag.

Dierdre rounded the table and took Randy by the hand, leading him to the dance floor. There were no other couples to worry about—yet. Randy's touch well above her waist and on her right hand was light but sure. He stepped with confidence into a lilting waltz. Dierdre was so surprised she could barely breathe let alone speak.

They moved around the floor as smoothly as if they'd danced together for years. Following him was easy for her because he cued where they were moving next with gentle pressure at her back and on the palm and tug of her hand. She was so impressed she wondered if before he became blind he might have been a ballroom-dance instructor. She didn't ask.

Lost in her thoughts, Dierdre realized their bodies flowing together to the haunting melody of "Stardust" made her sensually aware of Randy's muscle tone, his broad shoulders, the warmth of her hand in his, and the way his fingers sensitively grasped hers when he twirled her away then back into his arms. She stopped thinking about him dispassionately and drew in the scent of his cologne, the essence of his maleness, admired his chiseled jaw.

Oh, damn. I could fall for him if he could see. Hah. But then he can't watch me age either. Anthony will be amused when I relate this during my next Miami massage.

After several dances, the music ended. Only two other couples ever vied for space on the floor. Randy pulled some bills from his pocket and tipped the trio. Dierdre was impressed he dropped three twenties. *He may be blind, but he isn't broke.*

Without letting go of her hand, Randy faced her. "You're a wonderful dancer, Dierdre. I wish I could see how lovely you are, but I sense it. My daughter tells me you're beautiful. Thank you for braving to dance with a sightless man. Lead me back to Megan now, please."

"It was my pleasure, Randy. You're some dancer yourself. You'll have to tell me sometime where you learned to dance like a pro." Dierdre reeled from the physical and emotional connection with him. Trembling from the experience, she gathered her things and bid the Keenes goodnight.

In her cabin, Dierdre lay awake a long while doing instant replays of dancing in Randy's arms. With concentrated effort, she cooled the desires he aroused in her without getting out of bed and taking an icy shower.

* * *

Gregory followed in Taylor's footsteps behind the massive, black-needled pyracantha hedge, taller than the noisy row of Grand Pop's falcon mews. He loved being with the big man who'd become his new father, loved learning how to become a falconer—well *almost* loved it. The falcons still scared him more than he wanted Taylor to know. He kept the fear to himself in case he looked like a wimp and a coward, or like he didn't want to someday be a falconer like Taylor, Johnny, and Grand Pops—because he really did—more than anything.

They approached the cages' wire-mesh doors shot-through with metal bars and secured with combination locks to keep the birds in and vandals out. He heard cooing pigeons, fluttering doves, and the two falcons perched on weathering blocks each in their own mews. Roofed and sided from the sun and rain, but open to the air on the door-front wall, the mews' gravel floors were spattered with the birds' white droppings and a few feathers. In the falcon mews, fascinating cast pellets of indigestible fur, feathers, and bones lay among the pebbles. At first, before he learned how and why they were made, the lumpy upchucks gave Greg the disgusted shudders.

This morning he listened comfortably to the cooing pigeons and doves, but when the falcons greeted them with their shrill talk, the skin on the back of his neck prickled.

"They knew we were coming before they could see us, didn't they, Dad?"

Taylor's hand rested on his shoulder. "They're smart alright. Knowing food's coming or hoping to get out for a breather, falcons like to tell you to hurry up and get to it. Good thing the pigeons and doves don't know when they come with us they might not be coming back."

Gregory swallowed, knowing how raptors capture and kill their prey. *Pigeons and doves don't know to be scared 'til it's too late.* He didn't like thinking about the terrifying night Felon took his revenge on the kidnapper, just like the pigeons they brought down out of the sky. That night Felon shrieked and pecked until the screaming man's head was a bloody mess. The savage horror of it sometimes still played out in Gregory's nightmares. He wanted to hurry and grow up so he wouldn't be so afraid. *Taylor isn't afraid of anything. My real Dad wasn't either, not even about dying. Grown ups must not get so scared as us kids do.*

He hurried to keep up with Taylor's long strides. "Is your Pops coming with us this morning?"

"No, Son, he's at his heart doctor's office for a check up. Johnny and the boys are joining us though."

"Great! I'll get to be with Cloud. He's so cool." *He's a big kid, but he's not scared. Maybe 'cause he's an Indian. If I was Apache maybe I wouldn't be so afraid either. Not fair I'm just a white kid.*

Taylor ruffled his big hand through Gregory's hair. "Let's go to the barn for our gear. Our friends will drive in soon."

It's good to have a dad again. I wonder if he'll still care about me so much when Mom has their baby. It scared Gregory to think about that too, so he tried not to, but it was getting harder and harder to go to sleep.

Out in the field well beyond his step-Grand Pop's apple orchard and the fir-tree nursery, Gregory stood next to Cloud watching the empty sky. He listened hard to Taylor and Johnny talking because there was so much to remember about longwing falcons and his training to learn how they must be 'manned'.

Taylor had Felon tethered to the creance, a training line looped through the fingers of his heavy glove. "Speck's out of sight up there, waiting for lunch to be served."

"I'm ready to serve a pigeon when you say so," said Johnny. The purplish-feathered bird restrained in his hands had small eyes rimmed with pale pink lids. It blinked skyward adjusting to the light after being brought out of the dark bag.

Gregory's hand shaded one eye. "You guys want me to remember the 'serve' word, right Dad?"

Taylor nodded, then looked to Johnny. "Now."

Johnny threw the pigeon forward and up. It took off beating its wings rhythmically in freedom, heading away from the sun.

Above them, Speck appeared, a dot growing larger by the moment. He shrieked in his nearly two-hundred-mile-per-hour stoop to the pigeon. The prey either heard the shriek or noticed the hawk's shadow, switched direction and dodged this way and that, attempting evasion. The falcon pursued as if he and the pigeon wore magnets. The gap between the two birds blurred and began to close.

"Wow!" Cloud and Gregory chimed.

"Look at him dive," whispered Stellar, like they were in church.

"Stoop," corrected Gregory.

Cloud laughed. "Stellar's just learning, Gregory, he's not training to be a falconer like you are. Cut him some slack on the lingo."

Chastened by the teen he looked up to, Gregory felt his face grow hot. "Sorry."

Thwack. The sound of Speck's collision attack with outstretched talons made Gregory jump.

Speck brought the pigeon to the weedy ground, efficiently broke its neck with the tooth on its beak and folded his wings, settling down to the defeathering business of lunch.

Stellar groaned. "I'm glad he killed it quick."

"Me too." Gregory watched, fascinated while the falcon plucked fluffy breast feathers that caught on the breeze and floated about its head like fat snowflakes.

Speck tore into the breast flesh, drawing blood, tugging and tearing morsels free, lifting his head to gulp and swallow. On Taylor's gloved fist, Felon ducked his head repeatedly, chortling his own response to the show, restless with hunger.

Johnny's arm went around the shoulders of his boys, one on each side. "You fellows think falconry might be for you? Be happy to teach you."

Cloud raised his chin, a grin spreading across his high-cheek-boned face. "Maybe. How 'bout you bro?" He reached around Johnny and punched Stellar on the arm.

"No thanks." Stellar whistled for Radar, who rose from the weeds and came to have his ears scratched. "Okay if me and the dog head back to the barn? I'd rather practice wheelies on my bike. This bloody stuff kind of kills my appetite."

Johnny patted his shoulder. "Radar's flushing work's done. Okay by me if you take him. We won't be more than half an hour."

Taylor released the creance from the winding in his fingers, allowing Felon to lift his wings and fly to the extent of the lure. The end of it bristled with tied-on feathers, resembling the falcon's quarry. To gain muscle strength Felon needed regular exercise. The reinforcement of food rewards from Taylor's glove strengthened his trust. Gregory had been told he'd be well-manned before long.

He nudged Cloud. "Why don't Taylor and Johnny let Felon fly free the way they do Speck?"

Johnny bent to his ear. "Felon's not quite over his neglect and deprivation when he was birdnapped. Remember he was my bird. I'm not steady enough on my feet to resume his training. Taylor has to give Felon time to bond with him, feed from his fist, and work for his food on the creance. It's been nearly a year since we rescued him, and you, but Felon's still fearful. He could get confused or distracted by another hawk and bolt. We don't want to risk losing him—again."

With what he'd suddenly come to understand, Gregory dropped to his knees in the cheat grass.

Felon still gets scared like I do. We both have to learn to trust again, all because of the same bad man. I thought it was just Johnny and me. I was real wrong.

Cloud tapped him on the shoulder. "Let's ask if we can be the ones to carry the falcons back to the mews. Which hawk do you want to handle?"

Gregory didn't have to think twice.

"If it's okay with you, I choose Felon." He put on Johnny's big glove.

* * *

Taylor and Johnny layered dried cottonwood logs in the Armstrong's backyard fire pit, stuffing brittle twigs and brush between the layers for kindling.

Taylor said, "Let's explain this bonfire idea to the kids with something like, since we didn't get to complete our final campfire on our campout, we're going to do it tonight. Would you say it?"

"Sure." Johnny nodded in agreement. "We'll set things up for Cosma and whatever Cloud has planned for Gregory to try and put an end to his nightmares."

"Great idea."

Johnny pulled a box of matches from his pocket and set it by the fire pit. "If there's time, we can talk about Cosma and me getting married, too. Being a family with her and the boys is keeping talk buzzing around the house. Have you told your kids yet?"

"Nope, waiting for you two to do it. Tonight's campfire might be the perfect time." Taylor covered the logs with the domed fire screen and straightened up. "Guess you won't be needing my trailer house." He chuckled and winked at Johnny, who blushed.

Johnny ducked his head and brushed his crooked hands on his jeans. "I'll clean your mobile home 'til it shines. I promise. You've been great to let me rent it on the cheap. Think you can find another renter, since I'm not going to finish out our lease agreement?"

Taylor moved on to the Weber grill and flipped up the lid. "Actually, this timing works out great. I've got a new man coming on to team with Grif in my other truck, so I can focus on the residential and commercial business in Farr. They'll handle most of the orchard and ranch tree-trimming business in the rural areas. The new guy's not from Utah and needs a place to stay. I'll offer it to him before I put the word out."

"Good." Johnny leaned on the picnic table. "Hope his rent's stiffer than mine and helps you out better financially."

Taylor laughed. "Since I paid off both trucks, I've been saving what I would've been forking out for payments to use for Suzanne's birthday cruise, our honeymoon. You still keeping my secret?"

"What are friends for?" Sweeping a hand broom, Johnny cleared the picnic table of golden pollen from the linden branches above them.

Wielding a wire brush, Taylor scraped away the burned-on black residue coating the grill insert. "There, that's clean for burgers and dogs." He lit the charcoal and closed the lid with the vents open. "Want a beer?"

They headed inside to the kitchen.

At the sound of the back door opening, Suzanne hushed Cosma with a finger to her lips. She finished making hamburger patties at the counter while Cosma added cherry tomatoes to a tossed green salad.

"We're getting our picnic organized for you heroes while the kids finish a pirate video." Suzanne cocked her head toward the TV room.

Taylor kissed the back of her neck, then went to the sink and scrubbed his hands.

"We're ready with the fire pit. We stacked plenty of logs in it for tonight's . . . festivities."

Suzanne nudged him away from the sink with her hip. "I sure wish we didn't have to burn a single limb of our beautiful old cottonwood."

"Me too, Honey. But every time I lift a log I think of how relieved I am you and the kids weren't hurt when Bo made that massive old beauty go over."

He gestured out the window while drying his hands on a towel. "One day, that Mountain Ash we planted in its place will shade this side of the house again. It'll never be the same as that pioneer's cottonwood, but it'll give you something else pretty to paint." He patted the tummy of her apron on his way to the fridge for a couple of beers.

Johnny washed and dried his hands too. Cosma handed him a box of plastic wrap.

"Make yourself extra useful, big man." She steadied the salad bowl and smiled encouragement. With great concentration to his awkward fingers, Johnny stretched and sealed the cling wrap. He breathed a sigh of relief and followed her to the fridge.

Popping their beer cans, the men settled in at the table while the women cleared the counters and got out trays of plastic glasses, paper plates, buns, and flatware. Everything ready, Suzanne and Cosma filled glasses with iced tea and joined them.

Cosma lowered her voice and spoke near Johnny's shoulder. "Suzanne tells me Gregory's bad dreams still happen almost nightly. Let's send white light to surround him tonight and pray our healing ceremonies by the fire will put his terrors to rest."

Suzanne looked out the window where Cloud searched for something under the picnic table. "What's he doing out there?"

Cosma watched for a moment. "He's gathering pollen for his ceremony. Cloud's been reading many of my ceremony guidebooks lately. He'll teach us what he's learned and what is in his heart for his friend Gregory."

Johnny looked from her to Taylor. "I'm never sure how to do that 'sending white light' business this beautiful Indian woman tells me to do. Now Cloud's following close—in her moccasins—so to speak."

They laughed at his pun.

Grinning, Johnny shrugged his shoulders and stroked Cosma's cheek with his knuckles until she smiled and her dark eyes found his gaze.

"You have spirit light within you, John-Love. We all do. Just close your eyes and concentrate on sending the pure white light of love and peace Gregory's way. Believe me, it works."

Absently, she fingered the bead wrap on the braid at her shoulder. "Perhaps Cloud's plan will bring Great Spirit's power and sever Bo's hold on Gregory."

Johnny's broken hand closed over hers, his smile gone. "And me as well," he whispered, nodding to each of them in turn.

Suzanne shuddered. "To all of us. My God, to all of us."

* * *

The setting sun's golden disk dropped into Great Salt Lake. Glittering orange water swallowed the orb. Lavender twilight turned velvety black like a curtain poked through with stars and a rising moon.

Fire-pit embers glowed. Where marshmallow drips blackened from making S'mores, sizzles steamed and died. Away from the picnic table, Taylor and Johnny lit tiki torches planted in the ground. Flickering light spread out in pools on the darkening grass, friendly yet mysterious.

Gregory watched his Apache friend Cloud pouring a thin stream of corn meal from a carton, making a pale yellow circle on the backyard grass. Puzzled, he followed.

"How come your pouring cereal on the grass?"

Cloud smiled at him. "Stay outside the circle. I'm preparing for a ceremony. It's my first healing ritual. Someday I'll be a Shaman like my Apache Grandfather Blue Thorn and my Paiute mother."

Greg backed up a couple of steps, jamming his hands in his shorts pockets to watch.

"Yeah, but what kind of ceremony needs a giant circle? You sure it isn't a game? You're good at making up games."

Cloud laughed, connecting the corn meal line he was finishing with the place he started, completing the circle. "It's not a game. Corn protects the sacred space."

"Protects it from what?"

"Evil spirits. You'll see . . . very soon."

When all of the picnic leftovers were returned to the kitchen and the grownups and kids gathered outside in torch-lit semi-darkness again, Johnny cleared his throat several times.

"You kids know we didn't get to have our last campfire in the desert because I had trouble on our hike and went to the hospital. So we're going to have our ceremony now. Cosma, Cloud, and Stellar will make it special. Let's pretend we're still camping."

Overwhelmed by the longest speech he'd ever made to a group, Johnny lowered himself to the grass and leaned against the Linden tree, motioning for them all to settle nearby.

Taylor patted his shoulder in passing, and gave him a thumbs-up. He smoothed a quilt out for himself, Suzanne, and Mitzi.

Gregory squatted on the edge of the quilt. *I wonder what's going to happen and where I'm going to sit. Hope it's near Cloud.*

To his right, Cloud unzipped several pockets on his backpack, but didn't take anything out.

Barefoot, Cosma paused at the fire pit and whisked a bound sheaf of smudging-sage over the embers until tendrils of smoke drifted toward the stars. She stepped to the corn-meal circle and swayed all around it moving her smudging arm across the space, wafting the sweet burning sage from one person to the next. Gently, she blew smoky sage fragrance over their heads and shoulders.

When it tickled her nose, Mitzi giggled. Gregory coughed into his sleeve and blinked smoke from his eyes. His gaze kept returning to Cloud who moved in and out of shadow and torch glow sprinkling handfuls of Linden pollen inside the circle.

I wonder why he's doing that.

Cosma spoke. "We clear the circle and ourselves of all impure thoughts and prepare to connect in spirit. This circle is a Medicine Wheel, the place where the two worlds touch: Grandfather Sky above where the light of the sun, moon, and stars give the spark of life to the two-legged—that's us—here on Earth. Life is our divine gift from the Creator."

"I got two legs," blurted Mitzi, snuggled between Suzanne and Taylor.

Suzanne held a finger to her lips. "Shhh, we all do, honey."

Cosma continued, "The circle is unity, our oneness with the universe. Tonight the Medicine Wheel is an altar for healing. In ceremony we connect with Great Spirit. You may call the Creator: Great Spirit, God, Jesus, or Holy Spirit. All are One. We two-leggeds are one of a kind in nature.

"In your mind, let your body glow as if a layer of light covers you like the sage smoke. Let it flow under your feet. Listen to the drum's voice, the voice of Stellar's flute, and the music of the rattle." She handed Mitzi a lidded glass jar half full of dried peas.

"Shake it when I nod to you, Sweetheart."

Cosma seated herself next to Johnny and took up her drum, tapping it lightly while her voice rose.

"All this music we offer is our prayer moving us into this sacred place prepared for Cloud's ceremony.

"The prayer we send to Great Spirit gives thanks for our safety, survival, and bounty and asks for help in righting the upset balance of those on the Medicine-Wheel altar. We ask your help, Great Spirit, in restoring harmony to our loved ones on this Earth."

Gregory changed positions and sat, bringing his chin to his raised knees; curious, cautious. *Nobody's sitting in the circle. What's she talking about? I'm glad we're not really camping in the desert tonight. I don't care what Johnny says; I'm not pretending I'm back in the scary desert I hate.*

Cosma drummed with the flat of her hands and sang in a Paiute few-note voice:

"Earth is a sacred circle. The compass of the Medicine Wheel is the power of the four directions helping us navigate to the Spirit world. There are many medicine-wheel traditions. Great Spirit guides which ceremony is needed for the two-leggeds being healed."

"Mommy says we all got two legs." Mitzi held her jar of peas up in the light. Cosma nodded.

Mitzi shook the rattle jar until the dry peas sounded like popping corn. Stellar joined in, playing a wooden flute; his breath and moving fingers making low, soft sounds like an owl singing hoot melodies.

Spooky but cool. Gregory sat forward more curious than ever. *It's like being in the middle of a movie.*

Stellar's flute played on. After a while, Mitzi's rattle slowed and stopped. Gregory saw her eyes had closed where she rested against Taylor. The dried-pea rattle lat quiet in her lap.

Cloud got to his feet with the corn-meal container. Without a word, he stepped into the circle and sprinkled lines that cut the Medicine Wheel into four equal sections like pieces of pie in a round dish. He stopped in the space facing South and gestured an invitation with his hand.

"Suzanne Armstrong, please come and sit in the South direction. You are the Mom who loves like a mother bear protecting her cubs, and in the coming moons will bring a new child to love. You are called Stands For Truth in your transformation."

Suzanne stood, her face showing surprise while she entered the circle. She sat down in the South pie-slice shape and waited.

Cloud turned and gestured toward the Linden tree. "Johnny Carlisle, please come and sit with Stands For Truth. You bred hawks, survived a terrible test, bravely saved your captured hawk, and went to the aid of Gregory, the kidnapped boy, and his mother."

At mention of his name, Gregory stiffened. His head came up from his knees and his heart beat faster.

"Gregory—my friend—once the kidnapped child. You helped save your mother and yourself when you took away the bad man's weapons. Come sit with Johnny and your mom in the South place. It holds the past and the fears we don't want to talk about."

Cloud called me friend. I didn't think he remembered all that stuff about me. Gregory moved inside the circle and sat close to Suzanne facing Johnny.

The wavering torchlight wiggled across the scars on Johnny's face. Scars made by the same Bo who kidnapped him. Clammy sweat wet Gregory's fingers. *What's Cloud doing talking about fears? If this isn't going to be fun, I'd rather play a game.*

Cloud pulled a feather from his backpack. Grasping it by the quill end, he waved it through the air.

"This is a hawk feather from the falcon that shared your terrible night. Felon's molted wing feather stands for the North direction, home of the air, wind—like Felon's Irish name—cold, and snow. Freezing snow makes things hard and sharp, like Felon's talons and beak. Sharp enough to cut out evil and bring justice to us below."

Remembering Felon's bloody attack on Bo in the root cellar, Gregory shuddered and held his breath. *I don't like this.* The hair on the back of his neck prickled when he thought of the screeches of the bird and the screams of his bleeding kidnapper.

I want out of here. If Cloud's my friend, why's he scaring me? Gregory started to get to his feet.

Cloud put a hand on his shoulder and pressed him back to the grass. From his backpack, he brought out a mirror and propped it in front of Gregory's sandals.

"This mirror, like the corn meal circle, is a shield against the evil kidnapper of your dreams. Now you will be free to face your fears and take power over them, so you will no longer dread sleep."

"Wha . . . I, I don't know how," Gregory stammered, his mouth dry as a desert. He swallowed,

swallowed again. Tried to breathe. His heart hammered in his chest. Suzanne covered his hand with hers. He inhaled, released breath, and began to relax.

Cloud looked to his mother. Cosma nodded encouragement. He waved the feather again, this time over Gregory.

"Seek truth is the message of hawk's cry. Welcome hawk to your dreams, Gregory. The hawk is the messenger to and from Great Spirit, somewhere above Grandfather Sky. Soar with Felon to Grandfather Sky and look down on your good family from a higher place. Hawk's cry pierces your dark dreams and flies away with them to restore balance and harmony to you on Mother Earth."

He pushed the quill end of the hawk feather into the ground in the grassy place he'd named North for the wind, home of the hawk. From his backpack, Cloud brought out a shriveled lump of stuffed-cattail leaf stuck with four twigs. Holding it on his open palms, he brought his hands before Gregory.

It's the stuff he put together on our desert hike. It's all dried up now. What's it for? Gregory stared at what looked to him like a dead turtle with sticks too long to be four legs. He shook his head and shrugged. "I don't get it."

"In your mind when you talk to yourself," Cloud began. "What name do you give Bo, the man with a rifle who took you from your camp tent? I made this grass man with crooked-twig legs to be that crippled one who stole you . . . for this your healing ceremony. Hawk and Great Spirit demand you speak your truth."

Cloud really wants to help me. Gregory whispered, "I dream of Stinking Man. He hung me by my wrists in the cellar with rattlesnakes. But even if he leaves my dreams, Tracker, his big black dog Mom killed, chases me with sharp teeth to kill me. His panting behind me is so real I wake up . . . afraid."

Greg hung his head, biting his lip. He whispered, "Stinking Man killed my mother, Rehma. I didn't get to help save her like I did Suzanne."

Cloud looked at Cosma. "Oh, Mother. Have I failed my friend? I didn't know to make a dog symbol for his ceremony." His bright-black eyes glittered with unshed tears. His arms fell to his sides. The grass man dangled from his fingers, its crooked legs poking out at angles. "I didn't know about Gregory's first mother, either. I am sorry."

Cosma approached the Medicine Wheel, touched her son's shoulder and raised her outstretched hands to the starry sky.

"Great Spirit, what more do we need for Gregory's healing and for blessing the boy's spirit with peace for his dream time?"

In the darkness, Johnny spoke in a hesitant voice. "Is it something to stand for the black dog you need for his . . . healing?"

Cloud's face glowed in the firelight. His voice was all hope, "Yes."

From his shirt pocket, Johnny brought out something small. "Will Felon's cast pellet of packrat be good enough?"

Cosma lowered her arms and accepted the casting. She faced Cloud, her voice strong. "Felon still serves Great Spirit's purpose for justice, bringing harmony from nature to the two-legged on the Medicine Wheel altar."

Cloud placed his brittle, 'dead' kidnapper form and the packrat remains in Gregory's hands.

"My brother friend, hold Felon's casting of rat fur, bones, and teeth to be the Black Dog. Take it with the symbol of the kidnapper to the iron skillet on the fire pit. Cover them with screen to capture the ashes of these dead ones who will come no more to your dreams."

Cosma got to her feet. "Let's follow Cloud and Gregory and watch the burning death of Stinking Man and Black Dog."

Suzanne stood behind Gregory at the fire pit, one hand resting on his shoulder. The iron skillet with the dried-grass figure of dead Bo Rodman and the falcon's pellet grew hotter and hotter. The bad totems split. From the ruptures, wisps of smoke drifted skyward.

At Suzanne's back, Taylor held sleeping Mitzi against him. "Put the spatter-screen cover on top now, Gregory."

Cloud put the screen handle into his friend's fingers.

Across the pit from them, Cosma's drumming stopped. "Gregory, while Stinking Man and Black Dog die for the last time on this fire, let them leave with your fear captured in their ashes. You will be free."

Johnny raised his crooked hands over the spatter screen. "Gregory, Bo took so much from you and from me. I'm letting my frightening nightmares end right here too. Let's do this together." He took one of the boy's hands in his own. "He scared me plenty and I'm a big guy. There's no shame in being afraid."

As if Johnny's words magically made the grass and the fur ignite, the bundles in the skillet glowed and burst into flame, spinning and crackling.

Gregory jumped back. Gripping Johnny's hand, he gasped. "They're on fire!"

Suzanne and Taylor stepped respectfully away. Smoke rose through the screen mesh, bringing with it the stench of burning fur.

Gregory turned his head and bent his elbow over his nose. "Yuck! Stinking Man and Black Dog smell worse than ever." He grinned, then laughed. "They're burnt to nothing now. The ashes look like the white dust he walked me through in the desert."

It was the first genuine laugh Suzanne had heard from Gregory in months. She smiled up at Taylor and brought her hands together, pressing them to her lips. Closing her eyes, she prayed fervently in her mind. *Oh Lord, let this ritual free my son, Johnny, and all of us from these nightmares of Bo—and may his own soul rest in peace.*

Johnny pulled on hot-pad grilling gloves and lifted the skillet of ashes from the fire pit. He set it in the dirt to cool and removed the gloves.

Cosma nodded to her sons. Stellar played a gentle melody on his flute. Cloud said, "Gregory, follow me to the Medicine Wheel. We'll finish your ceremony now."

He led Gregory to the West section of the wheel and gestured for him to sit and for Johnny to join him.

"The West is where the sun dies and the black night welcomes the dream time. Sometimes, when we won't talk about our fears—even to ourselves—they enter our dreams and hold us hostage, like a kidnapping, until we honor them. Our prayer is for these three two-leggeds to become like the bear, sleeping peacefully through the long winter. Now you two are free to dream good dreams."

Cloud continued, "East is the beginning place where the sun is born each morning. It is no time at all or *all* time, for it is a space for higher spiritual purpose."

He gestured to the wheel section of grass bordered with corn meal across from them. "Now, Gregory, you and Johnny may move to this altar space. Your transformation is almost complete."

From his backpack, Cloud took out a deer-hide pouch, smaller than an egg, strung on a red cord. He hung it around Gregory's neck.

"My friend, do not open this Medicine Bag. It's for your protection. Inside are Earth gifts to care for you. Linden-tree pollen, tobacco, corn meal, salt, a red bead for Earth, a turquoise bead for Sky, the wing of a moth, and the claw of an owl for the night flyers.

"Besides the healing desert plants of sage, rosemary, and juniper, there are hairs from your head. I took them from your hairbrush in the motel. All these spiritual totems surround your hair, even your DNA with healing power."

Cloud stooped to his backpack and removed two more matching gifts. He gave one to Johnny and one to Gregory. "Hang these dream catchers above the places where you sleep. The circle of webs catches all your dreams. The webs hold any bad ones and let the good dreams pass down to you along the night-bird feathers. You will not always need your Medicine Bag or your Dream Catcher, but treat them with respect. When you don't need them, wrap them in a clean cloth you use for no other purpose and put them in a safe place."

Cloud sat down outside the Medicine Wheel, facing Gregory. From the North, he gave his friend Felon's molted wing feather.

"This feather can be tied to your Dream Catcher. These gifts are your armor, especially at night for sleeping. Imagine you are wearing an invisible space suit. My Indian brother, like your policeman father Stephen, you have courage. He watches you from the Spirit World where he lives now and waits for you. He is proud of your courage when the bad man stole you from your desert tent. You were clever to seek

Tarantula's help to frighten him and save you and your mother. Your courage saved Felon too."

Cloud signaled his brother Stellar with an open hand. Flute music drifted their way. Like the wind in the trees, Cosma drummed and sang Indian words. Cloud rose to his knees, his eyes at the level of Gregory's.

"My friend, you have not understood your own medicine. Now your hawk-like eye wants to focus on the powerful, happy dreams of the man you will become. Good, strong, kind, like your father Stephen in the Spirit World and your Earth-bound father, Taylor Armstrong. Gregory, you are a Price. You are an Armstrong. You are Cloud and Stellar's brother."

Coming to his feet, Cloud reached into the circle and pulled the boy up to stand across from him. From his jacket he put something in Gregory's hands.

"Gregory, I give you an Indian-brother name— Bold Heart. It is written on a paper wrapped with sage in this red cloth. This is your spirit name." They shook hands like two men.

Gregory swallowed hard—more than once.

"Stand, Johnny, my soon-to-be Earth Father, you will be called Hawk's Brother. You survived your spirit test and restored life to a stolen falcon. You birthed hawks into this Earth time to save raptor winged-ones from extinction. Great Spirit honors falconers for their compassion and protection."

The drumming and flute music ended. Cosma entered the circle and placed her hands on Gregory's shoulders. He looked into her eyes flickering with tiki lights, calmly, no longer afraid of her.

Her voice came out strong. "Gregory, you can let the wind scatter the feared ones' ashes to the far corners of Grandfather Sky or you can bury them in the Earth. Whatever you choose, they are truly dead and will not come again to haunt your sleeping time with scary dreams."

Gregory stood tall. He looked from Cloud to each of them, his gaze coming to rest on Johnny. He inhaled a big breath and let it out slowly. "I don't want the ashes to blow free and give someone else bad dreams like ours. Help me bury them."

Johnny nodded. Chuckling, he ruffled Gregory's hair with his best hand.

Gregory called into the dim light, "Taylor, could we bury them under the ash tree we planted where Stinking Man cut our cottonwood down? The one my Dad loved? I want them to be stuck feeding our new one even if they did kill my climbing tree."

Taylor eased sleeping Mitzi to her mother's lap and went to the fire pit for the matchbox. He returned and shook the long wooden matches into Stellar's hands, giving Gregory the empty box to use for burying the ashes.

Cloud poured water in the center of the circle, the soul place. The rest he used to douse the embers of the fire pit, until they sizzled and steamed.

Gregory went to Suzanne and knelt for a hug. His eyes glistened with happy tears.

"Johnny and I don't have to be scared to sleep anymore."

Suzanne's heart swelled with relief. "I'm so happy for you both. We'll all sleep better, Sweetheart."

"Bold Heart," he whispered.

"Yes," she agreed. "Bold Heart."

Much later, after the brief funeral and tucking Gregory in beneath his hanging Dream Catcher with Felon's feather above his headboard, Suzanne returned to the others.

Tired and hopeful, she entered the kitchen where Cloud sat next to his mother, eating the last of what appeared to be a peanut butter, mayo, and banana sandwich stuffed to overflowing in a bulging, multigrain pita. The ivory and brown goo oozed between his fingers, challenging her preparedness to fight nausea. She looked away and settled on a much more appetizing sight—bowls of chilled watermelon chunks.

Ugh, what kids won't combine in a snack. Poor Cloud, the darling only nibbled his cheeseburger at the campfire and left it to make his circle for the ceremony.

After what he'd done for Gregory, she looked on this young Apache-Paiute, almost-man with greater affection than ever. *If all the trouble Cloud went to works for Gregory tonight, I'll be on my knees in thanks to Jesus.*

Cosma, Johnny, and Taylor lounged at the table, forking bite-sized cubes of cold watermelon into their mouths.

Suzanne stopped at Cloud's chair. "I'm so impressed with the thought and effort you put into creating an amazing healing ceremony for Gregory."

Cloud nodded, his long hair obscuring his eyes. "Thanks." He took another bite.

Suzanne tried not to watch him chew.

"Gregory's embarrassed to tell you in front of the rest of us, but when I said goodnight to him, he held his leather pouch and told me how surprised and proud he is to be your brother. He didn't hide his tears of happiness. The meaning of the symbols you used and your special gifts all make sense to him now, even though he can't quite believe you went to so much trouble for him. The Bold Heart name you chose is perfect."

She touched Cloud's arm lightly before taking a seat next to Taylor.

Johnny put his fork down. "Cloud, giving the boy an Indian name made him feel he's past being a scared kid—becoming a young man." Rocking back in his chair so he could see Cloud past Cosma, he added, "Where you came up with all those ideas I don't know. They worked for Gregory and for me too. The name you gave me makes me proud to be a man and a falconer, both things I thought Bo took from me."

He cleared his throat. "I'll work hard to earn your respect as your stepdad. I couldn't be more proud of you if you were my blood son."

Cloud gave Johnny a high five. Eyeing the messy mayo marks on Johnny's palm, he blushed. Acting suddenly shy, he licked mayo from his fingers and his lips, rubbed his hands clean on a napkin and handed it to Johnny to use too.

Cosma brushed strands of black hair out of his eyes with her fingers. "I couldn't have performed a more powerful Medicine Wheel Ceremony if I'd tried, Son. I had no idea you'd practiced what you studied and made gifts for Johnny and Gregory. Your Grandfather would be proud you spoke with such confidence and remembered symbolic ceremony meanings."

Draining his glass of milk, Cloud stood and pushed in his chair. With his back to them, he rinsed his glass at the sink. "I'm glad Blue Thorn let me sit in on his sweat-lodge cleansing ceremonies last year. I tried to sound like him."

Cosma's rose and went to him, hugging him briefly from the back. "You did that alright. I'm still amazed." She sat back down, smiling at the others and shaking her head.

His back still to them, Cloud leaned against the sink and looked at the ceiling, the walls, the floor, anywhere but at the grownups.

The awkward silence continued until Taylor carried a dish of watermelon seeds to the plastic-lined wastebasket and emptied them. He clamped a hand on the fourteen-year-old's shoulder, only a head lower than his own.

"I don't know any man three times your age who could pour so much meaning into a ceremony and explain it so well. We thank you for easing Gregory's mind. He looks up to you and your brother."

Cloud offered a lopsided grin. "Thanks. He looks up to you, too. Told me so in the motel."

Taylor cocked his head. A pleased smile crinkled the corners of his eyes. A happy man, he returned to the table and pulled Suzanne's chair closer to his own until their eyes locked and their knees touched.

Johnny slung an arm around Cosma's shoulders. "I think Gregory's over being afraid of you now. Cloud put the boy's fears into words making it okay to be afraid. He did it for me too."

Cosma kissed his cheek. "You didn't do so badly yourself."

Suzanne sipped her cup of steaming chamomile tea. "Until after the solstice when we came home, I wasn't certain Gregory understood in the root cellar about the police discovering his mother's body. He mentioned it then before bedtime and never again until tonight during the ceremony. It broke my heart to hear the agony in his voice because he couldn't save Rehma from Bo the way he saved me. He's held in all that pain and guilt along with the terrible memories of what he went through."

Her hands gripped the cup. "I've had a hard time letting go of my anger toward Bo for putting Gregory and the rest of us through so much confusion and terror."

Johnny looked thoughtful. "Put himself through hell too. Wouldn't want to go the way he did."

Cosma toyed with the beaded sleeve on her braid. "But if we don't let all the dark go, there'll be no white-light healing."

Cloud walked toward the swinging door to the hallway. Hand on the push panel, he hesitated and looked over his shoulder at them.

"It's no secret we're doing this sleep-over to see if the Dream Catcher above Gregory's bed and his Medicine Bag stop his nightmares. Stellar and I put our sleeping bags on the floor in his room. If Gregory wakes up freaking, I'll get him back to sleep. He trusts me. If the dreams do come, I don't think they'll last beyond tonight. If he yells and scares Mitzi, somebody else better take care of her because she wanted to camp out with us and we coaxed her out of it."

Suzanne straightened her cup on its saucer.

"Let's pray the bad dreams don't return." She'd never admired Cloud more for his mysterious strength than she did tonight. "If your ceremony didn't bury Bo and his dog, there isn't much hope."

At the door, Cloud's inscrutable black eyes lingered on each of them in turn.

"Grandfather Blue Thorn told me 'when the smoke of the sacred fire blows to the four directions—if there are no secrets among the elders—there will be lasting trust.' I sense secrets in this room. Maybe it's time to clear the smoke between you like I tried to do for Bold Heart."

He pushed the door open and left them in a silence more awkward than before.

Cosma grinned and whispered, "If Grandfather Blue Thorn said that I'll eat my drum. I think Cloud made it up, suspecting something untold between us whispery grownups." She winked at Suzanne.

Suzanne turned to Taylor. "Sweetheart, I do have a secret I've been keeping from you. Well, maybe two, but they're really good ones. It's a perfect night to tell you while Johnny and Cosma are with us."

Taylor and Johnny exchanged a knowing look. Taylor leaned close and kissed Suzanne on the cheek.

"I have a secret too." He grinned broadly and winked at Johnny. "I'm sure you'll like mine."

"Spill it, you lovebirds," Johnny said, "but give me a chance to crack a beer. You want one, Taylor? I got a feeling this little exchange could take a while. I don't want to risk going dry in the middle."

The round of laughter eased Suzanne's tension about Gregory and his nightmares. Her energy lifted. For a moment she savored the anticipation of Cosma's surprise. *My shaman friend thinks she knows all. I'm so excited to finally tell Taylor and can't wait for the reaction of our friends who don't suspect my secrets involve them too.*

She caught a wicked grin on Taylor's face directed at Johnny. What on earth is Taylor's secret? It seems Johnny knows what it is and I don't.

Delighted Suzanne was finally going to tell Taylor her financial secrets, Cosma sat back to enjoy Taylor's reaction to the news. *Taylor has a secret too and my John-Love seems to be in on it, though he never breathed a word about it to me. Some kind of guy thing between them.*

Johnny returned to the table with a couple of cold beers. He popped his own and set the other can in front of Taylor. "You two going to flip a coin to see who goes first?"

Taylor laughed and squeezed Suzanne's bare thigh below her shorts with the hand he'd just gripped the cold beer can. She yelped. He pulled his hand away, laughing harder. "My secret can wait. I didn't know Suze had a secret, let alone two. Ladies first."

But before Suzanne could begin, his face wore a startled expression. "We're not having twins are we?"

Suzanne giggled. "No silly. Probably too soon to know anyway." She took a big breath, closed her eyes and exhaled. "I've *really* wanted us to have our honeymoon cruise with Dee for our thirtieth birthday."

She looked around the table. "With our whole family, not just you and me, Taylor. This week two miracles happened."

Taylor swigged a couple of gulps and swallowed dramatically. "If anybody's into miracles, Honey, it's you. Tell Daddy."

She punched him on the shoulder. "These are not little-baby miracles. I'm talking money miracles. The hospital foundation presented me with a bonus check for $7,000."

Cosma watched Taylor's face and the surprise registering in his eyes. Under the table, she pressed Johnny's arm in the certain way they communicated special moments. He patted her hand back and sipped his beer.

Taylor came up for air. "I know you're a fantastic mural painter, Suze, but you already have a juicy fee for the job you've nearly finished. Why the fat bonus?"

Suzanne beamed. "Because I went the extra mile and painted portraits of the founders' seven family members and their many kids in a border on the central mural for the new children's wing. I worked from archive photos going back ninety years."

Taylor spread his fingers on the table. "Is that the additional mural they decided on after your initial arrangement? The one you didn't even ask to be paid to design and paint?"

"The very one," she said. "I thought including the portraits would show today's kids the connection to the hospital's past and the children of the founders."

"Wow, Honey. I'm amazed you could keep a secret like that. What's the other one, a full-time job offer? Please tell me you said no. We're going to let you stay home and be a mom and paint your sweet little heart out, maybe creating a nursery mural." He pushed back his chair to stand.

Cosma held up a palm. "Taylor, stay seated. She's not finished."

Suzanne reached into her apron pocket and pulled out an envelope. "This came yesterday." She handed it to Taylor. "It's an advance check for $12,000. Greeting cards are being made from my watercolors in the Arbor Day Calendar and picked up by Catch Publishing in Holland."

She glanced at Johnny. "It's the competition I won last year."

Taylor's mouth dropped open. He shook his head. "Whew, Babe. My secret doesn't look like much compared to these two checks."

She hugged him around the neck. "Whatever it is, I bet it's a good one. Tell us."

Cosma felt Johnny's hand squeeze hers under the table. *This is it. John-Love knows what's coming.* She sat forward. "Yes, tell us, Taylor."

"A month and a half ago I paid off both of the Armstrong's Tree Service trucks two years early. I put the $1,200 and the two monthly stipend advances from the Golf & Country Club and City Parks & Recreation for the coming year's tree maintenance in the bank. My total deposit was $6,950. I figure on saving the $1,200 every month 'til after Christmas and the baby, barring any unforeseen emergency."

Johnny said, "I'm no math whiz but just the truck-payment amounts are going to come to over $8,000 by then. Nothing to sneeze at, my friend."

Suzanne brushed tears from her lashes. She kissed Taylor's cheek.

"Then my third secret is a cinch to be for a miracle for all of us." She looked at Cosma and Johnny, tipping her head coyly.

"Dee has arranged for our two families to get a group-discount-ticket rate. I'm going to teach watercolor painting on three mornings aboard ship when we're at sea and one *en plein air* class at a park when we land. She wants Cosma to offer three afternoon Tarot-card sessions for the cruise guests. Our two couples' cruise tickets will be comped." Her eyes darted from one to another around the table.

She hurried on. "We only have to pay for our four kids at the group rate. It's even possible for you two falconers to do a Power Point presentation on the art of falconry, but only if you want to. Taylor and I can put what's left of our miracle money toward making the attic into a bedroom for Gregory. Then his old room can become a nursery. Isn't this all fantastic?"

Cosma's pulse thundered in her ears. Bewildered, she fought for control, caught between the joy of a way to pay for her and John-Love's cruise and fear he'd refuse out of pride, thinking he couldn't help Taylor explain falconry very well. *If he thinks he can't contribute, I'm afraid he'll refuse to go.*

She locked gaze with him. Each reading the other's emotions, they sensed it could be an important time for both families to share.

"Oh, there's more for you two," Suzanne bubbled. "I think the best part is Dierdre's going to help arrange your marriage ceremony. Our cruise to Bermuda isn't just a twins' birthday cruise, it's a double honeymoon. You can't possibly say no."

"Bermuda?" Cosma and Johnny echoed.

"Yes, Bermuda." Suzanne got to her feet and went around the table to Cosma. She opened her arms.

"Cruise ships dock in beautiful places for people to get off and have fun. Don't you think playing on the world's most famous pink beaches will be awesome for us honeymooners, after your destination wedding?"

Cosma stood and embraced Suzanne.

Marriage to John-Love, my boys with a good dad, and the kind of honeymoon memories people with money make happen. These are miracles I dared not dream could come true for me and my boys.

Johnny clinked beer cans with Taylor. "Here's to falcons, babies, money, and other miracles."

"Here, here. Always imagined what a tropical isle would be like. Now we'll find out together." Taylor checked his watch. "It's half past two. Gregory's usually wakened with nightmares a couple of times by now." He grinned.

Suzanne released Cosma and stepped back. "I think Cloud has performed the greatest miracle of all. Let's make certain he understands this cruise is also a thank-you trip for his Medicine Wheel healing ceremony."

Much later, Suzanne lay quietly next to Taylor. She'd begun to doze, until a butterfly sensation deep in her abdomen brought her wide-awake. Alert, she held her breath willing herself to feel it again.

In a moment she knew the flutter of tiny hands or feet blossoming in her sacred-mother place.

Dear God, you've blessed us in so many ways. Thank you. Our new family is ready now. This time I ask for your protection so this baby is born healthy and strong.

* * *

The cruise's final stage show closed with rousing applause. Later, two decks up Dierdre crossed the dance floor to the bar area. She'd accepted Randy and Megan Keene's invitation for a farewell drink. As it was the Captain's last formal dinner evening—she wore an off-one-shoulder, electric-blue taffeta gown splashed with crystal beads at the bodice and accenting a single knee-high split. Her brunette hair secured with a crystal clip above one ear, Dierdre knew she looked sensational.

How disappointing. I went to so much trouble for my appearance and it's lost on sightless Randy. Get a grip, Dee. It's the last night to enjoy the hottie who can't see anyway. He's gorgeous, so what? Probably an impaired man hoping to meet a nursemaid for his golden years. Definitely not what I see for my future.

When she took the stool between them, Megan, sophisticated as ever, eyed her with obvious approval, which almost made up for her oblivious father.

"Dad," Megan said. "I wish you could see the vision who's joined us in a fabulous blue gown."

Randy held out his hand somewhat in her direction. Dierdre grasped his fingers briefly and did her best to ignore the tingle traveling up her arm.

"If she's half as lovely to gaze upon as the perfume she's wearing, I'm sure I'd be impressed."

The smile beneath his dark glasses dazzled Dierdre. "How sweet of you, Randy. It's a shame it's our last night." She glanced at Megan. "I've enjoyed getting to know you *both*."

Megan, in an emerald-green cocktail dress, matching shoes, and diamond ear studs, grinned impishly. "I've convinced Dad to get us tickets on the upcoming cruise to Bermuda . . . so he can continue his research."

"My novel, you know," Randy said. He brought his glass to his lips, found it empty, and set it on the bar. "Megan, can you get the bartender's attention for a refill? I'm sure our cruise director would welcome some refreshment as well. Dierdre?"

"Yes, I would. A frozen raspberry daiquiri, please and thank you." The high stool and her pencil-slim gown made sitting awkward, even with a split skirt. "Could we move to that empty table?" She gestured toward it. "Sitting in a row at the bar isn't very comfortable. It's like attending a tennis match with me posted at the net."

"Of course." Megan giggled and touched her father's elbow. "You don't mind, do you, Dad?"

Randy felt for his cane and slid off of his stool. "Anything to please the ladies. I'd appreciate back support and a table with more room anyway."

Once at the bistro table, when he sat down opposite her, Randy's knees brushed hers. She wasn't certain if it was accidental or if he was actually flirting with her. Not being able to read a man's eyes for a desire rating flummoxed Dierdre. Randy's broad shoulders in his white dinner jacket distracted her, too. She opted for a professional tone to keep her head.

"The Bermuda cruise leaves Miami in five weeks. It's my next CD assignment."

"We know." Megan winked. "We made certain you were the cruise director for it before we bought the tickets."

Dierdre was speechless, fumbling with her handbag, feigning deciding where to put it at the crowded table. *Why am I so rattled around this guy?*

"It's a first to have someone book a cruise to be with me, at least the first I know about."

Randy chuckled, then burst into a hearty laugh.

"You're rarely without a stage comeback, dear lady. Truth is, I told Megan I didn't want to break in another cruise director to wheedle more information out of her, or the gods forbid—him. Laying the groundwork to pick brains is a project. I'd rather do so with a charming dinner companion."

He continued to laugh in a rich baritone, rippling through Dierdre like mountain water in spring run-off. She thought of drowning and didn't find the idea terrifying in the least. *Maybe even a great way to go. Or come.* Dierdre laughed too, but not in response to what he'd said so much as the thought of him without a dinner jacket or any other stitch of formal clothing. She regretted only glimpsing him one delicious afternoon at the pool in bathing trunks. *Sounds like I might have the chance in the future.*

Megan punched him lightly on the shoulder.

"Don't fib, Dad. You also feared another cruise director might not be such a terrific dance partner."

"Or wear such sensational perfume." Randy reached in his breast pocket for his leather passport folder and opened it out toward Megan. "Use my ship's pass for these drinks. Snacks too, if you ladies are hungry."

Not for food.

The combo musicians returned from their break and tuned up their instruments.

"Ahh," Randy murmured. "Perhaps we can dance again?"

In your arms I'd welcome it. "That would be lovely." Suddenly, Dierdre experienced a sense of urgency, before the room filled with more sound. She wanted to tell them now while she could keep her voice low. There were staffers about who would love to spread her private family business to the entire crew.

She broached her secret. "The Bermuda cruise is a really special one for me this year. My twin and I are celebrating our birthday and sharing it with her family and their closest friends. It's sort of a honeymoon cruise they never had, coming from Utah. I'm so excited."

"Oh, Dad, don't look so disappointed. You're used to competition for your time."

His smile held something more. "You mean there are *two* of you?"

"We're not identical. Suzanne is lovely in that all-American-girl way. Married, children and expecting a baby. She's a professional watercolor artist. She'll be teaching some workshops on board."

Megan sat forward. "Really? That's great. Sign me up. Do I need to pack my painting supplies?"

"Yes, do. We'll have a few items in the gift shop, but you'll want whatever you're used to using."

Randy's eyebrows rose above his dark glasses. "When did you take up painting, Honey?"

"Uh, first year of college, Dad. Guess you've forgotten those paintings I thrust your way on every occasion." She ran her fingers through her swingy hair and drilled his dark glasses with a hard look.

Dierdre swirled her icy drink. "So, you haven't always been blind?"

Randy swallowed, pulled at his collar. "No, no I haven't. It was an accident in my, my . . . thirties. I don't like to talk about it. Hope you don't mind."

"Of course not. So sorry. It was rude of me to ask." Dierdre looked from father to daughter. Something awkward was happening, but she couldn't put her finger on what it was. *Just a feeling I guess. Leave it to me to be skeptical lately.*

The music started with a soft jazz number, lilting and intimate.

"Not rude at all. Shall we have the last dance of this cruise?" He stood and propped his red-and-white-tipped cane against the table.

Megan opened her handbag, removed a cigarette and lit up. "I'll hold down the fort while you two enjoy a dance."

Dierdre's heart beat faster, and it wasn't because of Megan's enviable cigarette lit with what appeared to be an elegant gold lighter like something out of *Breakfast at Tiffanys*. Already on her feet, she pushed her chair in and took Randy's hand.

"Lead me to the floor, please, Dierdre." He crooked an arm for her to grasp.

That voice. I'd rather lead you to my cabin. "My pleasure," she said, guiding him to the middle of the dance floor and resting her left hand on his white-linen shoulder. Her cheek close to his neck, his aftershave made her dizzier than the daiquiri.

Randy's arms held her so gentlemanly apart from him she could barely resist leaning into his chest. Their palms touched.

He's igniting something in me I haven't felt for a long time. It's beyond sexual attraction, something totally different, deeper somehow.

Her heart stirred. *I care about what this man feels and not just about me. He's not pitiful, so it isn't that. But what exactly could it be?*

* * *

PART II

Deep Water

Chapter Eight   *Secret Agendas*

Arnold J. Bloomquist mailed the stock-transaction details he'd just completed for a nonexistent client, alias Herb Dennison—himself. Sending them to a DBA account in his cousin Raylene's hometown of Roanoke, Virginia, he paid rent on a post-office box where his collected dividend checks and laundered money piled up. If shady deals were going well, the collection grew daily. The largest rentable PO boxes gave him wiggle room for particularly lucrative months. It was a new-to-him swindle activity but it had definite possibilities.

Since Arni began sending Raylene $50 in cash each month, her 'shopping and mad money' she called it, his package of Doing-Business-As mail came promptly the first week of each succeeding month. Before he'd sent the $50, it'd been tough convincing her his business mail mattered to an urgent degree. The mad money worked. Greed twirled on their family genomes.

A similar scam brought him success in Peru, Indiana with the help of a former college roommate. What Max collected from Arni's DBA post-office box for "Jim Patterson" was shipped to Arnold J. Bloomquist at cheap book rate in a cardboard container large enough to hold the entire month's mail. Max's service didn't cost anything; just the way Arni liked it.

He traded his silence about a grade-switch Max made to boost his point average for a scholarship while in college. The deed was accomplished during a midnight break-in at the Dean's office. Keeping Max's secret was the acceptable tender between them for having Arni's illicit mail collected and sent to him.

As Arni well knew, Max feared if word ever got out about his grade-changing escapade, he'd likely lose his upstanding city council position as well as his marriage to his wealthy, self-righteously bitter wife who owned title to their real-estate business, their upscale home, and his Lexus. Max couldn't afford to lose his lifestyle and reputation with Alma, and was thus motivated to be timely for Jim Patterson and never ask uncomfortable questions. Arni was glad it hadn't so far occurred to Max that aiding and abetting criminal activity across state lines is a Federal felony. To his added relief, Max apparently chose to believe his old college pal Arni's business was on the up and up.

Unless electronically transferred, Arni taped each mailing shut with impermeable postal tape before he sent it to his post-office boxes. When he received each collection in Vegas, he religiously checked for tampering. Having Raylene or Max open envelopes and discover his operation was way too risky. It could blow his whole gig to the Feds or inspire his friend and relative to blackmail him for a cut on his deals.

Arni didn't dwell on any confining thoughts of landing in jail. He considered himself invincible and his operation invisible.

Mr. Arnold J. Bloomquist managed legitimate stock funds by the book for an impressive handful of affluent and politically powerful clients in order to operate with no corporate or government questions asked. The honest figures made faking his books look plausible to the IRS.

Among his legit clients was a recent addition, Dr. Wesley LeChaminant. Wesley was a busy and extremely successful Las Vegas cosmetic surgeon for a bevy of showgirls and "showboys". His reputation for superb endowment expertise, sex changes, and magical facelift procedures spread like wildfire among members of the entertainment venues whose jobs depended upon drop-dead fabulous looks discreetly arranged at his private clinic.

Advertising was word-of-mouth. Wesley operated on a cash basis as much as possible, so paperwork and paper trails were minimized, and a lean staff was all that was necessary. From the beginning of their financial discussions, the cash fact impressed Arni. Keeping his staff organization at his private clinic simple, Dr. LeChaminant made a hefty profit, which he liked to invest. The surgeon's business dealings tempted Arni to plan a little hedge-fund embezzling for the future when the time felt right. Soon he'd help himself to select items in the LeChaminant portfolio. But he had to get a hold of it in private first. The good doctor was too careful on that point for Arni's liking. He'd have to watch for an opportune moment with the books in his hands.

When they'd lunched at Caesar's Palace a couple of weeks ago, LeChaminant mentioned he had a ticket for a Bermuda cruise in a few weeks. He suggested Arni join him, so they could meet and schmooze some charming ladies together. Easier to keep lively conversation going as a foursome, he'd said. Wesley didn't mix pleasure with Vegas business. When a vacation break could be arranged, he enjoyed dining, dancing, and romancing the ladies offshore where the particulars of his dalliances were less likely to attract Las Vegas attention, or confuse his flamboyant reputation in the City of Lights.

After lunch, they'd retired to Wesley's apartment near the Riviera Casino, where Arni drooled over a few documents in the LeChaminant portfolio so recently shown to him and not yet entrusted for selected investments. Barely able to contain his enthusiasm for what he had in mind, Arni agreed to join his client on the cruise. They wouldn't be sharing a first-class cabin, but their suites would adjoin with a door either of them could lock or unlock from their side. Thus they could watch the international stock markets together and plot the most profitable course of action for Wesley.

So Arni led Wesley to believe.

The following morning, Arni Bloomquist phoned his travel agent for a cruise ticket on the Sundancer bound for Bermuda, where he already had an offshore sheltered account at a Trade Ltd. firm. He had the ticket sent to his snazzy penthouse overlooking the Strip. Inking in the seven-day cruise on his day planner, he informed his secretary to block out those dates for meetings and conferences. She was used to following orders without question.

Who knows, this could be an opportunity to meet some rich old broad with a fat portfolio needing my management skills. If I'm lucky, perhaps she'll enjoy gambling, with her money, not mine.

In addition to evading the lion's share of his taxes for years, deeming them un-reportable because of "complications," his sidelines in money laundering, fraudulent stock transactions, and embezzlement schemes kept him comfortably enjoying his opulent lifestyle. A blue-black BMW Z-3 sports car convertible, his elegant penthouse professionally decorated with expensive paintings and imported sculpture, an enviable Italian wardrobe—he especially loved handcrafted-leather Brazilian and Florentine loafers—and his diamond-studded Rolex, not to mention international trips, made life especially good for Arnold J. (Arni) Bloomquist. His elegant business cards attested to his impressive expertise.

What did it matter if neither Arni nor Herb was his *real* name? He'd almost forgotten what it was himself.

* * *

Weeks later, Dierdre sipped an iced tea while reviewing Sundancer passenger reservation listings before the afternoon boarding for Bermuda. An important part of her job was matching names with passport faces so she could greet guests by name on their arrival. Out of time to memorize more, at a quarter to four, she assumed her place at the entry ramp and welcomed newlyweds, college coeds, anniversary couples, and family groups hung with cameras and carryalls. If she hadn't already been near delirium for her birthday cruise, their excitement was contagious enough to send her over the edge.

High with anticipation, she could hardly wait for Suzanne and Taylor's entourage to arrive, and kept scanning the crowd for a glimpse of them among the sea of guests. Hundreds cued up behind ropes to be checked through with their passports and cruise tickets. *You just had to make all of your plane and shuttle connections on time, Suze.*

A tall gentleman, probably her late mother's age, maybe fifty, smiled at the cruise cameraman with an "I'm used to this drill" expression. He approached Dierdre carrying only a celebrity magazine. *He must have hired a porter for everything else he's bringing aboard.* A gold, heavy-linked bracelet and an imposing diamond dinner ring outshined his professional manicure. *He enjoys being hard to miss. A man after my own heart.*

Only guys with money and a public following have their nails trimmed and matt polished. No doubt a celeb of some sort, or at least a man from the entertainment world.

She scanned her recent memory bank. *Has to be LeChaminant, Wesley, MD, cosmetic surgeon to the stars and showgirls of Vegas. No wonder the flamboyant wardrobe and accessories.* The salt air ruffled his professionally died hair, styled long on top and not at a street barbershop. *His passport pix isn't up to date but he's still quite handsome. A summer-weight Armani suit, if I'm not mistaken. Silk shirt. Subtly monogrammed pocket with his own initials. Wow.*

Her seven-second assessment complete, Dierdre held out her hand. "Welcome aboard, Dr. LeChaminant. We're so happy you could join us."

He tucked the magazine between his arm and his lean ribs, put a single finger to his lips and took her hand in both of his. "Shhhh, I see you've done your homework. I prefer Wes. Let's keep the doctor reference to ourselves. On vacation I'd prefer to not be on-call for medical emergencies."

He continued to hold her hand and peered directly into her eyes, while other guests moved on around them. "You look very familiar." His gaze moved to her nametag.

"Dierdre Ingram. Ingram, so familiar. Haven't we met?"

"No, sir." She withdrew her hand. "I would have remembered a distinguished gentleman like yourself." *Very smooth approach. Practiced charm. Intense and interesting.*

Dr. LeChaminant laughed and shook his head. "Distinguished. You are a classy lady. Thank you for not labeling me old." He stepped back. "I hope you'll introduce me to all the classy, single ladies on board."

"May I start with myself?" Dierdre countered.

"But of course!" He nodded vigorously. "I look forward to getting to know you. Is Dierdre, okay with you?"

"Yes, fine. Enjoy your cruise . . . Wes."

He departed and moved on up the ramp to the main deck. *Something about him is familiar, but I'm sure we've never met. I bet he's checked me out for every plastic-surgery procedure he thinks I need. Damned intimidating. Older, but could he be a man for my future?*

She stepped aside to let a decidedly chubby, red-faced fellow struggling with an enormous suitcase get by. "Mr. Campbell, welcome. You brought the whole family. Not in that suitcase, I hope."

He and his tiny wife laughed, followed by several children arranged like stair steps in height from tall oldest to trotting three-year-old harnessed—literally—to her mother by a leash. *Oh dear, this child is no well-behaved Mitzi or they are the most controlling of parental types I've ever welcomed aboard.*

Dierdre signaled a steward. "If you can spare a minute, please take care of Mr. Campbell's luggage, at least as far as the elevator." She held her tongue from adding, *before he has a heart attack.*

Mrs. Campbell blew the hair out of her eyes, yanked her charges into line, and brought up the rear of her brood. "Thank you so much," she whispered in passing. A distinct sour diaper smell lingered.

Below at the photo-op ship photographer, Dierdre caught sight of Suzanne's party. They'd just finished with check in. Her heart pumping with joy, she rushed down to meet them.

"Auntie Dreedra!" whooped Mitzi, sailing away from the others, up the ramp scurrying around people and into her arms. "We been missing you!"

Dierdre's heart filled with happiness. She kissed the bobbing curly head of her niece, realizing the darling had grown remarkably in the year since they were last together.

"Dee," called Suzanne. "Bring Mitzi and have your picture taken with the rest of us! Please, please. You simply must."

At last, my very own family. Holding Mitzi's hand she hurried further down the ramp, excusing her way through the crowd to hug her twin. Suzanne's baby bump swelled perceptibly beneath her loose sundress. Taylor waved a welcome with the arm that wasn't at his wife's waist.

Dierdre gasped, suddenly overcome by pangs of envy, pride, and concern that this cruise be a smooth sail for her pretty pregnant twin.

* * *

Further back in the passport-check line, Randolph Chandler Keene III heard the voice he'd most looked forward to hearing again—Dierdre—the stunning brunette cruise director he found so unforgettable. She offset his unsavory reason for this cruise with promised pleasure. His undercover situation was frustrating where she was concerned. Playing at being someone else wasn't his idea of getting to know a lady he found not only indescribably attractive, but someone he was inexplicably drawn to for the first time since his three-years-ago divorce.

Taking advantage of his apparent impairment, Randy urged Megan to guide him to the shorter line for the disabled. In moments his red-and-white-tipped cane, dark glasses, and her requests to staff had maneuvered them within sight of the complementary souvenir-photo stop. Megan whisked them through ticket check-in while Randy concentrated on figuring out who and how many were the guests in the twins' party being photographed three groups ahead.

Dierdre's twin watercolor painter had to be the honey-blonde mother with a son and daughter, appearing pregnant, and the rugged outdoorsman husband in a white Stetson anticipating her every need. The other woman, exotic, with jet-black hair fashioned in one long braid over her shoulder couldn't be a twin to Dierdre. Beautiful South American or Native American perhaps?

The Caucasian man at her side had survived some nasty ordeal by the scars on his face and hands and the need for the cane he leaned on. Two pre-teen boys, as different from one another as night and day, and a tall teenager with long hair tied back in a ponytail crowded close to the others for the photo with Dierdre. A blended family of some sort, the happy bunch talked all at once. The three boys jostled one another and pointed out aspects of the huge ship to each other, their eyes wide with amazement. The laughing family members hugged one another and, hauling mismatched bags and suitcases, moved on up the ramp behind Dierdre's swaying hips.

Randy turned to Megan and whispered, "The captain's confirmed Bloomquist's on the guest list as we hoped. I'm glad our cab got us here in plenty of time to board without being overly conspicuous in talking with the staff."

She tugged his sleeve, stopped by the cruise-ship poster, and turned to the photographer. Megan smiled at the camera, pinching Randy to do the same. The flash went off, sparkling across his dark glasses. They joined the milling crowd going aboard.

She held his free arm and leaned close enough for him to hear. "I'll do anything to see the low-down scammer pay for what he's done to my family. Mother's devastated."

"Play it cool, Meg. We won't get a better chance than this cruise to nail him for the government and for you. We've seven days to trip him up with the advantage of knowing which passenger he is without him knowing who we are. Stay sharp. Play the good daughter and the available divorcé with the fat bank account. He'll come to us in short order. Your beauty, motivation, and smarts toying with his ego should do the rest."

"Like cream for the cat?"

"Exactly. We'll catch him with cream on his sly whiskers." He adjusted his glasses, gripped his cane, and tapped his way up the ramp on her guiding arm.

His mind and senses for the moment on the cruise director's disappearing hips, Randy imagined holding her in his arms on the dance floor. *Her perfume, her hair, that smile. As soon as possible and often.*

When this case breaks I want to see where things could go for us . . . if I don't screw it up.

* * *

Dr. Wesley LeChaminant motioned for the steward to bring all of his bags into his luxurious cabin. This accomplished, Wes tipped him generously, closed the door behind him, and opened his briefcase on the bed. Removing his laptop, he plugged it into the charger and went about unpacking.

Meticulous about his appearance, Wes shook out every shirt, jacket, and pair of slacks before hanging up each item ready for steaming by the steward.

With his leather dopp kit open on the bath vanity and its contents arranged neatly on the counter, he went through his velvet jewelry bag to insure all pieces were undamaged in transit. Opening the wall safe, he set up his personal combination, deposited the jewelry, his money belt, passport, traveler's checks, camera, and credit cards before locking it. Ignoring his travel agent's warnings to not travel with anything but paste jewelry because of the danger of pickpockets, as usual, Wes had packed real gems.

He enjoyed causing a sensation when entering a gathering in tux, tails, or even a cape accented by fine jewelry. Considered ostentatious by many, he chose impressive pearl or diamond-studded crest pins for his jacket pockets accompanied by impossible-to-ignore dinner rings and bracelets, even for everyday. Known as a sort of Liberace presence in Vegas, he loved the notoriety and felt perfectly justified in drawing attention to himself for business as well as personal reasons. Entering a gathering late gave him the admiring reactions he lived for.

There was a sharp rapping on the connecting door to the adjacent suite. *Ah, Arnold Bloomquist is wasting no time in making contact. Not a hesitant knock either. This cruise gives me a sustained opportunity to observe my new broker. I may be a bit of a gambler, but I won't show him my entire hand or entrust my entire portfolio to his management unless, by the end of the cruise, I trust him completely.*

Wes passed by the bed and closed his briefcase, stashing it in the closet before unlocking the door and ushering in the broker.

"Hello, Arnold. Glad you've arrived to settle in before the cocktail hour. By the look of the crowd of unattached women, we should have a pleasant week meeting interesting new ladies. Let's hope many of them can afford our mutually beneficial services in Las Vegas."

The much shorter, expensively dressed man in his early fifties, entered and stuck out his hand, raising piercing, dark eyes behind tortoise-shell rims to meet Wes's gaze.

"Dr. LeChaminant, so glad to be rooming next door. What a great idea you had, cruising together while we conduct our . . . *your* portfolio business."

Wes noted the 'our' correction and gestured to a chair at the desk.

"Let's dispense with the doctor formality, please. I've already asked the charming cruise director to simply call me Wes. The fewer who know I'm medically competent, the better. I don't intend to spend my vacation catering to every hangnail and headache on board when there's a clinic staff. You do understand I expect you to keep my confidence?"

"Of course, of course." The stockbroker crossed one leg on his other knee. Patterned silk stockings on a neat ankle were exposed above a tasseled loafer. Wes watched Arnold's eyes appraise the suite, dart from stacked matching luggage to open door of the bath where custom-tailored formal wear hung on the glass shower wall. "You brought a lot of fancy clothes. You think we'll have that many Captain's Dinner events in seven days? Aren't there usually just two?"

Wes sat on the foot of his bed, his tall frame elegant in an open-neck custom-tailored poet's shirt he designed himself after those worn by Keats and Shelly. His cream-linen slacks were precisely creased and cuffed, despite the lap wrinkles from a lengthy belted-in plane ride. He faked a casual demeanor while rolling up the shirt's long sleeves and scrutinizing Arnold J. Bloomquist out of the corner of his eye. Without looking at him directly, Wes smiled the way he might have patiently smiled at a naïve child who didn't understand the perfectly obvious.

"My style is not determined by the captain or his formal dinner plans. I'll appear in a tux at dinner *every* evening. White tails for Captain's Dinner. I want the ladies to notice me, especially ones I care to dance with or to enhance cosmetically in my operating theater. I always travel with a duplicate of my secretary's appointment book."

Arnold blushed. "Of course. Always thinking about promoting your cosmetic-surgery business. Admirable. Explains why you're so successful."

Swallowing, he thought, *Good god, I almost said 'sir' to this pretentious fart. This fruitcake is so full of himself he oozes, and I smell his cologne from across the stateroom. If he weren't going on about women I'd swear he's gay. No matter. His bank account speaks my creative-investment language.*

Getting a grip on himself Arni continued. "Do you want to begin exploring your stock options in the morning . . . or do you think we should take it easy on our first day?"

Wes stood and moved to the courtesy fridge. Opening it, with his back purposely to Arnold he said, especially casually, "Yes, let's do take it easy tomorrow. Explore the ship and compare notes on the ladies and any prattle we hear about the most affluent on board. Care for a soda . . . or something stronger?" *What will he choose?*

He turned and pinned the broker with a questioning smile, surprised when Arni's shrewd stare confronted his own. *Well, well. Not easily intimidated I see. Good to know before signing any papers with this pompous little twit.*

"Diet soda, if you please." *The good doctor is checking me out for booze to see if I can do a sober job of his business dealings. Smarter than I gave him credit for, but then I've heard he's nobody's fool. We'll see about that by the time I help myself to some of his dough. My god, who says 'prattle' any more?*

Wes grinned. "Good, I'm having club soda."

So early in our arrangement, Arnold J. Bloomquist's not about to let me know if he's a drinker or not. We'll see if he trips himself up over the next few days and nights with loose lips I'd never trust with my financial investments.

* * *

Completing her guest-greeting responsibilities, including welcoming the Keene's aboard for the second time, she couldn't find her twin's family anywhere on the open-air decks. Dierdre hurried down familiar corridors below and tapped on Suzanne and Taylor's cabin door.

She thought she detected a soft "Yes?"

"It's Dee. May I come in?"

"Use the extra key I gave you."

She slipped inside and found Suzanne lying on her bed in a rumpled cotton sundress, pretty as ever. Mitzi pillowed on her shoulder, slept soundly.

Pointing to her daughter, Suzanne said softly, "The little darling's exhausted from all the traveling excitement of her first plane ride and coming aboard this amazing ship."

Dierdre leaned down for her twin's half hug. "I'm so thrilled we actually pulled off our dream birthday cruise."

"Me too. Thank you for all you've arranged to make it possible. Not to mention the anticipation of a wedding and a couple of honeymoons." Suzanne eased Mitzi off of her shoulder and sat up, combing fingers through her hair and smoothing the dress. "I needed a nap myself. I get unusually tired lately." She slid her feet into thongs.

Dierdre pulled out a chair at the tiny table and flipped open a notepad. "Pace yourself this cruise. Let everyone help, and you and the baby will do fine. Where are Taylor and the others?"

Suzanne laughed and sat down opposite. "Off exploring, I imagine. The boys wanted to check out the pool and the video-game room. The men . . . who knows? Plenty of bikinis on the Lido Deck to catch a man's eye. Cosma's unpacking her tarot cards and ritual stuff. She'll be here soon. Hope it's okay the men opted not to teach falconry familiarization. Taylor wants to devote himself to being my hero, especially where baby and Mitzi are concerned."

Dierdre nodded. "The finances between us all worked out fine." She scanned note pages and met her sister's eyes. "Gives me a minute to tell you the pre-registration for your watercolor workshop and Cosma's tarot readings each have more than a dozen signups. From my experience, that's really good. Once guests read their daily event promos and word of mouth gets out, these numbers will go up. Shall we close tomorrow's first session at fifteen?"

Suzanne rubbed her tummy absently. "Um hum. Fifteen's already pushing it to give painters some personal attention, especially the beginners."

"Okay, I'll brief the staff. Let's get with Cosma soon and hear her ideas for their wedding."

* * *

That evening, the first-seating entree choices pleased everyone at Dierdre's table. Happily nibbling a seafood salad and sipping iced tea she feasted on being surrounded by friends and family—her only family. Each of them took turns telling her what they'd discovered on board so far. Laughter punctuated the anecdotes going back and forth. After so long a separation by time and distance, soaking up the joys of belonging to her sister and these special people nourished her far more than the food.

Mitzi tapped her arm. "I like your pretty bracelet Auntie Dreedra. And I really like all these fat starberries." She stabbed one with her fork and brought it to her mouth.

Gregory at Dierdre's other side, tugged at her elbow, "My sister can say your name better than last year—sometimes—but starberries for strawberries is still, you know," He whispered. "Baby talk."

Dierdre hugged him, delighted he appeared to be a happy boy again. She'd have to ask her sister how his transformation had come about. Her eyes moved from her niece and nephew to their parents. Across the table, Suzanne and Taylor discussed her delicious macadamia-crusted halibut, while she fed him a flaky white morsel between his rib-eye bites. Their adoring attention to each other made Dierdre warm inside. Envious too. *Would I ever love to be in love like them.*

Cosma, dramatic in a bright turquoise caftan streaming multi-colored ribbons from shoulders to waist, urged Johnny and her sons to finish their cheeseburgers before the dessert cart arrived. Her exotic appearance with her customary beaded braid over one shoulder and flashing silver earrings caused many guests at nearby tables to whisper and nod toward her. Dierdre predicted Cosma's animal-tarot readings would be popular once guests figured out the unique Native American opportunities she offered.

Dierdre noted an increased buzz in nearby conversations. Her gaze followed the direction of the guests who were rude enough to actually point. At the doorway of the dining room, Dr. Wesley LeChaminant, a stylish cut above most diners in a white tuxedo had engaged a server in conversation.

Stellar nudged her. "Is that guy a movie star or something?"

Dierdre grinned at the boy and whispered. "Not exactly, but he does sort of work with professional Las Vegas entertainers."

"Wow." Stellar's fork bristling with French fries paused inches from his mouth like a hovering hummingbird. "How do you know that?"

She chuckled. "It's my job to know a little something about all of our cruise guests."

Cloud cocked his head toward them and back to the man they were discussing who walked across the floor in their direction. "You have to know who he is, but does he know you?"

Before she could answer, Wes had reached their table. Their eyes met and he winked at her.

"I'm happy to see you, Dierdre. You're looking especially lovely this evening. I understand you'll be the MC at tonight's floor show."

"Hello, Wes. Yes and thank you. This is my sister Suzanne's family and our dear friend Cosma's family." She swept her arm around the table. "We'll introduce one another properly soon, I'm sure."

"I'll wave tonight from the audience." He tipped his wavy-haired head in a brief bow. "Excuse me, won't you? My table partner is probably ordering dinner without me."

"Of course." Dierdre smiled while he moved on to a table not far away.

Stellar lightly punched his brother's arm. "I'd say he knows her alright."

Cloud's eyebrows furrowed over his deep-set dark eyes. "That's not all. He's wearing some powerful shaving lotion. If he goes out in nature the animals won't go near him—or they'll eat him."

Johnny laughed. "That goes for the hawks too."

Suzanne and Cosma shushed them all and changed the subject to the classes she would be teaching and how Cloud and Cosma would help her with carrying the painting supplies to the classroom while Taylor managed Mitzi.

Dierdre watched Wes seat himself with another man at a table for two. *His smartly dressed companion's a stockbroker, if I remember correctly,* she thought. *They aren't cabin mates but perhaps business associates? Lovers? Wes is a standout, handsome, confident, and rich. Wonder if he can dance. What is it about him that's so familiar?* As if he read her mind telepathically, he turned and looked in her direction.

She smiled at him. He grinned and waved a few fingers, the pinky sporting a sparkling amber gemstone the size of an almond. *No wedding ring.* Dierdre felt a blush climb from her throat to her cheeks. *Am I attracted to this older man? Well, why not? He's certainly attracted to me.* She checked her watch and interrupted the light conversations at her table.

"You'll all excuse me I hope." She rose and pushed in her chair. "Time for me to join the cast for tonight's show. Take your time over dessert. First performance doesn't start for fifty minutes."

"Mommy says I get to stay up late and come see your play 'cause I had a nap."

Dierdre bent and kissed the top of her curly head. "Don't be disappointed, sweetheart. It's not exactly a play with a story but we do a lot of singing and dancing."

"I like dancing. I'll wave to you."

Dierdre wiped strawberry juice from the child's chin. "Okay, Mitzi, I'll wave back."

Dropping the napkin by her plate, Dierdre's sweeping farewell gesture took in everyone around her. "See you all later."

She stepped away from the table and turned to leave, sensing Wes LeChaminant's gaze or someone else's. Glancing toward his table, his chair was empty. Nevertheless the sense of being watched persisted. Retreating between tables and around tray-laden waiters toward the lounge area and the nearest elevators, she checked the reflection behind her in the mirrored wall. Wes walked through the crowd in her direction. A thrill of excitement coursed like electricity from her head to the toes in her clicking high heels.

Dierdre slowed to give him time to catch up. At the elevator she hesitated before pressing the button in case he meant to join her and assure her safety. Elevators still made her nervous. *What will such a sophisticated and worldly gentleman say? Will he ask me for a dinner date or suggest a chat over a nightcap?*

* * *

Wes joined Cruise Director Dierdre Ingram at the elevators. While pressing the button for a downward deck, she smiled the so-familiar and deeply puzzling dazzler. The doors opened.

"Going my way, Wes?" she asked, stepping inside and moving toward the panel of button controls.

He followed. "Yes, Dierdre. I must talk with you. If not now, at a time you would find more convenient."

A young family hurried in, bumping a baby carriage over the transom.

"Excuse us," muttered the woman, appearing frazzled.

The man he assumed to be the father reached in front of Ms. Ingram to thumb a deck button and pull the carriage away from the closing door. The toddler jabbered, grasping at everything within reach, including the cruise director's skirt hem.

"No, no darling. Let go." The mother stooped and disengaged the tot's fingers, awkwardly smiling up at all the adults through the unkempt hair in her eyes.

Wes struggled to swallow his impatience with not only the interruption, but imagining the young mother thought nothing of appearing disheveled in public, which he found appalling. He noted Ms. Ingram succeeded in professionally hanging onto both her patience and her dignity. She brushed at her skirt and backed into a corner while the elevator arrived at the next level and came to a stop.

Good, they're getting off. Now if no one else gets on I can have the moment I need with this gorgeous woman.

The family departed. No one else waited to board. They were alone.

She eyed him, cautiously he thought, for she resumed her spot within reach of the button panel. "You *must* talk with me?" Her tone had an edge. "About what?"

As the doors closed and the ascent continued, Wes planted his feet to steady himself. He smiled warmly, hoping to disarm her protective attitude, so different than their resent exchange at the table with her family.

He spoke softly, "You're the second most beautiful woman I've ever met."

Her eyes flew open in a startled expression.

"*Second?*" she squeaked, then burst into giggles. "That's the most lame come-on I've ever heard, Doctor LeChaminant."

"Please, no doctor, remember our agreement yesterday?"

He shifted his feet and grinned. "It wasn't meant as a seduction. Let me explain. From the moment we met there was something so familiar about you. At dinner I watched you with the honey blonde, your sister? She's familiar too. I dated an Ingram lady, whom I'm convinced was a relative of yours. Perhaps a stunning aunt?"

She didn't look convinced, pursed her lips, and raised an eyebrow. "My sister and I don't have an aunt.

Never did, but you've proved you're not making a move. If I had an aunt, she'd certainly be your age and the age of our late mother."

"Ouch," he said. "I deserved that sarcasm for the awkward way I'm pursuing you."

Perplexed, he insisted, "But you are so like the gorgeous young Ingram girl I dated one summer. An absolutely uncanny likeness. You and your sister even gesture like her. Your voices have the same timber. Too amazing to be a coincidence."

The elevator slowed. She glanced at her watch. The doors slid open.

"Sorry I can't help you, Wes."

She stepped out, turned back and added, "I think it's the first time I've ever been flattered to be second at anything. Good luck tracking down number one."

* * *

Chapter Nine   *What Comes and Goes*

Gregory climbed down from their cabin's top bunk, deciding not to fold it back into the wall. He left his dream catcher and Felon feather hanging above his pillow because so far it was working. He hadn't had any nightmares about Stinking Man or Black Dog since Cloud's ceremony.

"Mom, I said I'd meet Cloud and Stellar at the ice-cream stand by the pool. Okay if I go now?"

Suzanne straightened in her chair, pressing a fist to her lower back. She put out an arm to draw him near.

"Have your key in case I'm napping?"

Gregory nodded. "Got it." He patted his shorts pocket.

She gestured with the handle of her paintbrush toward the lump under his tee shirt. "Is your medicine pouch keeping the bad dreams away?"

He smiled easily. "Haven't had even a scary one since Cloud made me his Indian brother."

Suzanne put the brush on the table and opened her handbag. "Here's my ship card, Bold Heart. After ice cream you boys might want to play some video games."

"Wow. Great, Mom. Thanks!" He hugged her. "Want me to check on Mitzi in the playroom?"

"Not necessary, honey. Taylor's picking her up in half an hour. I'm going to grab a nap before the energy princess returns."

* * *

Sundancer's gift shop hummed with customers. Arni pretended to study the magazine display while he edged closer to the woman named Megan. Her expensive couture wardrobe and genuine jewelry caught his eye on deck and in the dining room last night. An heiress he was certain, prompting him to follow her as surreptitiously as possible. Her sensational figure and sassy brunette haircut complemented her pretty face.

He'd followed her from above deck to get a handle on her activities. Her likes and dislikes would help him form a strategy for discussing financial opportunities as soon as he could get her alone. She was speaking to the gift-shop clerk. He moved closer.

"Is there a supply list for the watercolor class? I'm not sure I brought everything required from home." Megan swung a lock of hair across her cheek and tucked it behind her sparkling ear lobe with French-manicured nails.

The clerk gestured to the activity board posted on an easel.

Arni looked over Megan's shoulder, moving even closer, attempting to appear—he hoped—as inquisitive as she. Her luxurious perfume momentarily distracted him.

"Oh, did you need to see this art-supply list as well?" Megan moved her Hermes bag to the side, giving him room to step up to the easel. Jewelry at her throat, on her wrist, and on her tanned ear lobes expressed high-end taste to his practiced eye. Her fresh beauty had almost forced her gold and diamond earrings from his mind. Almost.

"I've been toying with the idea of taking up a childhood pastime," he managed to say, casually checking his diamond-studded Rolex on the pretext of caring about the time. "Have you already signed up?"

"Yes. It'll be fun. Why don't you join us? Class starts in an hour." She smiled warmly, looking directly into his eyes from her own dark pools fringed with expertly applied extensions making the sexiest long lashes he'd ever observed up this close.

His heart skipped a beat. *She spends hours and plenty of money in up-scale salons.* "You're very convincing. Will you mentor me through the . . . the brush technique difficulties?" *I mustn't press too hard too fast.*

"That's what the instructor is for." She laughed. "My watercolor skills are pretty rusty. I'm more of an encourager. But it will be fun to wield a paintbrush again."

"I'll take the class too. You can only sun yourself on the decks for so long, waiting for the ship to drop anchor in Bermuda."

He purchased the suggested watercolor kit, while Megan bought the most expensive sable wash brush on display. They nodded to one another and parted company.

Arni returned to his cabin loaded with watercolor paper, brushes, tubes of paint, a palm-size cosmetic sponge, and the resolve to make Megan one of his clients before the cruise ended. *Dressed to the nines and wearing real rocks, Megan's got to be loaded. I'll get her to invest with me managing her accounts.*

I'll manage them all right. If I play my cards right, perhaps I can even become intimate with more than her investment portfolio.

* * *

Arni arrived early while the group comprised mostly of women two to a table were arranging their art materials as directed by the instructor. She handed out triangular light balsa-wood wedges about a foot long to each person.

The pretty and obviously pregnant instructor wore a nametag, "Suzanne". She spoke in a pleasant voice, with neither southern nor northeastern accent, more like the western cadence he was used to in Nevada.

"I'll demonstrate for any novice painters what these board rests are for while you're getting organized. Please fill your water jars from the main bucket and put your brushes bristle up in the extra empty jar. Squeeze blobs of watercolor paint from your tubes onto your palettes in warm-and cool-color order. Follow the chart on your handout if you're unsure."

Megan placed her supplies near the window at the first table. Arni took the table next to hers, though there was room for a second person at her table. *Mustn't be too obvious too soon.* He flipped through the pages of the class handout and opened it to the Preparing the Palette chart. Relieved to see the color names were printed under each blob in the diagram, he began to squeeze dabs onto his palette following the names on the tubes. Out the corner of his eye he watched to see who would occupy the other half of Megan's table, putting a person between them.

He nodded a greeting to Megan, which she returned, adding a flutter of fingers in a girlish wave. They both set to making up their palettes. He watched Megan and the instructor to get it right because his red-green color-blind impairment would be a challenge in this class. *If I can pull off an investment arrangement with Megan it will be worth all the time, trouble, and expense of this cruise class.*

The remaining tables around them were soon claimed. Conversation murmured with people getting to know each other while they set up and prepared for class to begin.

Two chatty women running late followed one another. Traveling together, he surmised. They surveyed the room, exchanged disappointed looks and split up, the chubby dramatic one plopped giant tote bags at his table. The slim quiet one joined Megan. Both appeared to be in their early fifties.

Spicy perfume, too liberally applied, assaulted Arni's nostrils. *I'm going to smell like a French whore before this class is over. My tablemate doesn't have Megan's taste or pocketbook.* He swallowed hard, tied on the provided apron imprinted with the Sundancer logo, and ventured to meet the eyes of the bizarre creature who'd joined him.

"Hello," he said, seating himself. *Might as well be friendly.* "Great to be in the first row. We won't miss a thing."

"Hello yourself, you darling man, Arni by your name tag. I'm Hettie Klingle and I'm only doing this to please my friend Catherine Hatch at the next table." She tipped her head in her friend's direction.

Hettie's shocking black and white, spiked hair looked like a hacked paintbrush in sore need of reconditioning. "I'm quite an experienced painter so I don't need lessons. I'm here for fun." She cackled.

I thought people only laughed like that in cartoon and horror movies, like the wicked witch in the Wizard of Oz or Cruella Deville in a Dalmatian coat. Their screaming laughs could peel wallpaper, scaring children to death. I'll try not to be funny so I won't have to buy earplugs at the gift shop for next class.

Arni found Hettie fascinating though, noting her clothes were designer brands as outrageously expensive as they were amazingly mismatched. *I bet she figures she's a Bohemian artistic type.* Stretched over her considerable bulges, she wore stripes with prints, wild clashing colors, and her fat fingers were tipped with turquoise-glitter nail polish. Hettie fiddled with the tiny lids on her paint tubes. Her knuckle-duster rings were hideous. *Stones too big to be tasteful, but real gems.*

Suddenly, it was easy to forgive her overwhelming perfume and her maniacal laugh. *Money.* He could smell it. *A new target.*

Hettie leaned close and looked up at him through false eyelashes tipped with lime-green glitter. "I can't get these tubes open. Would you be a dear and help me?"

She fluttered her eyelashes. *Has she been living under a rock for years thinking silent-screen antics are cute? Pitiful.* He swallowed to keep from laughing.

"Sure," he said, quickly loosening the lids on all the tubes and laying them in a row. Despite her earlier remarks she acted as if she didn't know how to proceed, making him wonder why she said she was an experienced painter. He took one tube and showed her how to pierce the metal security seal with the sharp point in the lid, the way he'd observed Megan doing. He sent a grateful glance beyond Hettie's friend Catherine toward Megan, his elegant number-one target. She smiled and nodded to him.

Soft-spoken, classy, Megan appeared to be getting on well with Catherine, dressed tastefully and so opposite in appearance and personality to Hettie he wondered how the two could even be friends let alone traveling companions. *No flashy jewelry. Doubt Catherine has big bucks. But then you never know. Some wealthy women are understated.*

Suzanne returned to the front of the room and demonstrated propping their watercolor boards at an angle on the balsa-wood rests to control the paint washes with the aid of gravity. Everyone followed suit.

Mixing colors, layering washes and dry-brush techniques completed the demonstrations. With hair dryers speeding up the process, the class members experimented for half an hour with their brushes and various techniques until each had an array of samples drying on their table. Arni checked his Rolex, realized it was nearing quitting time, and dabbed at a puddle with his cosmetic sponge before it could run onto the table. He stayed in his seat arranging and rearranging his samples to hang around Megan. She was speaking to Catherine. He strained to listen.

"Suzanne is the cruise director's twin sister. Not identical twins of course, but this cruise is their birthday celebration and the honeymoon for Suzanne and her husband of a year."

Catherine rinsed her fan brush. "Isn't that just lovely. How romantic and she carrying their baby."

Hettie nudged Arni with a pudgy elbow and whispered, "Catherine's been a widow for several years. I dragged her along on this cruise to get her back into circulation. She's terribly shy and needs a person like me to charge her batteries and push her out of her comfort zone. Know what I mean?" She fluttered her lashes and continued raucously in her normal cackle. "Are you single?"

Arni choked. "Yes, yes . . . single. And you?"

She looked mischievous or devious, he couldn't decide, while scrutinizing him with tattooed eyebrows in danger of meeting in dramatic Frieda fashion over her bulbous nose.

"Single of course. Last evening I went to dinner without Catherine. She was woozy with seasickness. You dined with that handsome, flamboyant man in a white tux. Are you gay partners? I tried to describe you two to Catherine."

His gut clenched and heat spread from his neck up to his forehead. Arni wanted to choke Hettie or stuff a few brushes and a dry sponge down her fat throat.

"Wesley LeChaminant is a prominent Las Vegas . . . businessman and my esteemed client. I assure you, madame, we are most certainly *not* gay."

Arni bit his tongue lest in revenge he accuse Hettie and Catherine of some kinky relationship and live to regret it. He switched on the whir of a hair dryer to drown Hettie out and fanned it over his splotchy painting samples.

From his left he felt a tap on his arm. Catherine's stricken expression nearly dropped him in his tracks. He turned off the hair dryer. "Yes, ma'am?"

Her hand on his arm shook like a palsy.

"Did I hear you say Wes . . . Wesley LeChaminant?"

* * *

Megan helped Catherine sop up spilled paint water. *I wonder why the man's name upset her so much she tipped her water jar over.*

Megan had told Randy she was already onto their quarry and had pressed him to join the painting class. The fellow wearing the painting-class Arni nametag was the swindler Bloomquist. Watching his response to Catherine surprised her. He'd said, "Yes, that's my client's name," and shrugged his shoulders in a cavalier gesture. His dismissive arrogance made Megan want to pop him one for that on top of her other reasons. He seemed to change his mind, perhaps curious.

"Yes, I did say Wesley LeChaminant. We do a great deal of business together in Vegas. Do you know him personally?"

Visibly shaken, Catherine stammered, "A familiar name of an old . . . friend is all. It's nothing."

He seemed amused and gestured to the water pouring over the table and dripping on the floor. "Oh, guess you'll be busy a while. Want some help or can you two women handle it?"

Catherine grabbed a roll of paper towels and tore off several sheets. "We'll manage. Thanks for offering." Her eyes beseeched Megan. "I'm so sorry to make such a mess. How embarrassing."

Classtime over, Suzanne was joined by a striking Native American woman and a teenage boy with a thick, black ponytail reaching half way down his back. Megan noticed them last night at dinner, sitting with Suzanne's sister Dierdre. Randy's heartthrob, though Dierdre probably didn't know it yet. Moving from painting table to painting table, they helped Suzanne box up all the art supplies, balsa-wedge props, and painting samples brought for class. The black-haired boy with the high cheekbones and dark eyes did the carrying, making repeated trips to the entry area to stack the boxes.

Megan kept an eye on Arnold as discreetly as she could, not wanting her quarry to think her unusually interested in him and become suspicious before she had a chance to trap him for Randy and herself. Arnold was their reason for being on this cruise and it wouldn't do for him to figure that out. Not yet anyway.

His hands and a sleeve splotched with paint, she watched the shyster carefully remove his diamond Rolex watch and tuck it under his paint cloth, before picking up his wet brushes, his own jar of water, and heading for the sink across the room.

Catherine's spikey-haired friend, Hettie chattered a dramatic stream in his wake, punctuated with her cackling laughter. Matching her tipped eyelashes, her glittering lime-green fingernails sprouted wet paintbrushes like Edward Scissorhands.

Megan's gaze followed Hettie. *She is so comical. He deserves her driving him nuts.* Megan swooped spreading water into an empty jar with her paint cloth and dabbed the table and their supplies with more paper towels. She winked at Catherine.

"Accidents happen. Don't give it a second thought. I might do it myself next class."

Touching Catherine's hand briefly, she smiled in what she hoped would be taken for genuine concern. "More important than cleaning up our table, are you okay?"

Catherine wiped up the last of the dirty water on the floor and rose from her knees. "I knew someone by that name years ago. The coincidence was a bit of a shock."

Head down, with shaking hands on the table top, Catherine used her paint cloth to dry her tubes and the handles of her brushes. "I . . . I've not said his name for some time—years in fact."

Megan's curiosity pricked, she glanced over her shoulder. Arnold and Hettie were out of earshot, so she whispered, "He must have been terribly important for just his name to upset you so. Did he hurt you somehow, perhaps do something . . . unspeakable?"

Catherine tucked her brushes one at a time into her linen carrier's slots as if her life depended upon how perfectly she aligned their various handles.

She shook her head. "No, nothing nasty. Quite the opposite. Wes was my first love. The biggest regret of my life was breaking our engagement . . . under duress from his mother. Later, I married someone else. My husband died a few years ago." She let out a long sigh. "I loved him but it was never the same. Not like what I felt for Wes."

She sniffled. Tears quivered at her lashes. She blinked furiously to stop them.

Megan pursed her lips. "I'm so sorry. But isn't it possible Arnold's friend *is* the same man, your former fiancé? You have to admit Wesley LeChaminant is quite a unique moniker."

Catherine shook her head vehemently, dislodging long tendrils of light brown hair from the ribbon at the back of her neck. "That fellow said his friend was a Las Vegas businessman. Wes is a surgeon with an international reputation—definitely not a businessman. Even if he were a businessman he wouldn't be successful at it. He knows how to make money. He's just not very good at hanging onto it, generous and too trusting." She laughed, apparently restoring herself to coping level. "I'll be fine. Sorry to be so emotional."

Hettie and Arnold returned from the sink. He slipped his hand under his paint cloth and pulled it back, then snatched the cloth and shook it. His bright brown eyes widened in alarm and darted like search engines around his painting space. He slapped his empty water jar on the table and began methodically going through the pockets of his painting apron, his stained shirt, and his white slacks. He raised his arms, hands at his mouth megaphone style, like a booing fan at a football game. The tone of his voice rose to take in everyone in the classroom.

"My watch! Has anyone seen my watch? I only took it off for a few moments to wash my brushes and my hands. For god's sake it's a Rolex!"

He glared at Catherine and Megan. "You two were right here the whole time I was gone. Did you see anyone take it? Did one of *you* take it?"

Megan stood her ground, hands on her hips. "Of course not! Stealing is not *my* thing." She choked on almost giving herself away and bent to the task of storing her supplies in her pocket-lined tote, ignoring, while enjoying Bloomquist's panic. *Savor how it feels to lose something important, you devious scoundrel. Next you'll lose your fake sterling reputation and your real freedom. That will be a sweet moment.*

Frantic, Arnold patted down every item on the table. Stooping, he looked under his chair, under the table, rechecked his pockets and hurtled back in the direction of the sink. Hettie was on his trail like a beagle after a fox.

"Arni dear, I know I saw that watch on your arm," she soothed. "It's got to be here somewhere. Calm down. I'll help you look. You'll help too, won't you, Catherine?"

Catherine nodded but didn't move to help. She kept packing up her supplies.

Suzanne approached him. "We'll all help you look. A Rolex must be very expensive." The Indian woman and the boy who resembled her, probably her son, set their boxes on the floor and followed to help in the search.

While some members of the class stayed to help, others were leaving. Arnold rummaged in the deep wastebasket by the sink. He looked up at Suzanne with an expression of distain, quite apparent in his voice. "Expensive? Expensive!" his voice exploded in a shout, "Thousands of dollars worth of expensive! Gold and diamond expensive."

Rising from the wastebasket, he pointed an accusing finger at the teenager. "You shifty Indian kid. I bet you stole my Rolex!"

Megan's hand flew to her mouth. *Oh no. He's accused that darling boy unjustly.*

* * *

Cloud reeled at the man's accusation. His heart pounded in his ears. He jumped back fearing the guy would leap the few feet between them and punch him out. His mother grabbed his arm and yanked him behind her, forcing him to retreat several steps. Her grip on his arm loosened, but she didn't let go. He figured she could tell he was mad enough to defend himself physically if he had to.

"Stay cool, Cloud. This could get ugly," she whispered.

Suzanne approached the man pacing beside the wastebasket. "I know you're upset Arnold, but making wild accusations is uncalled for. So is your labeling. The young man deserves an apology. Since your watch has not been located, it's time to report the loss to security. I'm sure it will turn up in lost and found."

The man's face twisted in anger. "If you think the kid's not the thief, search him and everybody else too. Then we'll know for sure."

Cloud's heart beat faster and faster. *My pockets are empty, but will that be enough to convince him I'm not a thief?* He pulled the pockets of his jeans out, holding two quarters in his fist. "Mom, I swear I didn't take his watch."

Suzanne spoke in the soft voice Cloud had heard her use to chill Gregory. "As you can see, Mr. Bloomquist. Most of our painters have already left and the chef's team has arrived to set up the ice-sculpture demonstration. We need to leave now."

The woman with the wild hair tugged on the angry man's shirtsleeve. "You should file a report. Come on. I'll go with you."

The guy jerked his arm free. "I'll report this to security myself." He glared in Cosma and Cloud's direction. Turning back to the wild-haired woman, his voice softened. "No need for you to trouble yourself, Hettie. See you in class tomorrow."

He jammed his watercolor samples into a bag, closed up his kit, and hefted them in one hand, his watercolor board in the other. Nodding to Catherine and Megan he muttered, "G-bye. If you two remember seeing anyone around my stuff, let me know right away. Bloomquist. Call information."

He dropped his business card on their table and hurried from the room.

When his mother released her hold on him, Cloud began to breathe normally and accepted her hug, then Suzanne's.

She lifted his chin with her hand and looked him in the eye. "I'm terribly sorry Arnold behaved so rudely. You're a good honest person, Cloud. I wish he'd apologized to you."

"I don't think he's the apologizing type," said his mother. Her face was dark with an angry flush. She fingered the beads on her braid. "He could be real trouble."

Cloud piled two boxes on top of each other and steadied them with his chin. "It's not the first time somebody pointed a finger at me for being an Indian. Probably won't be the last."

Still it hurt way deep and he wouldn't soon forget it. He'd be watching for the guy and steering clear of him. Some white guys could be real trouble.

* * *

On deck following Suzanne's class, Dierdre joined her sister and Cosma, already settled in folding loungers soaking up the sun. Taylor stood at Suzanne's bare feet, polishing his sunglasses on his shirttail. His white Stetson shaded his handsome face. Dierdre gave him a brief hello hug and plopped into the lounger he'd just vacated.

Taylor replaced his glasses on his tanned nose. "I'll leave you ladies to your party plans while I go work out with Johnny. We've got to pump some iron to burn off calories and make room for tonight's Captain's Dinner. I'll check on Mitzi in the kids' playroom on my way." He tweaked Suzanne's dainty silver toe ring affectionately and blew her a kiss before sauntering off.

What a fine specimen of manhood. Suze's so lucky he's as good to her as he is handsome. I want one of those for myself.

Seated between Suzanne and Cosma, she turned to her twin. "So how'd your first watercolor class go? I didn't get a break to stop by and peek in but you maxed out your class size, which is simply great, especially for the first day."

"Great until it went to heaven in a hand basket." Suzanne squirmed and cast a furtive glance at Cosma.

What that's all about? Nothing that gets back to the captain I hope. Dierdre studied their faces and waited for an explanation.

Cosma put down her notepad. "One of the guests in her class accused Cloud of taking his Rolex. He made an ugly scene, practically calling him a thieving little Indian."

Dierdre caught her breath. "Seriously?" She swallowed hard, flushing with embarrassment. "That's terrible. How did Cloud take it?" *Oh god, this could get out of hand if the guy's a demanding jerk and takes it upstairs to the Captain.*

Cosma shook her head, her face tight, her brow furrowed. "Cloud's so upset and angry, I urged him to take Stellar and Gregory and play video games for some fun. I don't want him dwelling on bad feelings about himself. My son's a good boy."

She chewed at her pencil, her dark eyes troubled. "I hope the watch turns up soon or this cruise could be disastrous for him."

Suzanne spoke up. "We all know Cloud's an honorable young man." She rubbed her modest baby bump absently. "I'm just so sorry it happened.

Everything was going so well, better than I expected for my first teaching experience."

Cosma tapped her notepad with the pencil.

"Yes, *we* know Cloud's honest, but a man who can afford a diamond Rolex is probably used to having his way. I'm afraid he'll make trouble—racial profiling—if you know what I mean."

Dierdre smoothed tanning lotion on her legs.

"Has this man reported the loss?" Through her sunglasses, she noted the approach of good looking and elegant Dr. Wesley LeChaminant. She smiled and waved her tube of lotion. He grinned back and continued to walk their way.

I'd like to see more of this man before the cruise is over. Preferably without that sports jacket or less than that.

Suzanne lifted her hat brim. "I sure hope so. And without accusing Cloud."

Distracted by Wes, for a moment Dierdre puzzled at her twin's remark, then replayed their conversation in her head and caught on. "I'll follow up with Security staff," she assured them.

She nodded to the doctor, whose secret she knew. He paused at her lounger.

"Afternoon, ladies, Miss Dierdre." He removed his sunglasses and gestured with them toward the horizon. "Looks like we're in for a storm. It seems to be coming our way quite fast."

Dierdre noted his trim body, wavy hair blowing in the rising breeze, and his terrific smile. "Wes, this is my twin Suzanne and our friend Cosma I explained briefy in the dining room. Suzanne teaches watercolor painting and Cosma offers Native American animal-tarot readings for our guests."

He tipped his head to each of them in turn. "So pleased to meet you both. What three beautiful women you are. Your husbands and children as well, of course."

She knew his career expertise but didn't let on what a compliment he'd paid them, coming from a Vegas cosmetic surgeon. *There's something very sexy about his graceful manner. Odd to think of a man as graceful. Wonder if he's gay. If so it would be just my luck to be out of the picture already.*

Wes hadn't moved. "My late wife, who was also quite pretty, wouldn't have enjoyed sunning herself out here like you. She avoided the sun on her skin. Ironically, she died of metastasized complications of squamous cancer."

Late wife. Gay is unlikely, but that explanation about her sounded so clinical he's giving his medical expertise away without realizing it.

Dierdre's interest in him deepened. "Are you dancing this evening?" she said, hoping her intent sounded innocent.

"Yes, as a matter of fact I've been invited to sit at the Captain's table. Perhaps you'd save a dance for me later? My travel companion is put out about my dining plans, but I'm sure he'll manage to find a suitable table partner."

Cosma interjected, "Is that the man you sat with at dinner last night?"

"Why yes it is," Wes said, smiling at her. "He's my stock broker and financial advisor."

Cosma looked him in the eye, her own dark eyes bright as spear points. "He accused my son of stealing his Rolex—brutal about it too."

Wesley's face clouded. "I'm so sorry to hear that. I haven't seen Arnold since breakfast, so I didn't know his watch was missing." He put his sunglasses back on and buttoned his jacket in the rising breeze. "He does have a belligerent side, but I'm sure it will blow over. I hope his Rolex turns up."

Nodding to Dierdre, he stepped away. "This evening then. Good afternoon."

"There's something so familiar about him," Suzanne said. "I just can't put my finger on it."

"Funny you say that." Dierdre capped her lotion then helped load up magazines and towels in the wind. "I have that feeling too, and he said the same thing about me and even you."

Dark clouds obliterated the sun. The wind picked up, churning glittery blue swells to cold iron gray. The ship rose and fell sharply with the rising waves.

Suzanne paled, her face bordering on green.

Dierdre paused with her arms full. "You okay, Sis?"

Suzanne bit her lip and shook her head. "I need to go to my cabin. This motion is making me sick." She gathered her towel and beach bag stuffed with wedding magazines.

"Forgive me, Cosma. Can we go into your wedding plans after I've had a lie down?"

Dierdre helped them both with all of their things and followed them along the rolling deck to the doors. They were barely inside when the sprinkles began, followed almost immediately by crashing thunder and driving rain.

* * *

Dierdre crossed the dance floor; nodding and waving to guests she'd met. She was drawn to Randy's broad shoulders and thick, wavy hair defining his tan neck and well-shaped ears. *Must have had a trim today. He looks handsome as always. He's certainly careful about his appearance, despite being blind or perhaps because of it.*

Her insides stirred when she recalled his gentle touch, dancing in his arms. The chemical heat of reacting to his maleness came back to her along with her dizzying response to his aftershave and the wish to see the eyes behind his dark glasses. *Eyes tell so much about a person.*

Tonight he had his back to her. At his side, his daughter Megan smiled eagerly and motioned Dierdre to join them, prodding Randy on the arm. He didn't turn in her direction but said something in reply.

Reluctant to join them because she'd agreed to dance with attractive Wesley LeChaminant, she hesitated, casting her gaze around the other guests, looking for the plastic surgeon. In mid-step, Dierdre spied Wesley's white dinner jacket, or so she thought. He faced her, rose to his feet tall and commanding, and held a hand out to her. Surprised to note his dinner jacket was actually a white tux with tails and matching white tux pants striped with satin down the legs, she suppressed a gasp. *White leather dance shoes too.*

Good lord. Whoever dresses like that except Fred Astaire starring in old black and white movies? She moved toward him, smiling and winking as she passed near Megan who raised her eyebrows and whispered to Randy. For a moment, her feelings about Randy did a tug of war, surprising her.

Wes stood smiling by his chair. "Dierdre, I'm so glad you didn't forget to join me, as in demand as I'm sure you are."

"Wes, of course I wouldn't forget." Dierdre accepted his hand and allowed him to seat her.

He pushed in her chair and moved to the opposite one. "I excused myself early from the Captain's dinner table, hoping to get here in time to secure a table for two where you could join me."

He seated himself across from her and bridged his ringed fingers above his drink, gazing intently into her eyes. "I'm glad you remembered you'd save me a dance this evening when we spoke on deck today."

"I looked forward to meeting you for a dance. You weren't too difficult to pick out among the less opulently dressed men here." She laughed softly, placing her pleated evening bag on the tablecloth. "I've never danced with a man in tails before. I'll feel like Ginger Rogers."

Wes's lips pressed together in a wry smile. "I'm no Fred Astaire," he said. "But I always did admire his suave manners and his tux and tails wardrobe, even his cape, minus the top hat, of course."

"I'll try not to trip you." She chuckled, admiring his eyes, as dark brown as her own. They practically penetrated her soul. "Do you claim to be as romantic as you appear?"

Wes laughed heartily. "There is no doubt about it. My son Leland says I was born in the wrong century. I do enjoy beautiful things like you, Miss Dierdre Ingram. Though what I collect is in the vintage-art variety, hardly items with your intriguing youthful vitality."

She felt a flush of pleasure at his attentive remarks, restoring her confidence of still being appealing to a man. "Are you always so formal and effusive?"

He took her hand, brought it to his lips, and brushed her fingers with a barely perceptible kiss. "Sometimes." He raised his eyes to hers without dropping her hand. "They're playing a waltz, shall we dance?"

She shivered as if he'd run his lips across her body, knowing she'd like him—a distinguished older, very sensual man—to do that very thing.

He pushed his chair back and came to her, assisting her to her feet with an out-stretched hand, then led her onto the dance floor. Holding her right hand at shoulder level away from them, he whirled her into place at his side. His other hand at her mid-back guided her close but not too close. His liquid movements were easy to follow. To a lilting waltz, they flowed around the floor, maneuvering effortlessly between the other couples in a graceful, switching back and forth side step. Guided backward, Dierdre was delighted she could keep up with him without causing any awkward hesitations. She prayed she wouldn't fluff up since all was going well.

He whispered into the hair above her ear. "You are quite lovely you know, Dierdre Ingram. You've brought back pleasant memories of my youth."

"Coming from you, that's *quite* a compliment," she teased and concentrated on her steps, unaccustomed to such an accomplished dancer, even more polished than Randy. Many guests watched from their tables, poking each other and gesturing in their direction.

I think I know how Ginger felt in Fred's arms, so famously dancing backward in high heels. Older men are so smooth. I could get used to this charming man so easily. Younger men don't have Wes's finesse. Is his approach tonight just a come-on or would he be like this all the time? I intend to find out if I can.

He twirled her expertly away from him, her skirt a cloud of fluttering chiffon around them. Then he pulled her back into his arms. "Thank you for keeping my secret. I appreciate your discretion, Dierdre."

"I'll continue to do so, barring any unusual personal emergency." She laughed softly, flirting with him on the edge of outrageously. It felt like dancing on glass or ice, tempting him to say more, move her more tightly into his embrace. But he didn't, his upper body remained centered like a professional ballroom dancer. Dierdre tried not to be too disappointed. She'd simply have to work a little harder.

The waltz ended and they returned to the table. Wes seated her, signaled to a waiter, and sat down in his own chair. "What would you like to drink?"

"I need to be up early, so I think I'll just have an herbal tea, if you don't mind."

"Very sensible," he said and gave the waiter her order.

Wanting to freshen her lipstick, she reached for her evening bag. Looking around their table, she lifted her napkin, and finally peeked at the floor near her feet and his white shoes.

"Is something the matter?" Wes asked, waving the waiter away.

"My favorite evening bag. I know I left it here on the table." Perplexed, she looked at him in some alarm. "It's gone! I left something very important in it." Her voice shook.

Dierdre wrung her hands, fighting back tears. "How could I be so foolish as to leave it on our table?"

* * *

Having abruptly excused herself from Wes with apologies, Dierdre reported her missing evening bag to the ballroom serving staff and left for the security office. She took the elevator to the lower decks and hurried to Suzanne and Taylor's cabin, hoping they'd still be awake. She knocked softly on their door.

Taylor opened it. Standing damp from a shower in a white terry robe and bare feet, his wet curly hair getting a one-handed rub with a towel. "Hi there sister-in-law of shipboard fame, how goes the high-maintenance life?"

He gestured her inside with a hug and closed the door. "You certainly look and smell gorgeous. It can't be the state of your love life."

"Things aren't going so well I'm afraid." Her pulse pounded from rushing around to report her lost evening bag. Taylor's spontaneous compliments warmed her frantic heart and she began to breathe normally, emotionally detaching by practiced habit into professional mode.

Suzanne paused in her mending of Mitzi's bathing suit and patted the empty chair next to her. "Come tell us all about it, Sis. You seem pretty upset."

Dierdre collapsed gratefully and surveyed the cabin. Gregory and Mitzi, playing a board game on the fold-out Murphy bunk above, waved to her.

"Auntie Dreedra you look like a movie star," Mitzi bubbled. "I want to be just like you when I grow up big and pretty."

Gregory, intent on winning, mumbled, "Hello" but hardly looked up.

Dierdre wiggled a finger at the kids and managed a smile. "Sorry to keep you little darlings up longer, but I need your parents for a sound out."

"We're not little," said Gregory.

"But we are darlings," Mitzi asserted.

The twins and Taylor laughed. He leaned his hips against the sink counter, facing her while he finished toweling his hair. "What's up?"

"My evening bag went missing from our table while I danced with Wes LeChaminant. It . . . well, it has my gift for our birthday surprise in it, Suze. I'm absolutely sick about it. Not so much the $300 dollars I paid for the gift certificate, but the fact that whoever took my bag can use it for the fun I've been planning for *us*. Burns my buns!"

"Tell us about your secret," Mitzi peered over the upper bunk. "I just love secrets."

Gregory's impatient voice interrupted. "I'm almost the winner, Mitzi. Stick to the game. Grown ups don't tell their secrets anyway."

Dierdre looked from Taylor to her sister. Suzanne's fingers holding a needle stopped in mid-air trailing thread. "You mean Arnold's Rolex isn't the only thing missing on this ship?"

Confusion added to Dierdre's frustration. "I'd almost forgotten you told me about that watch and the jerk accusing Cloud of taking it." She fingered an earring, and shook her head in disbelief. "We do get cameras and laptops reported stolen but . . . I think these two thefts are out of the ordinary."

Taylor moved away from the sink and sat on a bunk. "Well, you're theft should put Cloud in a better light. As a teenager, he certainly wasn't in the ballroom. Sounds more like an inside staff job to me."

Suzanne resumed stitching. "Not to downplay your missing evening bag, but Cosma will be relieved her son will look less of a guilty suspect. She's nearly sick with worry we haven't heard the last of Arnold accusing Cloud of taking his missing Rolex, just because he's an Indian."

Taylor scratched his head. "You've reported this, I assume?"

"Yes, of course I have." Dierdre's pursed lips formed a grimace. "I suppose there's nothing more to be done tonight, but it really throws a wrench in my plans for you and me."

Suzanne reached across the table and patted her hand. "Dee, just knowing you had something extra special beyond this cruise planned for our birthday makes me not mind turning thirty quite so much."

Dierdre leaned over and kissed her sister's cheek. "Enough about me and my troubles. How are you and baby-in-waiting doing?"

Suzanne looked at Taylor and back at her. "Some discomfort and . . ." she glanced up at her children, then mouthed, "some spotting yesterday and today. I'm trying to take it real easy."

Taylor rose and put a hand on Suzanne's shoulder. He caught Dierdre's eye. "I'm riding herd on her to rest and let me do all the lifting of her art supply boxes when Cosma and her boys aren't around to help."

"We're a long way from my OBGYN," said Suzanne. "It isn't that I regret coming on this cruise, but . . . but . . . We want to keep this baby."

"We *will* keep our baby," Taylor said firmly. "Absolutely no question about that."

* * *

Moonlight danced across the waves and glittered a slash of silver where the velvet sky kissed the sea. Waves slapped against the moving ship's hull in a lulling rhythm. A swirl of stars pierced the night like scattered diamonds in a jewel box. After the squall the decks had been swabbed clean and the intense rain had freshened the night air. The ocean breeze felt soft.

Dierdre stood, forearms resting on the top rail of the deserted Lido Deck. Lost in thought about her missing evening bag with the birthday gift certificate in it, wedding plans for Cosma and Johnny, and her sister's pregnancy swarmed like bees in her head. Loosened wisps of her hair wafted around her face in the salty breeze; her chiffon evening skirt filmed against her legs, and the noise of the engines far below churned beneath her feet. Dierdre didn't sense someone's presence until a man's voice spoke nearly at her elbow.

"You're not as available on this cruise as last time." His voice was warm and kind.

She jumped. "Randy!"

"Had to track you down, or up as the case actually is, to get a moment alone since you didn't stop at our table tonight."

Greatly relieved it wasn't Daniel or Tyler, air whooshed from her lungs. "You startled me. I didn't hear you or your cane tapping up the stairs."

He laughed softly. "Seems one of us is blind and the other's deaf."

Laughing at his tease, Dierdre relaxed. *Why am I so attracted to this man? He's exciting and comforting at the same time. What on earth prompted him to come find me on the top deck?*

"It's after two in the morning and breezy as all get out. Still you found me. I'm flattered."

He grinned, moonlight glinting on his dark glasses and his even white teeth. "For some reason, I felt like coming up on deck. Unusual for me, couldn't sleep. What's your excuse, pretty lady?"

"No real excuse, just a lot on my mind." She touched his wrist and decided on a Tonto approach to tease some truth out of him. "So if 'you no see um', what makes you think I'm a pretty lady?"

His hand covered her fingers, trapping them against the sleeve of his dinner jacket, a ghostly white apparition in the moonlight. His deep laughter, caught by the sea breeze, drifted beyond them into the night. "Megan tells me you're gorgeous, and I trust my daughter's critical opinion."

Dierdre left her hand beneath his, warm and endearing, filling her with happiness she hadn't experienced in a long time. Confusing too. Hadn't she just decided to pursue a relationship with Dr. Wesley LeChaminant? *Why the electricity with Randy when I'm also attracted to Wes?*

He spoke to the crown of her head. "We missed your charming company. I hoped to dance with you tonight. Of course, I miss talking with you too about the details I need for my novel."

She lifted her chin and looked up at him as if she could fathom the man behind the dark lenses. "I'm sure you searched this ship high and low until you just had to come out in the middle of the night, without your daughter's help, to find me in the dark to talk about your novel." Her tease bordering on sarcasm played out in her tone. She waited for his reaction.

Then it occurred to her, the puzzlement, the missing logic. Pulling away and stepping back, she eyed him.

"Wait a minute. If you can't see, how on earth did you know it was me up here on the very top deck?"

"Perfume, my dear. The scent you wear is distinctive, plus I must admit to asking a steward near the pool door if he'd seen Ms. Ingram, our lovely cruise director."

"You had a navigator even without Megan or being able to read the stars."

"Exactly. Besides, it's always dark for me."

She moved nearer to brush his shoulder with her arm. He embraced her and tugged her close.

"Chilly?" he asked.

"Not any more," she said. *I'm nearly mad with longing to be intimate with this man. What on earth's come over me?*

Randy turned her to him, stroked his fingertips along her face, thumbed her lips ever so gently, and bent his head until she felt his breath upon her eyelids.

Moonlight touched his hair as if a paintbrush tipped each strand with silver.

Dierdre had heard a blind person's touch was exceptionally sensitive, had watched the portrayal of Helen Keller, in *The Miracle Worker* and the way a blind child learned to see with her fingers. *This must be what it feels like to be explored by someone who's trying to visualize you by touch. It's giving me shivers. Delicious ones.*

He leaned closer, lifted her chin with his fingers and whispered, "May I kiss you, Dierdre?"

Her pulse throbbed and her breath fluttered in her throat. "I think I'd like that very much." Her fingers slid up to the back of his neck and laced through his thick hair.

Randy's lips found hers so softly she could barely detect them. While he pulled her into his arms, steadying himself between the railing and his planted feet, his lips nibbled hers hungrily, then more insistently.

Dierdre returned his kiss. He parted her mouth with his tongue and gently flicked it over her teeth. She melted into him until nothing but their clothing separated their urgent bodies. Moaning softly, after a long moment she raised a palm to his chest and pushed to create space between them and catch her breath.

"It must be the starlight or something. We're behaving a little madly, for two people who hardly know each other."

"Then madness with you is intoxicating." His voice was husky with emotion.

She straightened and reached to adjust his glasses straighter on his face. "I'm glad we did that, but . . . but . . ."

"But what?" His lips explored her ear.

Dierdre pulled further away. "I'm feeling very vulnerable, perhaps foolish."

"I know all about how vulnerable feels. I wanted to hold you in my arms and dance with you but you don't have time for me this cruise. Vulnerable for me too. Nothing foolish about that."

"My free time's pretty absorbed with my sister's family and our friends."

"In the ballroom tonight, Megan said you were quite *absorbed* with the Hollywood-looking fellow. She didn't notice any of your family, so it's something else, isn't it?"

The spell was broken. They moved apart. Dierdre's fingers slid down his arms until only their fingertips touched. She wished they could look into each other's eyes.

"I had a previous engagement with Mr. LeChaminant. He's not Hollywood but Vegas. A very nice man and a smart one."

"Good dancer?"

"Great dancer."

"A budding shipboard romance even if he's more than a little old for you?"

"Possibly." Dierdre dropped her hands and leaned her back against the railing.

"Oh, Randy. I find you extremely attractive, interesting, exciting—but . . ."

"But you can't *see* yourself with me, right?"

His wry laugh stabbed her heart, underscoring his brutal pun. Determined to be strong instead of impulsively passionate as usual, which seemed to continually bring on more trouble than she wanted to handle, Dierdre chose honesty instead of leading him on. *I at least have that much respect for Randy.*

"Something like that," she said, as kindly as she could.

A shooting star shot past Randy's hair and disappeared into the waves. Dierdre caught her breath. Something about that unexpected star seemed so poignant, like an explanation mark on her dilemma of feeling drawn to this dear man while she toyed with the idea of a conquest for Wes. Wes fit the picture of the financially secure and glamorous future she imagined for herself.

Turning, she walked away and descended the stairs to the deck below, silly tears streaming down her cheeks.

* * *

Chapter Ten   *Mysteries of Life*

Why on earth I'm crying is beyond me. Dierdre wiped tears away with her fingers, stumbled blindly to her cabin, and collapsed on the bed.

Am I deeply depressed or what?

After crying herself to near exhaustion, she fisted the pillow and sat up. *This is NOT me. I handle situations, others' expectations of me be damned. I never fall apart. Why now?*

I've attracted Dr. Wesley LeChaminant who may be a little old for me, but he fits the profile of my goal for a husband: single, a gracious if flamboyant gentleman, a terrific dancer, financially stable even affluent, no children of school age. I bet he could offer me the lifestyle I'd like to become accustomed to without making minimum payments on my credit cards. Why did I fall to bits over Randy? For heaven's sakes I hardly know the guy.

She got up, undressed and took a steaming shower. While her eyes were shut tight—blind against foaming, stinging shampoo—the image of Randy floated to mind.

He can't see and yet he came alone, without Megan's help, vulnerable to someone taking advantage of him or even a dangerous fall, to find me up on deck and risk expressing feelings for me. We have such chemistry I felt shot through with electricity for him. He's bound to know it. If he could see he'd have read it in my eyes, not just my eager response to his kisses.

She adjusted the taps and let cold water rinse over her head, down her shoulders, and across her breasts until her nipples stood erect. The icy liquid spilled over her hips and thighs, her calves, shocking her into sober clarity. She turned off the water and stood dripping, shaking with cold, willing herself to consider her heart for emotional feelings besides sexual urges and promises she'd made to herself about the sort of man who could meet her criteria for a life partner.

I don't feel surges of passion with Wes. I don't feel any emotional chemistry for the older guy at all. Okay, so he's a way handsome man in his fifties, not a tottering grandfather type. Still, you'd think I'd feel something more than comfortable and flattered at his attentiveness. Some spark for our future intimacy has got to be there or our relationship could never work long term, no matter how spoiled, secure and cared for I'd be. I'd come to resent being tied to him. It wouldn't be fair to him and I'd drown in guilt.

Dierdre toweled dry. Before the mirror she savagely attacked clumps of wet tangles with a brush and a hairdryer, staring down the angry woman who faced her. She spoke to the stranger in a harsh whisper.

"You're crumbling because you're a frapping hypocrite. You, who can't abide hypocrites and often cruelly mock them, are nothing but a two-face. The worst kind of hypocrite."

The idea of personal hypocrisy was such a shock she broke into sobs. Grabbing a towel, she stifled them, eying herself above the terry folds until the heaving stopped and calm returned. The eyes in the mirror softened. Dierdre lowered the towel, defeated.

I haven't cried like this since Gregory was kidnapped. I take pride in being honest with myself and everyone else, brutally so if necessary. I'm detestable. That's why I'm so devastated.

I'm a scared, vulnerable woman about to suck up for security to a man who can see me and has surgical skills to keep me beautiful for decades. All while I'm falling for a handsome, blind writer who gives love without caring or even knowing if I'm beautiful.

"God, I hate myself."

* * *

Head down, her beaded braid falling over one shoulder, Cosma dealt the nine Animal Medicine cards face down in an arc on the table in front of them. She studied Dierdre's face for a moment. Without comment, she changed her mind, gathered up the tarot cards, removed two, and arranged them differently.

"Why are you starting over?" Dierdre sipped coffee, watching, wondering what would happen next while questioning her sanity. Why had she come to find her shaman friend for a reading? Yet, she knew why.

Torn to pieces inside, a life decision before her, she was desperate to get a handle on her life before she made another disastrous mistake about a man. After last summer's blessing ceremony at the Sun Tunnels in Utah, Dierdre had great confidence in Cosma Stargazer's spiritual abilities for direction and healing. Cosma wouldn't blab any personal thing she figured out about Dierdre. Inhaling, she focused on the moment.

Cosma arranged the cards in three short rows at angles: two cards, three, and two. She looked into Dierdre's eyes. "The Medicine cards are intended to improve your connection to the Great Mystery of life. I sensed you don't want to know your nine animal totems as much as you need to make an important decision. That's why I gathered up the first layout of cards."

Dierdre swallowed, nodded, and set her lidded coffee flask aside. "What do I do?"

Cosma smiled and folded her arms. "This spread of seven is known as the Pathway Spread. It's not so much a Native American system of divination as a Druidic one. It gives you information about your pathway in life."

Sighing, Dierdre pursed her lips. "That's apt, lead on."

Tapping the cards one by one, Cosma explained. Card one is your past, then your present, and card three is your future. This fourth card is the pattern of your life lessons. Card five is the challenge you've already conquered, number six is what's working for you and—perhaps most useful is the seventh card—what's working against you."

Dierdre chuckled ruefully. "*I'm* what's working against me. That much I know."

"Perhaps you'd like to know what works for you and how you're undoing your best efforts?"

"Yes, I would. That's why I came."

Cosma gestured with her hand. "Turn the cards over beginning with the past. I'll explain meanings to you as we go."

Dierdre picked up card number one. An elk. She lifted her shoulders in a question.

"Ahh, my friend. Elk wanders through the forest looking for a partner. Elk bellows his mating call throughout the forest, which attracts Mountain Lion and other predators. Elk's stamina allows him to outrun Mountain Lion. By the time Elk returns to the herd, he may or may not find an available, suitable mate."

Laughing, Dierdre remarked, "That's me alright. Let's deal with the present."

She turned over a snake.

Cosma inhaled deeply and sat straighter. "Snake medicine people are rare. Experiencing and living through multiple snakebites allows them to transmute poisons. Mental, physical, emotional, or spiritual."

"Oh," Dierdre said. "The shedding old skin idea, I suppose."

"It's far more than that," Cosma continued thoughtfully. "True, the life-death-rebirth cycle is represented by the shedding of skin, but Snake medicine is also creative power. It symbolizes sexuality, psychic energy, reproduction, and the ascension to immortality. The powerful ability to experience anything willingly without resisting it and survive to experience anew."

Tingles crept up and down Dierdre's spine. "Whew, that's heavy stuff."

Cosma's voice was kind. "Perhaps you are encouraged because Snake medicine is resilient, no matter how harsh the lesson?"

"Yes." Dierdre shifted in her chair. "Let's see if the Future card has some hope I might learn from my lessons." She turned over the Butterfly card.

Cosma relaxed and chuckled. "Butterfly medicine encourages us to observe our positions in the cycle of self-transformation. You are confronted with the ability to know your mind and to change it."

"Yes, but how to know which way to jump is my challenge." Dierdre sipped her coffee, now lukewarm. Disinterested, she set it down again. "So am I an egg, the larva, or a cocoon? I sure as heck know I haven't sprouted wings."

"If you are about to make a decision of importance," Cosma explained, "you are in the larval stage. To proceed to the doing-something-about-your-circumstances phase of decision making, you must become the cocoon."

Dierdre chewed at a knuckle. "So I have to understand where I am in the present to know what to do next, how to transform my situation, right?"

Nodding, Cosma answered, "Exactly. Shall we move to the pattern of your life lessons?" She tapped card number four. "Turtle. Ah, the oldest symbol of Earth, representing goddess energy and the eternal

Mother. You have conquered your adversities under the protection of your shell. You have relied on a shield from hurt, injury, deception, and the indifference of others. However, that shield can blind you to reality."

Dierdre digested the idea, consulting her watch. "I've fifteen minutes 'til I direct a group to the marine-life lecture before their shore tour in Bermuda. We've three cards to go. Should I reschedule with you?"

"No." Cosma shook her head. "Continuity matters. Card five is a challenge you've conquered."

Dierdre flipped it. "Moose?"

"Self-esteem medicine. You have survived on your strong sense of self and your ultimate wisdom." She pointed to card six.

"What works *for* me, is six, right?" Dierdre tilted her head toward the next to last card and turned it over. "Fox." She began to laugh.

"Wiley fox merges into its surroundings taking note of its powerful gift to observe others. Fox is quick of thought and action, sure-footed." Cosma hesitated for a moment then added, "Great Spirit honors Fox for keeping the family safe, even acting as a talisman for those traveling far from home."

Dierdre heard a soft tapping coming in their direction. Looking up, Randy approached with Megan. Her heart nearly lurched from her chest. "I think you said card seven is what *isn't* working for me." She lifted it, looked at the image and showed it to Cosma. "Squirrel."

Randy's cane tapped closer, side-to-side in front of his feet only a few yards away. She held her breath, for the first time grateful he couldn't see her, hoping Megan wouldn't mention noticing them.

Cosma pressed the squirrel into Dierdre's palm.

"I think since you've perfected gathering to prepare for future winters, Squirrel's contrary medicine is the hoarder. The fearful person who expects the worst and is stuck in waiting."

She took the card back and returned it to the deck. "Waiting for something to happen is a trap, Dierdre."

Megan guided Randy to a space even with their table, nodded in their direction and led her father tapping on down the lounge area beyond them. Dierdre's heart settled into a more normal rhythm. She looked steadily into Cosma's fixed gaze. "So what can I do differently? I need to stop screwing up and make wiser decisions. I feel like I'm falling apart."

Her shaman friend grinned, slid the deck back into its box and snapped the lid shut. With a twinkle in her dark eyes she winked. "Squirrel," she whispered. "Try hanging upside down on a branch and look at the world through opposites. If you hoard your thoughts of abundance and security the fear of scarcity takes hold. Honor your connection to Earth Mother from whom all things flow, including love."

Cosma reached across the table with both hands and took Dierdre's in hers.

"Remember, one of Squirrel's family borrowed Eagle energy, connected to Great Spirit, squirrel learned to fly."

She squeezed Dierdre's hands and let go, gathering up the Animal Medicine Cards. "Squirrel is not a fool and neither are you. Listen to your heart."

* * *

Cosma watched the two women approach her Tarot table. The quiet one so ladylike, her brusque companion the zany woman who tried coaxing the man with the missing watch to apologize to Cloud.

Great Spirit I need wisdom for these two-leggeds. I sense something unsettling between them.

"My name is Catherine Hatch," said the gentle soul, scanning the clipboard on the table. "I see you have my name on your schedule. I've tried to be punctual."

"You're right on ti . . ."

"And I'm Hettie. You don't have me down because I'm not into this game. I'm along for my friend's moral support. Besides, the things I could tell you about her when we were young." She laughed like sharp knives slivering the air.

"Hettie, please, for goodness sake that was decades ago," squeaked Catherine. Her blush rose from her prominent forehead to her silky gray-brown hair.

Cosma sensed a control freak and steeled herself to resist the harsh woman's negative energy. Indicating with a gesture the single chair opposite herself, she said firmly, "The healing Animal Medicine Cards are not a game. My readings are private, not a team activity." She tilted her head toward the lounge area across the wide corridor, spilling her beaded braid across her shoulder. "You might want to wait over there."

Hettie huffed indignantly. "Well I never. How rude." She stood her ground. "I don't have to sit. I can just stand here and listen. I promise not to interrupt."

Cosma struggled to allow matters to unfold, while her wristwatch ticked away Catherine's scheduled minutes. "You already have."

Hettie ignored the remark except for the grimmer set to her determined chin.

Catherine sat down, averting her eyes from her companion. "We'll meet for lunch, Hettie. Go shopping or something. I'm scheduled for fifteen minutes; you won't have long to wait."

Cosma dealt out four cards face down, spreading her hands across them in a protective gesture, leaving them covered. She looked intently at Hettie and waited until the woman *tsked tsked*, sighed dramatically, and turned away. The tension dissipated.

Cosma relaxed, and lifted her hands from the spread. "Select a card and turn it over, please."

Catherine's slim fingers hesitated many times over each of the four as if her choice might be life threatening.

Cosma waited patiently. *Something important is going on in this woman's mind.* With Great Spirit's help she concentrated on reading Catherine's energy and her thoughts.

After several minutes, returning to the first card on the left, Catherine turned it over. Her fingers lingered on the animal image. An expression of confusion on her face, she looked at Cosma. "A porcupine? That spikey creature seems more telling of Hettie." Her shoulders slumped and she sat back.

Cosma chuckled. "There's certainly a physical resemblance to your friend."

Fidgeting with the purse in her lap, Catherine sat forward and whispered. "She's not really my friend. I *trust* my friends." Straightening her shoulders, she appeared prepared, even eager to learn. "Tell me about my porcupine."

Pleased with her open attitude, Cosma began. "The porcupine's quills are only used when trust has been broken. Porcupine is a gentle, loving, playful creature like the otter. The card you chose is a nudging reminder to not be caught in the turmoil of fear and greed around you." She studied the woman's face. "Perhaps you are aware of this challenge in your life?"

Catherine nodded. "I'm on a painful fence about a decision I have little time to make on this cruise because of revelations I didn't expect. Is there more?"

Amused but kind, Cosma avoided laughing to not appear to trivialize Catherine's concerns. "There is always more. I sense the lesson porcupine brings is a simple one about trust, two-fold for you. Life dealt you a hard blow, maybe more than one. Fearing to stand strong in your values, you withhold trust for the undeserving. A very wise decision. For the deserving, a person from the painful past I think, you fear trusting to love again?"

The woman's eyes opened wide. Her eyebrows shot up. "What makes you think?" She gasped. "I fear being unable to take care of myself with someone."

Cosma gathered the cards and returned them to the box. She pinned Catherine with her gaze. "You are armed with honest quills to ward off complications with those who would use you for their own purposes. Let your courage rise. Speak your warning and create your boundaries. Someone unexpected will help."

Hettie approached, tapping the face of her wristwatch in irritation. She stopped a few feet away and stood tapping one foot.

Catherine unsnapped her purse and removed a few bills.

"Thank you for your insight and your kindness. You've helped me make an important decision." Her face brightened and her eyes sparkled. Standing, she pushed her chair under the table, suddenly quite pretty and about ten years younger.

Slipping the accepted fee into a zippered bag, Cosma added quietly, "When porcupine trusts, the quills lay back, exposing the vulnerable belly to be patted with love. Perhaps you are ready for such a safe bond with a worthy person."

"I'm a widow unlikely to connect romantically with anyone. The door to my heart is closed."

Cosma smiled. "Someone unexpected may open it for you."

* * *

Chapter Eleven *Puzzling Returns*

Sweaty and flushed, Dierdre tugged a hooded sweatshirt on over her stretch body suit. Her long bare legs extended from its hem to her slip-on Sketchers. She left the workout room less stressed than before coming in and completing two-point-five miles on the treadmill, all she could schedule. In a much better mood, she'd left time to take a shower, change for the day's events, and have Jody deal with her hair. After last-night's theft of her evening bag, she could no longer look forward to squeezing in sharing the scheduled birthday spa experience with Suzanne in the afternoon.

Entering the corridor, Dierdre pulled the hoody over her sweaty hair and headband and adjusted dark sunglasses to obscure her make-up-free face. She hoped to get to her cabin looking like any anonymous early-workout cruise guest.

No time for a sit-down breakfast. On the main dining-room level she stopped at the coffee bar for a hot chai. While the barista worked on her tea brew, she collected napkins and uncapped the cinnamon shaker.

"My dear Dierdre, don't you look devastating this morning."

She whirled. "Wes!" She clapped her napkins to her cheeks. "Heavens, I'm a mess. I hoped I wouldn't run into anyone who knows me."

He stepped closer wearing an engaging grin, a seersucker jacket, and precisely pleated white slacks.

I wonder if he sleeps in permanent-press pajamas. Wes shifted his folded *Wall Street Journal* to the other hand, offering his right.

"You have a fabulous showgirl figure. Nothing to be embarrassed about or hide, though it's an enticing disguise."

She graciously shook his hand then removed her dark glasses. "Seriously?" *He's looking me over with a practiced professional eye, probably imagining what he'd surgically improve first before the follow up.*

"Dierdre, I can easily picture how you'd look in a Vegas showgirl costume."

"Not a topless one I hope." *God forbid he's imagining my naked boobs.*

Wes chuckled. "You'd be stunning in such an outfit. You know the old saying; if you've got it flaunt it. I wouldn't recommend those elaborate forty-pound headdresses showgirls wear, however. Dangerous in high heels."

Wonder how many girls he's done boob and fanny jobs on. If he's imagining me topless, it's kind of creepy, but natural in his business. I've certainly imagined a few men without their clothes. She checked her watch and noted the woman was nearly finished with her order. "You're right, I wouldn't want to parade in platform stilettos down those formidably steep, Tropicana-stage stairs."

The barista handed her a foaming chai.

"Thank you," Dierdre said, stuffing a couple of bills into the tip jar and sprinkling her chai with cinnamon. She selected a plastic lid and a straw.

Wes waited then fell into step with her. "You know, my dear, the way you danced with me flowed like poetry. As the saying goes, I could have danced all night. We must do it again. Could we pick up where we left off when your evening bag was taken?"

He touched her shoulder. His hand lingered.

"Tonight when you finish with the second show? I'll reserve a table, perhaps have some champagne chilling?"

I'm not sure how comfortable I am with his intensified coziness, but it could work in my favor. I thought I'd have to work a lot harder to make him fall for me.

Dierdre sipped foam from her take-out cup so she could snap on the lid without making a dripping mess or wasting chai. She looked over at him, pausing to deal with the straw and the lid so the cup was capped. *He's really going for it this morning. Much more assertively than on the dance floor.*

"I'd like looking forward to that after a busy day, Wes."

"Excellent." He looked into her eyes. "May I?" He grasped her hand with smooth, strong fingers ending in expertly manicured nails. Bending, he languished over her hand, before briefly kissing her fingers.

Surprised and a little embarrassed at his old-world gesture of adoration, Dierdre withdrew her hand and grasped the chai cup with both hands. She wondered why her heart hadn't fluttered with his little intimacy. If anything, endearment by an uncle came to mind, except she didn't have one.

"Don't look so cautious, Dierdre. You're a gorgeous woman. I'm sure men fall at your feet with great regularity." He placed a knuckle gently under her chin and lifted it. Their eyes locked.

"Until tonight then, my beauty?"

Dierdre nodded and swallowed a steaming sip.

"Until tonight." *My beauty? That's sort of ownership talk isn't it?*

She turned and walked quickly to the nearest elevator. Checking her watch again, she barely had time to shower and change. No time for Jody. A ribbon-tied ponytail at the base of her head would have to do.

I've got to get a move on to not be late introducing Cosma at her animal-tarot session. Hope she didn't forget I had to schedule an extra morning one since she's so popular.

Thinking of Wes, Dierdre couldn't decide whether to take him seriously or not.

He knows how to put an industrial-strength move on. A skill he's practiced plenty no doubt. Still, he definitely seems to have a crush on me.

I wonder if we can take it to another level . . . or even if we should.

* * *

Following the first lecture where she'd introduced the expert and assisted with handing out information material, Dierdre introduced Cosma and departed, welcoming an hour to herself. She unlocked her cabin door and stopped mid-step before entering.

On the floor, just inside the doorway, lay a small envelope.

Another invitation from Megan and Randy Keene perhaps? *Looks like the same sort of envelope.*

She stooped and retrieved it, shut the door behind her, and switched on the lamp above her desk. Turning the sealed envelope over she could find no writing.

How odd. If it were from the Keenes it would surely be as elegantly addressed as the invitation they gave me on their previous cruise. She slit the envelope open with a nail file and withdrew the folded stiff card stock. Unfolding it, she gasped in surprise. It wasn't an invitation or even a note.

Dierdre held the $300 gift certificate from her missing evening bag, the one for the twins' birthday celebration at the on-board day spa.

I'm thrilled to have it back, but what on earth am I supposed to think about this?

She pulled out a chair and sank into it, bewildered. For a few minutes she sat stunned, unable to think clearly. Her mind whirled with possibilities. Dierdre opened a desk drawer and sorted through memos and correspondence until she located the Keene's invitation from over a month ago. Under the lamp she scrutinized the envelope and compared it to the new one. The size, paper quality, and ivory color matched perfectly.

Now I'm really puzzled. Having trusted the Keenes, she couldn't imagine what was going on.

If this is from Megan, she would have to be the one who could see to slide it under my door. Where did she find it in the first place? Wait a minute. Staff quarters are off limits to cruise guests. If Megan returned this, she had to bribe a steward . . . unless she has the captain's permission to enter all areas of the ship. If that's true, why and how did she get such access?

Dierdre closed her eyes, fingered the envelope, and considered every angle she could imagine.

Surely Megan couldn't be the one who actually stole it. Could she? But if she did, why? And if she had the bag too, why only give me back the gift card? Where's my evening bag?

Dierdre had no idea what to do next besides tell Suzanne their spa experience was back on schedule. In fact, they were due for their massages and mani-pedis at two o'clock. The date and time were printed clearly on the gift certificate. *Today after all.*

She punched in the numbers for the Armstrong's cabin. Suzanne answered, "Hello?"

"Sis, you're not going to believe this, but our spa gift card for us has been returned. Line up the childcare. We're on for two this afternoon."

"Did lost and found return it to you?"

"No, and I couldn't be more surprised. Tell you all about it later." Dierdre put both envelopes back in the drawer and switched off the desk lamp.

"I'm sure you're happy to have that lovely evening bag back," Suzanne added. "You always told me it was your favorite with the tiny pleats and crystal beads."

"That's the really odd part of this. Still no evening bag. The gift certificate was returned anonymously in an unmarked envelope. I think I know who shoved it under my door. What I don't know is who took my bag in the first place and why the gift certificate has been returned."

* * *

Megan finished her morning latté, picked up her newspaper, and walked toward the exit leading out of the dining room to the main corridor. A tall man in a blue-and-white-striped seersucker jacket, crisp white slacks, and a pale blue shirt open at the throat was just entering.

Ah, Mr. Wesley LeChaminant, if I'm not mistaken. Seeing him gave Megan the flash of an idea. She decided to pursue it.

She approached him and stopped him in his tracks. "Would you be Wesley LeChaminant?"

He smiled and inclined his head. "Indeed I am. And whom do I have the pleasure of meeting this morning?"

"I'm Megan Keene, and I wonder if you could solve a mystery for me, well actually for a friend."

They stepped out of the entryway so other passengers could come and go. At the side of the glass doors they moved to the corridor wall.

"Do you and I know each other?" he asked, polite and obviously curious. "As lovely as you are, I'm sure I'd remember if we'd met."

Megan laughed casually. "I've observed you dining with Arnold who paints at the table next to me in our morning class."

Wesley chuckled. "I'm flattered you chose to approach me instead of my friend Arnold. What mystery can I assist you in solving? It would be my pleasure."

Megan warmed to her scheme. "Could you come to our watercolor class at about 10:30 this morning and take a peek at Arnold's paintings? Then since I'm at the next table, you could simply move to view my paintings and . . . my tablemate's."

He shook his head, furrowing his brow. "This sounds mysterious to be sure, but I don't think I'm understanding what you need or what your friend needs to have solved."

"It's really very simple. If you recognize my acquaintance as an old friend of yours the mystery is solved. If you don't, then there is no mystery."

"Now I'm infinitely curious." His professionally groomed brows arched with his wry smile. "I've nothing else pressing at that hour since Arnold is occupied. I'll drop by on the pretext of looking to purchase some original art for my Vegas penthouse."

"The perfect ruse, Wesley." She shook his hand, amazed at the pistachio-sized, yellow-diamond dinner ring blazing at that hour of the morning. Coyly she asked, "Has Arnold located his Rolex?"

Wesley still held her hand. "No, and he's ranting about it at every turn. I hope he finds it soon so our dinner topics can become more pleasant."

"It would be nice if his watch turns up. It's terribly unfortunate for that Indian boy to be under such nasty suspicion."

"I agree, Megan. I've been tempted to buy him a replacement just to hush him up and get the unfortunate teen off the hook."

"How thoughtful of you." She withdrew her hand and grinned. "Perhaps the boy is already out of suspicion after the theft of the cruise director's evening bag, don't you think?"

"Let's hope so, but I so regret Dierdre's distress. She wouldn't tell me what was so important in her bag." He nodded an end to their conversation. "See you about 10:30."

They parted in opposite directions.

Megan smiled to herself all the way back to her cabin to collect her painting supplies for watercolor class.

Well, my dear Randolph. I'm doing my part to help in your romantic pursuit of our cruise director. If schmoozer LeChaminant actually is the former fiancé of Catherine, his affections may move from Dierdre to his old love. Wouldn't that just be ducky for you?

Megan chewed her bottom lip. *Such a rekindled romance might throw a wrench in Arnold's plan for swindling Wesley LeChaminant too.* Megan had no doubt it was exactly what the pompous little scamming creep had in mind.

Fowling up his plans would be truly satisfying and might even turn his hand in our favor. Arnold's already terribly upset about his missing Rolex. Anything that ups his tension could make him more likely to be careless and make a sting easier to pull off.

They were counting on careless. Tomorrow they'd land in Bermuda, the mid-point of the cruise. There wasn't much time to catch Bloomquist with sufficient evidence to get him arrested when they returned to New York or Vegas, however far he had to be pursued to get her mother's money back.

* * *

It was nearing ten o'clock in the morning when Wes finished explaining to his steward how he wished his black tux with the burgundy cummerbund to be steamed and pressed for the evening. He indicated which shoes were to be polished, and instructed how the finest champagne should be ordered chilled at his reserved table after the second seating. He wanted to impress Dierdre as favorably as possible.

It's good to get away from Vegas like this and totally relax in a different environment. Different people, no surgical worries. Beautiful Dierdre Ingram makes me feel younger and more vital than I've felt in

*years. I'm weary of being lonely. The difference in our
ages doesn't seem to be an obstacle for her.*

His only pressure was Arnold. They'd spent the
previous afternoon going over his stock portfolio.
Arnold had asked to keep it in his cabin to be able to
pore over "the details" in more depth, but Wes didn't
trust him totally yet. He'd discovered a more than
modest gin and tonic bar set up on a side table in
Arnold's cabin.

*Arnold's more than a casual drinker. It's not
wise to put my portfolio in his hands—out of my sight
and control—overnight. The fellow's shrewd. Must be
very smart because he didn't take notes. I watched him
run his finger along under each stock, its quantity, and
current worth. If he has a photographic memory, he can
research whatever he remembers of my investments
without me around. Could be good or bad, depending
upon his integrity.*

Wes's travel alarm buzzed 10:20. *Time to drop
in on the watercolor class and the lovely Megan.*

He planned to wander around viewing the
painters' work, eventually stopping by Arnold and
Megan's tables. He was supposed to notice a person
also painting who was of some mysterious
consequence. *Best get on with it. I gave the lovely lady
my word.*

In another ten minutes he peeked in the door of
the painting class, saw Dierdre's sister Suzanne
strolling around the room, stopping to discuss points
with various painters. He couldn't catch her eye to ask
permission appropriately, so he slipped in and moved in

Arnold's direction. Megan looked up from her watercolor board and winked, dipping her head toward the woman next to her. She'd told him he was supposed to notice her tablemate.

Ah, a woman. No doubt one of my former patients.

The slim lady's head was bent so he couldn't see her face. Brown hair artfully streaked with gray fell about her shoulders, loosely tied back with a pastel-green ribbon. It matched her cardigan and slacks. Wes shrugged his shoulders at Megan.

"Hello, Wesley," Megan said. "How nice to see you have an interest in painting."

Catherine's head shot up. She looked at Wes. Her brush dripped red onto the blue sky of her watercolor paper but she didn't seem to notice. Her eyes widened, her breath caught.

"Wesley . . . oh, Wesley." Her voice was a wistful whisper like a star-struck teenager begging for an autograph. She stood frozen staring at him, her brush still dripping.

"Catherine. Oh my God. It's really you isn't it? After all these years. Beautiful as ever." Wes's head reeled. He put a hand to his heart and opened his arms to her.

My sweet fiancée right here in front of me. All the years of longing . . . aching to know where and how you were, to hold you in my arms, kiss your soft lips as I once did.

She dropped her brush onto her painting, moved in slow motion around the table and into his embrace, clinging to him as if in peril and only he could save her very life.

"Catherine, oh my darling girl. I'm simply overwhelmed." He held her at arm's length, looked into her face where tears glistened on her lashes. *She's speechless and as happy to see me, as I am to see her. Amazing.*

"You two know each other, I take it." Arnold interrupted in a sarcastic tone. He plopped his brush into his water jar. "Does this reunion call for a celebration?"

Wes had eyes and ears only for Catherine. "Oh my dear one, are you . . . alone or is your husband aboard also?"

She still held him close, her face pressed tight against his pounding heart.

It doesn't matter to me that my wrinkling shirt is moist with her happy tears.

"I'm widowed, Wesley. My husband died two years ago."

He's dead. I'm divorced. Coming together unencumbered. Was it meant to be?

"My dear dear Catherine, I know I should express my regrets but I'm so grateful to find you after all these years—my first love—I must not lose you again."

It must be fate. Do I even believe in meant-to-be romances?

* * *

Suzanne had half an hour to rest after class before Dierdre delivered Mitzi. She was so looking forward to their spa pampering. She'd been stretched out on the bed with her swollen ankles raised higher than her hips on an extra pillow. Cosma sat beside her while they sipped iced lemon water.

"Cosma, are you half as tired as I am?" Suzanne sat up enough to drink more without spilling. "Thanks for taking such good care of me. Hauling all my stuff and just being there for support, even though you have your own sessions."

"Still having problems?" Cosma moved to the end of the bed and massaged Suzanne's feet.

"Yes, still spotting once in a while, but not constantly. I'll go straight to my doctor when I get home. This cruise may not have been timed very well for the baby. Taylor watches over me like a hawk."

Cosma laughed. "Appropriate metaphor for your falconer. Have you thought of baby names so we don't have to keep saying baby this and baby that?" She rubbed the puffy ankles gently.

"I didn't want to know the sex yet. The specimen test was thrilling enough to be sure I'm pregnant." She drained the water glass and lay back. "I'm having the first ultra-sound when I'm back home."

Continuing to rub the soles of Suzanne's feet, Cosma got a faraway look in her eyes. "I named my first born Cloud because for me he embodies the mystery of the ancient ones, full of portend like a cloud burdened with longed-for rain. His father had gotten in trouble by then and was gone from us."

She sighed, then chuckled. "Cloud can flash with emotional thunder and lightening or float above us all. Yet he's never oblivious to the struggles of others."

"How lovely. I've always wondered why you chose his name." Suzanne flexed her ankles. "That's feeling heavenly on my tired feet too. Thanks for the spoiling. What about Stellar, the star name?"

Cosma went to the table and began folding and stacking pool towels. "Stellar is my star child surrounding us with an orbit of care. He's love personified, our family glue. His father stayed around longer, but he wasn't dependable either, a hippy drifter."

"Symbolic names are great for Native Americans but I imagine Taylor and I will choose a more traditional name, perhaps Tabitha for a girl or Josh for a boy. Something biblical."

Cosma finished the towels and settled in a chair with her feet on the bed. "Isn't Joshua the one in the song who blew a trumpet and brought down the walls of Jericho?"

Suzanne nodded.

"Sounds like a symbolic name to me, the way you take down walls of prejudice. I bet some of your church folks wonder how our families can be close friends when we're so different."

Suzanne smiled. "We're not so different at all."

"I agree," said Cosma, nudging Suzanne's toes with her own and chuckling.

The door opened. Dierdre walked in holding Mitzi's hand. "How are Sundancer's two most popular teachers?" She squeezed Suzanne's raised hand and sat down in the other chair. "Well, sister mine, time for our spa session."

Turning to Cosma she added, "Thanks for agreeing to keep an eye on our princess for a couple of hours. Mitzi has been a darling, according to the kids' activity leader."

"I was really really good," said Mitzi. "We played games, and I made lots of new friends."

Suzanne sat up and slid her feet into sandals. "Great, Honey. I bet everyone wants to be your friend."

Dierdre turned to Cosma. "How are your boys getting along keeping Gregory happy?"

"The three of them have gone to the computer center to watch Cloud reconfirm all the Bermuda wedding arrangements on the Internet. You know how I'm superstitious about my energy going out over cyberspace without prayers to Great Spirit. It spooks me so much Cloud said he'd take care of it. He and Stellar love exploring Web sites and playing computer games. Not me."

She closed her eyes for a moment, then they flew open. "I can't believe I'll be Mrs. Johnny Carlisle in two more days." Her face was radiant. "Married for the first time and Great Spirit has blessed me with a dependable, loving man."

"And I'll be a flower girl in a pretty fancy dress and new pretty shoes." Mitzi beamed, twirling in front of the mirror, posing this way and that. She curtsied while the three women clapped.

"I'm so excited to be part of your wedding," Dierdre said. "I've helped arrange many ship and beach weddings, but I've never been a member of the wedding party before."

Suzanne combed her fingers through her hair. "Taylor's honored to be Johnny's best man. He bought a new shirt, jacket, and slacks for the occasion and promised to leave his Stetson on board."

Dierdre kissed Mitzi's cheek. "You and Cosma have fun practicing smiles in the mirror for the wedding photographer. It's going to be an amazing wedding. The album we put together afterward will be awesome."

At the door, Suzanne looked back at her little one and her best friend.

I hope everything goes well with this baby and me, so I don't cause any disruption in the ceremony plans. I didn't expect to be so tired all the time.

* * *

Cloud led the way into the computer room, already busy with grownups. The blind man sat across from the three available computers. He'd brought his own laptop and typed quickly with an expressionless face beneath dark glasses. The woman with the funky hair, who painted at the mean guy's table in Suzanne's class, read a magazine in a corner chair. He didn't recognize anyone else among the half dozen people talking quietly or reading. Cloud motioned for Stellar and Gregory to follow him to a monitor.

He sat down, brought the Net up on the screen, and mouse clicked to Google search. Stellar took the computer to his left, while Gregory stood between them saying something about trying to learn how to get around on the Net. The computer station on his right was empty.

Cloud had assured his mom he'd reconfirm the wedding arrangements on a Bermuda beach set for day after tomorrow. He figured she wasn't just superstitious about computers but afraid of them, though he'd never say so to her. Dierdre assured them completing final confirmations on line wasn't as expensive as ship-to-shore phone calls at International rates. He really liked Dierdre, not only because she was beautiful and sexy, but because she was kind and funny. More than a few times on the ship he'd dreamed about kissing her . . . and more, waking up sweaty and feeling embarrassed. It was getting uncomfortable for him to be around her. He couldn't seem to talk without getting nervous and bungling up his words.

Dierdre had wanted the captain to marry his mom and Johnny on board the Sundancer, but his mother insisted she wanted her feet on sacred Mother Earth when she made her marriage promise. Their travel agent back in Utah gave them their choice of three resorts and a couple of officiate names weeks ago. Once decisions were made, the agent arranged everything. All he had to do was reconfirm they were on board and soon to land.

Checking notes on the paper his mom had given him, Cloud went to the matching resort Web site and clicked on the homepage. It popped up with pictures of a pink beach and smiling people having dinner in a tropical garden. The hotel building's walls were painted pink like the sand. He clicked on the wedding-ceremony link next, where brides and grooms stood saying their vows before pastors in the resort chapel and on the beach.

Gregory leaned on the back of Cloud's chair and looked over his shoulder. "Can we play games on these computers?"

Cloud scrolled down through catering services to scheduled wedding ceremonies, looking for Carlisle Ceremony.

"If nobody else wants to use the one Stellar's on, maybe so. I can't help you look for games right now, sorry."

"Okay," Gregory said, and left to share a seat and computer with Stellar.

Someone entered behind them, casting a shadow on Cloud's screen. The shadow didn't move. Cloud turned and looked up. His stomach tightened. *The mean guy who hates Indians and thinks I stole his fancy watch. Why doesn't he move away?*

Cloud dropped his gaze back to the screen. Fighting for control, he drummed his fingers on the mouse pad so he wouldn't accidently hit the command button and lose the wedding site he'd brought up. He was glad he wore his hair long so the jerk couldn't see the hair on the back of his neck bristling like a coyote. *You don't scare me, mister, but I sure as heck don't like you. There's something bad in your heart.*

His accuser sat down at the empty computer chair on his right. Out the corner of his eye Cloud could tell the man's face looked like he'd been sucking lemons.

"Move out, you kids. These computers aren't toys." He spit the words out, glaring at them. "You boys should go play in the game room."

Cloud sucked in air and held it, then let the shaky breath out slowly through his teeth. "I'm not playing a game. I'm doing some research for my mom."

"Like hell you are," said the man in a bitter voice. "You're probably looking up Craig's List or some other place to sell my Rolex."

A feeling of rage filled Cloud's body and grew until his skin felt like it would split open across his chest. He bit down on his tongue to keep from saying some defensive remark his mother would disapprove of. Being Indian, anything he said could get him in big trouble with this rich and probably powerful white man.

Stellar and Gregory backed away from their computer. Stellar walked by the blind man and his laptop, glancing at his keyboard. He and Gregory flopped on the couch in front of Cloud. He liked knowing they were there for him like back up, even though the boys were a lot younger. Cloud wanted to act smart while his brothers watched to see how he'd handle the attack. *Grandfather Blue Thorn would tell me to hold my peace for a better time. There will always be a better time or there will be no time for words, he'd said more than once.*

Gregory squirmed on his cushion. "Lumpy thing sure isn't comfortable," he mumbled, scooching over a little to rest against the couch arm.

The wild-haired woman slapped her magazine on the nearest table. "I couldn't get comfortable on that couch either," she said. "A plush ship like this you'd think they'd have cozy sofas." She smiled at Stellar and Gregory, fluttering her silly looking green-tipped eyelashes.

Strange she's talking to my brothers. He focused on finding the Carlisle wedding scheduled for afternoon day after tomorrow. When he did, he hit the reconfirm box and carefully typed in the required letters matching the wedding contract confirmation code on his mom's notepaper.

Cloud logged out of the wedding site and got out of his chair. He nodded to Stellar. "I'm finished," he said. "Let's go."

Gregory's head bent while he ran his hand back and forth under the couch cushion.

"Arni, darling," the woman squealed, rising from her chair and walking over, making her way between other people in the room "I didn't see you come in. What a nice surprise." She came up behind him and placed her chubby hands on his shoulders.

"I'm busy, Hettie. Stocks you know. Don't bother me right now." The man she'd called Arni looked at his computer's screen, hunching his shoulders like a barrier.

He looks like he's trying to hide whatever site he's got up on the screen.

Gregory brought his hand out from under the cushion. He held up a gold watch.

Cloud looked from Gregory to the man at the computer.

Could it be the man's missing watch? Sure hope so. I want this bad man off my back.

* * *

Randy had been acutely aware of the goings on with his quarry Arnold Bloomquist, wishing he could see what Web site was up on the man's computer screen. He was acting secretive. When he logged out, Randy planned to pull up recent sites and get a bead on what the swindler had been up to. Monitoring phone calls with a planted audio device in Arnold's cabin, Randy overheard calls to a bank in Bermuda, which proved more than interesting. Arnold had scheduled a meeting for tomorrow afternoon with the international finance official who handled off-shore accounts. *Wait 'til I tell Meg we're finally onto something specific.*

The woman with the black-and-white spiked hair, who'd sat on the couch when she first came in, had moved to a chair some time ago. Positioned in the corner, it gave her an unobstructed view of the whole room and he thought she pretended to read a magazine. Like a vulture her head bent as if to focus on the magazine open in her lap. Her heavily made-up eyes never stopped sweeping everyone around her. *I wonder if she has a particular interest in someone here.*

Occasionally she smiled to herself. Randy didn't think it had much to do with the magazine.

When Arnold appeared she'd watched for a while, then after a few remarks to the boys on the couch, Randy recognized as the ones in Dierdre's sister's party, she pounced on Arnold. *Why connect with the kids? An excuse to move over to the scoundrel I'm after?* He continued to watch, grateful for his dark glasses allowing him to study everyone without being recognized for a too-nosy sighted person.

"Arni, Arni dear," she shook his shoulder.

"Don't dear me, Hettie. I told you I'm busy." Arnold didn't look up but scowled through his glasses and brushed her hand from his sleeve.

Smiling and undeterred, she whispered right at his ear, "Oh, I think you'll be *very* interested in why I'm bugging you." Her voice was as silky as a cartoon cat. "Somebody just found a watch. Could it be yours?"

"What?" Arnold's head came up abruptly. He pushed his tortoise-shell reading glasses up on his forehead and stared her down. "What'd you say about a watch?"

Ah, she's set the stage for this moment. Randy scrutinized her every move. *I don't get what she's up to. Wish Meg was here to give me her take on it.*

Hettie pointed to the boys on the couch. They were examining a watch Randy had seen the youngest one dig out from under a couch cushion. The teenage Indian boy stood aside, his black eyes riveted on Arnold, his arm protectively across the chest of the kid with the watch. Dierdre's nephew, if he wasn't mistaken. *This may get ugly. Arnold's a hot head. I hope the teen keeps his cool.* Randy glanced around at the others in the room.

Arnold bolted from his chair and confronted the boys, his hand poised to snatch the watch. "So now I suppose you're going to claim you've never seen my watch before! Am I right, you sneaky Indian brat?"

"You're right, sir, none of us have ever seen this watch before." The long-haired teen was controlled, his voice calm but firm. "How do we know this is *your* watch and not someone else's?"

Randy could tell the teen was barely able to suppress a smile, while making Arnold's stress level scream off the charts. *That is one smart kid.*

"I'll tell you how, you mouthy little savage. My name's inscribed on the back."

"What does it say, Gregory?" the tee-shirted teenager asked evenly, his piercing black gaze never leaving Arnold, his strong brown arm a bar between the belligerent man and the nervous young boy.

Others in the room stopped their conversations to eavesdrop or drew nearer for the show. One woman, obviously shocked, held a hand to her mouth.

Gregory's face flushed. He touched one hand to a little leather pouch at his neck, then turned the watch over and in a shaky voice read the name out loud. "Arnold J. Bloom . . . something."

"Mine!" Arnold grabbed it. "I'm going to report you sneaking brats for stealing my Rolex and wasting my time worrying about what happened to it for a couple of days."

Hettie stepped up to Arnold and put her arm through his. "Don't you think you could show a little more gratitude to someone who found your precious Rolex? I'm sure these nice boys are perfectly innocent." Her voice was soft, coaxing. She was actually fluttering her bizarre eyelashes. *She is one weird chick.*

Arnold looked at her with disgust before turning back to the three boys. "I'll see you pay for this prank and pay plenty. Where are your parents?"

Randy picked up his cane and stood debating whether or not to get involved.

I saw the youngest boy find the damn watch but I don't dare say so or I give away the fact I'm not blind. I can't let Arnold know the truth before he shows his hand. Son of a B. How can I keep these innocent kids out of the trouble Arnold's about to make with security when I think the witchy broad set them up? What's in it for her? He stood puzzling for a moment, then had a truly disturbing thought. *Is she a front for Arnold? Are they putting on a show for everyone's benefit?*

He pressed his pager for Megan. She answered almost immediately.

"Meet me at the coffee bar as soon as you can. We may have complications."

* * *

Chapter Twelve *Betrayals and Forgiveness*

Dierdre stashed her tote in her cabin, freshened her lipstick, and took an elevator to the ballroom level. *I wonder if Wes will be disappointed if my energy's only up to a few dances this evening. I'm bushed after this long, busy day. A glass or two of champagne is liable to put me under. Have to be careful not to get stupid.*

She entered the ballroom and scanned the tables. Her eyes searched for Randy as well as Wes. *What's the matter with me? Why on earth do I find that handsome blind man so damned attractive? Well, more than attractive. He's on my mind way too much.*

Spying them both on opposite sides of the room, it was easy to head for Wes's table without walking anywhere close to Randy's and Megan's.

As she made her way toward Wes's reserved table, her heart froze. The table was set for *three*. Another woman with her back to Dierdre was already seated. Wes held her hands across the linen, appearing totally absorbed in conversation.

Dierdre gasped. She stopped and steadied herself with a hand on a pillar, moving behind it to regain her composure.

What the bloody hell is going on? Our just-for-two evening plans are dashed. Another f-ing jerk has played me for a fool. Thank heaven I'm stopping just short of falling for it this time.

She whirled and retraced her steps, shaking with fury, too tired to care her face streamed with tears.

* * *

It was all Randy could do to not run after Dierdre whose crying escape from behind the ballroom pillar tore at his heart. He gritted his teeth and whispered across the table to Megan.

"We've got to nail Arnold quickly. This is the second time today I've had to rein myself in from giving away my sighted capabilities."

"You've got it bad for Dierdre, don't you?" Her voice kind, Megan rested her hand on his.

"That flamboyant twit has been playing up to Dierdre and had the nerve to invite another woman to their table. It wasn't a very pretty surprise for Dier . . ." He shook his head vehemently, unable to finish. "How could he embarrass and hurt her like that?"

Megan refilled his water glass from the pitcher. "It ought to make things easier for you to be the heroic knight on a white horse when the truth comes out."

"What I fear is she'll be turned off by men period, thinking we all betray her."

Randy wrung the cloth napkin between his fists.

"I'll probably look like the worst of the deceiving jerks for faking blindness, and I'm not even a passable writer, let alone a serious novelist."

* * *

Cloud told Stellar and Gregory they'd go for ice cream and video games after he let his mother know the reservations in Bermuda were all set. He knocked on their cabin door, since Gregory was along. His mom might be showering or trying on her wedding dress.

Cosma opened it, and brought him in with a hug, ushering the others in behind him.

"Hello boys. Cloud, were you able to confirm the wedding reservations?" She released him, her voice hopeful, her face smiling and excited.

"Yeah, Mom, it was easy." He handed her the notepaper with the reconfirmation code. "Everything just the way you and Johnny planned it."

She hummed to herself and tucked the paper under an empty glass on the table. Turning to him she said, "Thank you so much for taking care of something so important, Cloud."

Her eyebrows lifted. "You look upset about something. In fact, all three of you don't look very happy. What's up?"

Sighing, Cloud plopped into a chair. Stellar sat on the bed.

"Okay if I use your bathroom?" Gregory asked.

"Of course."

His mother looked at each of them in turn, then paused in front of Cloud and waited.

He folded his arms across his chest. "Gregory found the Rolex. It's back with the guy who accused me of taking it. He thinks I did it for a prank and put it where it could be easily found. Says he's going to talk to my parents and 'make me pay plenty for all the worry I put him through.'"

"Oh my dear one, I'm so sorry you were confronted and embarrassed again." She leaned against the bureau. "Don't worry, if he has his watch back there's nothing he can do but be a pain in the . . . you know." She chuckled. "Did anyone see this all take place? Anyone who can defend your innocence?"

"Yes and no." Cloud kicked off his sneakers and reached for his flipflops.

"I don't understand," said his mother.

Stellar reclined on the pillows and threaded his fingers behind his head. "There were some people around who didn't pay much attention until he got loud. The wacky black-and-white-haired woman from Suzanne's painting class was there. She tried to calm the dude down, but he wasn't having any part of it."

"Anybody else?"

Cloud laughed wryly. "The blind guy was there, but he couldn't see what happened, only hear it."

"I don't know about that," Stellar said. "By the look of his laptop keyboard, the guy's not blind."

Cloud sat forward and looked at his brother. "What makes you think that?"

"Well, bro, if he types on a Braille keypad, wouldn't all the letters have those little bumps that are usually just on the F and J keys? His keyboard is just like ours. I'm telling you, the guy's no more blind than we are."

* * *

About time for bed, Wes opened his portfolio of stocks and mutual-fund investments to review the pages he'd printed out in his office and brought on board. Before handing any of his investments over to Arnold, he'd decide which ones to risk and which ones to withhold. *Giving Arnold my entire financial picture to manage at this time is out of the question. His list of clients is impressive but he's a wily little fellow who makes my potential earnings sound too good to be true.*

Turning over page after page, he couldn't find the one he was looking for to put in a separate folder— the investments he planned to keep to himself. The printout for Breast Implant Techno-Research Ltd., his highest-yield investment was missing.

Wes sat dumbfounded, going back over the last time he'd had his hands on it. He remembered shifting that particular page to the back of the folder for safekeeping before he met with Arnold in his cabin two days before. *Could have sworn the folder has never been out of my hands. Did I lay it aside, turn my back?*

Then he remembered using Arnold's bathroom to wash his hands after lunch, before opening the folder with Arnold present for the first time.

Could he have taken it in those few minutes?

But why bother to steal it if I'd given him the impression he was going to manage all my finances? Didn't he trust me either? Good god, if he did take it, what's he done with my investment in two days?

* * *

Fighting back tears, Dierdre fled the ballroom. Forcing a smile she'd nodded to chatting guests and hurried along the broad corridor to the nearest elevator, trying to give the impression she was late to some sort of meeting. Unable to bear the thought of unburdening her pain and humiliation within the close quarters of her cabin, she chose instead to clear her head and calm her fury with a blast of cool night air.

The steady churning of Sundancer's wake matched Dierdre's pounding heart. She squeezed the railing since Wes's throat wasn't available. Inhaling salty air, she performed the stress-lowering breathing exercises generally effective on her condo balcony.

I'm livid, betrayed again. The way Wes looked at that woman, the adoration in his expression, damn him! How could he get that gaga over a woman he's just met? What am I, chopped liver? He didn't even give me the courtesy of a message to say he'd invited someone else for champagne, the jerk. Having the table set for three, what insensitive brass! His flamboyant ego's as big as this ship.

Maybe older men look at their romantic encounters differently, or maybe that's why he's single. She pummeled the railing with a fist.

She continued inhaling and exhaling ever more slowly until calm centered her. *Is my anger solely at Wes?* She swallowed hard, willing herself to consider all options. *I think I'm more upset with myself. Why?*

Dierdre puzzled, questioning her deepest feelings, putting herself through a self-examination ritual she'd been attempting to perfect lately.

Near her on deck, occasional embracing couples drifted close and moved on. An elderly pair held hands and walked along the deck grasping the railing to steady one another with the rocking of the ship.

They're an example of what I want, aren't they? To be a couple, to be with someone I can count on to be kind and loving, trustworthy and adoring into my golden years. Why should such an enduring relationship be so hard for me to find? I'm sick to death of these short-term flings never materializing into significant relationships I can count on.

The sea breeze loosened tufts of her hair, sweeping them along her cheeks. She released her death grip on the railing and caught a few strands with her fingers, tucking them behind her ear, all the while biting her lower lip.

I chose Wes because I thought an older man could be depended on. I'm annoyed with myself for rejecting Randy's attention when he sends my senses reeling and comforts me at the same time. Why did I let my misgivings about being with a blind man turn him away? I can be such a short-sighted dimwit.

She set her jaw with gritted teeth. *Now I've lost them both.*

"Dierdre, what brings you out here?"

Turning from the rail, with supreme effort she softened her expression. "Cosma, Johnny, how nice to see you two lovebirds strolling on a romantic evening."

"Thought you said this afternoon you were sharing bubbly with Wes tonight." Cosma pulled her wrap more securely around her shoulders.

"He appears to be enthralled with someone else at his table. I left without joining him . . . them." Her voice was light, but brittle.

"I'm sorry," Cosma said. "Would you like company, or do you want us to leave you alone?'

Dierdre started to decline, then swallowed her pride. "I'd love the company of friends. Could we take those loungers over there for a little while?" She gestured to an unoccupied row of deck chairs.

"Looks good to me," said Johnny. "Keeping my balance on this rolling deck is wearing me out." He tapped his cane and arm in arm with Cosma, followed Dierdre and took a seat between them.

Dierdre led off. "I'm kicking myself in the behind for rebuffing Randy's advances in favor of Wes. I'm powerfully attracted to Randy, a very big crush." She laughed nervously. "But, he doesn't fit my profile of the man I'm looking for."

Cosma slipped off her shoes and put her feet on the lounger. "Which is?"

"I want a kind someone who has style and charm, is dependable and financially secure so I can eventually give up this job. He'll have no children of school age and be trustworthy with loyal values and think I'm great just as I am. It would be ideal if he's a smart guy with a sense of humor and is curious for adventure. A good dancer if possible would be nice too.

That's about it." Dierdre sat back and looked from one to the other of her friends.

"So how does this Randy not fit your profile?" Johnny's eyebrows knit in confusion.

"He fits most of my want list, but he's blind."

Johnny's wry smile flashed crooked across his scarred face. "Sounds like a guy with disabilities isn't good enough for you. My bride-to-be has humbled me with her acceptance of a man on a cane."

Dierdre's stomach lurched. "Ouch. I didn't mean . . ." *Damn.*

"Yes, you did." Johnny said. "The truth can be a sharp knife. But it's good to know what you're willing to handle."

"The guilt of turning a good man away can be painful too," Dierdre whispered, wringing her hands. "I've been a fool."

Cosma took her hands. "Dierdre, remember what I said about a flying squirrel at your tarot reading?"

Dierdre nodded.

"You say you want a man who's smart and adventurous. Maybe he wants a woman who's smart and a risk-taker too. Why don't you tell Randy how you feel and ask his forgiveness?" Cosma let go of her hands, patting them kindly.

Hope flickered, but Dierdre despaired of expressing the ugly truth. "He'll think I'm only coming to him on the rebound from being dumped."

Cosma laughed. "Maybe he'll be happy about that and think you finally grew up."

"Do you think so? I'd leave him a note, but he wouldn't be able to read it. I'm not keen on the idea of his daughter being the go-between on something so private because she'd have to read it to him."

"Better be sure you wouldn't resent spending your life with a man on a cane," Johnny said kindly. "My former wife couldn't live with my impairments. It felt like hell between us even before she dumped me and took my boys to be with a new fellow with a pair of good legs."

He struggled to his feet, steading himself with a hand on Cosma's shoulder. "Put your fancy shoes on, my love. Let's leave her to handle her dilemma."

Cosma kissed Dierdre's cheek and slid her feet back into her sandals. "You're smart. You'll think of something." She rose and took Johnny's arm. "Goodnight, Dierdre. Try asking for guidance." She pointed skyward.

Dierdre leaned her head back on the lounger. "Goodnight. Thanks you two."

She felt the rumbling of the ships powerful engines below like a hidden need of her own, some formidable force driving her to find a lasting love. Staring out at the roiling white wake trailing into the dark sea behind Sundancer, she sighed at the enormity of her challenges—as endless as the ocean and the twinkling blackness above. She lifted her eyes to the constellations, so clear tonight. She envied their clarity.

I didn't even think to ask them about their wedding plans. I'm such a frapping idiot, too self-absorbed for my own good. Johnny sure gave me something to think about. Could I handle being with a man who can't see, who could care if I'm beautiful or aging? Wouldn't that be a plus so I could stop obsessing about my looks? Would love in the arms of a good, honest man be enough for me to alter and inconvenience myself to become the support person to an impaired man the way Cosma has, and loving it?

A shooting star, then another and another, streaked across the night sky and disappeared where sparkling sea and inky ceiling knelt on the distant horizon. She thought of the hurtling meteor she'd watched the night Randy kissed her with such tender passion. The sensation of his mouth on hers was so real she could practically taste his kisses. Her mouth watered at the thought. *There's nothing impaired about how he can kiss.* The exquisite memory stabbed her heart with fresh anguish at her loss.

He, a blind man for heaven's sake, went to a lot of trouble to find me on the upper deck that night. My struggle to meet him more than half way now seems only fair. I can down a big slice of humble pie if there's a chance he'd reconsider our getting to really know each other.

But what if he's still hurt and tells me it's too late? He might not be able to trust my fickle behavior. Then won't I be devastated by another rejection?

We land in Bermuda tomorrow. I must think of what to do while there's time. I want him to stay in touch and give us a chance to have a future—on land.

* * *

Just finishing his second cup of morning coffee, behind his dark glasses Randy caught sight of Dierdre coming down the carpeted incline in his direction. He scrutinized her face. *Her eyes are puffy. She's been crying or didn't sleep well after getting replaced with another woman by the Liberace ass last night.*

She came closer and he ached to call her name, say something nice to brighten her day, but she thought he was blind. He had to keep it that way. She was almost even with his table. Her gaze regarded him with a pained and anxious expression. He had the silly urge to trip her, make her fall at his feet so he could help her up and take her in his arms. Her perfume nearly made him dizzy. He had to act as if he didn't know she was within reach.

She slowed, looking at him intensely, then walked on by. Randy's heart sank because he didn't dare follow her. *I want this thing with Arnold over so I can be myself. If only I could hold Dierdre in my arms and tell her she's wonderful before this cruise is over.*

"Randy?" Her voice.

"Dierdre? Is that you?"

"Yes, it's me." She'd returned and took the vacant chair.

His pulse sped. He smiled and set down his cup, opening a hand to her, hoping she'd take it.

She laid her hand in his open palm. "Randy, I'm so sorry I treated you badly the other night. I wouldn't hurt your feelings for the world. I hope you can forgive my rudeness. You didn't deserve it. You're a . . . a kind and charming man."

"Of course you're forgiven. I came on too strong. I've regretted . . ."

"You didn't come on too strong." She sat forward so all he could do was inhale her intoxicating scent. "You may have noticed at the time my response was pretty enthusiastic. I've been afraid you wouldn't speak to me after the way I ran off in tears."

His fingers closed over her hand and he massaged it gently. "I wish we had more time to get to know each other, give ourselves a chance to . . ."

"Find out if we could fall in love?" she finished.

Her eyes were all soft like her voice. His heart filled his chest so he could barely breathe.

"Well, why not?"

She didn't pull her hand from his, but she did reach up with the other one and stroke his cheek slowly, sensuously.

"Dierdre," he whispered, too choked with emotion to say anything more.

* * *

Slowly, Dierdre withdrew her trembling hand from Randy's firm palm. Her eyes searched his handsome face for any nuance of emotion she could read below the lenses of his dark glasses. He had spoken kindly to her, even reacted to her presence with what appeared to be genuine pleasure. At her apology he seemed moved. His chin quivered for the briefest moment. *Is it possible he cares about me as profoundly as I care about him?*

"I truly wish I could stay and talk. We land in Bermuda this morning. I must assist guests with sight-seeing information. I hope you understand."

He nodded, taking in a breath so deeply his broad chest expanded. Exhaling slowly, he said, "Your perfume is sensational."

She laughed. "I don't know what I expected you to say, but that wasn't it. Thank you. Glad you like it."

His manner shifted to his usual easy confidence as though he were relieved in some way she didn't understand. "Megan and I are going ashore for a few hours. We have some business around noon to two-ish, but after lunch? Would you . . . could you join me in town if I send her off shopping? Then you and I could start getting to know each other better." He cleared his throat and sat up straighter, folding his napkin across his half-eaten breakfast.

Dierdre stood and rested a hand on his shoulder, wishing she could twine her fingers through his wavy hair. She didn't know if she imagined it or not, but the air between them felt electrically charged. Her hand tingled and she left it there.

"I'm going with my sister to Victoria Park so she can plan how to set up her outdoor painting class tomorrow." She squeezed his shoulder and reluctantly let go. "After that I'm free. Meeting you would be terrific."

Randy's smile lit up her heart.

"Tell me where and when." His voice grew husky. "Make it easy for Megan and me to find you—before I send her off."

"I'll wait near the big iron lantern gates of Victoria Park. There's a bench there."

Chuckling, Randy brushed the air with his hand. "Off you go until I have you all to myself."

She clung to his words. *Wouldn't that be great forever?*

* * *

Sun pennies sparkled on the harbor water when Sundancer docked at Bermuda's Hamilton pier. On deck, Dierdre delighted in the fact their ship was less than seven-hundred feet in length so passengers could walk off the ramp into the heart of downtown Hamilton. The bigger cruise ships moored across the harbor at the Naval pier, in her mind a transportation inconvenience for Suzanne and her boxes of painting equipment.

White clouds chased one another across a brilliant blue sky. Birds chirped and trilled sounds not heard at sea. Soft warm air caressed her face and bare arms. This island paradise was Dierdre's favorite cruise destination. A sense of anticipation filled her with elation, a welcome change from recent troubling happenings and thoughts.

I'm feeling so happy and hopeful. My mind revolves around Randy in a good way. Funny, I'm looking forward to our time together more than anything I've planned in a long time. I'm relieved Wes dumped me, in spite of how much it hurt to be so publically replaced. A table set for three, another woman in my place without warning. Humiliating torture.

As if she'd conjured him into her presence, Wes and his new lady friend moved toward her in the crowd of departing guests. Dierdre's stomach tightened. *Just the man I didn't want to deal with any time soon, if ever, the flamboyant twit.*

She forced a professional cruise-director smile and offered them island maps, dining coupons, and transportation information, expecting Wes to be savvy enough to accept them and depart without a scene.

"Dierdre," he nudged the petite woman ahead of himself with a hand at her dainty waist. "I want you to meet Catherine, my fiancée. I didn't get a chance to introduce you the other evening. You didn't join me . . . us as I thought you and I planned."

Dierdre's polite smile faded. Incredulous, she gasped. "Fiancée? But haven't you just met?" She laughed nervously, gripping her sheaf of Bermuda packets to keep from smacking his jubilant face with the lot of them.

She swallowed, took a breath, and said more sweetly, "Catherine, how nice to meet you. Are you certain this charmer isn't rushing things a bit?" She almost regretted the ice in her tone. "He does have a suave way with words."

The little mouse didn't appear to notice or take any offense, but smiled warmly and extended her hand. "Wesley tells me you and your lovely twin sister are exceptionally familiar to him somehow. I'd hoped to get to know you personally."

Awkwardly, Dierdre shook hands and promptly let go. Passengers heading for the gangway crowded near, reaching for her Bermuda info packets. Handing them out, she smiled, muttering, "Have a great time," while they moved on with shopping totes, eager to get their land legs and their souvenirs.

Suddenly, Megan and Randy were among the crowd. Sickened that she couldn't speak to them personally under the circumstances, she and Megan exchanged waves.

"See you later," Megan called out. "About two-thirty," she added.

Dierdre waved and nodded, hoping Wes and Catherine would move on with the others. *No such luck.*

Wes plunged on. "Catherine and I were engaged years ago when I was in the Army. We were separated by time and distance; haven't seen each other in decades. It's like we've never been apart. Can you believe the little lady never stopped loving me?"

He kissed her forehead impulsively. "We're going to a jeweler to pick out the second ring I'll be placing on her finger. This time for good. I adore this little lady. Perhaps we'll get time with you to explain how the first engagement got bolloxed up."

"And what happened to that first engagement diamond," Catherine said, leaning into Wes's seersucker sport jacket, inspiring an affectionate hug on his part.

Forgiveness coursed through Dierdre like a welcoming wave of relief. "Yours is a shipboard romance to treasure. I hope you'll both be very very happy." She meant it and watched them depart hand-in-hand like a pair of young lovers.

How really sweet. I want a romance like theirs. So that's why the table was set for three that night. He wanted me to share their reunion joy. There I go again, reacting as though everything's all about me. I hate that in other people. Why do I do it myself?

I really am as self-absorbed as Suzanne tells me. Makes me cautious of assuming anything about Randy's feelings for me. He'll have to be direct and clear or I'm not going to fall prey to imagining what might not be in his heart—only in mine.

* * *

Chapter Thirteen   *Altered Plans*

Shading her eyes under a floppy sunhat and sipping her bottled water, Suzanne waited at the ship railing while Dierdre ushered off departing stragglers.

"Are you free to leave for town now?" she called to her twin. She winced, not wanting to let on her stomach was still queasy and her lower back ached right down to her toes. Checking out where to have her students arrange their painting chairs tomorrow was about all she thought she could handle before a late afternoon nap. This pregnancy made her more tired than the first one. She tried not to think of how it had ended and what she feared this time. Perhaps the more intense discomfort was due to her being a decade or so older and further along.

Suzanne hoped to finish the painting class and get comfortably through Cosma and Johnny's wedding with flower girl Mitzi the following afternoon and the reception in the evening. After those responsibilities were accomplished, she planned to spend the remainder of the birthday cruise with her feet up on a deck chair, following take-care-of-herself orders from Taylor. Having already held this baby several weeks beyond her previous pregnancy and miscarriage, she had no intention of risking overdoing it this time. Cosma and Taylor anticipated her every need. Suzanne couldn't imagine coming on the cruise without her steady friend

Cosma let alone her precious husband to manage their active five-year old and her painting equipment.

Dierdre waved her closer. "I brought my tote. Let's walk to the park."

"Is it far?"

"No, not too far. A walk will do us both good. We'll skip the hike up the steep garden stairs to the moon gate and go around the other way." Dierdre acted especially sparkly, sort of coltish. Suzanne suspected something was up. It would become clear soon enough, if she knew her flirty twin.

Dierdre embraced her lightly and kissed her cheek. "Don't worry, we'll take our time. Where's the rest of your high-energy entourage?" She paused, a look of concern pinching her brow. "You feeling okay? Your face is awfully pale."

Suzanne laughed it off, adjusting her carryall to the other shoulder. "I'm fine. Morning sickness is a bit of a challenge but I'm getting used to it. Taylor, Cosma, and Johnny left with the kids hours ago. They're touring the Royal Naval Dockyard to see the bigger cruise ships, then on to the Bermuda Aquarium. We're meeting for a late lunch, traditional British teatime at four. After that, Cosma, Johnny, and I are off by bus to the beach wedding site for a quick peruse. Want to come along?"

"Lovely of you to offer and I really should, but . . . well." Dierdre appeared awkward, looked away across the water, unlike her usual super-confident, breezy self. She brought her gaze back. "Please forgive me for ditching you. I've a date with a special man."

"Oh?" She laughed. "What's new? You always have a date with somebody. The old-world Wes guy in white tails this time?" Suzanne rolled her eyes and swept her arm, taking a dramatic pose from the movies.

"Surely he won't dress like that on the streets of Hamilton or St. George."

Dierdre giggled. "No, Sis. I'm not meeting Wes. He's otherwise occupied with his fiancée. They're ring shopping on Front Street as we speak." She turned Suzanne by the elbow and gestured toward camera-laden tourists strolling past pastel harbor-front shops.

"Fiancée? You can't be serious." Suzanne protested, unsure she'd heard her clearly. "Please explain."

"Forget him. I have." Dierdre pointed none too discreetly. "See the tall fellow with the wavy hair and his brunette daughter just passing that luggage shop?"

Suzanne focused. "The blind guy with the cane? The man I've seen you dance with a couple of times?"

"That's Randy. Don't you love those amazing athletic shoulders and the way he carries himself?" Dierdre's voice held a note of rapture, an unusually vulnerable quality.

Frankly puzzled, Suzanne stopped with a restraining hand on Dierdre's arm. She removed her sunglasses, and studied her twin's expression, concentrating on her eyes.

"Sis, this is a little uncharacteristic for you, isn't it?" She spoke cautiously because she didn't want to hurt her nor experience Dierdre's indignant temper. "Dee, he's handsome, yes, but definitely not the charismatic heartthrob you usually attract. I wonder if you've imagined what caregiver difficulties his blindness will mean if your relationship becomes really serious."

Suzanne sighed, reconsidered the possible consequences of angering her only sister, and went for the additional assessment anyway. "You have to admit, putting yourself out for others has rarely been your strong suit."

"Ouch!" Dierdre chuckled cheerfully. "I've earned that remark. Since I'm always brutally honest with you, I'll forgive you—in honor of our thirtieth birthday. Time I matured a bit, don't you think? I'm not proud of the way I often behave. Turning over a new leaf isn't easy but we'll all like me better."

Surprised, Suzanne nonetheless still had misgivings. "You seem genuinely taken with this Randy in spite of his impairment. How come?"

They resumed their stroll toward lush Victoria Park, prospective tropical garden site of Suzanne's *en plein air* painting class the next morning.

The silence grew. They passed beneath the iron Victoria Park archway suspended between stone lantern-topped gateposts. She retreated to a bench beside the cobbled walkway to rest her swollen ankles, drew her sister down beside her, and repeated, "How come?"

"I heard you."

Dierdre actually blushed, which Suzanne hadn't seen for years. Prompted to pay extra attention to her twin's words, even between the lines, she welcomed the less protected, less-caustic woman who first reappeared from their teen years after Gregory's kidnapping, only to evaporate again. This was the sister she missed most since then, whenever they were apart by distance or out of touch by phone.

Radiant with what Suzanne took for a woman in the flush of new love, Dierdre faced her with a sincerely sweet smile.

"Suze, I know I sound like a drooling teenager, but try to understand. Randy's chemistry with mine is simply mind-blowing. It's like what I see between you and Taylor. What I've envied." She fiddled with the handles of the tote at her side.

"More than that, he's someone I trust to be kind, respectful, and genuinely loving. It doesn't matter he's not the wealthy man I wanted to take care of me. Wes could have been that before he was reunited with his old flame, but I didn't feel toward him what I feel for Randy. It's a good thing Wes dissed me before I had to do the dumping and suffer the guilt.

"Randy's open honesty is what's so different about him. I'm finished with men who lead me on and betray me later with a hidden agenda. I'll never let myself be so stupid again."

Suzanne sipped from her water bottle. *I think I've heard her make that vow a dozen times. She's always gone back on it and gotten hurt. Why should this time be any different?*

* * *

When Suzanne left by taxi to meet her family, Dierdre was already at Victoria Park and a little early for Randy. She checked her pager to make certain the batteries were still charged and was returning it to her tote when a taxi pulled to the curb. Randy's profile in the window made her heart race. Rising to her feet, she walked through the gate in his direction.

She watched him get out, his wavy hair first, then the broad shoulders she loved. He said something to Megan who remained inside waving to Dierdre out the window. Randy closed the cab door and turned. She stopped staring at his fine round ass and watched him steady his cane. He called out,

"Dierdre, Megan says you beat me here. Come take my arm, please." He grinned and waited for her to join him on the pavement.

She went to him with pleasure, offering a cheery, "Hello, Randy," and stretched to give him an impulsive kiss on the cheek.

"Mmh, nice. Hello to you too." His voice was husky. "I've looked forward to being with you all day."

She went soft inside and took the offered forearm gladly. With effort she shifted her gaze to his daughter. "Bye, Megan. Have fun shopping. I promise to take good care of your dad."

The taxi pulled into the flow of bicycles and mopeds. She led Randy back through the gate and across the cobblestone path to the bench where she and Suzanne sat earlier. She pulled him down beside her. "What would you like to do so we can get better acquainted? I know what I'd like to do but I'd lose my job for behaving intimately in public."

He covered the hand she placed on his arm with one of his own. "I'm feeling like a teenager eager to park with you for half the night. I don't want to share you with anyone in a restaurant setting. Let's sit here and talk a while, then I've arranged for a romantic expedition. It was Megan's idea and I thought it brilliant."

"Are you going to tell me what it is?"

"Soon. I promise."

She edged closer on the bench. "Until then, let's talk about you and me. You know what I do for a career. I want to know how you earn a living with time to pursue writing a novel and taking cruises. Isn't that what people do when they retire, unless they live in a chilly attic somewhere and never scrape up the money for anything but cigarettes and typing paper? I didn't think wannabe writers could afford to go on a luxury cruise, let alone two of them in one season."

He threw back his head and laughed. "You are one sharp cookie. I guess you could call me a private consultant on fat retainers from corporations who pay for my financial advice."

"So money isn't an issue, even though . . ."

"Even though I'm blind? I'm comfortable, let's leave it there . . . for now." He released her hand and walked his fingers up her arm. "What would you be doing in the City of Hamilton on a sunny day like this without me or your sister's family and friends to fill your free time?"

"I'd be golfing. I'm pretty good at it and the challenge on every shot is always fun."

"I love golf too." He looked suddenly extremely uncomfortable, fidgeting and loosening his collar. "At least I used to." His expression had turned sour or sad, she wasn't certain which.

Wanting him to be happy again, and avoiding the topic of how and when he became blind, she said, "Tell me about your novel."

Randy hesitated but only for a moment. "Okay, I trust you to keep the plot a secret. It's about a private investigator on the tail of an unscrupulous hedge-fund manager who swindled a sweet old widow out of most of the fortune her hardworking husband left her. Her daughter hires him to catch the guy and get her mother's money back. In disguise, the hero PI stalks him, finds out the crook's taking a cruise, and follows the shyster onto the ship, soon discovering who the next victim is. Things get twisted and really interesting from there . . . to the end."

Folding his hands across his lap and feigning a smug expression, Randy added,

"That's where you and Sundancer come in and why I wanted to cruise long enough to gather information to make my story believable."

"So does the bad guy get caught in the end?" She sat forward completely captivated, her hands squeezing his arm.

"Oh, yes he certainly does. Justice will be served." He pulled her close and she snuggled into him.

"Well, Miss Cruise Director, do you know of a likely wealthy target on board our cruise? Somebody I could use as a character example, anonymously of course, with celebrity connections who's not only a likely victim but one who can lead a bad guy to other vulnerable targets' and their bank accounts? Maybe somebody like that showy fellow you danced with for a couple of nights."

"The one walking this way with his fiancée right now, you mean? Wish you could see the lovebirds. Kind of charming to know older people fall in love like younger ones."

"Do you think they'll stop and talk?" His head turned in the direction of approaching steps.

Wes walked over to their bench leading Catherine by the hand.

"Dierdre Ingram, we were just wishing we knew someone with whom we could share our exciting news, and here you are. You met Catherine earlier today."

I can't figure out how old she is, well-preserved but no spring chicken. Don't think he'll have to make adjustments to her face or body for quite some time.

"Yes, of course. Randy Keene meet Wesley LeChaminant and Catherine?"

The petite woman stepped closer. "Hatch," she said, breathlessly.

"Soon to be LeChaminant," Wes added. "Show off your ring, dear."

Catherine stretched forth her left hand, smiling shyly, her soft brown hair streaked with gray blowing about her face and shoulders.

Dierdre was surprised she could lift her arm.

"My goodness, that's quite an impressive diamond. You must be proud to wear it." *If it weren't such a clear sparkling diamond I'd swear she dropped a quarter in a bubblegum machine. Must be five or six carets. He has some very deep pockets. Certainly filled my criteria for the ideal man.*

Catherine's eyes widened with excitement. "It's five times as big as the first one when we were broke college students. I tried to talk him into a less dramatic ring but . . ."

Wes shifted his feet. "We have dinner reservations and must hurry on, but Dierdre I've been meaning to ask. Is Ingram your mother's maiden or married name?"

"My mother Marissa never married. Ingram is—was—her maiden name." Dierdre chuckled nervously. "Suzanne and I sometimes joke about our virgin birth. Our mother never would tell us who our father was. We don't even know if she told him she was pregnant, before they went their separate ways."

The silence was awkward. Dierdre hadn't intended to let on she was born out of wedlock as the old saying goes. *Oh well, it's the twenty-first century, we're all grown up, and he's a doctor. Probably doesn't shock easily, especially if he has Vegas showgirls for clients. Not sure I wanted Randy to know it though.*

"You said Marissa?" Wes softly asked. "Well well. Right after Catherine and I broke off, I spent a summer surfing and dated a sweet and gorgeous

Marissa Ingram, until I changed majors and went off to med school. You must be her daughter. No wonder you look and behave so much like her, your sister as well." His eyes searched Dierdre's. "She's no longer living?"

Dierdre looked at his face, his eyes, his smile even more seriously, imagining him thirty or so years younger. "She died in an accident a few years ago. I believe I've seen a picture of you and a group of friends at the beach. At least there's a Wes in the line up of handsome men in swim trunks on a beach with her."

"What a small world it is. Mystery solved. Your mother was a very special lady whom I had a hard time leaving that summer to return to university." He hugged Catherine. "Of course, she tried to help me recover from losing my darling Catherine."

Randy interrupted. "Wesley, aren't you a close friend to Arnold Bloomquist?"

"Why yes, we're traveling together in adjoining suites and considering some business arrangements. Why do you ask?"

"I'd be careful of doing business with him." Randy betrayed nothing beyond a sober expression. Surprised, Dierdre vowed to ask him about it later.

Wes's face grew equally solemn. "We should continue this conversation privately at another time—but soon. Thank you for the tip. I shall be careful." He steered Catherine back to the walkway. "Best to you both, we must catch a taxi."

"No wonder he's seemed so familiar to me," Dierdre said. "I've seen that photo of him as a young man a hundred times."

"He must've looked different in a bathing suit without a tuxedo." Randy joked, rubbing a thumb across his watch. "About time for my surprise. Let's go out the gate to the street." He stood, held out a hand to her and kept her fingers entwined with his while he tapped the walk with his cane.

A horse-drawn carriage pulled out of the motorcycle traffic and drew up at the curb. The matched pair of chestnut geldings shook their caramel manes, setting their bridles to clinking. The driver in a proper suit and top hat called down to them. "Mr. Keene, perhaps?"

"Sounds like our chariot has arrived. Lead on, my lady. You can explain the sights to me. Actually I promised a larger tip if he'd let us talk privately without the guided-tour spiel. I figure you know the island quite well and I can't see it anyway."

Moments later they settled into the carriage seats holding hands while the driver, having served them glasses of champagne, climbed back to his seat and lightly flicked his whip at the horses' flanks. The carriage took to the shore-line road. Randy's thumb made gentle circles on the top of her hand. The sensation was exciting and comforting at the same time. It was a good thing they were in a public place. She could hardly resist unbuttoning his shirt and getting down to some passionate business.

"Why did you warn Wes about Arnold? Do you know something suspicious about him?" She so wished she could see his eyes and determined at their first intimate opportunity she'd remove those damned dark glasses and find out the color of his eyes.

"Nothing to worry your pretty head about. We'll go into it another time. Right now we're all about us."

She relaxed into his arm around her shoulders and gazed out at the passing palm trees, lush magenta bougainvillea draped around gingerbread porches, and colorful chirping birds. Listening to the steady clip clop of the horses' hooves on the pavement, sipping champagne, she realized she hadn't been this content, or ever felt this safe with any man.

"You're on my mind about twenty-four-seven, Dierdre."

"Ahh," she said, laughing deep in her throat. "We are similarly afflicted. Do you think it's terminal?"

Randy's firm thigh nudged hers. "Definitely. It's probably a good thing I can't see or I'd really get myself in trouble. Megan tells me you're more than pretty, really beautiful. I know you feel wonderful in my arms on the dance floor and smell like flowers and spicy sweetness, even when I can't hold you against me—like now in public."

He leaned his head close to hers. "Do you think we could see each other after the cruise? I mean, often?" He kissed her temple and whispered, "I can't imagine not being with you after we return to New York and our ordinary lives."

Dierdre's heart squeezed with happiness. "I can't think of anything I'd like more than seeing you often. I live in Miami and travel back and forth to New

York. You live in Virginia by your guest bio. Where? Where could we meet?"

He lifted her palm to his lips and kissed it. She thrilled to the goose bumps tickling all the way up her arm and wished they were in her king-size bed with the scent of jasmine blossoms wafting in a sea breeze over their bare bodies.

"I work from home on my farm when I'm not in D.C." He kept her palm to his lips, and his breath moving between her fingers nearly drove her mad. "You could come stay with me for weeks at a time. I have horses. There's a pool nearby and a golf course. We could move the furniture out of the way, roll up the carpets, and dance every night after dinner."

"Would we have to live on Chinese take-out like a Woody Allen movie?"

Chuckling, he shook his head. "You make me happy when you're ridiculous."

A buzzing from her tote told Dierdre she was being paged. "Oh dear. Excuse me, it must be a ship call. No one else would know to contact me."

* * *

Suzanne had left Dierdre at the entrance to Victoria Park and hailed a taxi. She hoped her sister wasn't making a terrible mistake with her heart. She knew better than to interfere any more than what she'd risked saying already.

Arriving first at the Hungry Bear Café on Chancery Lane, the kids' choice that morning for its wild-animal name, she ordered iced lemonade while waiting for her family and friends.

Under an umbrella at a patio table with enough chairs for her group, it was good to take a load off her aching feet and remove her sandals. Taking a sketchbook from her bag, Suzanne's colored pencils recorded hibiscus flowers and palm trees, teal-blue harbor water, boats and yachts, charming pastel buildings with their distinctive water-collecting roofs, and shutters like eyebrows above windows. Without cars the streets were busy with people going by on bikes and mopeds. She'd never been in a place with only taxis and public transportation before. It was a welcome relief from noisy car traffic in America. *Something to be said for living on an island,* she mused.

Soon the pages of her ring-bound book began to fill with local men in colorful Bermuda shorts and smart sports jackets, sunburned tourists roped with cameras and souvenir bags, and bright birds flitting among the trees and roosting on roof tops.

"Mommy's here already!" She heard Mitzi's voice first and lifted her head to see her daughter bouncing along in hand with Taylor. Her heart stirred as it always did when he came into view. *How dearly I love you, darling man. You are so good to these children, and I'm so happy we're making a baby together.* As if it knew, the baby within fluttered fists or feet against her belly, which tightened in response. She chuckled and held out her arms to her children.

Chairs scraped as everyone began talking at once while finding a place to sit. She passed out menus, accepting a hug from Taylor and a kiss on the lips, which knocked her hat askew when his Stetson bumped her brim, making them both laugh. He patted her tummy bump. "Missed you two, Mommy."

She bopped him on a broad shoulder. "You too, you big galootin' daddy."

"Mom, you should've seen the Galapagos tortoise and the giant lizards at the aquarium," blurted Gregory, wearing a new tee shirt emblazoned with tropical fish. Stellar had one like it. Cloud had tied a bright bandana decorated with animals around his ponytail but his shirt was the white one he'd worn that morning. She loved its contrast to his brown skin.

"The monkeys looking like little lions were the bestest," chattered Mitzi. "I didn't like the bats so much but the fish were pretty colors and some huge ones were bigger as me."

Cloud and Stellar studied menus, obviously starved. Johnny propped his cane against the table edge and shoved his hat back on his forehead. Cosma looked as fresh as if she hadn't walked all over the island for hours. Her exotic appearance with magenta, yellow, and blue ribbons fluttering against her caramel skin and shining black braid drew many glances from nearby diners. Suzanne sketched her friend while she had a few minutes to capture her beauty.

"How are you holding up, Suzanne?" Cosma asked. "I've wondered if your sister wore you out today."

"I'm doing fine, puffy ankles, just a little tired, the usual for expectant mothers. I'll be ready to hit the sack after we visit the beach at the Fairmont Southhampton and make sure you're happy with the ceremony arrangements."

"Can I go too so I can see where the flower girl gets to walk and scatter rose petals?" Mitzi asked wistfully.

Taylor intervened. "No, Sweetheart. Johnny and I are going to whisk all you squirrely kids off to the ship so you can shower, play some board games, and rest up for tomorrow's fun."

Within half an hour they were served what the boys wanted, familiar American cheeseburgers, while the adults savored fish chowder, codfish potatoes with a side of bananas, and something called bangers and mash, which made them all laugh. They shared tasty bites from each other's plates and coaxed the kids to taste a few bites without much success.

Suzanne picked at her platter, putting most of it on other people's plates while she listened to the children discuss the aquarium peacocks, lemurs, flamingoes, and parrots. She fought nausea at their descriptions of an octopus and the suction cups on its many writhing arms.

They were gathering up their belongings to leave when Mitzi called out, "It's Auntie Dreedra in that big baby buggy with the horses!"

Suzanne whirled to look, caught the expression on her sister's face, and gasped in alarm. Dierdre swung down from the carriage and hurried toward them leaving Randy and the driver at the curb. She made straight for Taylor with a paper in her hand.

"Taylor, I'm so glad you're still here," she said, nearly out of breath. "I'm so sorry to interrupt with urgent news but I had to find you quickly."

"What do you mean?" Taylor took the envelope she handed him. He unfolded a telegram, skimmed it, and dropped back into his chair.

He looked up at Suzanne. "It's Pops. Damn! He's suffered another heart attack, is in ICU. Mom begs me to come. . . . Doctors don't give him much time."

* * *

Dierdre leaned down and encircled her twin's shoulder with an affectionate half hug, a gesture of comfort for what was to come—the shattering of all their birthday and wedding plans. "I'll be right back, just let me bring Randy . . ."

Suzanne nodded. "Of course, go to him." Her soft and shaky voice broke Dierdre's heart. Her sister was so upset. *This was supposed to be a happy trip. Now it's all falling apart.* Steeling herself to prevent her frustration from dissolving into tears or anger, she hurried back to Randy.

At the curb, he pulled a bill from his wallet and handed it to the driver. "Keep the change. I'm sorry, sir. Family emergency. We'll have to taxi from here."

She touched his arm, feeling guilty his plans for their romantic afternoon were shot to hell, and feeling guilty for resenting Pops Armstrong for having his damn heart attack in the middle of their birthday vacation.

He turned to her. "How's your brother-in-law taking the news?"

Dierdre led him by the elbow to the restaurant.

"He's doing better than my sister. They're all stunned and trying to figure out what to do. Hope you can handle it if it gets emotional."

"I'm here for you. Just ask. Megan and I will help however we can." He squeezed her hand more firmly to his arm. "I've been in love with you for weeks. You can count on me."

Her heart struggling with tender emotions, she squelched the urge to grab him around the neck right on the street. "Oh, Randy. What a time to tell me something so wonderful when I can't respond the way I'd like to."

"I know." He chuckled. "You'll make it up to me in the near future I'm sure."

They joined her family and friends. "Excuse me, everyone. I'd like you to meet my dear friend Randy. We'll do proper intros later, after we deal with the current crisis."

They all nodded their hellos, which she wished he could see. Cloud gave up his chair. "You can have my seat, Randy."

Randy took it, eased himself down, and held onto his cane. Cloud stood behind him and gave a peculiar rolling-eyes look to Stellar and Gregory who winked in return.

Wonder what that's all about. They'd better not do anything rude to Randy or I'll skin them all within an inch of their little lives.

A long sigh erupted from Taylor squatting next to Suzanne's chair, his hat on one knee. He held her hand. "Honey, I'm so sorry but you know I must get the first possible flight back to the mainland."

Her sister's chin quivered. "Taylor, I know your mother needs you beside her with Pops, but I want to go with you."

Dierdre wrung her hands. "But Suze, it's our birthday cruise. We haven't even had our cake and party yet, and I've scheduled your painting class in the park tomorrow."

Taylor stood. "I could maybe take Mitzi to make things easier for you here. My sister-in-law wouldn't mind adding one more to her brood 'til you get home, if I can get two plane tickets."

Mitzi's glass went over, spilling ice across the table. "Then I won't get to be a flower girl and wear my new pretty shoes!" She burst into tears.

Cosma pulled her onto her lap. "Suzanne, we can take care of the kids and help with your class tomorrow."

"I can take care of myself," Gregory insisted. "I'll help take care of Mitzi. She's no trouble. 'Specially when she takes a nap."

Suzanne brushed tears from her cheeks with her napkin. "Your wedding. How could I put your lovely beach ceremony out of my mind? Forgive me, Cosma, Johnny." She shook her head and gasped. "Taylor, you're to be Johnny's best man. You even bought white slacks and a new shirt."

"And promised not to wear my Stetson during the ceremony." Grinning, Taylor ruffled Gregory's cowlick. "Sorry, just a little attempt to lighten the mood. The kids will do their best to be helpful and good, won't you?" He checked the faces of each one nodding fiercely.

Cosma stroked Mitzi's curls away from her face, rocking her gently. "The wedding can be put off until we're all back in Utah."

Cloud stepped to his mother's chair. "No!" His proud Apache face appeared stricken. "Mom, you and Johnny just have to get married while we're here. You just have to—like we planned. I told all my friends at school you were . . . finally getting married."

He sucked air in gulps. It was the most vulnerable emotion Dierdre had ever seen him express. He jammed his hands in his pockets and bit his lip, willing his mother to reconsider with a beseeching look.

He bent to her eye level and in an urgent voice, added, "Besides, I helped you two fill out that Bermuda's Notice of Intended Marriage form. It's been published in two local newspapers to make it legal, and the three-month window closes in a couple weeks. You'd have to go through stuff like that again in Utah if you don't get married here."

Stellar moved next to his brother, nudging in front of him. "I'm scared you'd never get around to it. I'm supposed to be the ring bearer and that's so cool.

You've got to go through with it, Mom. Cloud and I want to be Carlisle brothers."

"Party reception's all paid for," said Taylor. "My wedding present, remember?" He slapped Johnny on the shoulder. "Better go through with it like the boys say, my friend. We'll be a couple of old married falconers when you get back to the States."

Johnny cleared his throat. "Cosma, you said yes. I'm holding you to it. We're getting married as planned. Please make me a proud and happy man." He leaned close above Mitzi's head and kissed her cheek.

"John Love, we'll do it. I do want to be Mrs. Carlisle." Her big dark eyes looked into his with the adoration most people see in the eyes of a Golden Retriever. Dierdre swallowed the lump in her throat.

"Thank you, Sweetheart," Johnny whispered.

"Great!" breathed Cloud. His relieved shoulders dropped. The gust of air he blew out between his lips could have extinguished Suzanne and Dierdre's birthday cake blazing with thirty candles.

Taylor adjusted his Stetson back on his head. "Maybe Randy here can be my stand in as best man."

"Any way I can help, count me in," said Randy.

Johnny reached across the table and shook his hand. "You're on. Thank you."

Everyone sat stunned, as if stuck in mud. Dierdre's professionalism kicked in. "Taylor it's less than three hours from here to Atlanta on Delta. Once there you can catch a direct red-eye to Salt Lake City. Can someone meet you for the drive to Farr?"

Suzanne moaned, holding Taylor's hand firmly.

Dierdre hurried on. "I've assisted with emergency flights many times. I'll use the restaurant phone to call Wade Airport across the bay and arrange your ticket. We'll need a couple of taxis too, unless one of those pink buses comes by. You'll want your passport and a carry-on from the ship. We can send a telegram to your mother to say you're on the way."

Suzanne tugged Dierdre's blouse hem. "Just because I wanted to go with him doesn't mean I think any less of all your planning and money to celebrate our birthday and these honeymoons."

Her eyes glistened with welling tears, and a trickle slid down her cheek. "But the kids, my class, the wedding, our party—all without my Taylor. It's so unexpected, so overwhelming." Her hands spanned her round belly while she fought for control. "This is going to take a lot of prayer."

Dierdre skirted the table on her way to use the phone, Taylor at her heels. "We'll all get through this. Right now we need to help Taylor get on the way to his father."

She brushed a hand across Randy's shoulders in passing and leaned close to his ear. "Sit tight, handsome. I'm not finished with you yet."

"I sincerely hope not," he said, smiling beneath his dark lenses.

* * *

Chapter Fourteen *Victoria Park*

Beneath a brittle-blue sky, sunlight flirted through fragrant pines, blossoming oleanders, and swaying palms, dappling Victoria Park's manicured lawns with golden speckles. Pristine pathways webbed across green oceans of clipped grass leading to the park centerpiece, the fretwork-gingerbread, cupola-topped gazebo. On its shady stage, clipboard in hand, Dierdre compared Sundancer's *en plein air* sign-up sheet with her sister's notebook list.

Beside her, Suzanne pressed a fist to her lower back, sighing with apparent fatigue. As painters arrived, she checked off their names. A soft sea breeze lifted the brim of Suzanne's sunhat, revealing dark circles under eyes weary from lack of sleep and probably weeping about Taylor having to leave. Dierdre's heart went out to her twin. She handed the notebook back and gave the dome of Suzanne's tummy a loving pat.

"Sis, everything's going to go fine. You'll be reunited with Taylor in a few days and the world will stop spinning out of your control."

Suzanne gave her a grateful look. "I hope you're right. We've never been apart since our wedding night. I'm absolutely lost without my man." She lifted a swollen ankle and massaged it. "I didn't get one of Taylor's marvelous foot rubs last night either."

She forced a laugh. "I'll try really hard to be upbeat for our birthday celebration and Cosma and Johnny's wedding. I promise. Though birthday cake tonight will probably make me swell up even more like a toad than I already am."

"You'll be the prettiest toad at the ball. All of us will help make it as easy and fun as possible for you. We'll keep Mitzi busy for the next couple days so you can sandwich in a few naps."

Suzanne pointed to her son carrying a big empty box in one hand, leading Mitzi and her art bag across the grass with the other. "Could you go see if he needs any help with her? He's taken care of her since breakfast while everyone else helped get my supplies and chairs ready for class here."

"Sure. Be right back." Dierdre descended the steps, picked up a couple of folding chairs, and followed the kids.

"Hey you darlings, what's your plan?"

"Auntie Dreedra, Gregory's making me a art table like for grown ups." She cocked her head, spilling curls to her shoulder. "I need my kiss."

Dierdre bent and pressed her lips to Mitzi's cheek. "There, did that help?"

The curls bobbed with the little girl's enthusiastic nod. "Yep it did."

After hugging Gregory, Dierdre opened a folding chair. "Show me your idea." She placed the chair out of his way.

He set to work. "See I'm turning this box upside down. Mitzi, hold your paper while I tape it." Gregory tugged a roll of masking tape from his shorts pocket, picked the starting end free, and secured the paper in place on top of the box.

"There. Now you can paint like an artist too." With a satisfied expression on his grinning face, he planted his feet wide apart, and folded his arms across the leather pouch at his chest.

Mitzi arranged her paint box, two brushes, and a paper cup of water at the side of the box table. She skipped in a circle. "I'm going to make a real pretty picture like Mommy's."

Cosma joined them and dragged both folding chairs into place on either side of the cardboard table. "Good morning everybody."

She hugged Dierdre and touched the boy's shoulder. "Gregory, you've taken such good care of your sister I think I can manage from here. Johnny will come after his workout if I need help. My boys finished unloading your mother's painting supplies from that long cart. Why don't you go have fun with them for a while?" She nodded toward the gazebo.

"Come on, Greg," said Dierdre. "Let's go hook you up with the guys while I see if my sister needs any more help from me. See you ladies later. Paint something special, Mitzi girl."

"I'll make it just for you." Mitzi opened the paint box and sat, her sandal toes swinging rhythmically across the grass.

Dierdre winked at Gregory and sped up her pace. Laughing, they fast-walked in a mini race to the gazebo and mounted the steps two at a time. "You win," she said, laughing at him. "Make your energy last. I might need to borrow some of it."

He gave her a high five and strolled over to Suzanne.

"Mom, Cosma says she'll stay with Mitzi. Can I go play with Cloud and Stellar for a while?"

"Okay by me. Your dad would be proud of you for helping with your little sister. Thank you, Honey. You're going to be the best big brother to this baby." She ruffled his hair and gave him an affectionate shove on the shoulder. "Off you go. Don't wear yourself out trying to keep up with Cloud."

Dierdre smiled at her twin. "He's becoming quite a helpful young man. You must be proud of him too. I wouldn't think it's been easy being stepparents."

Chuckling, Suzanne collected her art materials and moved to the table where she'd demonstrate techniques. "It's not always easy, but it's worth all the struggles we've been through to see Gregory happy again. I hope the dark times are behind us."

Together they watched the watercolor students set up the provided folding chairs, their art supplies, and their painting boards in the nearby grass. Most of them chatted with one another while surveying their surroundings and picking out what tropical subject matter they wanted to paint.

"Here comes Catherine with her fancy man carrying her art box. Hope he doesn't mess up his seersucker suit." Suzanne put a check by her name and waved hello.

"She usually comes with her traveling companion. Wonder where Hettie . . . oh, there she is entering the gate. Now if Arnold would just show up, everyone else is accounted for and we could get started while the early morning light is lovely."

Dierdre giggled. "Can't miss Hettie's wild-skunk hairdo. She doesn't seem too happy to have lost her milk-toast sidekick to Wes's devoted attention."

Seeing another arrival, her energy went into overdrive. "My heartthrob is now on site. If you can do without me for a while, I'm in need of a cure for my adrenalin rush."

"Hah," Suzanne poured water into her demo jar. "You've been an adrenalin junky since we escaped from the womb. I'm fine. Go get your morning fix."

Dierdre gave Suzanne's shoulder a squeeze and hurried to descend the steps. Randy stood talking with his daughter. She thought they both wore extremely sober expressions. She felt a pang in the pit of her stomach, but dismissed it and joined them.

Megan checked her watch and said something to her dad. Before he could reply, Dierdre slipped an arm around Randy's lean ribs and smiled at Megan.

"Hope I'm not interrupting something serious."

Randy wrapped his free arm around Dierdre's waist, pleasuring her body and warming her heart. It'd been difficult to part with him the evening before to help Taylor get to the airport in time to make his flight. This morning, her imagination sent her into raptures of the night to come. At last they'd be alone together after the birthday party. *It's time I helped him remove his dark glasses and every stitch of his clothing.* She trembled with anticipation and wondered if he could tell her mind had gone to bed with him.

"Good morning, my sweet," he said, his smile a white slash in the handsome tan face beneath his sunglasses. "You're not interrupting a thing."

"Morning, Dierdre." Megan brushed her cheek with a kiss. "Did your brother-in-law make it to his plane okay?"

"Yes, everything went off without a hitch. I imagine his sister's driving him from Salt Lake Airport to Farr as we speak. He'll be at his dad's hospital bedside before we have lunch."

Hettie tromped past them grumbling to herself. Dierdre and Megan backed out of her way. Her powerful perfume lingered in the air. Overtaking Catherine and Wesley, the woman set her bulging art tote down, opened a folding chair, and flopped into it. Loudly she blurted, "Cathy, why the hell didn't you wait for me?"

Dierdre and Megan paused their conversation to eavesdrop on the drama. Wesley unfolded the legs of Catherine's French easel and steadied it in the grass, while Catherine, her face flaming with embarrassment, tightened the wing nuts before the easel could collapse.

"Wesley offered to help me carry my things and I took him up on it." She faced her friend, her voice pleading. "Hettie, please don't make a scene."

"Well excu-u-s-e me! Once Arnie comes, maybe I'll have a handsome assistant too, if he doesn't follow Miss Beauty Queen Megan over there with his tongue hanging out."

Wes went to Hettie's side, lifted her sparkling green nails to his lips, and whispered something calming. Her shoulders relaxed and she smiled.

"Oh boy," whispered Dierdre to Megan. "She's a handful. Those women's personalities are so different I can't imagine how they're even girlfriends. Nice of Wes to calm the waters for Catherine and all of us."

Arnold hurried to set up his painting station next to Megan's. "Good morning, gorgeous," he gushed. "I wouldn't have missed a lovely morning with you in the park for anything. You look sensational as always."

Megan teased, "Flattery isn't likely to get you anywhere, Mr. Bloomquist. Looks like Dierdre's sister is ready to start class now that the last of you stragglers has arrived."

"Then may I accompany you to the demo, my dear?" Grasping her arm, he guided Megan toward the gazebo. "I trust you'll have dinner with me—alone—this evening."

She didn't answer.

He nodded to Wesley as he passed between Catherine and Hettie.

"Aren't you even going to say hello?" Hettie demanded, trigger happy with dissed outrage.

"Hello, Hettie my dear." Arnold strode past her, shielding himself with Megan.

"Well that's a fine how do you do." Hettie followed in their wake, cackling her bizarre laugh as if something funny were apparent to everyone.

Dierdre nudged Randy. "Do you mind if we go watch the demo for a moment?" He carried his cane and allowed her to lead him. "I'd go anywhere with you. Lead on."

Standing center stage, Suzanne raised her voice while the painters found places around her table to watch. She gestured toward three boards with taut stretched paper displayed before them.

Holding up a plastic viewfinder window, she said, "Once you've selected your subject matter, define your focal point with your finder, and decide where it will fit on your paper. Begin with a light pencil sketch as in this example, unless you prefer to skip that step and paint directly."

She pointed to the second board. "Then paint your light washes for sky, grass, water, and tree foliage, layering them up from light to dark as shown here. You can work wet on wet and wet on dry as we've practiced in class. Remember to slant your board and let gravity move the watercolor washes evenly down the paper. As painted areas dry in the breeze, experiment with dry-brush techniques to add detail."

Sloshing a mop brush in water, then swirling it in blue watercolor, Suzanne moved it across her third paper from one side to the other, leaving a slight puddle all the way across. She returned to the water jar and her palette and working directly underneath the first row, repeated the process. She captured and incorporated the puddle on each pass, adjusting how much slant was necessary to make the paint run where she wanted it for a graded-wash effect.

"Now return to your set ups and get started. I'll be coming around to see how you're doing and to give you whatever suggestions you need. Have fun. Tonight we'll display your finished paintings along the gallery wall outside the dining room."

The group dispersed to their chairs and supplies. Megan came down the gazebo steps with Arnold at her elbow. On their heels, Hettie whined like a dog. Megan rolled her eyes at Dierdre in passing, raising her finely arched eyebrows in a secret message of amusement between them.

Dierdre, standing in the grass next to Randy, called up to her twin. "Good job, Sis. Are you all set for a while?"

Suzanne picked up her camera and moved to the gazebo's balustrade. "I'm going to take pictures of their progress while they work. You two go off and do . . . whatever." She waved them away, grinning impishly.

"Catch you later," Dierdre said. "I won't be far if you need something before it's time to return all your gear to the ship."

Taking Randy by the hand, she said, "Let's move into the shade of those hibiscus shrubs. I can keep an eye on Suze from there."

"Okay, babe. I'm all yours."

"Don't I wish." She squeezed his fingers, thrilling to the tingles running up her arm and through her mind. *I am so crazy about this man I'm nearly delirious.*

Beneath the massive shrubs dotted with saucer-sized pink blossoms, they paused.

"Do you ever wish you could see everything beautiful around you?"

"At the moment, I sure do wish I could see something beautiful, starting with you." He kissed the hair billowing at her temple. "Most of the time, I try not to think about not seeing what I want—too depressing."

Now why did I ask such a stupid question? Thank God he doesn't appear to be insulted by my rudeness. "Thank you for coming to stay with me while I'm here for Suzanne this morning." She leaned into him, inhaling his musky aftershave and his personal man scent, loving the feeling of his firm muscles nudging occasionally against her hip and thigh.

He chuckled. "So you want me to admit it's you and not my daughter I came to be near?"

"It would be very flattering if you could do that for me, even if you have to fib."

She reached up and stroked the deep cleft she loved in his cheek, formed when he grinned. Out of the corner of her eye she noticed Wesley walking away from Catherine and coming in their direction. He stopped to speak with Arnold.

"Randy," she said. "Wesley's talking with Arnold but I think he's coming to talk to you. We'll have to ask Megan what they're talking about since she's close enough to hear."

"We certainly will." He practically went on alert, turning his head in their direction. "Let's walk back that way right now."

She wondered for a moment how he knew which way to incline his head, but realized the murmur of their voices was audible if indistinct. They returned the way they'd come, Randy moving quickly, sweeping his cane back and forth over the grass.

Suddenly, Arnold started ramming his materials back into his art bag and hurried off with it to the walkway toward the park's big iron gate. Left behind, Wesley stood rubbing his forehead, apparently deep in thought.

Wonder what that was about.

They reached Megan, who seemed distracted, her sketch of the gazebo barely started. Randy spun toward his daughter, his cane in his hand. "Now what do we do with him leaving so abruptly, Meg? We didn't anticipate he'd take off before we could put the squeeze on when his crush for you is so obvious."

She put down her pencil. "I guess we can't very well follow him now."

"But *we* can," came a voice behind them. Cloud stepped forward and put his hand on Randy's arm.

Dierdre was completely confused.

In a soft voice, Cloud said, "Stellar and I figured out you're not blind. Whatever reason you have for wearing fake glasses and using a blind person's cane, it must be a good one. That mean man Arnold's a rat. If you want us to find out where he goes, the guys and I will tag him and help you."

Randy released Dierdre's hand and dug for his wallet. Unfolding it, he pulled out three twenties, American. "Rent some pedal bikes outside the gate. Tail him and report back. Thanks and keep my secret."

Dierdre protested, "What's this all . . ."

But Randy held up a hand. Addressing Cloud he added, "Try to look like you're just out having fun. Buy some ice cream, pop some wheelies, just don't lose him. Tell me specifically where he goes and how long he stays along the way."

"You can count on us." Cloud made a follow-me gesture to Stellar and Gregory. Over his shoulder he called back, "Dierdre, tell Mom and your sister we'll be back after we go bike riding."

Dumbfounded, Dierdre's heart thundered in her ears. She nodded an okay to the boys. *Of course I'll tell your mothers. Now's not the time to upset them, you little twits.*

Her eyes flicked from Randy's face to Megan's. "What in hell's going on?" She choked out the words, "You're not really blind? You've both been faking it, lying to me? Why?"

"I can explain," Randy said, his voice ragged with emotion. He took her by the shoulders. "Please, Dierdre. We can't talk here but I will come clean with you very soon. Trust me."

"Trust you?" she sputtered. "Trust a big-time betraying liar? I may have fallen hard for you, but I'm not a complete idiot." She wrenched away from his grasp. "God, I'm such a fool."

She turned to Megan. "I suppose you're not even Randy's daughter. Probably his girlfriend, just helping him set me up to suck my brains for his damn novel."

Megan's face was ashen, her eyes darting from Dierdre to Randy and back again. Her lips a tight line, she picked up her pencil and turned back to her sketch, her hand shaking as if palsied.

Tears gathering on her lids, Dierdre brushed past the two, only to plough—unseeing—into Wesley's shirtfront, nearly knocking them both to the ground.

"Give Randolph a chance to explain," he implored. "He's too good a man to throw away in a fit of temper. He has his good reasons for deceiving you."

"Oh, to hell with all of you, Wes."

She stumbled blindly toward Cosma and her little niece.

* * *

Humiliated, betrayed, stunned beyond comprehension, Dierdre gravitated toward stability—Cosma. The wise friend she trusted to help her cope whom she believed could keep her from drowning in confusion and misery. Misery she'd brought on herself over yet another man.

Following electric attraction and her own idea of what a man was really like instead of using common sense had devastated her again, this time profoundly. Even after only a short time, she'd fallen deeply in love with the Randy she thought she knew. *I'm a smart woman, why in hell have I done this to myself again? He isn't blind, but I sure as hell am.*

Furiously, she wiped tears from her lashes with trembling fingers. It won't do for Mitzi to see me crying. She'll be onto me in a heartbeat and worry her mother.

Cosma sat beside the child. The long black braid with its beaded slide lay across one shoulder while she leaned close to watch Mitzi absorbed in painting another watercolor. Two bright paintings lay drying in the clipped grass.

Dierdre cleared her throat and did her best to sound cheerful. "Give this little artist a paint brush and she's apt to fill a gallery."

Cosma sat up and met her gaze. Her brow furrowed with what Dierdre took for concern.

She's read me already.

"I painted you a pretty flower picture," Mitzi bubbled. "See it's all dry too." She pointed near her box table with her brush toward the grass.

Dierdre bent and picked it up. "For me?"

"Yep. It's almost my bestest one."

"Did you paint one for me and Cosma yet?" The deep voice behind them came from Johnny, leaning on his cane. His damp hair glistened and smelled shower fresh. *He's become a different man than a year ago in the desert, clearly happy and healing in Cosma's love and her boys' admiration.*

Mitzi bounced out of her chair. "Um hum. It's a present for your wedding. Cosma knows it's this one I just made." She pulled her painting free of the tape on the box and presented it to him with a curtsy.

Johnny laughed and held the masterpiece up, dripping paint from one corner. "It's beautiful, Honey. We'll treasure it." He handed it back and leaned down to give her a hug. "My turn to have you all to myself. How about we go get some ice cream while it dries?"

"Oooh. I like ice cream. Can I have starberry? Auntie Dreedra knows it's my favorite."

Cosma stood on tiptoe and kissed Johnny's cheek. "You two go have fun while Dierdre and I help clear everything and load up after class."

"See you back at the ship in a couple hours." He took Mitzi's hand and led her chattering toward the gate path to the street.

Cosma folded chairs. "What's up? You don't look like your happy self."

Emptying the dirty-water cup in the grass, Dierdre crushed it with a vengeance. "I just found out Randy's been lying to me," she whispered. "I'm so upset I can't think straight." She turned the box right side up and stored Mitzi's paint box and brushes inside with the damp paintings on top of the trash.

"I'm so sorry." Cosma inclined her head to the gazebo. "Distract yourself with your sister for a moment. She's struggling today. Something's not right. We've got to get her back to the ship as soon as possible."

"I've never . . . given birth." Dierdre said. "You have and you sound worried. That scares me. Suze is terrified she might lose this baby too. Especially without Taylor here to lean on."

Even from a distance, they could see Suzanne slumped, seated on the gazebo steps with her camera in her lap, her swollen ankles bulging at the sandal straps.

"I'll go see what I can do." Dierdre carried the folded chairs to the ship's dolly parked nearby. She stacked them with others and took icy bottled water from the cooler.

"Hey, Sis." She handed the water to Suzanne. "I think you need this."

"I'm not feeling so good, Dee." Her twin removed her sandals. "I think I've walked around enough, coaching them on how to finish. They're getting a kick out of tourists stopping by to snap pictures and praise their work."

Dierdre sat next to her and put on a cheerful face. "You've done a great job making this outdoor painting experience a success. Makes me look savvy to the staff, too. Thanks for a job-security vote. By the time other guests view the display tonight, I wouldn't be surprised if you were invited to do this on another cruise."

Her twin didn't respond.

Dierdre stood and brought Suzanne's demo chair to the bottom of the steps. "Let's elevate your feet. I'll borrow your camera, take pictures, and spread the word if anyone needs your advice they'll have to bring their art boards to you."

"You're a life saver. I'm light-headed and nauseous. If Taylor were here he'd insist I go back to the ship and lie down."

"It won't be long now. Another half hour and we'll call a halt. Some have already packed up in time to join the Arboretum tour." Dierdre took the camera. "Drink the water, do your deep breathing, and I'll return as quickly as I can. Here comes Cosma to stay with you. Johnny's taken Mitzi for ice cream while we clean up after this group. I promised we'd leave the park as pristine as we found it."

It had taken a while, but eventually Dierdre had visited all the painters except Catherine, Hettie, and Megan. *I sucked up believing in you too. Betrayed me, you little witch.* She'd leave her until the last possible moment so she wouldn't show how much she'd like to pour a water jar over Megan's perfect hair and outfit.

Having glanced in the imposter's direction occasionally, she'd noticed Randy and Wes had left Megan and been talking on a shady bench for more than an hour. *I'd love to listen in on that conversation.*

Approaching Catherine and Hettie, she prepared the camera for a candid shot when she realized the women were arguing. Dierdre stepped behind the hibiscus shrubs to avoid interrupting something heated. The last thing she wanted to experience was more negative energy. She hadn't had a moment to come to terms with Randy and Megan's ruse. Trembling inside, Dierdre paused to decide what to do.

Hettie's hard-edged voice cut through the tropical air. "Of course I stole Arni's watch and made sure he got it back. How else was I going to look like the heroine so he'd notice me?"

"But you let that poor boy be treated like a common thief. He and his mother were terribly humiliated." Catherine's cultured voice sounded bewildered. "I simply can't understand you using people like that."

Dierdre listened with sudden avid interest, capping the camera lens and holding absolutely still.

"Oh, don't go all high and mighty self-righteous on me, Catherine. The kid'll get over it." Dierdre could hear Hettie ripping tape from her board. "I can clear his name if it comes to that."

"Hettie, is it wise to become involved with a man who would cruelly label someone a thief? Especially without a shred of proof. Why would you want such a man?"

"Oh grow up, Catherine. Arni's handsome, exciting, a great dresser, and a super-smart character. He gives me sparks. We're cut of the same devious cloth. He's intriguing and so adorable."

"You *must* keep this to yourself. I'm warning you for your own good. Wesley confided to me Arnold Bloomquist is probably a genuine crook. You could be making a terrible mistake."

Catherine's confidential whisper had been so much less strident than Hettie's, Dierdre had to strain to catch every word. Her mind reeled with the domino effect of what might be true about Arni, Wes, Randy, and Megan. If she could figure it out.

Hettie finished slamming lids on her paint box and clicking her water bottle shut. Her voice held such fake-sweet acid, Dierdre imagined a nasty smirk accompanied her reply and wished she could see through the shrubs.

"So what kind of a crook and how bad?" Hettie cackled a raucous laugh. "I'm a crook too. Didn't know that did you? But it's fun. I get off on the risk."

"Whatever do you mean?" Catherine's sweet voice had gone up a notch.

"I mean, my sweet goody-goody friend, crime is the spice of life. I'm a klepto and have been since I was a teenager. Swiping stuff gives me a high. Little stuff like a lipstick fits in my pocket. But a mink coat?"

She cackled a long rumble of shrieks. "Walking out of a fancy boutique in a $3,000 collection of stitched-together furry little skins—for free—well that's the bomb."

By her silence, Dierdre assumed Catherine was obviously struck as dumb as she was. Her own mouth had dropped open and she was sure her eyebrows reached her hairline. She put the camera strap over her shoulder before she dropped it in surprise at whatever else she was about to overhear.

There was a *kalump* noise of a folding chair collapsing. "Fortunately, you know good old Ralph left me with very, very deep pockets," Hettie continued. "So far, whenever I've been caught leaving with something or trying to return my rip-offs, I've been able to buy my way out of being arrested." Another shrieking cackle split the air.

"Of course there are some shops I can never return to, by orders of the management, but the thrill was worth it. There's always another opportunity for fun. That's why I love to travel."

"I'm shocked, Hettie. Reuniting with you at our class reunion after all these years I had no idea . . . traveling together, I never would h . . . Arnold being a criminal doesn't even make you nervous?"

"Nervous? He's a man after my own heart. Risk takers are like magnets to each other. He may think he has the hots for gorgeous Megan, but wait 'til Wes and the authorities tell him he's in trouble for whatever he's done. I'm going to look like Santa Claus. Only I get to be there on Christmas morning. You just wait and see."

Her heart outpacing her thoughts, Dierdre realized a lot more was going on with Randy and Wes than she'd imagined. *Is Randy really writing a novel or is that fake too? Maybe he's an undercover cop. That would explain faking blindness.*

She stepped around the hibiscus, uncapped the camera lens, and brought it to her eyes before adjusting the focus. Dierdre straightened, affecting a cruise director smile.

"Ladies, would you like me to photograph you with your finished paintings? I've already taken almost everyone else."

Catherine gaped, the art board propped on one hip. Her free hand shook above the taped painting of a lady walking under a sun umbrella. A jar, knocked over at her feet, dribbled gray water into the grass. Her naiveté appeared to have ebbed away with it.

Hettie held her wild painting of a strolling peacock under her chin and posed, grinning like a skunk with a shock of black and white fur on her head.

Dierdre knew the only way all mysteries would be cleared up was if she swallowed her pride and allowed Randy to do what he asked of her, let him explain. Even if their romance was crushed in the bud, her curiosity could be satisfied and their dignity restored.

She clicked the shutter. "Thank you, ladies. We'll be certain you get copies of these pictures before the cruise is finished. Don't forget, tonight your paintings will be on display outside the dining room. Great work, thanks for coming out to paint."

She nodded goodbye and walked down the cobbled path toward Megan.

Cutting across the grass closer than she'd like to the bench where Wes and Randy still sat in deep conversation, Dierdre neared Megan.

"Don't bother taking my picture." Megan busily replaced her capped paint tubes and rinsed brushes into her carrier.

"Oh, why not?" Recapping the camera lens, Dierdre wasn't about to simply walk away without any information and leave her with the last word.

"More important things are going on, if you haven't guessed by now." Megan's eyes met Dierdre's. They were disturbingly kind.

"I can't blame you for being upset with our deception. None of this is what you're thinking. It will all come out soon enough. I hope you'll give Randy the courtesy of an opportunity to explain."

She gathered her carrier and lifted her art board by the handle. "I may not be his daughter, but I am not his lady friend either, at least not romantically. The man's head-over-heels in love with you. This whole thing he's doing for me will break his heart if he loses you over it."

"Doing what for you?" Dierdre grasped for logic, genuinely puzzled.

"I can't explain now, but it will become clear before this cruise is over."

"Dierdre, Dierdre, come quickly." Cosma yelled to her from the gazebo. "Hurry, it's Suzanne!"

She turned to see her twin lying in the grass. Her heart nearly stopped.

"Oh, my God!"

She took off running, the camera bumping her chest. Everything blurred in her panic. She was barely aware out of the corner of her eye that Megan, Randy, and Wesley all ran toward her sister as she did.

* * *

Chapter Fifteen   *Secrets Old and New*

It took the boys a few minutes to rent pedal bikes, pay with Randy's money, and flip a coin to decide which way to go looking for Arnold.

Cloud rode in the lead down Hamilton's Front Street along the harbor businesses. "We saw him walk out of the park. He can't be far unless he caught a cab."

"What do we do if we find him and he goes inside somewhere?" Gregory pedaled close behind the brothers. There wasn't room to ride three across in the street busy with mopeds, taxis, and pink buses. Searching for Arnold made him feel like a real detective on a dangerous manhunt.

Stellar called over his shoulder. "I guess we hang around 'til he comes out."

"Or follow him inside if it's a place kids can go." Cloud's head moved from side to side, searching storefronts and alleyways between colorful pastel buildings.

"Hope we haven't lost him." Breathing hard in heavy tropical air so different than dry desert air, Gregory pedaled fast to keep up, his leather medicine pouch bouncing on his tee shirt. Glancing as far as he could ahead of them, he saw a businessman in slacks instead of Bermuda shorts, carrying an art bag. "Hey, I think he just came out of that yellow building."

"Hang back." Cloud pulled up to the curb and got off his bike. "The HSBC sign says it's a bank. Remember it guys. He must've gone there first. Randy will want to know."

Stellar walked his bike next to his brother. "It's him alright, hurrying and not heading back to the ship. He looks up a lot like he's reading signs, looking for a certain business maybe."

Gregory got off his bike and followed, trying to think like a detective. "Arnold doesn't have any shopping bags either. Just his art bag stuff."

"Follow him closer, Greg. In case he sees us he won't recognize you by yourself as fast as he does me with Stellar. Keep your sunglasses on." Cloud let Gregory move past him.

Hopping back on his bike, Gregory took off, excited with the adventure of doing something secret and important with his idols. "I'll signal if he goes in somewhere else."

His adrenalin pumping, Gregory no longer thought about the air. He pedaled fast enough to cover at least a block and rolled within ten feet of the fast-moving Arnold. Noticing his own reflection flicking by in store windows, Gregory didn't want the guy to realize he was being followed, so he kept a big space between them.

Arnold paused at a doorway and polished his shades on a handkerchief. He tucked them in his shirt pocket, smoothed his hair back, opened the door, and disappeared inside with his art bag. Gregory pedaled within a few feet of the entrance and stopped. He read

G-Trade Services Ltd., 129 Front Street on the sparkling window. He had no idea what kind of business it was, but the fancy lettering sure seemed important.

Looking back the way he'd come, he waved to his friends in the distance and pointed to the door. Cloud and Stellar pedaled fast to join him.

* * *

Her heart pulsing in her ears, Dierdre dropped to her knees next to her sister's outstretched body. "What happened? She didn't fall down the gazebo steps I hope."

Cosma cradled Suzanne's head and shoulders in her lap, fanning her with the floppy hat. "We were deciding which boxes to load first when she felt dizzy. Then her eyes rolled up in her head and she collapsed. I caught her before she hit the ground."

"Thank God you did," Dierdre said, her heart beating like a drum. "A fall might have spelled the end of this pregnancy." She took her sister's face in her hands, patting flushed cheeks. "Suze, wake up, honey. You're going to be fine."

Suzanne eyelids fluttered and she mumbled, "So dizzy. Should have finished Gregory's mural . . . he'll be disappointed." Her fingers pulled at her shirt.

Dierdre's anxiety grew. "Sis, you told me you finished his attic-bedroom mural before the cruise."

Cosma fanned harder. "She's confused, delirious."

"I'll take over from here." Wesley knelt at Suzanne's side and put his fingers to the sides of her throat. "Her pulse is thready. No time to waste."

Cosma protested, "Why are you . . . ?"

Dierdre moved aside to give him room. "It's okay, he's a doctor. How can we help, Wes?"

"She's dehydrated, needs fluids as soon as possible. Empty that dolly and we'll load her on it. It's too far to carry her out of the park, and we could injure her or the baby even if we tried. No time to wait for help to come this far inside the grounds." He checked her ankles and fingers. "Any of you have a way to call a taxi or an ambulance to meet us outside the gate?"

Randy and Dierdre chimed, "I have a pager." They looked at each other.

No dark glasses. His eyes are hazel, beautiful— and they work. Dierdre pulled herself together and pager in hand punched in numbers. Listening, her panic rose. "Dispatcher's line's busy." She watched Randy talking to a cab company.

Wes had his ear pressed to Suzanne's belly. "I'm quite certain she just needs her fluids restored. Sundancer's close, less than five minutes." He lifted his head. "Dierdre, does your clinic have IV capability?"

"Yes. Oxygen, defibrillator. The basics. I even told them to be prepared for my pregnant twin."

"Tell them we're bringing her in and to get an IV drip with potassium ready."

She coded in the ship doctor on her emergency list and contacted him.

Randy finished his taxi request and pocketed his pager. Cosma and Megan unloaded boxes and chairs from the dolly. Megan stacked them in the grass and moved her carrier and Randy's cane to create one central location for all their belongings. Wes and Randy lifted Suzanne onto the empty dolly. She babbled something about Taylor and Mitzi while they cushioned her head with her hat.

"She's semi-conscious and talking," said Wes. "That's a very good sign. With an IV she'll bounce back quickly."

Randy pushed the cart off the grass and onto the paving, bumping through the park with Wes hurrying along side. Dierdre and Cosma followed. Catherine, lugging her art supplies, hurried across the grass to join them.

Catching sight of Suzanne being wheeled down the gate path, visitors crowded around to see the drama. When the dolly passed under the Iron Gate, a cab whipped to the curb and stopped. The driver ran around and opened the rear door. Wes and Randy loaded Suzanne inside as gently as they could.

Randy supported Suzanne's legs while Dierdre slid in on one side of the back seat under them and unfastened the sandals.

He whispered, "She'll get through this alright. So will you." His lips brushed her cheek before he backed away.

Her heart squeezed and her face tingled. She couldn't meet his gaze for fear of falling apart and squelched all muddled feelings about him to focus on Suzanne.

"Dierdre, elevate her feet across your lap," ordered Wes. "Massage her ankles gently to dissipate the swelling. I'll ride up front. I can reach back to monitor her pulse from there."

Dierdre rolled down the window. "Cosma, if you and Megan reload the dolly I'll send staff to help you get everything back to the ship."

The taxi merged into the stream of mopeds and bicycles driven by smiling people Dierdre couldn't emotionally identify with. *Was I ever the kind of happy that actually lasted? This dreadful day has gone from bad to worse.* Her twin breathed shallowly, her swollen feet in Dierdre's lap. *Tonight is . . . was our birthday party. That's gone to heaven in a hand basket too.*

Suzanne' anklebones were nearly impossible to feel inside the soft, bloated tissue. Dierdre did her best to tenderly massage as Wes directed while she prayed for God to save Suzanne and her precious baby. She prayed for Taylor to be brave for his dad. If anything went wrong with her sister, no—she wouldn't put her worst fears into specific thoughts.

She begged God to forgive her for being irritated with Taylor's Pops for having a heart attack and ruining their birthday cruise. She prayed for herself to be brave and smart and helpful instead of a selfish pain in the ass. She prayed the same things over and over while the trees and buildings and people blurred outside the taxi window in a rainbow of color and movement. *Dear God, I simply can't lose her. Suze's all the family I have.*

They reached the Hamilton port and came to a stop. Dierdre breathed a sigh of relief knowing Wes would take over and help her sister. The ship's doctor met them at the gangway with a wheeled gurney and an assistant. In minutes babbling Suzanne was transferred aboard Sundancer and rolled to the medical clinic.

Dierdre paid the cabbie and hurried past concerned bystanders to catch up with her only blood relatives alive on the planet—her twin and the infant growing in her body.

* * *

Wes stripped off his jacket and threw it to Dierdre. He unfastened his cufflinks, stashed them in his slacks pocket with his rings, and rolled up his sleeves. At the basin he scrubbed his hands to his elbows and rinsed them under running water as hot as he could stand.

The ship's doctor came to the sink. "I'm told you're a licensed physician. Is that true? I'm responsible for what goes on in here. The guests are my patients. Policy . . . I'll need verification for. . ."

"Dr. Wesley LeChaminant is a practicing surgeon at the Las Vegas Surgical Center," Dierdre spoke from Suzanne's side. "We have his file on the ship roster."

Sundancer's doctor frowned but nodded, apparently accepting he'd have to endure the presence of another doctor in his space. Wes empathized with him. He wouldn't take kindly to a strange doctor walking into his operating theater in Vegas either.

The ship's doctor adjusted the drip speed on the IV tube trailing to Suzanne's hand. His assistant had swabbed antiseptic and taped the needle securely into place. The restorative liquid trickled into her vein.

Dierdre held the hand that didn't have the IV. "I'm here, Sis. You're going to be fine, just a little over-tired. Hang in there, Honey."

Her eyes swimming behind her closed lids—still mostly out of it—Suzanne mumbled Taylor's name and the word "baby" over and over. At least that's what Wes thought he heard.

Pulling on surgical gloves, he moved to the table where Suzanne had begun to breathe more normally. Her color had improved in a matter of minutes—a good sign.

He unbuttoned her blouse, exposing her swollen belly below her straining bra, its blue veins prominent in the powerful overhead light. "What's her blood type?"

"B negative, RH factor probably, same as mine." Dierdre answered.

"First pregnancy?"

"No," Dierdre stumbled for facts. "She miscarried her first a decade ago."

"Not necessarily bad but definitely not good. Has she been spotting?"

Dierdre nodded. "A little. Nausea too, but today she complained of feeling ill, clammy, light-headed—just different."

"Dehydrated. If she needs a transfusion, I assume you're willing. Matching B negative isn't always easy, and O from a universal donor may not be available without getting her to a hospital on the island. We'll know soon if it's going to be necessary."

"Do what you have to. I'm all for a hospital check up when she's in less danger."

Running a stethoscope over Suzanne's abdomen Wes moved an inch at a time, pausing to listen intently at each place on the rising and falling mound beneath his hands.

"A hospital visit may not be necessary if she comes around quickly, is coherent, and has no other complications."

He repeated the stethoscope process, wanting to be absolutely sure the fetal heartbeat was strong and the infant was in no distress.

Finally, sliding the instrument to the right lower quadrant of her belly, he settled it over an irregular shaped brownish birthmark the size of a fifty-cent piece. Sharply he sucked in his breath.

"What's wrong?" Dierdre asked. Her beautiful face, so like he remembered her mother's, etched with anxiety, like the long-ago face when he said he was transferring to med school at the Mayo Clinic hundreds of miles away.

"Nothing's very wrong with Suzanne, beyond more edema in her body and limbs than is healthy. And too much stress perhaps?" He swallowed, took a shaky breath, and unhooked the stethoscope from his ears. As casually as he could manage, he asked, "Do you have a birthmark like hers?"

"Sure. We're twin sisters. Not identical of course, but sisters born within minutes of each other." Her eyes pierced his. "Does that pose some kind of problem?"

"Not for you two, my dear."

Wes closed his eyes for a moment and took another shuddering breath. Opening them he regarded her thoughtfully before turning to the ship's doctor.

"The fetal heart beat is *quite* strong."

He began removing Suzanne's under clothing; fearful he'd find signs of hemorrhage. "I think it prudent to do a pelvic exam to see if she's effacing, which I doubt. We'd better be certain we don't have to rush her to a hospital and administer injections to stop premature labor."

Dierdre's face registered alarm.

Suzanne's feet were lifted into stirrups freeing her knees to part. "Without rest she could miscarry. I must insist on complete rest, absolutely no lifting, even after the cruise and flight home. You must convince her of my warning."

Wes looked away from Dierdre's eyes brimming with unshed tears, which tugged at his heart in ways he'd nearly forgotten. He removed Suzanne's panties, looking for fresh bleeding. Nothing unusual. Expertly his fingers explored her swollen vagina and cervix. He assessed everything normal. Humbled, he hadn't felt so relieved about a patient's wellbeing in a very long time. He nodded to the medical assistant.

"Put her legs down and replace her clothing and a light blanket. Keep up the IVs. She's not in danger of premature birth right now."

Suzanne's eyes fluttered open a few times and moments later remained open. She seemed to be trying to focus. "Dierdre? Oh, Sis, what . . . what happened?" Her face looked anxious. "My baby?" She stroked her belly with her unencumbered hand.

"You and baby are going to be just fine." Dierdre smoothed the hair back from her twin's forehead. "Rest now, sweetheart. We've all had a scare, but you've come through it beautifully."

"Am I in a hospital?"

"No, Honey. You're back on Sundancer in our clinic."

"The children?" Suzanne's eyes widened with concern.

"All accounted for and under supervision. All you have to do is rest."

Suzanne sighed deeply. "I am pretty tired. So nice to not be so dizzy. Okay if I take a nap?"

"Absolutely," Dierdre said. "Doctor's orders anyway."

Wes nodded to the assistant and handed over a small tray with a syringe. "Give her a little something to assure a good nap."

He removed his gloves and dropped them in the biohazard receptacle. Sighing with relief, Wes waited until Dierdre stepped away from the bed before taking her shoulders in his hands.

"By late afternoon she should be wide awake, rested, and talking with more energy. At that point I think we can move her back to her cabin if you'll stay with her tonight. Suzanne and your infant niece or nephew are going to be fine as long as she takes it easy from here on to full-term delivery."

"Thank God for that." Dierdre's shoulders relaxed. Meeting his steady gaze she whispered, "Wes, I'm so glad you gave up your secret about being a doctor to help my sister. . . and me. We'll be forever grateful you took charge in this emergency. Taylor will be grateful too."

"My dear Dierdre. It won't be the last time I help you twins, I assure you."

He was amused with the way her face and the knit of her eyebrows expressed confusion. She didn't understand in the least his light banter or the broad grin on his face at this critical time with her twin.

Dr. Wesley LeChaminant anticipated divulging a secret bigger than being a medical doctor. He'd decide when the time was right to let the cat out of the bag. A cat he hadn't even known about until moments ago. *Many bittersweet Ingram mysteries solved, at last.*

He wondered how his precious Catherine would take more changes in their lives than either of them had imagined while dreaming of their future at breakfast that morning.

Finished signing the official responsibility and disclaimer forms Sundancer's doctor insisted he fill out,

Wes hugged Dierdre's shoulder. "I'll check on you two in an hour or so. If she's awake again by then a catheter won't be necessary to relieve pressure on her bladder and the baby."

Nearly bursting with his secret, he hurried away to find Catherine.

* * *

Chapter Sixteen   *Worries and Surprises*

Dierdre pulled a chair over to the clinic bed where she could hold her sister's hand. Watching healthy color return to Suzanne's cheeks, Dierdre's anxiety evaporated in gratitude. Several of her prayers had been answered, thanks to Dr. Wesley LeChaminant. *How strange life is. Who would have thought . . .*

Gregory appeared at the clinic door, his face flushed and his spikey hair sweaty. His eyes opened wide. "What's wrong with Mom? Why's she got a needle in her hand?"

Dierdre released Suzanne's fingers and stood, opening her arms to her nephew.

"Come here, Sweetheart. Your mother's going to be fine. Once the sedative wears off, she'll be awake talking to us and back to your cabin."

Pulling away from her, Gregory stepped to Suzanne. "She's just sleeping, right? I mean she's not hurting or going to die or anything—is she?"

"No, Honey. She's resting while the doctor's IV solution restores her chemical balance. You don't have to worry. She's going to be fine."

"I've got to be sure." He pulled the leather cord at his neck over his hair. "Lift her head so I can give her my medicine pouch to protect her and the baby."

Dierdre's throat tightened with tender emotion. "Your mother told me Cloud made it just for you. Are you sure you want to be without it for yourself?"

He nodded so hard his hair fell into his eyes. "She almost got killed saving me last year. Taylor told me I had to be the man while he's gone. It's my turn to make sure she and the baby are safe from anything bad happening."

Tears rolled down his sunburned cheeks. "I hate being a kid. I don't know how to make her better. I couldn't stop Dad's cancer or my mother from getting killed. Suzanne's . . ." He snuffled. "My Mom's got to be okay."

"Your necklace will be perfect. What a thoughtful boy you are." She held Suzanne's head above the pillow while he put the medicine-pouch thong over his sleeping mother's hair and settled it onto her chest. Together they replaced the pillow under Suzanne's lolling head.

Dierdre hugged him close and didn't let go until he squirmed free.

"Who told you your mother was taken to Sundancer's clinic?" Dierdre asked, smiling at his independent spirit.

"Randy and Cosma. After us guys returned the bikes, we all crammed into two cabs and got here pretty fast. They're putting Mom's art stuff away, then they'll come check on her too."

"You got here first. I'm proud of you." Dierdre wished Suzanne could see the fierce love her stepson had for her.

"I didn't wait for the elevators," Gregory said, wiping his tears into dirty streaks. "I just ran down all the steps so maybe I could save her."

"My darling nephew, I'm sure your medicine pouch will make her well." *Your love alone is powerful enough to save any of us. My Sis is one lucky woman.*

* * *

Dierdre pushed a kitchen cart stacked with a dozen watercolor paintings layered between sheets of butcher paper. At the end of the corridor, she and Cosma arrived at the mezzanine lounge outside the main dining room. It overlooked the open stairway where groups of chatting guests came and went.

"Terrific," Dierdre said. "The staff delivered the easels so all we have to do is set up the display and report oohs and ahhs to Suzanne. We'll collect the paintings after second dinner seating."

A few guests stopped to watch what they were doing. Cosma carried several matted, unframed watercolors while Dierdre positioned the easels and clipped the art into place on each one. "Suzanne so wanted to arrange this exhibit herself."

Dierdre rolled the butcher papers and secured them with a rubber band. "Yes, but she's relieved she's come through her scare and is safely back in her cabin. Let's go pick up the cake and party things."

Cosma's dark eyes met hers. "Do you think your sister's up to a birthday party?"

"She said we need to go through with it for the kids more than for us twins. 'Just let me kick back on the bed while everybody celebrates,' was her suggestion, since we've had to scuttle the banquet-room plans. So that's what we'll do. Keep it simple."

They surveyed their display handiwork. Cosma touched her shoulder. "A lot of plans have had to change. How about you and Randy? Cleared the air yet?"

Dierdre shook her head no. "I suppose we're both wondering who should make the first move. I'll be forever grateful he helped with Suzanne. Thanking him is easy. If only I understood what all the secrecy is about. It's hard to trust him. What to do about my heart is the tough part."

A few minutes later on a lower deck, Suzanne's cabin door stood ajar. Soft voices and giggles drifted into the hall.

Cosma rolled the pastry cart inside so Johnny could make room for it at the end of the bed.

"They're here," squealed Mitzi, "Oooh, look at the pretty birthday cake, Mommy. It's got your favorite daisies all over it."

Dierdre followed, her arms laden with a yellow box tied with blue ribbons, her twin's favorite colors. She held paper Happy birthday crowns and set the box on the bed. "Come get your party hats on."

Mitzi popped in line first, except no one leaped in behind her.

"Do I have to?" Stellar groaned.

"Just for pictures," Dierdre said. "Then you can take them off."

"Where's your mom's camera?" Cloud asked Gregort, trying on a crown at a rakish angle in front of the mirror, his long black hair poking out the holes.

Dierdre gave the box to Suzanne. "Happy birthday, Sis. Want help opening it?"

Suzanne grinned. "Let's do it together."

Cosma gave them scissors and held out her hands for the wrapping paper.

"A linen-bound photo album and one of those fancy new digital Polaroid cameras!" Suzanne removed the instant camera from the molded Styrofoam box. "Did you think turning thirty means it's time to record our wrinkles and keep them for posterity?"

Their laughter was interrupted by a rapping on the doorframe. "Flowers for Suzanne Price and Dierdre Ingram," said the deliveryman.

"Wow. That's enough flowers to cover a float." Stellar backed to the porthole window to make room.

Suzanne craned her neck. "I wonder who . . . Taylor?"

The man placed two vases of long-stemmed pink roses on the vanity. Dierdre handed him a ten-dollar bill and he departed. She examined the matching gift tags and read aloud: "Happy Birthday to the loveliest twins on board. Best wishes, Randy."

Cosma hugged her. "You have two more reasons to thank the secretive man."

Dierdre's longing for Randy deepened but she didn't dare think about it until alone in her own cabin.

"Help me put the candles on," she said to Gregory. "This party has to be the quickest one in history. Doctor's orders."

"Which doctor?" Suzanne chuckled. "You said Mr. LeChaminant's secret career is medical. Did he give the order?"

"Yes, he did." Dierdre lit the thirty candles. "Help Suzanne and me blow these flames out before the automatic sprinklers activate."

Laughing, Cosma cut slices for everyone, Johnny poured punch, and Dierdre scooped ice cream onto paper plates. The party was in full swing when Wesley and Catherine squeezed into the room.

"We dropped by to wish you twins Happy Birthday and to make a few announcements."

"Thank you, Wes," the twins chimed.

"Announce away." Dierdre handed them each a plate of party food, which they declined.

One arm around Catherine, Wesley said, "You're all invited to our wedding as soon as arrangements are finalized. I'll cover travel expenses to Vegas—after baby-birth time."

"That's very generous," said Johnny, "but . . ."

"No buts," Wes interrupted. "I'm the patriarch here."

"I'll be part of your family, too." Catherine winked and looked fondly at Wes.

"I don't understand." Suzanne's brow furrowed, as she handed her plate of half-eaten cake to Gregory. She fingered the medicine pouch at her throat.

Wes chuckled. "I'm as surprised as anyone." He lifted Suzanne's hand, reached for Dierdre's and brought them together.

"My family birthmark perfectly matches the ones you twins have on your abdomens. Same size, shape, color, and location as my own. I'm the grandfather of that baby you're carrying."

"You're—you're our *father*?" Dierdre pulled her hand away. "Oh my God! That's quite an announcement." She met Suzanne's look of stunned surprise with one of her own. "So much for our virgin-birth fantasy." She giggled.

"Well, my darling daughters, there's just one more thing." He kissed Suzanne's fingers and replaced her hand on the blanket.

"You and that son-in-law of mine need to come up with more names. You're carrying my twin grandbabies."

* * *

Suzanne's head buzzed and her insides quivered with fatigue. "Twins? It's difficult to believe. Wait 'til I tell Taylor our news. Wish I could be there to see his face. Some birthday surprise."

When the hubbub subsided, Wesley spoke in a professional tone. "This is more than enough excitement for one expectant mother. What's the plan on clearing this cabin so Suzanne can rest?"

Johnny stood. "Okay boys, the overnight's a guy thing starting now. Video games and my place for snacks before bunking out. My bride-to-be is staying here with Dierdre and Suzanne tonight."

"And me, don't forget me." Mitzi patted her crown.

"We're set here, Wes," Dierdre mumbled. "I still can't believe we finally know we have a real dad—and he's *you*."

He kissed her forehead. "Good night, dear one. Take good care of your sister." His hand at Catherine's waist, he said, "Let's go have dinner with champagne, darling. I'm still adjusting to being a father, let alone a grandfather of this burgeoning brood."

"I'm getting used to the idea of an instant family myself after saying yes to becoming your wife." Catherine hugged Dierdre and patted Mitzi's curls.

Wes guided her out the door behind Johnny and the boys, who chattered about the idea of a grandpa that wasn't Pops and a new grandmother too.

Suzanne caught Dierdre's eye. "To think you were considering our father for . . ."

Dierdre put a finger to her lips and pointed to her niece. "Some other time."

Mitzi crawled up next to Suzanne. "Can I stay with you?" She snuggled against her mommy's tummy. "There's really two babies in there?"

"Um hum. Now we girls have tomorrow's wedding plans to discuss after I have a little nap." Suzanne sighed, closing her eyes. "How about you rest with me?"

Cosma rose to close the door but Megan walked in. "I'll only be a moment. Happy birthday you twins. Dierdre, could you step into the hall with me?"

In the corridor, Dierdre closed the door behind them. "Thank you, Megan for all you and Randy did in the park for Suzanne this morning. We couldn't have gotten her to the clinic so quickly without you both swinging into action like you did."

"You're more than welcome." When a few people passed by, Megan's voice dropped to a whisper, "I have to tell you why Randy's pretending to be a blind man. I hired him to catch that thieving Arnold Bloomquist and get my mother's money back. He swindled her out of hundred's of thousands. She's not only embarrassed; she's devastated. With her bad heart, I fear this mess could bring on a fatal attack."

She took a deep breath and rushed on. "Randy's an old family friend. My late father and his dad were business partners. When mother was widowed, Arnold had weaseled his way into their country-club social circle and took advantage of her vulnerability. I've been working in Europe and didn't figure out what he'd done until a few months ago. I called Randy and without hesitation he agreed to help. We thought up the disguise so he'd appear dependent upon me, his phony daughter. We could coordinate our efforts to catch Arnold doing something shady."

Dierdre chuckled "With you as the wealthy and beautiful decoy."

Megan nodded. "Please believe he doesn't want to lose you over my family's problems." She grasped Dierdre's hands.

"Give him a chance to put Bloomquist behind bars where he belongs. Then he'll be free to be himself. He's absolutely crazy in love with you."

* * *

Pulled along the corridor as if by a magnet, Dierdre slipped into the Lido lounge and paused just inside the doorway. Easy conversation and laughter, the tinkle of barware, and Caribbean marimba music swirled around her.

She put a hand to her hammering heart for courage while she scanned the crowded tables for Randy. Seated by himself at the end of the bar, he faced her. His eyes behind dark glasses, Dierdre knew he watched her from across the room. She tried to read his inscrutable face, gave up, and walked between guest tables to reach his side.

Wishing she could crush him to herself in a passionate embrace, she squelched the urge, keeping in mind the guests knew her as professional Sundancer Cruise Director. Also, she couldn't be absolutely certain Randy had forgiven her initial betrayed reaction when she learned he'd lied to her. At least until she apologized.

"Thank you for the birthday flowers, Randy. I, *we* appreciate your extravagant thoughtfulness. Two bouquets of long-stemmed roses must have cost a bomb."

"My pleasure," he said. "I would have delivered them personally, but I wasn't sure I'd be welcome. Figured you twins would each want your own flowers in your separate cabins." He grinned and patted the empty stool next to him. "Sit, please."

She hiked herself onto the seat and balanced facing him. "Megan explained your persona and why. I'm sorry I jumped to conclusions and treated you badly in the park. You were our hero in getting Suzanne here quickly. I can't thank you enough."

He chuckled and set his drink on the bar. "I'll help you thank me." He leaned close, his voice husky, "Let's get out of here."

"So we can be friends again?" She laughed with relief.

Randy stood, and she slid off the stool at his side. His arm circled her waist. "We can surely do better than that, my sweet." He handed her his cane. "I'll tell you where to go if you'll navigate to my cabin. I'm not permitted on your staff corridor, and I can't wait a minute longer for a make-up kiss with you in private."

Dierdre thrilled to his nearness and the anticipation of the freedom to share an intimate kiss— for starters. Their bodies brushed one another in the corridor, on the stairs, and along the cabin hallway until she was dizzy with desire to touch and be touched.

In his cabin, Randy switched on the bedside lamp and closed the door, pinning her against it with his hands on her shoulders and his hips pressed to hers. She couldn't escape had it crossed her mind to try. Their hearts pounded against their clothing. Breathing like freight trains careening toward each other down a single pair of tracks, their mouths sought each other hungrily, parting lips, mingling tongues.

Randy pulled his face away for a moment.

"Take them off," he whispered the command.

"Your shorts?"

He laughed. "No, Dierdre. These damn glasses."

She lifted them away from his face and tossed them on the bed. "I've been wanting to do that all week."

"Toss something on my bed?"

"Oh shut up." Her lips parted and met his kiss. Their tongues mingled and set her on fire.

He walked her backwards to the bed. "Better move the glasses so we don't break them. The charade's not over 'til Bloomquist is nailed."

"Mmh," she murmured. "You have amazing eyes. I'm trying to get used to knowing they see me."

"Sometime very very soon, when you don't have to work a cruise for a living, they want to see every inch of your lovely body."

* * *

Even with the dream catcher hanging above his bunk, and the cruise ship sailing out on the ocean where everything was quiet except for the thrum of the engines, Gregory couldn't quit thinking scary stuff about his family and go to sleep. His wide-awake dreams were almost as bad as his old nightmares. Just a different kind of scary. The all-day all-night worry was getting worse. He'd loaned his mom his medicine pouch to keep her and the baby safe, for sure until they were back home in Utah and Taylor could take over. But now it turned out there were two babies growing inside her. *Will my Indian medicine be powerful enough to keep a grown up and two babies safe?*

But that wasn't really as big a worry as the other one whirling in his head.

His Aunt Dierdre tiptoed across the room from the other bed and shook his shoulder gently. She whispered, "Are you still awake like I am?"

"Yes." He rolled over and finally found her face in the dim light.

"I have an idea," she went on. "Climb down and we'll share a secret while your mom, Cosma, and Mitzi are sleep."

Moments later with a sweatshirt over his pajamas, he took his Aunt Dierdre's hand and walked with her down the corridor to the elevator. While they rode up several decks, she said, "You mustn't tell what we do to Mitzi or your friends. They'll think I wasn't fair to only take you with me tonight. Do you understand?"

Gregory nodded. "What's the secret thing we're going to do?" He was just a little bit nervous and hoped it wasn't anything he didn't know how to do, like being a ring bearer in somebody's wedding.

"It's midnight," she said, when the elevator doors opened. "There's a buffet on the main deck and you can have anything you want to eat."

"Even if I want a cheeseburger with ice cream?"

"You've got the idea. Once your stomach's full you'll probably be able to sleep."

With a cheeseburger and fries on his plate, Gregory sat down at a table across from her. "I'm going to wait 'til I eat this stuff before I go for a banana split."

"Good," she said. "Then it won't be a puddle of cream with a floating banana before you get to it." She sipped a glass of iced tea and bit off the chocolate ends of a couple of strawberries.

"You must not be as hungry as I am." He chomped into his burger.

"I'm not growing like you are. At my age the only way you grow is rounder and rounder."

He laughed a muffled chuckle so he wouldn't choke before he swallowed.

"I wanted time to listen to what's been bothering you, Gregory. Remember how we talked about some tough things last year? I think you trust me to keep your secrets, don't you?"

Uh oh. He put his sandwich back on the plate without taking a second bite. "Do I *have* to tell?"

"Don't you think sharing what worries you would make it get smaller, maybe even disappear if you let me help you?" She munched her last chocolate-dipped strawberry and dabbed at her mouth with a napkin. Her smile made him feel braver.

"Have another bite before your food is cold. When you start filling up you can rest and tell me."

Half way through his sandwich Gregory began to talk and once he started he couldn't seem to stop— until he got to the scariest part. He took a big breath.

"I'm not Suzanne and Taylor's real kid, you know, like by blood. I'm not cute like Mitzi either. What if Mom and Dad won't love me as much or need me any more when the baby comes? Now there's even two of them and they'll be babies by blood, not just step kids like me and Mitzi."

His eyes blurred with unshed tears. "I'm scared I won't be good enough to be their son any more. If they don't want me, where will I go?"

His Aunt Dierdre handed him a Kleenex from her pocket. He blew and wiped his nose. She reached across the table and took one of his hands in hers.

"I was afraid you might think their love for you could go away. Your parents have been through a lot to make you feel safe and loved. They love you alright."

She let go of his hand and smiled the kind of smile when people care about you a whole lot. "Love multiplies, you know. Every time you add somebody, you get some more."

Gregory thought about what she said while he finished most of his burger and a few fries. Suddenly he felt better and really tired.

"Can we go back now? I'm awful sleepy. I don't have room for a banana split any more."

He liked that nobody could see him holding her hand all the way to his cabin.

* * *

The next morning while his mom and Mitzi took their showers, out on deck Cosma patted her drum softly with the flat of her hand. Gregory was less tired so the steady rhythm didn't make him sleepy like it did at nighttime. He didn't want to miss a word of the story she was about to tell. Cosma's Indian stories always made him feel better.

Her drumming made some people stop by and stand close to listen.

She began. "Once there was a grandfather who wanted to teach his grandson a lesson from the Good Red Road, so he could grow up to be a wise leader of his people.

'There are two wolves inside you and they are having a battle,' grandfather said.

'Tell me about them,' said the boy, and the grandfather did. 'One of the wolves was kind, fair, and cared about other people in his village as much as about what he wanted for himself. The other wolf was greedy, sneaky, and mean to everybody. Each wolf wanted to be the boss of the boy. The two wolves fought all the time until the boy was worn out with the war on his insides."

The drumming grew louder and stronger like a battle going on around and inside them too. Gregory,

Cloud, and Stellar looked at each other while they waited for her to finish the tale. The drumming stopped. Cosma was as silent as her drum.

The passengers that had stopped to listen looked at each other and some shrugged their shoulders.

Stellar said, "But Mother, which wolf won?"

"That's exactly what the little boy in the legend asked," she said. "Grandfather told the boy the wolf he fed the most would be the winner."

Cloud rubbed his chin. "So I guess it means if you think and act kind to your family and other people you feed the good wolf."

"And if you are greedy and mean you are feeding the bad wolf," said Stellar.

Cosma looked at Gregory. "What do you think the story means?"

He thought for a moment. "I think when Bo was a little kid he started feeding the worst wolf. He must have done sneaky mean stuff like being a bully until he grew into a mean grown-up, a criminal even."

"Our brother Bold Heart is very wise," said Cloud, patting Gregory's shoulder.

Passengers walked away nodding and smiling, talking to each other about the story. Gregory's fears were down to one. *What do I have to do to be a ring bearer in the wedding this afternoon, since Stellar backed out yesterday?*

* * *

Having sent Catherine off with his credit and ship cards to go shopping for a new wedding outfit, Wes cornered Dierdre in the corridor after breakfast.

"Please, may I have a moment alone with you?"

She fell into step with him. "Is there some sort of problem with Suzanne I should be aware of?"

"No, not at all, my dear." He pulled her toward an empty sofa near the window overlooking the sparkling pool. It was crowded with families having splash wars. He was grateful they were in a quieter place.

"Hear me out and feel free to explain what I'm about to say to Suzanne when you're alone together. I wasn't sure she'd be up to such a serious conversation right now. I think you both ought to know."

Dierdre lowered herself next to him on the sofa. "Now I *am* worried."

"Don't be. I simply want to set some things straight about your mother without Catherine around to be hurt."

"I'm listening."

Wes ran his hands through his hair and looked at her a long moment before speaking.

"A few months before I met Marissa, Catherine broke our engagement. I was destroyed. To put her out of my mind, I went to the shore for a few weeks of surfing fun with some buddies. I met the most gorgeous woman I've ever known, Marissa Ingram. You are so like her. All of us fell for her to one degree or another. Your mother and I were like lightening together. She knew I was broken-hearted and did her best to make the summer fun, for me and for all of us.

"She chose me to actually date. One night after a sea-side dinner dance, our passion got the best of us—we became intimate."

Dierdre swallowed, not really wanting to hear more. "That's putting it discreetly, Wes. You don't have to go into the details."

He laid a hand over hers. "Yes, but I do. Marissa deserves to have her reputation preserved with her daughters, our daughters."

"I'm still listening."

"As an almost-doctor, I should have had protection on hand."

"Or she should have . . ."

"She said she had a diaphragm, but she didn't. We were only intimate that once, though we continued to swim and date for weeks afterward. I think we were falling in love with each other, but I had my medical career to pursue. I didn't see her again after I returned to the Mayo Clinic. I wrote to her, but she never answered, so I quit writing. I had no Idea she was expecting a baby. She knew I was facing my plastic surgery practical exams at Mayo and I think she didn't want to distract me. Perhaps she even hoped I'd show up on her doorstep and want to pick up where we left off, even marry her."

"How tragic. Mom must have really loved you because she never even dated anyone seriously. She just focused on us twins."

"You can only imagine my shock at discovering I have children I never knew about. I was overcome with guilt and joy in a crazy mix."

"I'm amazed she didn't write to you." Dierdre had a puzzled expression.

"Perhaps she did. Because Catherine's letters begging my forgiveness and asking me to reconsider our engagement never reached me either. You see, I gave both women my home address with my parents while I was in med school and the Army.

My mother intercepted all those letters. Catherine tells me it was my mother who pressed her to return my ring and break our engagement in the first place. Since Catherine wouldn't give up her own university scholarship to marry me and be with me in med school, Mother altered the course of my life to suit her own dreams for me. All this I've learned since reuniting with Catherine. My Mother slipped off the pedestal I've had her on all my life. It's by the grace of God you daughters and my first sweetheart have been restored to me. I deeply regret not being able to apologize to Marissa. I hope you twins will let me try to make it up to her and to you."

Dierdre leaned back into the cushions and shook her head, her gaze never leaving his face. "I have new admiration for my mother. Anything else I should tell Suzanne?"

Wes grinned. "I guess you could let her know you two have a half-brother Leland."

* * *

Chapter Seventeen   *Chickens Roost at Home*

After pacing the floor of his cabin for more than ten minutes, Wes willed himself to stop consulting his watch and sit facing the closed door to Arnold Bloomquist's adjoining suite. For the second time that day, he removed his cufflinks and rolled his sleeves to his elbows. It had already been an emotional roller coaster of a draining day, but one more vital matter remained to be addressed before he could even consider relaxing. Too agitated to stay seated, he rose and filled a glass with ice water, then returned to the chair. He sipped, letting the liquid cool his throat and calm his nerves, as was his ritual prior to a challenging surgical procedure. He breathed deeply, releasing each breath with a slow whoosh, wishing he could calm his spinning thoughts as effectively.

How could I have been so gullible as to trust that smooth-talking wolf in sheep's clothing? He nearly succeeded in ripping off a healthy chunk of my investments. My blood boils at myself as well as him. It's going to be a great pleasure to confront Arnold Bloomquist with what I put a stop to this morning, thanks to Randolph's warning tip.

A muffled tap on the inner door brought Wes to his feet. He crossed the carpet in three strides and opened to Arnold. "You're late." His tone was crisp and he didn't care he might be giving himself away too soon. "Come in."

"Sorry I'm late, Wes." The swindler carried two icy tumblers. "I took a moment to pour us a couple of double scotches on the rocks. Had to knock with an elbow."

"Take a seat. You may want to drink them both yourself by the time we finish our business." He chuckled to himself and gestured to the small table where his cufflinks rested, not waiting for Arnold to sit first. *The worm doesn't deserve gentlemanly courtesies.*

Arnold's hands shook almost imperceptibly, but a few telltale drops of scotch dribbled down the sides of both tumblers.

He's more uptight than I am. Good. So much the better.

Wes was pleased his about-to-be-fired financial advisor was obviously uncomfortable and out of his depth. He waited to hear what the buffoon would say to begin their meeting, studying his every nuance of character as he would one of his less-than-forthright patients when discussing their desires for unnecessary repeated cosmetic surgery.

Arnold took a considerable swig of his scotch and set the tumbler down. He cleared his throat and adjusted his tortoise-shell rims. "In the park today you said, and I quote, 'I'm on to you Bloomquist. I suggest you make things right while you can.'" He picked an invisible speck from his shirt. "What exactly were you referring to, Wesley? We're business partners, aren't we?" His voice squeaked on the word *partners*.

With tremendous effort, Wes bit an irrepressible smile into a thin, sober line on what he hoped was his inscrutable face. Parting his lips, he spoke like he might explain the direst of medical prognoses. "I contacted my breast-implant corporation to check on my shares of stock this morning."

He eyed Arnold coldly and was rewarded with beads of perspiration forming at the louse's temples. "Someone 'from my organization' attempted to move $350,000 of my investment into a subsidiary fund which I did not know about nor authorize. I wonder who that someone could have been?"

Arnold downed half the amber scotch in the first glass. "I'm sure I have no idea. Perhaps you're being scammed. We'll have to . . . investigate. Was there a name?" he asked innocently, casually shrugging his shoulders and fingering the band of his Rolex.

"You're a brassy son of a bitch, I'll give you that for balls." Wes chuckled. "My organization be damned. I froze that one and all the rest of my accounts so the *someone* couldn't be so free with any of my money, correct stolen account-code numbers provided or not."

Arnold straightened in his chair and pushed the second scotch in Wes's direction.

"If you're insinuating I had anything to do with adjusting your accounts, you're out of your mind. We're just starting our arrangements with me brokering for you. I wouldn't do such a thing." He began to nurse the last of the drink.

"Oh, but I have it on the strictest confidence you have indeed done so before—successfully swindling hundreds of thousands from a trusting and vulnerable elderly widow." Wes looked at his watch and counted with the second hand, holding his breath.

The corridor door opened and Randolph entered—exactly as planned. He handed the room key to Wes who let out a sigh of satisfaction and didn't even turn his head. He was too busy enjoying the look of astonishment on Arnold's face and the scotch leaking from his gaping lips down his expensive rumpled shirtfront where it pooled on his slight paunch.

Randy tucked his sunglasses into his jacket pocket, closed the door and propped his unnecessary cane in the wastebasket by the writing desk, glad to be rid of it. He walked to the table and stood looking down at the miserable excuse for humankind. Drilling him with a withering stare, he said, "Hello, Bloomquist. I've looked forward to this moment for three months."

Arnold sopped at his shirt with his handkerchief, his skin reddening from collar to his brow. He didn't look up, hoarsely whispering, "So, you're not blind after all."

"Not as blind as I was to trust you," said Wesley. "Lucky for me, Randolph here was on board to warn me what a skunk you are before you compromised my accounts and sapped them."

Arnold fidgeted with a jerky index finger swirling ice cubes in his near empty glass. "I don't know what you two are up to with your accusations, but I'll sue you for defamation of . . ."

Randy laughed. "As if you had redeemable character to defend. If there's any suing to be done, it won't be by you." He leaned on the edge of the chest of drawers. "Megan tells me you attempted several times this week to talk her into letting you handle her financial affairs." He smirked. "You had plans to handle them right into your own pocket."

Shoving the glassware to the center of the table, Arnold pushed back his chair and stood. "You can't blame me for offering to financially act on behalf of a beautiful young woman. I certainly had no intention of defrauding your daughter."

Randy leaned forward and shoved Arnold's soggy shirtfront so hard he landed back in his chair. "Sit down you scamming bastard."

Arnold's face went pale. Twitches flickered across his right eyelid. "Who the hell do you think you are, you faker?" His eyes narrowed and he sat forward. "You some kind of private investigator?"

"Let's just say I'm a not-to-be-messed-with family friend. I'm here to wrench out of your hide every dime of Megan's mother's estate you swindled and see you turned over to the SCC's fraud division for securities and affinity fraud." Randy stabbed Arni's sagging shirtfront with an index finger. "You're going to go to prison for a long time."

"Megan's . . . mother?"

Wesley slid his loafers off and flexed his toes.

"Didn't you tell me, Randolph, Megan's mother

lost $750,000 to our fine, upstanding inebriated friend here?"

"I do believe that's the figure I've been quoted," Randy said. He winked at Wes.

"Now how do we get this piece of shit to cough up that kind of money before we turn him over to the authorities? We'd hate to lose our opportunity to square things—financially—before the judges get involved, wouldn't we? Court proceedings can drag on so long. Compensation delays would be too much for Megan's mother."

Arnold squirmed, dabbing his sweaty face with his stained handkerchief. "It will take me a while, but I'll get it somehow . . . if you give me time. No need to get legal authorities involved."

Randy moved quickly and squatted next to Arnold's chair. He looked from Wesley to the twit on his eye-level. "Your ass is grass. You see, Arni old boy, that's just what we don't have—unspecified time for you to scrape your shekels together. Megan's mother is unwell. She needs those big bucks to keep from losing the family home on that golf course you weaseled your way into joining, so you could run your Ponzi scheme on members of her country club."

"You guys have got to give me time . . . I have some foreign accounts I can draw from." Arnold pulled a pen and pad from his pockets and nervously flipped to a clean page. "I can estimate some figures . . ."

Randy cut him off. "Yes, you spent half an hour at the Trade Corp. this morning." He practically spit the words in Arni's face. "Any luck moving somebody else's money around?"

"How'd you know I went there?" Arnold choked. "You having me tailed?"

Randy smiled and stood. "You could say that. I guess you struck out at the ATM too. You weren't there nearly as long."

Tears formed at Arnold's white-lashed lids and began to course down his tanned cheeks to his jowls. "God almighty," he mumbled, "I'm in some deep shit."

There was a sharp rapping on the corridor door. Randy expected it might be Megan come to share in a bit of personal satisfaction at Arnold Bloomquist's demise.

Wes went to answer it, opening the door. He stepped back in surprise and alarm.

"Hettie? Is there something important you need? Catherine's okay, I trust."

Randy was dumbfounded to recognize the skunk-haired traveling companion of Wesley's fiancée.

Damn. Just what we don't need is some witchy woman throwing a wrench in the works when we're turning the screws on this swindling SOB. What in hell is she doing here?

Immeasurably irritated by the interruption to their confrontational meeting, Randy was surprised by Hettie's confident attitude. He wondered how Wes would get rid of her so they could get on with putting the screws to the schemer at the table.

Hettie pushed her way in, shutting the door behind her with a hip thump.

Brassy broad. What's she up to?

She smiled at Wes, whose hand still rested on the inside doorknob. She actually fluttered her fake lashes almost under his nose. "Catherine confided I should be careful not to trust Arni." She inclined her head toward the fidgeting scammer.

"Since I've watched you and Randy often talking the last couple of days, I assume he's in trouble and you . . ."

She has the gall to stare at me and grin.

Shrieking with laughter like a cartoon witch, Hettie shifted her shoulder bag, set it on the bed and continued. "No dark glasses? You're not a blind dude after all. A police detective or a government agent?" She stopped in front of Randy at Bloomquist's elbow.

"PI," Randy said, comfortable with the fib.

She smiled at each of them in turn, her eyes flashing with amusement.

Wes broke the awkward silence from where he stood, dumbfounded, by the door. "Why are you here, Hettie?"

She giggled like a teenager. "I came to offer my help to darling Arni."

"In regard to what?" Wes insisted.

She waved her flashy nails toward the rat in the chair and turned on a seductive voice. "Why to rescue my darling Arni out of the sticky little mess he's gotten himself into, of course."

Bloomquist erupted in a harrumph. "I am definitely *not* your darling," adding in a rush, "However nice a woman you are, this is men's business. Better be on your way."

"You see, darling," she giggled and rambled on. "I'm terribly afraid you'll be on *your* way—to prison— if you don't hear me out."

"What the hell?" Arnold reached for the second scotch. His eyes beseeched hers and his hand shook when he slid the tumbler closer to himself.

Wes left the closed door and returned to his chair. He looked at Randy and lifted his hands in a futile question.

Staying where he was at Arnold's side, Randy had the odd sensation of being in the middle of a hokey movie or on the stage of a questionable off-Broadway play. He had no idea how it the whole scene was going to play out but it was a fascinating culmination to months of research into Bloomquist's financial affairs by he and Megan. He wished she were here to witness what was coming down.

"There's nothing *little* about the sticky mess this rotten scammer created. It's a big one," Randy said.

"He's been ripping off other people's money," Wes added.

Hettie cackled. "As I suspected. Did you pull a financial fast one on Randy's beautiful daughter you've been panting after like a lost puppy?" She twirled an index finger through the hair at his collar. He pulled away. Undeterred, she moved in closer opposite Randy.

"We can handle this," Wes said. "You'd better leave now, Hettie. Go shopping with Catherine or something. She kindly warned you about him, so leave him to us now. Your investments are safe."

Chuckling, Hettie perched a chunky hip on Bloomquist's chair. "I wouldn't think of leaving Arni in the lurch under such serious circumstances." She leaned in and planted a bright red kiss mark on his cheek. "He needs *me* now."

Arni recoiled, looked bewildered, and gulped a couple swallows of scotch.

"Just how much have you filched?" She coaxed, taking his chin in her long-nailed fingers and turning his head to meet her gaze.

"What makes you think . . . I . . . I," he stammered.

"Come off it, Arni." Her voice took on a hard edge. "You're charming but you're a crook, and not a very good one. I'm here to offer you a way out of the mess you've gotten yourself into. But only *if* you take my offer, *all* of it."

Randy put a hand on her arm to pull her away from Bloomquist. "He's going to jail. You can't get him out of it."

Ignoring Randy, she wheedled in an annoying tone, "How much do you owe Megan?" She tapped his shoulder. "Spill it."

Arni looked her in the eye, flushed, and looked away into space. "$750,000."

Randy banged a fist on the table, making Arnold jump. "That's not all he's swindled. There are two others I know of in the country club. How many more trusting victims have had their life savings stripped away into his off-shore accounts?"

Bloomquist began to smile crookedly, back peddling. "I . . . I haven't been conducting this line of business but ten months or so. My intent was to pay everyone from my newest clients as I went."

Randy shoved his hands in his pockets before he punched the bastard out. "Classic Ponzi scheme, you thieving scammer."

Hettie scooted closer until her hip met his shirt pocket. "You're a money man, darling. What's the grand total?" She tugged on his ear as if he were a naughty child.

"About a million and a half," he whispered.

Randy choked and fisted his hands in his pockets, hard enough to burst seams. Thinking better of his best slacks, he took them out and wiggled his fingers for circulation.

"Good lord." Wes's face turned ashen. His knuckles whitened where he gripped the table edge. "Could have been me. Thanks for the warning, Randolph. I'd have had little security to offer Catherine or my children when he finished with me."

Hettie chuckled. "Are you going to spend a few years behind bars or do you want to hear my proposal?"

Laughing as if she'd given the punch line to a funny joke, she took the scotch from his hand and downed it herself. Replacing the empty glass in front of him in a ladylike gesture, Hettie added, "You're bound for jail—unless . . ." She let the words hang in the air for all of them.

What's she up to? "Hell of a lot of money to throw a drowning man." Randy's hands in front of his belt buckle repeatedly palmed a fist like a catcher with a baseball mitt. The urge to have a go at the loser's face was becoming irresistible.

Arnold pushed his chair back, nearly dumping Hettie to the floor. "Unless what?"

She regained her balance and crossed her arms over her bulging cleavage.

"Unless I pay your way out of the growing mess you're in."

Randy wasn't buying it. "Even if you could afford it, what's in it for you?"

Feet in high-heeled wedgies planted shoulder-width a part, she stared into Arni's eyes and said coyly, "I want to be Mrs. Arnold Bloomquist. You can have the lifestyle you want with me and you won't have to cheat for it. I have a huge home on a golf course, another in the Adirondacks. We can travel, have a great country-club life, all the scotch you want."

Arnold's face registered shock. His eyes bulged wide. The brown irises in white orbs behind his tortoise-shell rims resembled monogrammed golf balls. He appeared to be struggling to make his tongue work.

Hettie walked to the bed and sat down, rummaging in her handbag. She brought out a checkbook and waved it in his direction. "That's my offer. Take it or leave it." Her shrieking laugh rippled through the cabin loud enough to shatter glass.

Twisting his Rolex wristband, Arnold sat dazed for a long moment. He closed his eyes while his index finger tapped the face of his watch.

Wes shook his head. "Well I'll be damned, Randolph. Assuming she's got the money, if he takes her offer your problem is solved without an arrest. No way to be sure either one of them's telling the truth, however. That snake can't be trusted for sure."

"The truth can be ascertained," said Randy. "What'll it be you shifty bastard?"

Randy wondered if Arni sat considering which fate was the worst of the two commitments. *In his shoes I might choose life behind bars to life with that cackling, skunk-haired shrew.* He sucked in a deep breath and waited a few seconds before letting air out between his teeth.

He interrupted the uncomfortable silence. "Arnie, just in case you're considering simply jumping ship—so to speak—Sundancer's Captain has informed Security to prevent you from leaving this liner until we dock in New York. Our plan is for you to be arrested by the SCC or US Federal authorities before your luggage is unloaded."

"Shit!" Arnold pushed his chair back further and stood; his eye tick-flickered in spasms. His shoulders drooping, he looked from one to the other and stepped toward the door to his suite.

Wes spread both hands on the table and stood.

"Where the hell do you think you're going, Bloomquist?"

Arnold's defeated shoulders lifted. His grim jaw relaxed into a scornful smile.

He's been had. Randy flexed his fingers, eager for the climax he, Megan, and Wes had put into motion.

Arnold's sarcastic smile twisted into a lopsided grin. "I'm going after the rest of the scotch and a couple more glasses. Might as well lift a toast to my bride."

Hettie rushed from the bed to embrace Arnold like a fullback going for a touchdown. "I'm moving out of Catherine's cabin and into yours, Arni darling. I intend to keep a close eye on you, until we're married by the captain this evening, long before we dock in New York." She cackled. "Afterwards too, I imagine."

Her checkbook skittered across the carpet and came to rest against the tasseled toe of Randy's loafer.

Retrieving the checkbook, he experienced a rush of relief. "She's a clever one, Arnold. Once married she can't be made to testify against you in a court of law."

Mission for Megan accomplished. I'm free to work out my own romantic future with Dierdre sooner than my wildest hopes.

Randy shook hands with Wes to celebrate their victory. Declining Arni and Hettie's toast, he left his cane in the wastebasket and departed. Dark glasses in his pocket, his heart lighter than in months, he went to report the amazing turn of events to Megan.

* * *

Chapter Eighteen   *Joys of Two and One*

Dierdre spoke softly from her chair at Suzanne's cabin table, where she forked the frosting away from a slice of birthday cake and dabbed crumbs with the tines.

"Cosma, count on me for whatever you need to make your beach wedding your dream come true. Randy will help us." She inclined her head toward her sleeping twin within arm's reach. Mitzi snuggled close, napping. "Let me take care of details my sister was in charge of so you won't have to worry about a thing and she won't stress."

Raising her eyes from the yet-to-do list and wedding-plan-agreement papers, Cosma smiled like a Madonna. "In spite of canceling a rehearsal run through, this reads all we have to do is show up with the wedding party. I'm not a bit worried."

"Your serene attitude under every horrendous circumstance is nothing short of awe-inspiring."

Most of yesterday, from the moment Dierdre discovered Randy had deceived her, followed by Suzanne's collapse, she'd experienced her first longing for a cigarette in weeks. Her fingers had absolutely ached to hold a slim cylinder of nicotine and suck it into submission. Even though she and Randy had patched things up, and her twin had come through her crisis beautifully, the roller coaster of emotions from horrid to wonderful was taking its toll. Deep breathing wasn't calming her because there wasn't time to slow life down enough to go through the process.

A stirring from the bed interrupted her thoughts. "What are you two plotting?" Suzanne yawned and stretched, easing herself free of Mitzi. She stood and gestured to the bathroom. "Give me a moment. Two babies nudging my bladder spells urgent."

Cosma chuckled. "I remember those feelings and I only carried one at a time."

Dierdre envied both women. *Will I ever have a baby of my own?*

Leaning close, Cosma whispered, "Suzanne would feel so much better if she could talk to Taylor. Can you arrange it? It would make John-Love and I happier going through with this wedding in Bermuda instead of waiting until we're back in Utah where he could be part of it like we planned."

Dierdre nodded. "I'll use my Sundance account and insist she spoil herself at my ship-to-shore expense. Back me up if she resists."

* * *

Unable to unwind after feeding the falcons on his return from the hospital to give his mother a break, Taylor flipped on TV evening news. He missed Suzanne, imagining her sleeping since it was several hours later in Bermuda, unless the women were up late with last-minute wedding details. He hated missing being Johnny's best man. *I really wanted to be there for my buddy.*

The phone rang. His heart raced for a split second with the thought of Pops having a setback just when he'd come through his crisis and was on the mend after surgery. Worried at the late hour, he cranked his tired body out of his easy chair and hurried to pick up. *Good thing I wasn't already asleep. I'd really panic.*

"Hello?"

"Taylor, darling, I'm so happy you're home." His alarm changed from concern for his dad to his Suzanne, except she sounded so happy. *Must be something extra important or she wouldn't spend money for an expensive call.*

He pulled up a kitchen chair and straddled the seat so he could rest one folded arm on the back. "I sure miss you, Honey. Hope the birthday party was fun."

"Went fine. We all miss you too." He heard her sigh as clearly as if she were in the next room. He wished her sigh and her body were there in the house with him. Sleeping alone was the pits.

"Everything okay with you and the baby? The kids giving you any trouble?" He found himself hanging on her every word.

"It's all okay now. I had a little crisis this morning near the end of class in the park. Overtired and not drinking enough water, I guess." Her soft laugh had a hollow quality. He bolted from the chair and paced the kitchen with the phone to his shoulder.

"But you're alright now? Did Dierdre call a doctor for you?"

"Funny you should ask." She chuckled like her usual self and he relaxed a little.

"Actually, my father volunteered his services in spectacular fashion."

Taylor wasn't at all sure he'd heard her right. The silence on the line grew lengthier until her laughter exploded. He held the receiver away for a moment. Recupping it to his ear he said, "I don't get it. Can you go over that again?"

"Hold on," Suzanne said. "Mitzi just woke up and wants to tell you something."

"Put her on."

"Daddy, guess what. The bestest secret is Mommy has *two* babies in her tummy." She giggled. "Aren't you sprized?"

Taylor nearly dropped the phone. "I'm surprised alright, Sweetheart. I better talk to that mommy of yours, please."

Struggling for control of his competing emotions, Taylor gripped the receiver firmly, standing stock still in the middle of the kitchen while the TV news droned in the living room. Never had he wanted to hold Suzanne and see the sparkle in her eyes as much as he did at this moment, thousands of miles away from her. His heart surged with tender love for the mother of his child—his *children*. He could barely comprehend what two little ones at once was going to mean in just a few months. A sense of awe overtook him.

When she came back on, he sputtered, "Suze. Start at the beginning because I thought you said your mystery father is your doctor . . . and Mitzi says we're having twins, so whoever he is he must have medically confirmed it."

"Remember the guy who dresses like Fred Astaire?"

* * *

A sea breeze riffled fingers of palm fronds against a brilliant blue sky. The afternoon sun kissed pink sand with delicate sparkles in every direction along the shore, stuttering across seashells washed up on the wet beach. To Dierdre it seemed a picture postcard of a paradise. Four horse-drawn carriages withdrew to a shaded waiting area after delivering the wedding party to the moon-gate ceremony site, one of many dotting the island of Bermuda.

"Those horses are way bigger than Queeny on Pop's farm." Mitzi scampered toward her, then slowed to watch her feet. "I better be careful or Mommy says I'll scuff my new pretty shoes."

Dierdre snapped a photo of her niece in her pale-peach dress, white patent-leather Mary Janes, and her crown of bobbing curls scooped high in a daisy clip. "Be careful not to spill your basket of flower petals."

"I'm being careful to pieces." She caught up to her mother walking on ahead, flanked by her new grandfather and Catherine. Dierdre laughed at her precocious niece.

Earlier, Wes had assured Dierdre he'd be keeping a diagnostic eye on Suzanne. Dierdre wasn't to worry. In no way would he allow her twin to overdo and put herself and the babies back in crisis. Watching him be so attentive to her sister was deeply comforting.

"Wow," gushed Cloud. "Who thought of the orchids?" He pointed to the spray of creamy pink-and-white blossoms fastened with ribbons to the peak of the moon gate. "I helped Mom and Johnny pick the ceremony package. That choice wasn't in their budget."

Dierdre hugged him with a free arm. "I think I know who the romantic culprit is." She nodded at Randy. "Flower angel, I should have said."

Randy grinned and winked, but admitted nothing aloud.

Cosma touched his shoulder as she passed.

"Thank you, Randy. The pastor just said we get to take the flowers after the ceremony. You are a special man to give us such a beautiful surprise."

"Not half as beautiful as the bride," Randy said, turning to Johnny. "I'm sure the groom agrees."

Johnny chuckled, fingering the handle of his cane nervously and loosening the white-shirt collar at his throat with his other hand. "You know I do. Thanks for standing in as best man for my buddy Taylor."

"I'm honored." Randy stepped aside to let him pass. "I'll join you in a minute."

Cloud nudged Gregory who Dierdre noticed was unusually quiet in the carriage.

"Did Stellar give you the rings yet? He told me you have to take over as ring bearer since he got a chance to play the wedding march with Wilson. He can't do both things."

Gregory patted the slight bulge in his pocket. "I've got 'em. Hope I don't mess up 'cause I wasn't expecting to do this. Wish you were doing it."

"Nah," Cloud said. "It's always the youngest boy's job and I'm the oldest."

"Oh," said Gregory.

Dierdre made her nephew pause and force a smile for a picture, then he scuffed his Sunday shoes down the path behind his mother. *That young boy has some very big thoughts going on today. I thought we covered everything last midnight.*

Dierdre and Randy remained near the back of the party filing to the beach, so she could take pictures with Suzanne's new digital Polaroid as well as the one used for photographing paintings in the park. Randy collected the instant shots and stacked them. Making certain they were dry, he tucked them in a fabric folder for later. "Why didn't they get married in one of the island churches?" he whispered. "I'm told there are more churches here per square mile than in any other country in the world."

Dierdre capped the lens on the art camera. "Two reasons. One, Cosma wanted a wedding out in nature instead of in a building or at some resort water feature. Notice she's barefoot? The physical connection to Mother Earth is important to her. Two, Johnny's divorced and not many churches in Bermuda allow marriage of divorcees."

Now that they were out of earshot of the bride and groom, Randy spoke in a normal voice. "I guess it makes sense they want to get married on the beach. Wonder why Johnny has bare feet too?"

"Sand in his boots," Cloud said, passing them as he hurried to take his place. He laughed and so did they.

Down on the beach, Stellar rehearsed his flute with Wilson and his guitar. Dierdre had complimented the disco musician on his new hairstyle when she hired him that morning to play for the wedding. She turned her lips to Randy's ear. "Doesn't he have amazing blue eyes and thick black lashes a woman would die for?"

He knuckled her waist in a tease. "Yes, he does. You sure have a thing for eyes."

"Especially ones looking at me with deep affection." She pretended to peer through the camera lens while a mischievous smile played about her lips.

"Is a lusty look permissible?" Randy asked in the deepest sexy baritone he reserved for intimacies between them.

She lowered the camera with a sober facial expression. "Not at a wedding."

"It will be at ours I assure you."

Her heart squeezed with hope. "You think we might go that route, do you?" Her voice had a vulnerable quiver.

Randy smiled the smile she loved, sending her heart pounding with desire to kiss him right there in front of everyone. He raised her chin with a bent finger. "Positive, my sweet. Teasing aside, I'll propose properly, I promise—and it will be soon."

Heat rushed to her cheeks. *Is this really happening to me? The M word?*

She overheard the pastor's voice. "Shhh. He's giving instructions to you members of the ceremony."

She pressed Randy's hand, released it, and shoved him in the direction of those gathered near the moon gate.

"Couples make a wish as they walk hand-in-hand through the moon gate after the ceremony, a Chinese tradition brought to the island by a sea captain years ago," explained the pastor. "This ritual assures they will be granted happiness and good fortune during their marriage."

Dierdre uncapped Suzanne's professional camera and had fun photographing everyone, starting with the young pastor in his white shirt and slacks, his lei of island flowers, and his shoulder-length dreadlocks buffeting in the rising breeze.

Randy took his place next to Johnny, whose face reflected his adoration for Cosma waiting to join him after her Wedding March walk. Their backs to the sea, the men faced the others further up on the beach.

Gregory joined them and stood to the side as he'd been instructed, ready to hand Johnny the rings at the proper moment. Mitzi scattered flower petals from her little basket making a fragrant path through the moon gate. When her basket was empty, she skipped through the sand to stand by her mother.

Stellar's flute pierced the sound of the waves lapping the shore with the first notes of the Wedding March. Wilson joined in on the guitar. Their harmony was so eerie and lovely it brought tears to Dierdre's eyes. They played the first few strains before the pastor gestured for the bride to approach for the official repeating of the vows. The music embraced them while Cosma walked barefoot from the back of the group down the path of flower petals.

Dierdre raised the camera to capture the moment. Her father had left Suzanne's side to give his arm to the bride, accompanying her to the steady beat of the Wedding March, giving her away as tradition required of the bride's father. Cloud beamed with pride and gave his mother a two-thumbs-up gesture, his stunning white smile lighting up his ruddy Apache face.

Cosma is the vision of an exotic island princess. Her shiny black hair circled with ribbons entwined in tiny orchids—the first time I've seen it unbraided— drifting in the breeze from her shoulders to her waist like a dusky halo. She's the most stunning bride anyone could imagine. Her white spaghetti-strapped dress and its skirt billowing against her bare, brown ankles makes a gorgeous sight.

Dierdre snapped pictures until the pastor led the exchange of vows, the couple kissed as man and wife, and returned hand-in-hand through the moon gate.

It could not have been a more perfect wedding if we'd practiced all week. She couldn't help wishing for a wedding as meaningful for herself and Randy.

Dare I hope?

* * *

Chapter Nineteen   *Reception Surprises*

Sundancer sailed out of Hamilton Harbor at seven pm, right on schedule, headed for New York City. With her previously arranged night free, the ship's captain assigned the Hotel Manager to host the evening floorshow, allowing Dierdre to enjoy the Carlisle wedding reception. Becoming a lively duo, Stellar's flute and Wilson's guitar melodies set a unique romantic mood. Passing guests paused at the doorway to view the reception. Chatting amiably, invited tarot-reading enthusiasts of Cosma's and members of Suzanne's watercolor class, with the exceptions of the disinvited—Hettie and Arnold—milled about balancing their tiny dishes of finger food. The catering-crew servers posted near the displayed wedding cakes awaited the ceremonial cutting and plating.

Dierdre followed Bermuda tradition in ordering the bride's cake and the smaller groom's cake, each decorated with tiny cedar saplings. Usually planted next to each other in a secret place on the island to embody the couple's growing love, these would be packaged for Utah and planted somewhere important to the bridal couple. *With sacred ritual performed by Cosma and Cloud no doubt.*

Cosma, radiant in the coral dress and shell jewelry she'd changed into after the beach ceremony, strolled the banquet room arm-in-arm with Johnny greeting their guests. Her unbraided hair flowed to her waist, captured at the crown with delicate bridal blossoms.

She's a vision and Johnny is bursting with pride. He can't keep his eyes off her. Without that cane I think he'd have both hands around her even before the dance. Sundancer's photographer is equally enchanted. He gave Dierdre a thumbs-up and went on shooting. *What an album they'll have.*

The newlyweds joined the twins and guests at the buffet table.

"Dierdre, Suzanne, this is so much more elaborate than what we discussed," Cosma said. "Thank you for all the trouble you've gone to for our lovely wedding and this reception with *so many* people."

"I'll say." Johnny's sweeping arm included the many guests in the room. "Who's paying for the extras?" he whispered, his brow furrowed in concern.

Suzanne fussed with a fan of folded napkins on the linen table drape, realigning forks with vases of flowers. "Not to worry. Our dad insisted on 'throwing his two cents in' as he put it."

I know Suzanne's wishing Taylor were here as we planned. She's being so brave for Cosma. Dierdre set her glass on the table and hugged the bride and groom. "Mr. and Mrs. John Carlisle; sounds wonderful doesn't it?"

"IS wonderful," gushed Johnny. He kissed his wife's temple, just below her tiara of blossoms.

Cosma beamed. "We can hardly believe it, right John-Love?"

Dierdre's happiness for them underscored the joy of her maturing love for Randy. Across the room, the light of her life stood tall and delicious in a blue summer suit with a rose at his lapel, talking to her nephew and Cloud.

I can trust this man to be honest and good. Perhaps we'll have a day like this. He's what I want and none of the things I don't want. Thank heaven we've overcome my terrible accusations about his secrecy.

Catherine, in a green linen dress with a massive gardenia corsage at the shoulder, and Wesley, still wearing his white tux and tails from the wedding, spoke with Mitzi flouncing and twirling in her flower-girl dress. She gestured toward her aunt and stopped dancing to the music. Hands on her hips, she posed for her new grandparents. "I know you say Dierdre but I say Dreedra 'cause I always do. It's my special name for her since I was little."

"You're more grown up now, I see." Wes chuckled. "Charming, isn't she Catherine? And to think we feared never getting to enjoy grandchildren together."

Wesley stepped close to Suzanne. "Since I'm both your doctor and the grandfather of those twin babies, I insist you take Amtrak home from New York instead of flying. Sitting for hours in a pressurized jet cabin, when your legs can't be elevated to prevent swelling is not a healthy idea. On a train you can get up and move around or lie down with your feet up in a Pullman car. Catherine and I will ride with you."

Suzanne's chin lifted. "It takes so much longer. I already miss Taylor terribly. And, it's too expensive to change transportation plans, especially at the last minute."

"Arnold Bloomquist and her Hettieness are not the only people on board affluent enough to make things happen their way. It's all settled. Dierdre helped me make the arrangements. We've already notified Taylor to meet our train."

"I'm grateful for your concern, Wes, er Dad, but I'm not used to people making things happen for me without talking it over." Her eyes flashed in a way Dierdre recognized as a warning. She caught her sister's look and pressed a finger to her own lips, a code between them to hush.

Their father continued in a professional voice.

"If I weren't a doctor I wouldn't know the danger of clotting complications you could face trapped in a tiny airplane seat for hours. Catherine's coming with us, as far as Salt Lake City. She'll leave us there and prepare to put her home on the market. You and I will go on to Farr. Taylor will meet our train."

Suzanne cocked her head and rested a hand on her baby bump. The fingers of her other hand toyed with the Medicine Pouch at her throat. "The kids? I suppose you've taken care of getting them home without me as well?" There was an edge of annoyance to her tone.

Dierdre put an arm around her shoulders. "Mr. and Mrs. Carlisle are escorting their children and yours back to Salt Lake with the round-trip plane tickets they came on. No money wasted there."

Suzanne sagged into a chair and threw up her hands. "You've all thought of everything. I don't even have the option to argue."

"That's my girl." Wes chucked her chin with a knuckle. "Call it a day soon and get your pretty feet up. You've been pushing it."

Her twin caught Dierdre's eye. "Dee, the Carlisle boys are with me until morning so the newlyweds have private honeymoon time. Can you stop by and rally the troops before you turn in? I'm afraid I'll sleep right through their racket. The steward's liable to turn up with security staff and straight jackets for three rowdy boys."

"Count on me, Sis." Dierdre brushed her cheek.

"You've been a trooper. It will be over soon and you'll be back in Taylor's arms."

Megan approached with two glass punch cups. "I wish Poppy were here to meet all of you."

"Who's Poppy?" Dierdre accepted one of the punch cups.

"Randy's daughter. She's at soccer camp this week." Megan smiled and took a sip. "I thought Randy would have told you all about her by now."

* * *

Chapter Twenty *Candlelit Dilemma*

Shaken but not wanting to spoil her friend's wedding reception with an outburst at Randy, Dierdre finished her hostess responsibilities in a blur of suppressed emotion. The wedding guests drifted out while the newlyweds prepared to follow the cake cart to their cabin. Suzanne and the four children headed to the Armstrong cabin.

Poppy. How can there be a daughter Poppy? Mutely Dierdre followed Randy out into the corridor, her thoughts of love and betrayal in painful turmoil.

"I've reserved a table upstairs at the ballroom, hoping to hold you in my arms for a couple of dances."

He guided her through the ship's casino where laughter, tumbling dice, and the calling out of numbers jumbled in her ears.

"I hope you'll take a chance on me—on us." Randy squeezed her limp hand.

"I've vowed not to gamble on relationships ever again." Dierdre stiffened her shoulders and withdrew her fingers on pretense of securing her shoulder bag. "I want a sure thing or I don't want to play."

"Love isn't a game, Dierdre. True love may be a crap shoot sometimes, but it's definitely more profound than a game."

Soon, he led her to their reserved table for two. Rose petals scattered on the tablecloth scented the air, champagne chilled in an ice bucket on a stand, and candlelight flickered across gleaming china, stemmed glasses, and flatware.

"It's so beautiful. You've thought of everything." *He plans to propose. I'm sure of it. We've patched things up, but now I find out about Poppy. I doubt Randy will want more children. I didn't think I wanted babies of my own, but I do. Am I destined to be the aunt who never found the right man she could trust and truly love? Damn, here I go again. I have to keep him from proposing before I understand what life would be like with him. What he expects. I want to be able to say yes. What if I can't?*

He broke the uncomfortable silence. "When Megan mentioned Poppy your face changed from joyful to . . . I don't know, concerned maybe?"

"I didn't know you have a daughter. I'm surprised, stunned really. You never mentioned something, someone so important. It makes me want to know what other secret problems you have I should know about?"

"I don't have problems. I solve problems." He reached for her hand grinning, his eyes crinkling at the corners.

"Is that arrogance or a fact of your job? I don't even know what you really do for a living."

"Dierdre, give us time. We have a lot to learn about each other. Things have gone so quickly between us. There's no doubt in my mind we share the kind of love that gets deeper with time. I adore and love you."

Though her resistance was melting, she determined to be wise even if she lost him. *I will not sacrifice my dignity and myself over lack of foresight ever again.* "Tell me about Poppy . . . and your wife, and your home in Virginia, and your job."

He ran his fingers through his hair. "I should have told you. Poppy's twelve, a spunky redhead who'll take some corralling in a few years I suppose. Her mother lives with the lover she left us for, a ski instructor in the Swiss Alps."

Dierdre swallowed and pressed on. "Divorced?"

"Yes, of course. Poppy has a nanny, so you don't have to worry about raising her. We live on my family estate, which I manage in the rolling hills of Virginia. There are horses to ride, a swimming pool, tutors."

Wow, he must be loaded, which I didn't expect, except for the way he spends money. He's meeting far more of my want list in a husband than I imagined. Nevertheless . . . "She'll probably compete with me for your attention and devotion."

"You know I'm crazy about you. Will you marry me?" He gently squeezed her fingers.

Her heart warmed with the love in his voice, his touch, and her longing for a love and lover to believe in. "I love you too, but I've learned to ask more questions, not assume what someone means. Be patient with me."

"Shoot. I've given you reasons to doubt my trustworthiness. I'll answer honestly."

"It isn't that I don't want to be married, but I'm scared. I don't know much about raising kids. I'd hoped to find a man without kids to worry about. You have Poppy. She'll probably hate me. Daughters of divorcees want no interference from another woman."

"I've watched you with Mitzi and Gregory. You have terrific instincts about kids. Poppy will adore you as I do."

"Why two cruises?"

"Whew. Talk about changing the subject and catching me off guard." He chuckled. "It's simple. Swindler Bloomquist changed his plans because Dr. LeChaminant had a medical emergency requiring them to take a different cruise. It was too late for Meg and me to change our tickets without a massive penalty. Besides, I really wanted to get to know you after spying you in that enormous sun hat and that snug blue bathing suit at the pool. Megan realized I was serious about pursuing you and agreed to go along on both cruises, so I wouldn't blow my cover over falling for you. We made up the story about me working on a novel and needing more time for plot development on a cruise ship. She wanted to make sure I got her mother's little fortune back as quickly as possible."

Randy took a breath, swallowed three times from his water glass, and perked up. Dierdre could practically hear the wheels turning in his head.

He said, "Why not give the captain notice of a family emergency? It really is a sort of emergency don't you think? Or you could just resign and go to Suzanne in Utah. Help her with the kids so she can carry those twins full term. Meantime, I can fly in to

Salt Lake a couple of times a month on weekends, rent a car, and join you."

Her head spun with the barrage of ideas he expressed so urgently. She wanted things to go a little slower and yet she didn't because his prospects were so exciting. She imagined Tiff coaching from the sidelines somewhere behind the champagne bucket.

'Go for it girlfriend, this is the big chance you've been waiting for. Don't screw this one up.'

Randy continued, "I can't be apart from you for too long a time. When the babies are born and your sister can comfortably care for them, you can come home to me in Virginia."

"Now who's changing the subject?" Dierdre wagged her head in disbelief. *I just listened to my father shoving plans at my twin. Why are men like this? For heaven's sake, can't they wait for our input?*

"Slow down, Randy. What will I do all day on an estate in Virginia? I'm used to being busy."

"Play golf at the country club? Supervise the staff, or not. Ride my—our—thoroughbreds; buzz into Washington and shop for Vera Wang gowns and Ferragamo shoes; attend Embassy functions with me; throw lavish pool parties in the garden or dances in the ballroom; plan visits to Suzanne in Utah; make babies with me."

Astonished, Dierdre tried to take it all in. "You have a ballroom? You're invited to Embassy events?" She fingered the rose petals nearest her glass. "Make babies with you? Did you really suggest you wouldn't mind if we had children of our own?"

Her heart hammered in her rib cage. She could almost swear she heard little peeps from a nursery somewhere close by.

He reached across the table and took her fingers into his, stroking slowly from her fiery red nails down and around each one. His eyes never left hers. He turned her hands palm up and gently rubbed his thumbs across their hearts. She knew he watched for her reaction to this little intimacy he was risking in public.

Dierdre's arousal was immediate. Warmth and desire flowed from her palms up her arms and down her thighs, making her light-headed. Her insides burned to be entered by his body. Face flaming, she struggled to breathe.

"Randy, you must stop or we'll be publically humiliated when I rip your clothes off and help you with mine."

"You're so quiet this evening, I was only checking to see if there are live cells in that beautiful body of yours."

She gulped for air, laughing, leaned forward and whispered, "They're not only alive, they're begging, simply screaming to be satisfied."

"I'd take you to my stateroom to work on that . . . but you've given me a problem."

He massaged her palms, moved his fingertips to her wrists and stroked in circles, driving her absolutely mad. "I could be doing this on every square inch . . ."

"You've got to be kidding." She pulled her tingling hands back to her lap. "What have I done or not done to . . . to stop us?" Dierdre scrambled to imagine obstacles to their lovemaking she'd somehow created. Not sure if he was teasing or serious, she inhaled and waited, trying to let her breath return as much as possible to normal.

Randy took a tiny box from his pocket and set it amid the fragrant petals. "You haven't said I can put this ring on that finger you just took away from me. We haven't toasted our engagement and our future with this chilling champagne either. I've given up on dancing— at least here in the ballroom with our clothes on."

Dierdre's eyes filled with tears. She blinked them back and focused on the blurred vision of the man she could spend her life with, fulfill her dreams with, and melt into his touch whenever they wanted. *All I have to do is say yes.*

Wanting to with all her heart, she was nevertheless terrified she'd make some disastrous mistake or perhaps had already misread some critical red flag to future problems. She knew a moment of sheer panic and fidgeted with the napkin in her lap.

The image of Cosma explaining the significance of her squirrel totem came to mind. She'd said Dierdre was so like squirrels always preparing for winter, fearing to be the squirrel that risks flying. Her wise friend urged her to take a chance and trust goodness would come from her choices. 'You are not a fool,' she'd been assured.

With quivering lips, Dierdre struggled to form words. She gave up, took her left hand from her lap and placed it amid the rose petals within his reach. Their gazes locked while her heart thundered in her ears.

Randy's tender smile broadened to a grin. He lifted her hand to his lips and kissed each finger.

"Steady the box, please," he whispered. When she did, his free hand opened it and removed the ring from its velvet nest.

Arranged like a daisy, each marquis gem sparkled around the central rose-cut diamond the size of Randy's pinky nail. Dierdre gasped. "When? Where did you shop for this stunning engagement ring?"

"Megan and I ducked into the same jeweler's shop we watched Wes and Catherine exit on Front Street. I hope it pleases you, if not . . ."

"Oh, it pleases me alright." She could barely breathe for the thrill of it.

He slipped the diamond flower onto her ring finger, turned her hand over, and kissed the palm. "Now, my sweet fiancée, we can adjourn to my cabin and make mad passionate love—after a champagne toast."

"Without dark glasses?" Dierdre teased.

"Without a stitch of anything fake or otherwise between us—now and always."

"Suzanne gave me a curfew." She giggled and held up her stemmed glass while he poured her champagne.

"I'll give you more than that." Randy filled his own glass and clicked it gently against hers.

"I'm counting on it—soon and always," Dierdre whispered.

End

ACKNOWLEDGMENTS

The author wishes to acknowledge the invaluable assistance of critique partners Amy Jarecki and Christine Perkins; beta readers Peter Wilks, Carolyn Moore, and Sue Leth Stevenson; front cover design by Killian Group; back cover and spine Aaron Campbell; and David Smith, publisher of Synergy Books.

As in the prequel, *The Wind Remembers*, falconry experts' resources and advice as listed in that book's acknowledgments were referred to frequently in the writing of *Waves of Deception*. The intriguing book *Medicine Cards* by Jamie Sams and David Carson inspired the animal tarot scenes in this book.

To her muse or muses, whoever they be, making these characters talk in Shreeve's head and revealing their dreams, worries, and triumphs, she says: *Thank you and keep talking!*

At the urging of several of her readers who have come to know her colorful characters, book three, *Winds of Promise*, with many of these same characters ten years later, is in process.

Made in the USA
San Bernardino, CA
14 November 2014